The L

1976

John M. Tallon

THE LAST SKINHEAD 1976

Copyright © John Tallon, 2016

Cover art, Adam Tallon, copyright © 2016

All rights reserved in all media. No part of this book may be used or reproduced without written permission, except in the case of brief quotations embodied in critical articles and reviews.

All characters and places are entirely fictitious. Any resemblance or similarity to persons living or deceased is purely coincidental.

Also by this author:

Natural Born Skinhead 1971

Something to Do 1972

and

Never a Dull Moment 1973

Available on Kindle and in Paperback
at Amazon.com and Amazon.co.uk

Find us on facebook @
John M Tallon

or

https://www.facebook.com/pages/Something-to-Do-1972/427764967346581?fref=ts

**Dedicated to my beautiful wife Clare,
thanks for the past forty fantastic years**

CONTENTS

PREFACE

CHAPTER 1 – Spirit in the Sky **1**

CHAPTER 2 – Whiskey in the Jar **21**

CHAPTER 3 – Police and Thieves **54**

CHAPTER 4 – All Gone to Look for America **81**

CHAPTER 5 – Across 110th Street **114**

CHAPTER 6 – Mona Lisas and Mad Hatters **142**

CHAPTER 7 – Them Never Love Poor Marcus **173**

CHAPTER 8 – Jeremiah Johnson **209**

EPILOGUE

MUSIC (**end pages**)

GLOSSARY

Preface

All the books in this series of novels relate to the original English Skinheads of 1969 through to 1971/72 approximately, which arguably saw the demise of the first incarnation of this unique, working-class youth subculture.

There is no reference to the abhorrent issue of racism either overtly or as a subtext, as this would be contextually inappropriate and entirely incorrect; not in any way pertaining to the Skinhead ethos of that period. It would be a ridiculous paradox to suggest a fashion which was heavily influenced at its core by Ska and Reggae of West Indian origin and Soul from the motor cities of America, would at the same time discriminate against the very people who produced the soundtrack of their young lives. These youths were a working-class proletariat group and would identify themselves more along social class lines than any other differentiation.

As in the previous books *Natural Born Skinhead 1971, Something to Do 1972* and *Never a Dull Moment 1973,* the following preface should be considered as a content advisory notice.

This is a graphic tale depicting incidents that range from the seemingly innocuous to extremes of sadistic violence, including that of a sexual nature. From the start there are references to the prevailing cultural mores and perceptions of that time. There is no attempt to glorify them in any way but rather to reflect the formative climate in which the youths have developed and, find themselves living in. The atmosphere is essentially machismo-driven, homophobic and misogynistic and, by today's standards would be totally unacceptable but arguably renders a true portrait of that time, 'warts and all.'

The four books of this series may be read as individual volumes, each with self-contained tales and conclusions, or as one continuous narrative. Together they provide a complete picture of the colourful, exciting, violent world of the Original Skinheads and the spirit of 1969.

The Last Skinhead

Chapter 1

Spirit in the Sky

Friday 23rd November 1973

A thin flurry of snow swirled angrily about the small, sombre group of mourners standing on the cold, damp earth surrounding the edge of the freshly dug grave.

"Ashes to ashes, dust to dust ... and so we commend the soul of our dear departed brother..." the old priest paused momentarily, removed his thick-lensed spectacles and wiped them, unsuccessfully, with a stained, well-used, checked handkerchief. He utilised this brief hiatus to gather his thoughts, hoping to recall correctly the name of the deceased, having erred previously during the short, cobbled eulogy which he had delivered with an economy of sincerity.

"John... er, yes... our brother John." he continued, furtively looking about the mourners as if expecting some acknowledgement of his accurate naming of the soon to be interred remains of the young male.

When the cheap wooden casket was finally lowered into the dark, narrow chasm, a handful of soil was passed to each individual by the funeral director's representative.

Throwing his portion into the void, Patrick 'Irish' O'Hare spoke a few brief words. "I'll see yer on the other side Jay Mac. Take it easy mate." He was about to step away from his long-time friend's grave when a strong hand caught hold of his right arm, at the crook of the elbow and gripped him firmly.

"Aye, that's about right from you. Yer've gorra few kind words now but where were yer when he needed yer?"

Irish wheeled about and stared into the watery eyes of his angry, aged questioner, instantly recognising John 'Jay Mac's' veteran uncle. The youth had a bitter response already formed and waiting on the tip of his tongue but respect for his friend's old soldier uncle would not allow him to speak, instead he merely nodded his head as if in agreement.

Jay Mac's guardian pressed on, "Yeah, I thought so, no fuckin' answer, 'cause you know I'm right. You and the rest of yer Crown Team Skinheads, that's why he's ended up 'ere, like this. He never had a chance once he fell in with you lot." Still seething with rage the elderly male paused to catch his breath. This time Irish could not hold back, "That's where you're wrong boss! Jay Mac never had a chance from the moment he was born; we were *all* he ever had." Pulling his arm free from the vice-like grip of the temporarily stunned sexegenarian, Irish quickly moved away from the graveside and joined two other members of their crew; Billy 'Blue' Boyd and Daniel 'Glynn' who were waiting nearby, at a respectful distance.

Dressed in their three-quarter length dark leather coats, flared trousers and clumpy, colourful platform shoes and sporting the latest cut-and-blow dried, collar length hairstyles, the pair looked in stark contrast to the dour Irish whose own unkempt hair now reached almost to his shoulders and beyond the collar of his well-cut, black Crombie. With his matching black twenty-two inch parallel trousers, turned up just above his unpolished black, eight eyelet 1460's Dr Marten's boots and his white Ben Sherman shirt, Irish could almost have been mistaken for a scruffy member of the undertaking staff; almost but not quite.

His grim countenance bore the scars of numerous violent encounters. Some of the older markings were souvenirs of a brutal school 'education', the most recent, however, served as permanent reminders of his vicious beating and sickening assault at the hands of Jay Mac's murderer, the evil sadist known as 'Morgo' Jones. A former senior henchman and cell-mate lover of the sexually ambivalent, late Crown Team leader Sean 'Devo' Devlin, Morgo had fled the scene of Jay Mac's murder and was still at large, a fact that constantly tormented the already tortured soul of Irish.

"Fuckin' hell Irish, Jay Mac's uncle's really pissed off. I thought he was gonna give you a dig and that we'd have to jump in an stomp the arl feller." Blue observed as Irish joined him and Glynn.

Irish looked at his naive garrulous team mate like a parent about to scold a child, "Blue, stop talkin' bollocks will yer. Jay Mac's uncle might be old but he's as tough as fuck. I doubt if he'd have a problem with seein' the three of us off, what do you say Glynn?"

Glynn, who had never fully recovered from his near-fatal clash with a leader of another crew within the Crown Team, now steered well clear of any possible physical violence. "Yeah, too right Irish, I wouldn't fancy our chances against that arl bastard.

Blue persisted, "Come off it Glynn, you must be jokin' mate, y'know what am like when I get started!"

"Yeah Blue, we all know exactly what you're like." Irish acknowledged with a wry grin.

Although it was only just midday, with the sun having failed to punctuate the dense voluminous, grey clouds that hung ominously in the dark sky, it felt as if it were a late winter's evening. Only the occasional light flurries of snow added a faint bright dusting wherever drifts gathered about the mournful trees and aged gravestones. The three team mates were keen to leave this gloomy place as soon as possible, particularly with the prospect of an impromptu wake being held in the much warmer, more convivial surroundings of the Eagle public house.

"Hey you there, the one thee call 'Irish', come over here, we're after havin' a quick word with y'self." a tall heavily built, late thirties male wearing an expensive tailored overcoat over a suit of equal quality and price, called to them as the youths approached a highly polished, black limousine, parked on the nearby gravel path. Irish complied without objection; he knew exactly who he was dealing with, having already recognised the three elder cousins of Jay Mac who, together with the remainder of their thirteen-strong siblings, both male and female, were referred to collectively as the notorious 'Gerard Boys.'

Blue and Glynn made to accompany Irish but the older male signalled to them not to do so, he held out his large hand, palm upwards and spoke, "Not you two fellers, yer not required. Go on now and wait where yer are."

Both youths stopped at once, they too now recognised the speaker, having also met him previously and knew better than to argue.

"Alright there Irish; Patrick isn't it?" he paused then added, "I'm Niall by the way." Irish acknowledged his own name and that of the speaker then shook the heavy hand that was offered to him. "A sad day Patrick, to lose one of our own like this." Niall began, "Aye that'll have t'be taken care of." Irish looked into the battered face of this menacing bruiser; pity or sadness were not emotions that he read there.

"Yeah too right it's sad, that cunt Morgo needs to be sorted good and proper." Irish responded angrily.

A brief smile appeared on the thin lips of Niall, "Ah, now that's what we thought yer might be contemplatin', so it's lucky we're havin' this little chat." Niall who had been casually leaning against the black limousine stood up straight to his full height and leaned forward into Irish, "Y'see John there was family and *only* family can sort this out 'properly', not just friends, d'yer get my meaning?"

For a moment Irish made no response, leading Niall to place his hand firmly on the youth's shoulder. Suddenly a familiar voice called out from nearby, "Is everythin' alright there Irish?" Irish turned to look over his right shoulder and was pleasantly surprised to see their heroic team leader Tommy (S), standing in the path immediately to his rear. Although he was supported both by the aid of a walking stick and his formidable female companion, Joan (M), necessitated as a result of life-threatening injuries he had sustained in the Crown Team's epic battle with their once bitter rivals, the Kings Team Skins, he was still a formidable character. Niall moved his hand from Irish's shoulder and addressed the ferocious looking Tommy (S), "Now then wee man this doesn't concern you, so go on yer way, there's a good feller.

The redoubtable leader remained exactly where he was standing, perfectly still, as if rooted to the spot. Two of the doors of the car now opened and a pair of similarly well dressed large males stepped out to join their brother, Niall.

"Are yer a bit deaf there feller, or are yer just fuckin' soft in the head?" Francis, one of the new arrivals asked with his partner quickly adding, "Don't fuck with us wee man, or yer'll not be leavin' here today."

Tommy stared into each of their grim set faces in turn, fixing them with his own steel-grey, glass splinters of eyes, then without even the slightest flinch or gesture of acknowledgement of their presence, he continued, "Like I said, are yer alright there Irish?"

For his part though Irish knew full well the awesome scrapping ability of the Crown Team leader, he also doubted that in his present weakened state he could possibly have a chance against these three vicious thugs.

"Tommy, I'm fine thanks mate. Just havin' a quick word with Jay Mac's cousins like, so, er... see yer later in the Eagle for a drink, if yer can make it."

Whatever passed through the minds of these three senior Gerard Boys, they made no comment, revealed no emotion only remained staring at the stocky, five foot nine bullterrier of a youth, watching him intently even as he turned and walked away, with the aid of his female partner.

"Now that's a mad wee fucker, with some balls on 'im," Niall acknowledged approvingly, his brothers nodding their agreement. "Right Patrick, so you remember what I was tellin' yer, you leave that Morgo problem with us." He paused and waited for Irish to acquiesce then moved on. "One more thing Patrick, you were a good friend of our John's and we know you can handle yerself in a scrap so we've got a little business proposition for yer. We can always use a handy feller like yerself, someone we can trust to do a little bit of delivery work now and then, how does that sound to yer?"

Irish looked first at his prospective employer then to each of his brothers. He was well aware of their violent reputation, both from Jay Mac's first hand accounts and through the wider community to whom they had become urban legends of terror, he chose his words carefully before replying. "Thanks for the offer Niall, I really appreciate it but I think I'll pass for now, no disrespect like." Irish began, then on receiving no discernable response other than their unsmiling expressions, added "I'm just not up to it right now, y'know what I mean, with what's happened with Jay Mac, Devo an all that, yeah?"

Niall spoke for the trio, "Alright young feller, we'll leave it there for now." He held out his hand for Irish to shake. As the youth grasped Niall's outstretched paw, he felt the painful crushing power of his grip, with the Gerard senior increasing this while he delivered his final words, "Don't leave it too long Patrick, that offer won't be there forever. Time waits for no man and neither do we." He released Irish's hand then all three brothers returned to their gleaming vehicle.

Irish walked back towards Blue and Glynn rubbing his pained hand as he did. "What was all that about Irish, thee didn't look too happy?" Blue asked.

"Dont tell me yer gonna offer to jump in and stomp them three fuckers as well?" Irish asked with a grin. Blue chose not to reply, Glynn laughed out loud.

As the trio walked the hundred yards or so along the loose gravel path, towards the tall, rusty wrought iron gates, past headstones of varying age, some of which had long since been visited and whose inscribed epitaphs were barely legible, the light flurries of snow had ceased but in their place a freezing thin grey mist had arisen. All three had the uneasy feeling that they were being watched and in this instance their sixth senses proved correct.

"Hello Boot Boys, come to visit me here at home have you?" the unmistakable creepy voice of Mal 'the Pig' called to them. Standing surrounded by snaking tendrils of mist, under the weeping boughs of an ancient willow was Malcolm Chadwick, a genuinely disturbing character who had a morbid obsession with death and the occult. Mal had acquired his sobriquet 'the Pig' after being thrown through the windscreen of a stolen car, that he was driving and having the fleshy tip of his large nose sliced away, leading to several unsuccessful cosmetic surgeries that only served to exaggerate the disfigurement of his exposed nasal cavities. Because the accident had occurred not long after one of his more elaborate Ouija board séance sessions, in which he later claimed to have received messages of impending doom for several members of the Crown Team, many of his chronological peers believed his dabbling had directly led to his own unfortunate incident. As a general rule they all sought to avoid him whenever possible.

"What d'you want weirdo, what are yer doin' here?" Irish asked in reply.

"I don't want anything Irish, not from you. This is my place, where I belong, I don't need a reason or your permission." Mal responded, changing his usual obsequious tone to a more angry humour, adding, "Been saying goodbye to Jay Mac have you? I told him he didn't have long left and that he'd be next but the fool wouldn't listen."

"You fuckin' say that again and *you* defo will be next, you cracked cunt." Irish snapped. "You better watch out for the Raven Skins, this is their ground, thee give yer a good kickin' last time, if thee find yer in 'ere again, hopefully thee'll finish the job."

Mal stepped out from under the shadow of the tree and moved towards Irish. Wearing his blue-grey RAF great coat with its deep collar fully turned up and with his lower limbs partially obscured by its length and the thin mist, it appeared as if he glided in their direction. He stared directly at Irish with his small blood-red eyes and a cruel smile formed on his thin lips, fully revealing his yellow and brown tobacco stained, decaying teeth.

"You're the one who needs to be careful Irish. My master has revealed his plans for you. I see a lot of sadness and pain coming your way soon." Mal almost hissed his words as he uttered them.

All three Crown team mates felt a shiver run down their spines at his bitter prophecy.

"I'm just going to pay my respects to Jay Mac then me and him are going to have a good chat later tonight." Mal sneered and was about to turn away from them, when Glynn suddenly caught hold of his right arm.

"You fuckin' go anywhere near that grave an I promise you, yours will be in the next one thee dig!"

Mal pulled his arm free and laughed then drifted away along the gravel path. They could hear him talking to himself in a low voice, as if in conversation with another. "Yes that's right master... he touched me... I know he must pay, thank you..." His voice trailed off into the distance and the youths made their way to the exit, glad to be free of that morbid place.

"Fuck me, let's get down to the Eagle and gerra few beers." Irish suggested.

"Yeah, before our luck runs out." Glynn added, only part in jest.

Within twenty minutes of leaving the municipal cemetery and their unsettling encounter with Mal the Pig, Irish, Blue and Glynn were comfortably ensconced in the more convivial surroundings of the lounge bar of the Eagle public house. By mid afternoon the trio had been joined by several other members of their crew, who were either unemployed, or casual labourers, or happened to be absent from work for any number of 'legitimate' reasons. The impromptu wake was in full swing and although last orders had been called, with the towels briefly placed over the taps as a nominal gesture of closure, the savvy landlord knew better than to even suggest any of the drinkers should leave.

They presented an eclectic mix of styles with older crew members who clung to elements of the original Skinhead-look including Crombies, Levi's denim jackets and Ben Sherman or Jaytex shirts, even if their hair was no longer cropped to a number one length. The majority of Irish's chronological peers including Blue and Glynn had morphed into the hybrid fashion of the Boot Boy, with leather coats and jackets of varying length, wide parallel trousers or even wider flares. Only one unifying feature remained almost without exception, the wearing of Dr Marten's cherry red, 1460 eight eyelet Airwair boots. Some brave souls opted for the latest pre-requisite footwear, the platform shoe or boot but these were only ever worn as a fashion statement for an evening out or a formal event, such as Jay Mac's funeral. For any serious violence and the delivering of a good kicking, only one item would suffice.

"Come on, come on, come on, come on..." Stevie 'Johno' Johnson, the immensely strong, blond haired farm labourer, was leading the community singing as Gary Glitter's *I'm the Leader* began to play on the busy juke box in the corner of the boiling, hazy room. Several other 'choir masters' had already taken their turn including; Terry (H), an old school friend of both Irish and Jay Mac; Tony (G) a core member of the Crown

Team's Lambretta scooter crew and both of the two diminutive boxing brothers, Bobby and Liam Anton known collectively as 'the Ants'.

Irish had run the full alcohol induced gamut of emotions, from pleasant contentment with an initial feeling of almost universal fraternity and bon homie to extreme paranoia, accompanied by a raging desire to fight every other male in existence, including those in his present company. He was now drifting into a more tolerant mellow mood somewhere between pragmatic acceptance of the status quo and maudlin lamentation for that which had passed.

"He was the best of us that lad." Irish suddenly announced trying not to slur his words.

"Who was, who are yer talkin' about?" Blue asked with a mild curiosity while unsuccessfully trying to throw a salted peanut into his gaping mouth.

"Jay Mac yer fuckin' tit, who d'jer think I mean?" Irish responded angrily.

"Oh yeah, yer right there Irish. Oh yeah, the *very* best." Glynn concurred, from Irish's left hand side where he was casually watching a heated arm wrestling contest; one of many that afternoon between the champion Johno and his nearest possible rival, Terry (H). Several empty glasses and brown ale bottles crashed to the floor as a result of both parties' titanic efforts and either shattered on impact or lay as if stuck to the beer soaked, cigarette-burned remnants of the well-worn, originally fitted carpet.

The landlord and his bar staff did not remonstrate with the crew but merely moved amongst them like unseen phantoms, cleared the debris and refreshed the drinks as required.

"Fuckin' bullseye!" shouted the permanently unemployed Joey 'Tank' Turner with his 'winning' dart, striking the centre of a particularly stubborn brown patch of nicotine staining, that stood out from the general coating covering most of the once gloss cream walls and which several of them were using as an ad hoc dart board.

"Yeah, he was the best of us." Irish began once more, languidly blowing three consecutive smoke rings, punctuating his words.

"What about old Tommy (S) there, 'ey? He looked fuckin' rough don't yer think?" Blue asked rhetorically, "He's out the game now, who'd have believed it, Tommy (S), the last skinhead."

Irish looked to his right with a quizzical expression "Oh no Blue that's where you're fuckin' wrong. Tommy (S) is still with us, he'll bounce back, yeah." He paused and took a lengthy draught of his pint of Guinness then continued, "We've just buried the last real Skinhead over there in the municipal cemetery."

Blue and Glynn nodded in agreement and all three sat silently for a few moments before they were swept into another wild, enthusiastic burst of community singing, as Fairweather's *Natural Sinner* loaded onto the exhausted juke box. At the chorus they all erupted into a deafening rendition of their own parody...

> *"I'm a natural Skinhead, born a Skinhead's son,*
> *Evil's been my motto, fuck up everyone!"*

The hours slipped away and a boozy afternoon merged into a serious drinking evening, topics of conversation became more philosophical and inane by equal measure. Irish, who had by now quaffed sufficient Guinness and whiskey, found his thoughts drifting away from the present with his mind constantly returning to the events of that fateful night, almost three weeks earlier. He could clearly see the heaving interior of the recently opened Lucy in the Sky bar, hear the dreadful performance of the live band above the roar of the crowd; taste the bitter ale and even smell the powerful, pungent mix of cheap scent and aftershave combined with warm beer and even warmer body odour.

The one thing he could not do was touch. If that sense had been somehow still available to him, he knew he would have stopped Jay Mac from leaving their company, made him stay with them not walk into those stinking toilets, where Morgo would pounce. *Blockbuster* by The Sweet had replaced the live performers, the juke box having no real competition, as Irish happened to notice the incongruous bald-headed, limping figure pushing his way through the heaving throng en route to the exit. His movements were made all the more surreal by the staccato effect of the pulsating strobe lighting that was accompanying the blaring juke box. Whether it was a sixth-sense or a primal instinct, Irish wheeled about and stared in the direction that the scurrying figure had come from, only to see an agitated youth calling for help, mouthing the words, "There's been a stabbing!"

In an instant Irish was out of his seat and forcing his way through the raucous crowd, who were totally oblivious as to what was occurring. When he raced into the filthy toilets the sight that greeted him was almost too much to bear. Bathed in the dim flickering glow of the low wattage lighting, lying on his back in a growing pool of his own dark life's blood mixed with the overflowing piss from the blocked urinals, was his long-time school friend and Crown team mate. Irish knelt in that sea of despair gently closing the unblinking eyes of the motionless Jay Mac. He knew that his soul had departed him but Irish's own Catholicity suddenly spontaneously rose to the surface and for the first time in many years he prayed.

When the irate senior bouncer, who had been circumspect about admitting both Irish and Jay Mac because of their Skinhead garb, charged into the small, foul smelling chamber, the kneeling Irish totally ignored his angry protestations.

"I fuckin' knew I shouldn't have let you two pricks in, well yer done for now yer little cunt, the bizzies are on the way..."

Irish spoke only once but it was not to the doorman, "Wherever yer are, I'm gonna find yer and when I do I'm gonna gut yer good and proper." he called out aloud.

"Who are yer talkin' to Irish?" Blue asked lazily, instantly snapping Irish back to the here and now, sitting in the blue-grey cigarette smoke filled, boiling lounge of the Eagle public house. Irish stared directly ahead and said, "Anyone whose listenin' Blue, *anyone* whose listenin'."

A number of regular Friday night civilian punters had now taken their usual places in the lounge and the Crew's increasingly boisterous antics were rapidly wearing thin the already overstretched patience of the landlord. The point at which it would snap was almost arrived.

As Irish finished the dregs of his pint he casually looked to his left and then right, trying to recognise the sea of faces that swam about him. His unsteady gaze was drawn to a member of the Eagle crew who had suffered the loss of an eye in the same epic battle, with their Kings Team rivals that had nearly cost Tommy (S) his life. The visually challenged Brian 'Brain' Dent was sat three places to the right of Irish and was busily constructing a well packed herbal cigarette for immediate use.

Just as he was about to light his considerable joint Irish called out "What the fuck d'you think yer doin' Brain?"

Brain fixed Irish with his one functioning orb and replied "Rolling a joint *officer*, what the fuck's it gorra do with you?"

Irish now responded angrily, "Hey, dickhead what have we all said about stoppin' drugs on this estate?"

Brain laughed, asking "Who made you a fuckin' bizzie? Anyway yer dead mate Jay Mac didn't mind doin' a bit of dealin' when it suited 'im."

Irish was already on his feet demanding satisfaction "Let's have it cunt, c'mon."

Brain was normally a quiet member of the crew but he was still a Skinhead at heart like the rest of them and could not let this challenge pass. As The Rolling Stone's *Paint it Black* began playing on the juke box he leapt up to face Irish, snatching hold of an empty brown ale bottle as he did intent on smashing it across his opponent's head. Irish was too quick even in his drunken state, his right fist thumped into Brain's open mouth splitting his bottom lip and sending him crashing into a nearby table of older civilian drinkers dropping his weapon in the process. Brain came back with both fists swinging wildly, catching Irish in the gut and on the left side of his jaw. Snatching hold of Brain's feather-cut hair, Irish slammed his head down into his rapidly rising knee, repeating the movement several times for good effect. Bleeding and in pain as he was Brain grappled Irish round the waist. Both combatants fell to the sticky sodden floor, where they immediately began punching and gouging each other in an ugly spectacle of primal rage.

"Fuckin' pack it in now, the pair of yer." demanded the purple-faced landlord who burst through the ranks of imbibers, armed with his foot long, dark wooden club, retrieved from its secured place beneath the bar. "Gerrup and gerrout the fuckin lorra yer, I've had enough of your shite!" he bellowed.

"Alright George, calm the fuck down before yer 'ave a heart attack." Terry (H) warned whilst he, Tony (G) and Johno separated the two sweating, bloodied opponents.

"Come 'ed shake 'ands you two fuckers, we're all on the same team 'ere." the sagacious Terry (H), their senior player instructed.

Both parties reluctantly did as they were ordered and the whole Eagle crew rose to leave as one, donning their Crombies, leather or denim jackets, ready to face the outside elements. Just as they were filing out into the freezing night George the landlord, decided to remonstrate further, "That's right, do what I tell yer, I don't want yers in 'ere no more, yer all fuckin' barred!"

Terry (H) who was at the rear of the column turned about angrily, closing the distance between him and the older, much heavier male in an instant, "Watch yer mouth there George, just 'cause you've got yer fuckin' period doesn't give you the right to speak to us like that. We spend a wedge in this fuckin' shit hole, this is 'our' alehouse. Gerrit straight."

George had the height and weight advantage but staring into the cold, dead eyes of the Crown Team's seasoned scrapper, his rage dissipated, like the heat that was rapidly escaping through the open door to the darkness outside. Caution proved the better part of valour, he said no more. Terry (H) walked away to join the rest of the crew waiting in the ever-empty car park of the eponymous alehouse.

After a prolonged heavy drinking session there was only one obvious place to go for the much needed deep fried sustenance, Mr Li's Golden Diner. Situated at the lower edge of the bleak, post-war overspill housing estate, this particular fish and chip shop was considered the superior eatery of the two that were located in this area.

It was run by a formidable Chinese gentlemen whom all the youths were wise enough to be wary of, consequently they usually curbed their more outlandish behaviour and moderated their language in his establishment. No one wished to appear disrespectful and risk annoying this oriental warrior.

As the crew strolled down the main central road through that bitterly cold, late November night they were generally in good spirits, apart from Irish and Brain. Still seething with rage Irish constantly replayed his team mate's words over in his mind, causing him to consider how much of a 'team' they really were. For his part Brain, who had rapidly begun to sober as the inclement weather assaulted his senses, appreciated his good fortune that the fight had been stopped before he had sustained any further injuries, other than a split lip and bruises. He knew under normal circumstances he was no match for Irish, deciding to keep his distance and his mouth closed for the time being.

"See yer lads, I'm off." Glynn shouted on nearing his home, which was positioned half way along their route.

"Aren't yer 'ungry Glynn, yer gonna miss out on Mr Li's." Johno called to him as he crossed the road to the opposite side.

"Nah, I don't fancy any fish and chips, me ma's got a big pan of Scouse keepin' warm in the oven, so am gonna drop that, see yers." Glynn replied then hurried on towards his neatly painted residence.

Both Irish and Blue knew the real reason why Glynn had departed, he did not wish to encounter the crazed psychopath Weaver, now sole leader of the Heron Crew who together with two of his fellow commanders had gang-raped Glynn's mother.

"It's all a fuckin' mess." Irish observed speaking to Blue who was alongside him.

For once Blue understood perfectly what Irish was actually saying. "Yeah, I know what yer mean, it's fucked up. We're all walkin' round like we're still kids, like when we was fifteen and started as a Skinhead crew." He paused leading Irish to nod in agreement. "Look what's 'appened in the past year; those cunts Yad and Devo are dead, Macca (G)'s crippled for life, Floyd's fucked, Tommy (S) is in a bad state, Dayo and Quirky are away... inside, an our mate Jay Mac's been stabbed t'death by some psycho twat who's gorroff with it." Blue concluded his depressing summary just as they arrived at the famed Golden Diner.

Irish almost lost his appetite when he considered Blue's final comment. A burning hunger for revenge was gnawing his soul with an intensity far greater than any temporary physical desire, his corporeal needs could easily be satisfied but that which tormented his spirit demanded only one resolution.

The crew poured into the welcoming shop, ordered their fish and chip suppers, sausage dinners, meat and potato pies with extra gravy and the usual nominal supply of chop suey rolls for a healthy balance; all were saturated in vinegar and thoroughly doused in salt.

As each one was served they quickly exited and took up their places on the low walls outside the shops and the perimeter of the adjacent Heron public house. For a brief time there was little or no conversation, as the serious business of demolishing their food took precedence.

"Fuck I needed that!" Johno announced, immediately reinforcing his statement with an emphatic belch.

"Me too." said Blue, greedily eyeing the fare of those team mates who had not yet completely devoured their deep-fried comfort food. "Yeah, another couple of pies wouldn't go amiss." he concluded before abandoning his 'seat' between Irish and Johno and hurrying back into the Golden Diner.

"Gerrus a sausage dinner while yer there Blue an I'll keep yer space 'ere." Johno called, flicking a well-aimed new fifty pence piece to his corpulent team mate.

"Alright ladies... come down 'ere to a proper chippy 'ave yers?" Weaver, the crazed psychopath leader of the Heron Crew shouted to the Eagle players, as he approached from the rear of this eponymous alehouse, accompanied by a small retinue of Juniors.

"Watch who yer callin' ladies Weaver!" Terry (H) shouted in reply. "We're down 'ere havin' a bit of decent scran, we don't need any shit from you."

Weaver laughed, even unhinged as he undoubtedly was, he was still sufficiently cognisant to be wary of this veteran Crown Team scrapper.

"Nice one Terry, pity yers weren't down 'ere earlier, we've just been over the Lancs Road on the Kings ground, doin' a bit of 'work'."

Irish stared at the grinning madman with growing incredulity. "Can I just ask yer Weaver, why the fuck you'd wanna wind them up again now that business is all sorted?" He was referring to their long-standing blood feud with the Kings Team that had proved so costly for both sides and had only recently been concluded.

Weaver moved some loose strands of his coarse, scraggy mane away from his face and rubbed his stubbly chin, fixing Irish with his own intimidating, piercing stare. "Are you takin' the piss Irish? You come down 'ere to my fuckin' ground and start askin' *me* why am doin' what am doin', yer cheeky cunt." He quickly positioned himself in front of the seated Irish, watching for the slightest tell-tale movement.

Before Irish could reply, Terry (H) intervened, "'Ey nut-job he's not the only one askin' yer..., am fuckin' askin' yer, why *are* yer tryin' t'kick it all off again?"

"An me, I'd like t'know that." Johno added.

"Yeah Weaver, we're *all* askin' yer." Tony (G) concluded, speaking for the group.

Weaver stepped away from Irish, backed up a few paces, staring at them all intently "So that's the way it is, is it? Alright, I'll tell yer why I do it, seein' as yers 'ave all asked me nicely." He drew up a quantity of thick phlegm and spat it forcefully onto the pavement in front of them, "I do it for the buzz... I do it 'cause I've got the balls... an, I do it 'cause I'm Weaver!" He roared the final part of his answer and raised his clenched fists on either side of his head.

"Alright Weaver, what's happenin', what 'ave I missed?" asked the ever chirpy Blue as he emerged from Mr Li's establishment, clutching two meat and potato pies and a large portion of chips in one steaming package and Johno's sausage dinner in another.

The Heron leader glared angrily at the Eagle player who had accidentally but effectively deflated his dramatic moment.

"D'yer wanna chip mate? We're all starvin' 'cause we've been drinkin' all day for our mate Jay Mac."

Weaver smiled at the garrulous Blue and asked sarcastically, "Why, what's that cunt been doin' now? The last thing I heard was... he was dead!" He laughed loudly at his own humorous remark.

Everyone else remained silent, until Irish spoke. "We've been at Jay Mac's wake in the Eagle, he was buried today up at the municipal."

"What the fuck are yer tellin' me for, that doesn't mean anythin' to me." Weaver responded, returning to his usual grim expression.

One of the Juniors began to speak, "But Weaver you told us all..."

"Shut yer fuckin' mouth you, before I shut it for yer." Weaver snapped angrily.

"Hiya lads, giz a few chips." a familiar female voice called to them, announcing the arrival of Molly 'Skank' Brown, accompanied by four of her 'business' associates, including the badly scarred, obliging Donna.

Not far behind Molly and Co. in her wake and image, was her marginally younger sister, Little Jane with two of her friends, all eager to learn the trade.

The new arrivals were dressed in a similarly eclectic mix of styles to their male counterparts, including grubby Crombies, denim jackets, or leather coats of varying length. Their one unifying item of apparel was their ridiculously short skirts, which left little to the imagination. Worn with dark tights and tall platform shoes, they combined the old out-dated garb with the latest fashion prerequisite. Their arrival excited and animated the male members of the combined crews, who were keen for any possible entertaining diversion on this bleak, cold night.

"What's on offer t'night, Molly?" Weaver asked, slipping his arm around her waist, quickly feeling her bottom while he was in the general vicinity.

"Nothin' for free t'you, that's for sure." Molly replied, deftly stepping away from the aroused team leader.

Everyone laughed except Weaver.

"How's about one of yer ten pence tosses? I haven't had a wank for two days, me balls are turnin' blue." he asked expectantly.

"No chance, anyway its fifty pence a pull now." Molly announced much to everyone's surprise and disappointment.

"Fuckin' hell Molly, that's a bit steep, talk about the cost of livin' goin' up?" Terry (H) observed with a sly grin.

Weaver pressed on "Tell yer what Molly, I'll give yer all the loose change I've got in me pocket for a quickie in the alley now, how's that sound?"

"Piss off Weaver, you're always too fuckin' rough anyway." Molly replied sharply.

Weaver laughed, "Yeah an that's the way you like it, that's what Macca used to always tell us but then he's no fuckin' use to yer anymore is he?"

Molly was furious, she would accept no criticism of her sadistic lover the now permanently paralysed Macca (G).

The fact that he had totally abandoned her and his unacknowledged child, constantly humiliated her in front of the crews, a practice which ultimately led to his own violent assault and, used her for his scheming purposes, did not even slightly detract from her infatuation with the former Heron team leader.

"Fuck off Weaver, don't you even speak about my Gary, he's still twice the man you'll ever be." She spat her words at the temporarily stunned psychopath, then added "*Anyone* else fancy a bit of fun in the alley, I'll do yer a good price." Her colleagues quickly made similar offers which were instantly accepted by Johno, Blue, Terry (H), Tony (G) and several others.

As the prospective paramours moved away towards the reeking alley at the rear of the shops, with a raging Weaver watching their departure, Little Jane moved towards him, "I'll do yer Weaver... if yer like."

Weaver's face lit up with delight, "Gerrin that fuckin' alley now girl."

Molly was still within earshot and called back angrily, "Go home, our Jane, I'm warnin' yer."

Her younger sibling smiled slyly, "You can piss off our Molly, I do what I want, *you* don't own me." She turned to her two friends, "C'mon girls, don't be shy, we can make a few bob here."

Irish, who had finished his meal and was standing almost alongside the monocular Brain, received an offer he found difficult to refuse, "Listen, sorry about before in the alehouse, I was out of order. If yer fancy a go on one of these bitches, I'll pay, how's that?" Brain put forward his hand once again as he spoke.

Stood in front of the desolate, vandalised shops on this bitterly cold night, following the day of his best friend's funeral, Irish broke with tradition. He shook his team mate's hand and said, "Why not, I could do with a bit of relief meself." Within moments he too had joined the queue in the litter-strewn, filthy alley, waiting his turn to be serviced.

Moans and groans of passion temporarily warmed the frigid air as partners reached a climax and were instantly replaced by another urgent pleasure seeker. Irish watched the fumbled couplings, frantic masturbations and fevered fellatio montage like a disaffected voyeur at a Roman orgy. Casually unzipping his black twenty-two inch parallel trousers, he stepped forward to take his turn. A light, cold rain began to fall steadily. The smell of wet hair, unwashed bodies and damp clothing mixed with that of decaying refuse and heated sexual activity filled his nostrils. Irish tilted his head back letting the rain spatter on his face and said quietly to himself "I don't know where you've ended up Jay Mac but God I hope it's better than this shit hole."

Not far away across the other side of the main highway, the Lancashire Road, in the uncultivated, abandoned farmer's field, considered as Kings Team territory, Danny (H), the leader of the Anvil Crew, from the south sector of that huge sprawling estate, was standing with a dozen of his peers studying the work of Weaver and his Juniors. Having been alerted by two of his younger associate members, Danny had hastened to the spot where most of the gang's inflammatory propaganda was displayed, the massive concrete slab stanchions of the bisecting fly-over that spanned both territories.

There above them in two foot high letters were the freshly painted threats, insults and statements of Weaver. "CROWN TEAM GUNNERS, KINGS TEAM RUNNERS" was one of his classic pieces, supplemented with "CROWN TEAM RULE

OK!" "KINGS TEAM SHITS" and the mandatory "I'M WEAVER I DID THIS".

"D'yer want us to do them all same as usual Danny?" one of his talented team of artists asked.

"Yeah do them all, blank the fuckin' lot, all except this one." Danny ordered. He had moved onto the tarmaced pavement just beyond the field's edge and was staring up at one of the huge monolith supports, which faced directly onto the busy dual carriageway. "R.I.P. JAY MAC, CROWN SKIN" was the epitaph that he read there, on this monumental headstone.

"Leave that one." he said, stepping forward with an aerosol can of gloss black paint in his hand. "He was one of our own, Jay Mac." Danny observed as he added the words 'FROM THE KINGS ESTATE' beneath the original inscription, acknowledging the deceased's unique status, living on one estate and fighting for another.

Danny looked out across the wide road of speeding outward and inbound traffic, over its central reservation and into the Crown Team's equally abandoned field beyond. Even as Weaver and the others were being vigorously entertained, the Anvil Crew leader warned "He just won't let it go, that Weaver prick, he's gonna have t'be taught a fuckin' good lesson."

CHAPTER 2

Whiskey in the Jar

January 1976

January 1976 found Irish entering his twenty first year. Although he would not achieve that milestone birthday until the summer, he was making every possible effort to turn his life around and become a credible adult member of society. Almost since the day of his long-standing friend Jay Mac's funeral, Irish had been having less and less contact with the crew, severing his links wherever possible. For the past two years, having enrolled in a local college for night school sessions, he had gradually been gaining the education denied to him and the other poor unfortunate 'pupils' of the *Cardinals School for Catholic Boys*, which he, Jay Mac and Terry (H) had attended.

In stark contrast to his previously scruffy unkempt appearance throughout his official Skinhead, Suedehead and Boot Boy period, he had now embraced the original look wholeheartedly, even as it completely vanished from the ever-changing, ephemeral youth fashion scene. Whether it was an unconscious homage to his dead friend, who had been the embodiment of the smartest elements of the early Skinhead style, or merely a happy accident, Irish, with his regularly cropped hair, professionally laundered well-cut Crombie, immaculately pressed parallel trousers, with razor edge creases and new highly polished gleaming cherry red 1460 Airwair, looked the business. When his older team mate and scooter enthusiast Tony (G), progressed to a four-wheel mode of transport, Irish was able to secure his magnificent Lambretta LI175, replete with its array of dazzling chrome accessories, at a good price and no longer needed to rely on the infrequent, packed-to-capacity, slow moving, public bus service.

Racing from the construction site where he was unofficially employed as a labourer for three, four or five days of the week, depending on demand, to his series of self-improving evening classes on his uber-cool Lambretta, Irish felt on top of the world, he could see a way forward, he was in control of his life.

When the terrible day came in the middle of that freezing first month of the year, that he received devastating news it would prove to be the first of more upsets yet to come.

Returning home from his day's work for a quick snack before attending his further education college, Irish was summoned into the rear parlour of the open plan, small, corporation terraced house where he lived with his parents, two sisters and two brothers.

"Patrick yer need to come in here now." his mother called to him in a stern voice that quivered with emotion.

"Ma, can't it wait, I'm in an awful rush." he shouted from the stairs, heading towards the bathroom.

"No Patrick, it can't, come here please." she replied quietly.

When he entered the living room and found his four distressed siblings assembled, heard their sobbing, witnessed their grief, his gaze sped to his mother who was standing in the parlour to the rear. A terrible nausea and weakness suddenly overcame him, he was rendered unable to speak and could not ask that dread question. His tearful mother spared him the need.

"It's yer father... he's had a massive heart attack at work today..."

"What hospital is he in, how is he?" Irish interrupted, finally able to ask the desperate question he knew there was no answer to.

"Yer da's gone Patrick, he died where he was... at his machine." Mrs O'Hare answered softly.

For a few moments there was total silence then the denial began.

"No, not my da, he's fit and strong, he's never had *any* heart problems, *never*." Irish began.

His long-haired, ex-hippy brother Dermot stood up and joined his younger sibling and mother in the rear of the room, "Now that's were y'wrong Patrick, da's had trouble f'years, you should know that seein' as how you're partly to blame."

"Not now Dermot please, not now." Mrs O'Hare pleaded.

Irish sprang forward almost, face touching face with his elder brother asking "What are yer tryin' t'say Dermot? Don't hold back, let's have it straight."

Dermot, who was several inches taller than his brother, leaned over him saying "You well know what I'm talkin' about, the trouble you caused when you was hangin' around with all those bloody Skinhead fellers, you and that clown, John Mack, yous were always up t'no good, yer pair of ejits. Da never stopped worryin' about yer. He was broken hearted, the way yer turned out t'be a nobody."

In a blur of movement Irish pounded his tremendous right jab into his senior sibling's stomach, before seizing and throwing him to the floor, "Stay down Dermot or I'll hurt yer." Irish warned. His instinct and training was to put the boot in but his mother's shrill scream of despair stayed his action, jolting him back to reality. He fled the room, snatching up his Centurion helmet as he did, flung open the front door and charged into the street. Leaping onto his Lambretta he quickly started the engine, revved the accelerator, let out the clutch and sped off into the enveloping darkness. There would be no evening classes that night or any other.

A freezing fog was slowly settling onto the bleak estate, causing Irish to use his array of additional spot lamps to supplement the scooter's single main beam. He had no plan or destination in mind, only a desire to blot out the pain of the unbearable truth. Within minutes he was alongside The Hounds public house and pulled into the empty car park, intent on obtaining some liquid escapism from the off-licence store attached to the main building. Quickly purchasing a half bottle of Johnny Walker whiskey, he left the small shop, striding with urgent purpose towards his parked Lambretta.

"Alright Irish, what are yer doin' with Tony (G)'s machine?" a vaguely familiar voice called to him.

Irish recognised the speaker as Ste Turner, the younger brother of his Eagle crew mate Tank; two other youths were standing immediately to his rear. In no mood for conversation, Irish pushed through the trio stating brusquely "It's my bike, I bought it off Tony, right!"

"Yeah ok mate, no need t'get narked. We was just wonderin' if yer needed a little blow, if y'wanted to score, y'look like yer could do with chillin' out."

Irish spun round sharply; he knew only too well how the estate had long since been flooded with every manner of drugs, with an army of dealers increasing in number daily. His desperately futile attempts to organise a local resistance to this unstoppable wave of self-destruction, had been totally abandoned in the face of overwhelming odds by all those who had offered even a token effort. A doomed youth raced headlong to its own demise.

"You offerin' me drugs, lad?" he began.

"Depends on what y'fancy mate, we can sort yer out at a good price." Ste replied smiling.

Irish leapt forward and caught the youth by the throat in a powerful grip, "Don't ever offer me your fuckin' poison boy, I don't like you, I've never liked yer and if yer brother wasn't on the old team, I'd choke the fuckin' life out of yer here and now".

Nobody moved as the terrified youth gasped, "Alright, alright, just let me go."

After a few agonising moments while he increased the intensity of his grip, Irish released his victim then turned and walked away. He slipped the half bottle of whiskey into his Crombie side pocket, mounted his scooter, turning on the engine and prepared to ride off.

The angry youth called after him, "Yer alright with yer own poison are yer? Y'cunt, don't worry we'll see *you* again but you won't see us."

Briefly raising two fingers in victory salute, Irish rode away in the thickening fog.

A short time later he pulled over, stopped his machine, turned off his array of lights and parked alongside the aged walls of the municipal cemetery on the southern edge of the Crown Estate, bordering its equally bleak, huge encircling walled counterpart, Ravens Hall. He unclipped the strap of his white with black peak, Centurion helmet, letting its plastic chin cup hang loose. Quickly unscrewing the metal top of his

Johnny Walker whiskey, he took a series of deep swallows of the golden brown, warming liquid.

The more he drank the angrier he became, there was no solace here, no refuge at the bottom of this bottle. As his brain flooded with the intoxicating fluid, his inner vision became increasingly clouded, images he sought became indistinct and those he wished to avoid acquired a crystal clarity. Though he tried desperately to see his father's face one more time he could not, instead a horrible tableaux of his beloved parent's final moments occupied the centre stage of his mind, illuminated by garish footlights. Irish could see his father clutching at his chest in mortal agony, slumping over his machine surrounded by his fellow drones, ignored by all until his production of vital washing machine parts stopped and threatened to impinge on the day's quota for his section.

The angry foreman's ugly face appeared before him cursing and swearing, "Get old Paddy of that fuckin' machine, we've got targets t'meet here, we're on piece rate! No one's gettin' a bonus today, because of this cunt."

Irish visualised the other dead-eyed drones momentarily focusing their deeply imbedded anger on the hated overseer then turning back to their machines, obedient automatons for the rest of their shift. His tormenting vision was not far from the reality of the day's actual events. Mr O'Hare had always been a grafter, a provider; even now just short of his sixtieth birthday he worked every hour that was available, every minute of overtime, his family came first. Struggling as he was after years of hard physical toil, served under a raft of fat-cat bosses, he tried to keep up with the younger men. Finally his huge heart gave out and the Irish giant collapsed where he stood, still in harness to a new generation of factory owners, their forebears and his chronological peers having long since retired in comfort, enjoying the splendid fruits of the labour of others in their own golden years.

"'Ey lad giz a swig of yer bottle there!" Irish heard suddenly from a few yards distant behind him.

He was too drunk to even care who was calling to him, replying "Piss off, get yer own drink."

"That's not very nice is it? Y'come 'ere to Raven's ground, get yerself bevvied and won't even share yer booze, that's fuckin' disrespectful. I think we'll have t'be takin' that scooter off yer."

Irish turned around and launched the near-empty bottle into the middle of the six Ravens Boot Boys then started up his Lambretta and sped forward a few yards.

"Shithouse, wanker!" they unwisely called after him, "Go 'ed run off, yer fuckin' queer!" their leader taunted.

They were mistaken; Irish was not leaving, merely building up speed. He spun his magnificent machine around in a sharp u-turn and raced towards the half dozen tightly packed human skittles. Even though they dived to either side to avoid the speeding scooter, those nearest the centre were struck painful blows at its passing, all six fell to the damp ground in an array of poses.

Irish had not finished with them. Bringing his Lambretta to a stop he dismounted and strode back to where they lay, "C'mon who wants some, let's have it." he demanded, holding his hands out in front of him, palms upward.

Those Ravens Boot Boys who could rise, quickly scrambled to their feet ready to meet the raging madman. If they had been original Ravens Skins or members of their senior Boot Boy crew, Irish would have been in serious trouble but these youths were their younger siblings, no more than fifteen or sixteen years of age, the equivalent of the Crown Team's juniors. The two bravest came at Irish from either side; the foremost receiving a tremendous head-butt straight to the bridge of his nose, from the helmet-enclosed head of the Eagle player. Seeing his crew mate so easily dispatched, with his shattered nose spurting a stream of red blood, the next opponent drew a razor sharp Stanley knife from the pocket of his denim jacket.

"Fuck boy, you better have somethin' better than that if you're gonna threaten me." Irish sneered; lunging forward under the boy's wild slash, which merely glanced off the top of the white Centurion helmet and exposed him to Irish's punishing fists. Down he went to his knees receiving a vicious boot to the jaw as he did.

The pair who had been struck by the scooter had not yet fully risen, leaving only two Ravens players fit for the game. They both hesitated and that vacillation was their undoing. Irish removed his helmet as if to improve their chances but in reality to utilise it as a weapon. Charging to his right he smashed his reluctant opponent on that side fully in his face, almost snapping his neck with the force of the blow. He now joined his friends on the ground, falling like a marionette that had suddenly had its strings cut.

"Please mate, I didn't say nothin', I don't want no trouble." the terrified remaining youth pleaded, to no avail.

"Yer've already got trouble boy, too fuckin' late." Irish answered with an evil grin.

"Fuck this!" the youth shouted, turning to run from the scene. Within two paces the well aimed helmet struck him fully in the back of the skull with a terrific 'crack'. All six Ravens players were either on the ground or trying to rise from it.

Irish launched into a whiskey-fuelled, frenzied, delirious dance of rage, leaping from one victim to another lashing out with his gleaming cherry red Airwair, booting in faces, breaking teeth and noses and cracking ribs, until with his aching legs exhausted his anger was finally assuaged. Drenched in his own sweat he stood with heaving chest gasping for air, like a black-coated demon rising out of the freezing, grey fog, blood lust sated. "Look da, I *am* good at somethin', I'm not a failure!" he called out before picking up his helmet and walking back to his waiting Lambretta. None of the wounded Ravens youths would disagree with him.

Pleased with his bloody victory, Irish decided to enjoy a triumphal circuit of the perimeter road that encircled the huge municipal cemetery. He raced away from the scene leaving a trail of exhaust fumes to mingle with the natural vapours, the throaty roar of the scooter's two-stroke engine fading into the night, confirming his haste. Drunk and driving almost blind, having not bothered to switch on his lights, it was surprising that he even made the distance he did. Just as he approached the tall, rusty, wrought iron gates of the main entrance, less than half way around his course, his luck abandoned him.

Suddenly a dark misshapen figure stumbled out of the cemetery directly into Irish's path. Too late he called out his warning, "Gerrout the fuckin' way!"

Scooter, rider and casualty combined in one awful, fatal incident. Bones were broken, vital organs ruptured, a tenuous existence snuffed out with a sickening thud that rebounded off the aged cemetery walls. Irish raised himself from where he lay a few yards from his damaged Lambretta and staggered to where his victim had been thrown. "I'm sorry, I'm sorry mate..." he began, kneeling alongside the shattered body wrapped in its blue-grey R.A.F great coat. He took off his Centurion helmet and listened for any sign of remaining life, looking in horror at the blood-drenched, mutilated face of Mal the Pig. A stream of dark red fluid gurgled from the distorted mouth, two reddened eyes opened and a gasp of recognition escaped into the ether.

"Irish, it's you... why did you do this... to me?" Mal asked through the remnants of his rotten teeth.

"It was an accident... I didn't mean to do it... I've been drinkin'." Irish offered by way of a combined apology and explanation. "I'm really sorry Mal..."

Another scarlet splutter erupted from the disturbed youth's mouth, this time quickly followed by two trails of tears, streaming from his half-closed eyes, "It's ok Irish... I'm glad it's finally over..." Mal's breath was coming in short laboured bursts, "Do somethin' for me... when I'm gone... please."

"Anythin' Mal, anythin, what is it yer want?"

"Pray for me... pray for my soul... I'm afraid... I've seen that place." He began to convulse involuntarily, opened his small blood-shot eyes fully and beckoned with his right hand for Irish to come closer then spoke one last time, "He's ok... he's smiling... yer dad..."

Mal's tortured spirit fled into the great darkness. Irish made the sign of the cross and began "Eternal rest give unto him..."

For a brief period of time that seemed like an eternity, Irish did not move but remained kneeling by Mal's lifeless body, trying to absorb the enormity of what he had done. A sudden charge of adrenalin shuddered through him, preparing the distraught Eagle player for fight or flight. He knew the right thing to do was contact the emergency services, somehow call for an ambulance and the police. With equal certainty he knew that he must escape, hide the evidence, cover his trail or his own young life would be ended before it had begun.

Rising to a crouching position he grasped Mal's corpse by the shoulders of his heavy great coat and dragged him within the grounds of the forbidding gates, he ran back to his scooter, righted it, and quickly assessed the extent of damage it had sustained, all the time praying it would start. After pulling the mud guard and right front shield into a functioning shape, he manipulated some of the more severely bent mirror stalks so as to cause the least obstruction and picked up the fragments of his shattered, Perspex fly-screen which had cracked in two.

When the engine finally turned over, breathing a massive sigh of relief, he rode away from that place of death, 'No one must ever know what happened here tonight' Irish told himself as he sped through swirling fog, this time with all his remaining working lights cutting a hazy yellow swathe before him.

Finally arriving back at his home in the middle of the Crown Estate, he frantically dragged the damaged vehicle into the converted storage room that ran alongside the house, where his older brother tended to study and sometimes sleep. Fortunately for Irish on this particularly freezing night Dermot was sleeping on the comfortable old couch, in the front room. Irish covered his Lambretta with a heavy tarpaulin sheet then entered into the house, through a connecting door to the kitchen at the rear, trying to act as if nothing unusual had occurred that evening.

"Where the fuck have you been?" Dermot called angrily on hearing his arrival.

"Nowhere, I just went for a quick drive that's all. I haven't been near anywhere." he lied unconvincingly.

"Well that's lucky for you 'cause there's been a bad accident, some cunts been killed." Dermot advised.

Irish froze where he was standing in the kitchen, in the process of making a huge sandwich of corned beef on thick sliced bread. "What accident, where was this? I don't know anything about an accident." he blurted out defensively.

"Alright Patrick, calm down will yer, there's been enough upset in here today and don't think I've forgotten about that sly dig yer gave me either." Dermot paused then added casually, "Yeah, up on the Lancs Road, been a pile up, lucky there was only one fucker killed really."

Once again Irish breathed a huge sigh of relief, then called through to his reclining brother, "Not so lucky for that poor twat." He joined his brother in the front room and handed him a mug of steaming tea, "'Ere yer are arsehole, don't say I never give yer nothin'." Sitting down in an equally battered old armchair, Irish lit a cigarette, "I s'ppose we'll have t'start makin' the arrangements for da's funeral."

"No, ma's already got it all sorted, we're goin' up to the municipal tomorrer, to have a look at the plot, you can come with us, its about time you started takin' on a bit of responsibility." Dermot suggested.

Irish took a long drag of his cigarette before replying, "Nah, I don't think I'll be goin' anywhere near that awful place it gives me the creeps."

Within a week Mr O'Hare was laid to rest. His funeral was well attended by both friends and relations, with many elaborate floral tributes. One particularly large wreath caught Irish's attention. It was wrapped around with a broad silk band in the national colours of Eire and had a scallop-edged card attached which read 'Farewell and God bless, from the Mack family.' Irish was momentarily curious as to what possible connection the vicious Gerard Boys could have with his own gentle, deceased father. After a brief period of speculation, he idly slipped the card into his Crombie pocket and gave the matter no further thought for the present.

In stark contrast when the broken body of the troubled Mal was interred, a few days later, apart from the disinterested curate who performed a perfunctory rite expeditiously, only the devastated Mr and Mrs Chadwick stood at the side of that restless grave.

The police were still appealing for witnesses to the tragic hit and run, that had occurred on the night of the sixteenth of

January but as yet was without any response, or possible leads. They insisted that their enquiries were ongoing stating they were following a number of avenues and were confident of making an early arrest, or arrests.

Irish had read the detailed account of the terrible accident in the local press, the *Liverpool Echo* and had seen the printed appeals fastened to several telegraph poles and street lamps but was certain there were no witnesses and that he had sufficiently covered his trail, so no one or nothing could incriminate him. He was ashamed and remorseful for what he had done but his deeply ingrained self-survival instincts, convinced him he could not change the events and that no good would come of his voluntary surrendering to the authorities.

Irish was morally, legally and spiritually wrong but he was also incorrect in thinking that there were no witnesses. His six injured Ravens Boot Boy attackers had all read those same graphic newspaper accounts and the police appeals. Tradition meant they could not co-operate with the authorities but also demanded some suitable revenge for the insult they had suffered. For the moment they waited, biding their time until the right opportunity to inflict maximum damage presented itself.

Barely two weeks after the interment of his father, Irish's grieving mother summoned him once more into the rear parlour to advise him of another downturn in their families' fortunes.

"So there it is Patrick, with yer da gone and Dermot back down in Northampton for his studies, you're goin' to have t'become the man of the house." Mrs O'Hare announced then reiterated her urgent reasons for making such a bold but necessary decision, "Y'da was a good man but never very wise. He's left us with no pension, no money, nothing. Now that the factory is laying people off or puttin' us on short time, I'll be lucky to get even three days a week." She paused to allow him to ingest the financial consequences of what she had said. "It's down to you Patrick, yer've got two sisters and little Sean relyin' on yer, they can't go without. My wages will barely cover the rent but there'll be nothin' left for food, heatin' or anythin' else. We need you son, yer've got t'get more hours on that site and bring in a man's wage, can y'do that for us?"

Irish looked at his tearful mother then glanced into the front room were his younger siblings were seated. Both girls were busily engaged in their homework and Sean was playing with his toys, whilst intermittently watching the television.

"Of course ma, of course I can do it." he replied, smiling, "Don't you even worry yer head about money any more. I'll take care of it; I'll take care of us all."

"God bless yer son, I knew yer had the makin's in yer, yer old da will be lookin' down on yer and smilin' right now."

The following morning Irish made an urgent extra trip to the construction site where he was unofficially employed as a casual labourer. It was eight a.m. on a cold and frosty day with only a pale sun hanging in a grey sky. Irish trudged across the frozen, muddy ground, cracking pools of ice as he did and up the steps of the white-walled, plasterboard hut of the site foreman's office.

"Alright there Peter, what are yer doin' here t'day? This isn't one of yer day's lad. What's happened, pissed the bed again 'ave yer?" asked the cheery, red faced, late forties male, clinging to a steaming mug of Bovril in his equally weather-worn meaty hands.

"No I haven't thanks... and me names Patrick, not Peter." Irish began, "I need t'ask yer for some extra work, a couple of days is no good t'me anymore, yer see..."

The foreman raised his right hand, took a sip of his beefy drink then said, "I'll stop yer right there lad. Well am glad yer came in t'day, it'll save me tellin' yer tomorrer." He paused and took another drink; Irish did not like the direction the conversation seemed to be heading in and waited impatiently for his boss's next words.

"Yeah, y'see Peter there's been some cutbacks, with one thing an another and the main contractors haven't been gettin' paid by the top fellers, so we're gonna 'ave t'let a few lads go." the older male announced, continuing "No point in delayin' matters an fuckin' about, you know the score it's last in, first out. That means *you* Peter... yer not needed anymore."

Irish tried to protest then pleaded, "Please Mr Arnold, I'm desperate, really desperate... me arl fellers just died and me ma's..."

Again he was cut short. "Like I said, yer out... there's a few bob waitin' for yer in an envelope in the cash office, that's the best I can do, no hard feelin's lad." He stood up, held out his right hand and smiled.

"There's a few bob waitin' for me... that's it. I bet your job's safe yer cunt, fuck you!" Irish snapped.

"Go 'ed, gerrout before I..." the older male warned but was interrupted by the raging youth mid sentence.

"Before you what? Stay in 'ere fat arse where it's warm, drinkin' yer brew, yer've done the bosses' dirty work for them. By the way, me name's Patrick not fuckin' Peter, yer tit." Irish stormed out of the small cabin, slamming the flimsy door behind him.

"Aye, well fuck off then Patrick, 'ave a nice life on the dole, yer little prick." the grinning foreman called after him, simultaneously allowing a loud, protracted fart to escape into the confined space of his office. "Fuck! That's better, I needed that" he said, much relieved.

After hurriedly collecting his severance pay from the wages office, Irish tore open the small, brown envelope and carefully counted the cash within.

"Twenty fuckin' quid, you tight bastards!" he called out as he approached his waiting Lambretta. Whilst driving back to his home he tried to formulate a plan of action and concoct a convincing story to tell his mother.

When he entered the house he found Mrs O'Hare busily working in the small kitchen, washing the dishes, "Hello son, how did it go, did thee give yer those extra days?" she asked, expectantly.

"Oh yeah, no problem." he lied then took three of the four £5 notes he had received, out of his pocket and passed them to her, "There yer are ma... fifteen quid. The boss give me this as a little bonus, 'cause they're that pleased with me work an he said there'll be plenty more comin'."

"Patrick, what can I say? Saints be praised. Always have faith son, look how the Lord's provided for us, just when we needed Him most." his tearful mother declared, gratefully accepting Irish's offering.

"Too right ma. It must've been all that extra prayin' I've been doin'," he laughed adding, "I'm gonna go out for a bit now, got to sort a few things. Yer've no need t'worry no more."

Irish left the kitchen and went upstairs to his bedroom, where he quickly changed from his work clothes to his smartest Skinhead kit. In his white Ben Sherman shirt, dark patterned Fair Isle jumper, twenty-two inch petrol-blue parallels and gleaming cherry-red Airwair, he looked sharp. When he added his well-cut Crombie with scarlet silk handkerchief held in place in his breast pocket by a sparkling faux diamond stud, his transformation was complete. Surely no prospective employer could turn him down, he told himself as he admired his appearance in the full length mirror fixed to the back of his bedroom door.

The naive Irish was about to learn a harsh lesson in the fundamental, determining principle of economic success or failure of any individual or enterprise, the law of supply and demand.

Setting off on his repaired and modified Lambretta with new fly screen, reduced selection of chrome extras attached to the front rack and most of Tony (G)'s gold, adhesive-backed lettering removed from the iridescent red and white side panels, he was heading in the direction of what was previously enemy territory, the vast Kings Estate.

Split into four huge, compass point sections, each of which dwarfed the Crown Estate, this sprawling post-war, overspill, corporation housing development provided a captive workforce for the dozens of manufacturing factories, that encircled its perimeter. 'If there's any jobs goin', the Kings is the place they're gonna be.' he convinced himself riding through the cold morning air, along the Lancashire Road towards its southern boundary.

Irish's first port of call was the giant automotive parts complex. He waited hopefully outside the main office, after providing his details to the disinterested security staff. The frosted glazed panel, in the wall adjacent to the office door, was suddenly opened.

A bald, rotund male peered out into the hallway, "Are you the lad askin' about work?" he asked curtly.

"Yes mate, I'll take anythin' yer've got, am not fussed." Irish replied politely.

"You're not fussed! Fuckin' hell lad, you'll be lucky." he laughed then added, "You wanna try *readin'* the newspapers instead of just lookin' at the pictures in them. There is no fuckin' jobs, nowhere. We're layin' fellers off every day, nobody's safe nowadays." He laughed again then slid the window closed.

Irish moved on to the next factory, downhearted but determined. For the rest of that day he travelled from one to another of the dark, concrete and steel cathedrals of industry, in each case receiving the same negative response, if any at all. The disconsolate youth had no understanding of the real politik of the conflicting factors that had produced a national economic slump and were ushering in a change in the global hierarchy of manufacture.

In the previous decade a disgruntled worker could quit a job one day and secure a new position the next. Those days were gone, labour intensive systems were becoming obsolete, at least in the western hemisphere; no one could expect a 'job for life'. There would be many bitter disputes leading to widespread union action and brutal official responses, before the leviathan of the original industrial revolutionary would cease its struggle and accept a new, pared to the bone progeny as its heir.

"Fuckin' hell, I just want a job." Irish protested as he was forcefully expelled from his final destination that day, the foul smelling, smoke belching; chemical dye works to the north of the huge estate. 'I've gorra get some work, any fuckin' work.' he told himself. Throughout that week he pursued his objective relentlessly only to be frustrated at every turn and utterly rejected. He was becoming increasingly desperate and angry.

Friday, 20th February 1976

As the second week of Irish's futile quest drew to a close he began to accept that regular employment was not to be found, he had exhausted all possible legitimate avenues. It was a Friday evening, pay day and he knew his mother would be waiting for his vital wages. Irish checked his pockets for cash then began to rummage through every drawer in his bedroom furniture, for any loose change.

'Three pound and seventy five pence, that's it. What the fuck am I gonna tell me ma?' he asked himself. Next he undertook a frantic search, tipping the contents of his chest of drawers and bedside table onto the cold linoleum floor. Digging through a growing pile of socks, underpants and tee shirts, he accidently found a discarded item that he speculated may just offer a possible, if dangerous, solution; the scallop-edged funeral card from the Gerard Boys.

Recalling his graveyard conversation with three of their seniors on the day of Jay Mac's funeral, Irish knew exactly what he must do, whatever the result. He changed into his twenty-four inch parallel Fleming's jeans, pulled on a clean white tee shirt, clipped his half-inch black, elasticated braces into place, before donning his Levi's denim jacket, with bleached collar and pocket flaps, followed by his black Crombie. After giving his gleaming cherry red Airwair a cursory polish, he raced downstairs almost colliding with his waiting mother.

"Patrick, are you goin' out, aren't yer forgettin' somethin'?" she asked expectantly.

"Sorry ma, I'm in a rush, thee paid us a bit short this week. I'll give yer the rest later, honest." he offered, passing his frowning mother all the cash he presently owned.

After dragging his Lambretta out from its secure hiding place to the side of his house, he was about to put his Centurion helmet onto his head when he heard a familiar voice calling to him, from his left.

"Alright Irish, hold on mate!" the ever chirpy Blue shouted, hurriedly approaching from his parents' house, which was located further along the same street.

Irish glanced at his corpulent former team mate as he came towards him. With his long, carefully coiffured hairstyle, plastered into place with a generous dousing of Cossack hairspray and his drooping blond moustache, wearing his broad lapelled calf-length leather coat, excessively wide, large checked Oxford bags and tall platform shoes, he was a long way from his original Skinhead days.

"What d'jer fuckin' want Blue, am dead busy right now." Irish snapped, in his usual surly manner.

"I haven't seen yer in a while and I was wonderin' if yer fancied a few bevvies in the Eagle and maybe gettin' a bit of scran down at Mr Li's after... I'll be payin' like, what d'jer think?" Blue asked hopefully.

"Not tonight Blue, I've gorra bit of business on the go. Some other time, maybe, see yer." Irish replied mounting his scooter.

Blue persisted, almost stepping in front of Irish's machine. "Please mate, am fuckin' goin' mental, I can't take no more, what with Beryl and the twins and me mum and dad. It's like a fuckin' mad house in ours now, can't I come with yer, go 'ed, it'll be just like the arl days?"

"The arl days is dead and gone Blue, where I'm goin' tonight could get a bit lively, yeah?" Irish warned.

"Fuck! I'll take the chance mate, it couldn't be any worse. The twins never stop eatin' and shittin' and cryin' then shittin' some more." Blue added to support his case.

"Blue, you're the one who wanted t'dip yer wick all over the fuckin' place, yer was bound t'get caught out sooner or later, so don't cry about it. Go 'ome t'yer bird and yer kids." Irish responded coldly.

Resigned to his fate Blue turned to walk away, ready for another long evening of domestic bliss. He knew Irish was correct, he had always been 'active' whenever the opportunity arose and never that selective about his choice of partner. Beryl was a new associate of little Jane when her more than ample bosom first caught Blue's eye, soon he became a regular customer of hers. When she withdrew from the business without explanation he was initially, momentarily disappointed but not as much as he would be several months later when she presented herself at his parents' house with his two chubby, blonde haired, twin daughters. Thrown onto the streets by her own uncaring, abusive mother and father, Beryl pleaded for refuge and assistance. Mr and Mrs Boyd did the decent thing and soon all six were playing 'happy families' at least on the surface, to the viewing public.

Irish watched the famous 'bird bandit' trudging off towards his fate, 'Caged at last, poor cunt' he thought, then shouted, "Hold on their Blue, I could do with a bit of company, c'mon."

Blue raced back to his friend and received a spare helmet from him, which he had quickly retrieved from the side room where he stowed his Lambretta.

"Here, put this on, Tony (G) give me the two lids when I bought his bike, never used this one before." Irish advised adding, "fasten it on properly, I don't want yer havin' an accident."

"But it'll ruin me hair." Blue moaned, whilst carefully placing the white with black peak helmet onto his coiffured head.

"Blue that's already fucked. Anyway I don't want anyone thinkin' I've got some fat bird on the back." Irish laughed and brought the uber cool machine into roaring life.

Within half an hour they had reached their destination, London Road, the once thriving shopping district in the heart of the city. Now a pale spectre of its former bustling self though most of its major attractions had long departed, its classic collection of traditional ale houses remained, catering for the wild revellers or lone, maudlin drinker as needed. The Gerard Boys either owned or had major shares in almost all of them.

After parking his Lambretta in a side street off the main road, Irish led the way to his first choice of the evening, The Swan Hotel. They presented an incongruous pair, the Skinhead and the 'disco king' carrying their Centurion helmets. In the boiling, smoky bar however, with The Band's *The Night They Drove Old Dixie Down* blaring out from the juke box, the raucous crowd paid little notice to them as Blue ordered their drinks. It was not until Irish began to ask the barman about the infamous brothers, that they became the focus of attention.

"Yeah I was... er... just wonderin' if yer happen to know where I might find Tommy or Francis, or Niall Mack, I'm a good friend of theirs?" he asked casually, before sipping the creamy head of his pint of Guinness.

"I've never heard of anyone round here by that name." the surly barman replied, leaning his heavy frame against the badly stained, aged wooden counter.

Blue thought he could assist by clarifying the position, blurting out "No mate, that's because everyone calls them the Gerard Boys, they're a bit lively!"

The nearest drinkers on either side of the new arrivals moved away, turning their backs as they did, the barman drew himself up to his full height and leaned forward across his counter. "Drop those fuckin' drinks fast and gerrout."

Irish and Blue did as instructed swallowing their ale in rapid gulps and departed in silence.

As they walked through the cold night towards their next hostelry, Irish turned to Blue and warned "Let me do the talkin' from now on, before your big mouth gets us fucked." Blue decided to follow his angry friend's advice and did not reply.

After visiting two more similar establishments, receiving the same negative response, they arrived at The Central public house, a venue they had often visited either as a precursor for an evening's 'drunk watching', or a Saturday afternoon's female spotting. This was a narrow three-storey establishment with the main bar at street level, a two-chambered lounge above and a sparse, large basement imbibing chamber. All were usually crammed with serious drinkers.

Irish squeezed through the tightly packed crowd to order their drinks, which the silent Blue continued to pay for. Whilst lighting a cigarette he glanced about the room looking for any of the three senior Gerard Boys, with whom he was familiar. Apart from the usual motley collection of hardened alcoholics with their ale damaged features belying their actual age, there was no one who looked even vaguely like the three notorious brothers. Bobby Darrin's *Mack the Knife* was currently playing on the juke box but nobody appeared to be listening, all were either engaged in their own conversations, or sitting alone staring blankly into the void.

Irish decided to be a little more circumspect with his approach and waited until he and Blue had almost downed their pints, before casually asking the barman his urgent question, "Alright there mate... I was just wonderin' if any of the Mack brothers were comin' in t'night... Francis or Tommy or...?"

"I'll stop yer right there lad." the barman warned angrily, instantly changing his originally placid manner. "We sell ale and bar snacks in 'ere not fuckin' information. Yer better finish yer drinks and piss off before..." he stopped mid-sentence, his face becoming visibly pale, "I didn't say nothin'." the man suddenly blurted out, staring beyond Irish and Blue at two huge, stocky males who were now positioned immediately behind the Crown players.

Both youths felt the weight of heavy paws on their shoulders then heard "Yous two pricks, up them fuckin' stairs move yerselves."

Wisely they decided to comply rather than resist and allowed themselves to be led up the short flight of stairs to the two-chamber lounge above. They had sat in this same bar several years earlier when Jay Mac had been confronted by his violent cousins and both recognised their ominous surroundings. Pushed through the first crowded room into a smaller parlour, they were abruptly brought to a halt by the same restraining grasp of their grim escorts.

"Evenin' officers, gotcha warrant cards 'ave yer?" a seated male of similar age to them asked, with a familiar smile. "Bit obvious for a pair of bizzies aren't yer, what sort of shit disguises are they?" He took a drink from his pint then added, "Who are yer supposed to be, fuckin' Starsky and Hutch?"

Irish was momentarily unable to answer, struck by the uncanny resemblance of their questioner to his deceased friend, Jay Mac. In fact this was the youngest Mack sibling, Daniel or 'Danny Boy' as he was known and whose photograph had been supplied for the late Crown Team player's passport because of his remarkable likeness. With his dark feather-cut hair, angular features, piercing hazel eyes and athletic rangy build, apart from a recently acquired, still red raw scar running down the right side of his forehead and ending just below that eye, he could easily have been mistaken for Jay Mac's twin.

"We're not bizzies mate, honest." Blue called out nervously.

Danny laughed, "I know that soft arse, even the plod aren't fuckin' stupid enough t'be goin' round our alehouses askin' knob 'ed questions lookin' for us. So my question is who the fuck are yer?"

Irish stared at the young man in his deep collared, colourful patterned shirt and expensive dark green, wide lapelled leather jacket. What particularly caught his attention was the large, gold St Michael medal he wore around his neck on an equally heavy gold chain. "That's a crackin' St Michael medal yer've got there; yer cousin had one just like it but not as flashy." Irish observed, finally breaking his silence.

His comments intrigued their questioner, "So you knew my cousin did yer, the one thee all said looked like me?" he asked, instantly changing his demeanour, "I think yer part of the crew that done 'im in, yers look like a pair of sly bastards. Yous 'ave come 'ere tonight lookin' for trouble haven't yers, bringin' a message from that Morgo cunt, is that it?"

"No, no yer wrong. I was just lookin' for work, that's all." Irish called out.

"What d'yer think this is... the fuckin' dole office yer cheeky twat?" Danny asked angrily. "Alright lads when yer ready." He signalled to his henchmen.

Irish and Blue were struck tremendous blows simultaneously in their lower backs at kidney height then thrown to the floor. "Get their coats off an search them." Danny ordered, warning the downed Crown players "Don't even think about gettin' up."

Their coats were roughly dragged from them and thoroughly searched. "Nothin' Danny, just some cash, keys, a comb, some chewies and this card." the lead searcher announced.

"Let's see that card Liam." Danny asked reaching for the scalloped edge condolence token. "Where did yer get this from yer cunt?" Danny addressed his question to Irish.

"It was from me da's funeral, your family sent it." Irish replied honestly.

"Nah, I don't think so, you've nicked this to try an gerrin' close with us but am not havin' it." Danny was unconvinced suspecting a rouse, a trap, "Take these two cunts into the back alley and give them a fuckin' good kickin' until thee come up with the truth."

"Please mate, he's tellin' yer the truth, we don't want no trouble." Blue pleaded.

"Too fuckin' late, yers have already gorrit. Get them out of 'ere."

Just as they were being dragged to their feet, with Blue trying to appeal to Danny's better nature, an older harsher voice with a distinctive Liverpool-Irish accent called out.

"What the fuck's goin' on 'ere? Are these the two gob shites who've been askin' around for us all night?" Niall the eldest of the Mack clan stepped into the room followed by Tommy and Francis with a hard faced female of similar age accompanying them. All of the new arrivals were smartly dressed, the men in well-cut suits with a certain sheen about them and the woman wrapped in a leopard skin coat over a clinging, red satin dress.

"These are the two little pricks Niall." Danny advised. "That one wearin' the arl Skinhead gear says he knows our family, he was a mate of our cousin, John."

Niall moved directly in front of the dishevelled Irish, instantly grasping him by the lapels of his denim jacket. He stared into Irish's face searching for recognition. "I don't think I've ever seen this cunt before but he's got a look of someone that I just can't recall."

"I'm Joseph O'Hare's son, Patrick, I was at Jay Mac's funeral a couple of years ago and you spoke to me." Irish offered quickly.

Niall studied the youth with his number one crop and razor trench haircut, "The lad I talked to was a scruffy bastard, hair all over the place, I think yer fuckin' lyin'."

Danny interrupted the proceedings and inadvertently assisted Irish's cause, "He had this bit of a card with 'im, says it was from us, 'ere yer are."

He passed the distinctive card to Niall, the elder of the Gerard Boys, "I fuckin' wrote this, didn't yer recognise my writin' Danny Boy?" Niall asked of his younger sibling.

"'Course not, I'm not one of those fuckin' handwritin' fellers." the aggrieved Danny replied.

The atmosphere began to warm rapidly as Irish's credentials were accepted and his lineage acknowledged.

"So you're Joseph O'Hare's lad." Niall began, "There's been a bit of a misunderstandin' here but no harm done. That's your fault Danny Boy, yer'll have t'start learnin' t'trust people and not be so fuckin' quick with kickin' off."

"Yeah, that's how I got this by trustin' some cunt, so yer can keep yer advice thanks Niall." Danny answered, pointing to the raw scar on his forehead.

Irish and Blue were given back their coats and invited to sit with the Gerard crew in the cosy parlour.

"Right, a round of drinks is needed 'ere," Niall decided.

Irish remembered what Jay Mac had previously warned, never to accept a drink from his cousins because they would expect a lot more in return. "Yer all right Niall thanks, I just wanted t'ask yer about somethin' and then we'll be off." he tried, in vain.

Niall's mood changed in an instant, "Yer won't accept a drink from us, where's yer manners boy, yer not tryin' to insult us are yer?" he asked angrily.

"No, of course not Niall." Irish hastily responded.

The Gerard senior smiled once again, "That's more like it, we'll get a round in, then you can get one, ok?"

It would prove to be an expensive night for Blue with 'rounds' consisting of pints of Guinness with Jameson's Irish whiskey chasers and generous measures of brandy with Babycham, for the formidable female, whom Niall introduced simply as Shirley.

Before broaching his actual purpose for being there, Irish was curious about the Gerard Boys' relationship with his late father. "I was wonderin' lads, how yers happened t'know me da?" he asked politely.

"Oh we knew yer da alright, a long time ago when he was a young feller, he had the divil of a temper on him, we were only boys at the time back in the old country. Some people wanted him to help 'The Cause' but Joseph wasn't havin' any of it, he was his own man, he knew his own mind. Sure he got himself back off t'sea probably just in the nick of time and we didn't even realise he was the same man, until we heard about the death notice in the paper. It was our own sainted ma who told us. God, she loves readin' those notices, she says she knows she's still with us if she's readin' about some other poor bastard dyin." Niall advised laughing.

All the while that they were talking, with a selection of Frank Sinatra, Dean Martin and Tony Bennett records playing on the juke box as a suitable background, Shirley, who had removed and carefully folded her fabulous coat made from the pelts of formerly magnificent animals, sat alongside Blue who on his left was next to Irish, flanked as *he* was by the Gerard seniors and Danny Boy to his own left. Shirley smiled whilst smoking her king size cigarettes studying both Crown team players, allowing her smooth, crossed legs to regularly rest against Blue's, watching his reaction.

Irish felt the time was right to pursue his objective, "The reason I'm 'ere t'night Niall is to ask yer about that work yer offered me a couple of years ago."

Niall thought for a few moments then replied, "I remember now we did wanna give yer some work after our John got done by that bastard Morgo but that was then. Now we've got more fellers than we need, it's the way it is, the law of supply and demand yer see." He paused and threw back his whiskey chaser. "Yeah, y'see if the government keeps fuckin' everythin' up... closin' factories all over the place, throwin' loads of lads out of work, well we can pick and choose, so sorry Patrick me boy, that job offer is no longer on the table... Sliante." When Niall had finished talking he began gulping down his pint of Guinness and turned away from Irish.

The desperate youth could not let the issue rest and unwisely pressed on, "Lads I don't mean no disrespect but I really need that work, I'll do anythin', fuckin' anythin'. Give us a chance for the sake of me arl da and Jay Mac, y'know yers can trust me."

Tommy, who was in the centre between Niall and Francis, spoke quietly to them for a few moments then offered his solution, "Are you a sportin' feller there Patrick, a bettin' man?" he asked slyly.

"Er... yeah... I am... I'll take me chances, for the right bet." Irish replied stepping fully into their snare.

"Well that's grand because we're gonna give yer a sportin' chance an if yer win, yer get the job." Tommy offered.

"What if he loses?" Blue asked, now sufficiently intoxicated to become emboldened.

Tommy laughed, "Who rattled your cage blondie? If he loses the pair of yers can fuck off and never show yer faces round 'ere again, right?"

Irish knew this was his only chance and equally that the odds of his succeeding in whatever task they presented, were probably slim to none existent.

"I'm in, tell me what yer want me t'do and I'll give it me best shot." he responded resolutely.

"Good man Patrick, you're Joseph O'Hare's son alright, no doubt about it." Francis acknowledged, continuing "We've got a feller in 'ere drinkin' in the basement bar who was a contender, he's an arl piss 'ed now, in his sixties but he can still throw a decent punch even if he can't see straight. All yer've gotta do is put 'im on the deck, just once mind and we'll be happy with that. Is that a bet?" He held out his hand after spitting into it and following a few brief moments of hesitation, Irish returned the gesture, shaking his hand firmly.

"Good luck t'yer!" said Niall.

The two Crown Team players, the Gerard seniors, Danny Boy and the increasingly friendly Shirley, stood up gathered their belongings and decamped down to the subterranean drinking den. Two flights of stairs later they were in a different world, the domain of the professional imbiber. Irish had become Theseus in search of the Minotaur, with no real idea of what he would be facing in this large, dank cellar. Despite the blaring juke box which was currently playing *That's Life* by Frank Sinatra, being fully audible in this blue-grey smoke filled room as elsewhere, no one in this audience was listening.

Tommy looked about for his prized pugilist, calling to him "Barney, where the fuck are yer? Show yerself."

An aged drunk slumped across a small circular table at the far end of the rectangular room, slowly raised his silver-grey and incongruously dark haired head. "Whose shoutin' me, is that you da?"

"Gerrover 'ere now you!" Tommy instructed.

After stiffly rising to his unsteady feet the slim, broad shouldered, early sixties male shuffled between the seated drinkers at their tables, eventually coming to a wavering halt in front of Tommy and the rest of his party.

"Here's yer man, Patrick. Meet Barney 'Rumble' Flynn, once upon a time welterweight champion of all Ireland, so he'll tell yer."

Irish looked at the pathetic figure who preferred to be known as Errol, after the famous heart-throb star of silver screen and matinee idol. In hope of creating the illusion, the imposter wore a dreadful, badly fitting, black-haired toupee combed into a rakish side part and had drawn a thin moustache in his white stubble with a dark eyebrow pencil, above his upper lip. At five foot ten with an athletic build, Barney had indeed been a contender and was famed for his lightning fast movement and tremendous, pile-driver, knockout punches. If his early meteoric career success had not given him more access to the temptation of the bottle, if his self-discipline had been stronger he may not have drunk his prize money and prospects away to nothing.

Standing in front of his latest opponent, dressed in a filthy collarless, striped shirt, wearing thick braces to support his equally stained heavy corduroy trousers and old army boots, Barney fixed Tommy with his watery gaze, asking, "Who is it yer want batterin' tonight?"

Tommy laughed, "That's the spirit Barney, yer a game one I'll give yer that." He turned to Irish, "Alright Patrick do yer best t'knock this fucker down and the job's yours."

The Crown player did not reply he was neither stupid nor naive enough to believe this would be an easy fight. He watched while Francis, Tommy and Danny cleared punters and their tables away from the central arena, towards the perimeter unplastered, brick walls of the room.

"C'mon piss 'eds, move yer arses... then yers can watch the show." Danny called, herding the shufflers, clutching their ale, to their 'ringside' seats. The Gerard crew took their places forcing other spectators to vacate their positions. Irish passed Blue his Crombie and denim jacket then raised his fists walking forward, ready for the bout to begin. Barney took a final swig of his whiskey, removed his top and bottom set of false teeth, placing them in the empty tumbler for safety, he cracked his knuckles, shook his head from side-to-side and stood facing his opponent with his own bricks of fists at the ready. As The Dubliner's *Whiskey in the Jar* began to play on the juke box, Tommy tapped a coin sharply on an empty pint glass as a signal for the contest to commence.

Lunging forward Irish threw a straight right at his opponent's jaw, which he dodged with only the slightest movement, responding with a thumping left to the youth's stomach. Irish felt the force of the blow and stepped back a few paces to recover his breath. Barney came on with surprising speed, unleashing a punishing combination of crosses that again drove into Irish's aching gut. It was all one-way traffic for the opening moments of the bout, with the Crown player on the receiving end of Barney's painfully accurate punches.

"C'mon Patrick, show us what yer've got." Tommy called out laughing.

Irish was trying to do just that as he leapt into Barney, caught him around the back of the head with his hands and made to force him down onto his rising knee. The older man knew all the tricks; he was a scrapper as well as a boxer and instantly booted Irish in the shin of his supporting leg, while pounding his mid section once more. A lightning fast right uppercut smashed into Irish's jaw, jolting his head back and dropping him to the floor, for the first of several visits. Irish had no time to recover as Barney launched into a vicious kicking assault with both heavy boots.

The previously apathetic crowd now began to respond enthusiastically, sensing that one of their own drunken army was enjoying a brief moment of triumph.

"Fuck 'im, fuck 'im Barney, do the little shit!" a number of them shouted.

Rolling quickly out of range, Irish leapt back to his feet, trying to clear his spinning head, receiving Barney's next sequence of punches on his raised forearms. Opening his guard for a split second, Irish smashed his right fist fully into Barney's face, to no effect. The elder male's repeatedly broken nose was almost without sensation, as if it were made of rubber. Irish's powerful punch barely registered, unlike Barney's devastating right cross that spun the youth's head violently to one side.

For a few moments Irish became a human punch-bag, receiving strike after strike to body and head as Barney chose to target. Seeing his man on the ropes the professional pugilist changed tactics, launching his stone-hard head directly onto the bridge of Irish's nose. Even as the audible crack and accompanying stream of blood and snot announced the breaking of bone and cartilage, Irish lost his footing falling to his knees once more. Again Barney transformed into a kicking machine booting his bleeding, defenceless, downed opponent repeatedly, until his own legs were aching.

Eventually he stepped away, wiped the sweat from his brow and warned, "Stay the fuck down boy, I don't want t'kill yer but I will if I 'ave to."

Blue echoed his advice, "Stay down Irish, he's fuckin' killin' yer."

The Gerard Boys sneered in agreement "'Aye, yer might as well stay down where yer are, yer no fuckin' use to us."

Wiping the blood and snot from his face Irish rose to his feet once more "Come on you arl bastard, I'm a Crown Skin, so let's have it." he shouted defiantly.

Barney smiled before responding with a barrage of rip-cracking body blows.

Gasping for air Irish clutched at the top of Barney's head inadvertently dislodging the 'film star's' black toupee.

"Me hair, me fuckin' hair, y'cunt!" he called out in alarm, reaching for the dreadful hairpiece.

Irish sprang into him, punching for his life, throwing left and right combinations without respite, depriving his frantic opponent of breath. One tremendous uppercut to the jaw now rocked Barney's head back in an explosion of bright light. He moved a few faltering paces to the rear, dropped to one knee and prepared to receive his penance. Lurching forward Irish stood over his stunned adversary, ready to deliver the *coup de gras*.

"Finish this sad cunt, or yer'll not be workin' for *us*." Niall warned.

Irish felt a wave of pity pass over him as he gazed down at the toothless, pathetic figure with his bald pate, swaying to and fro without a care for his fate, no plea for mercy on his lips. "Sorry old timer, I really need this fuckin' job." he announced before unleashing his own torrent of vicious kicks to face and body, using his gleaming Dr. Marten's to good effect. Finally as the unrecognisable mush of Barney's battered face slammed down upon the old weathered floorboards, spitting blood and gore from the ragged mouth, Irish stepped away. "Is that good enough for yer?" he shouted triumphantly, with heaving chest.

Irish left Barney where he lay, rejoining the Gerard contingent and Blue. Niall threw the victorious youth a bar towel to wipe his face and Tommy passed him a good measure of Jameson's to revive his spirits, saying "Y'done alright Patrick... against an arl man but don't get too cocky." Turning to Blue he ordered, "Ok fatso, you're up next."

The colour drained from Blue's face as he protested "No... er no thanks... I just came 'ere with me mate..."

Tommy interrupted, "Don't be talkin' bollocks. Yer don't think you came here just to watch do yer?"

Blue stood up nervously and began to remove his leather coat, still trying to appeal, "Please... I don't want any work... please."

As he stepped away from their table, looking across into the zombie ranks, wondering who his opponent may be, Tommy slapped him hard on the backside, "Sit down yer fat fuck, I'm only jokin' with yer." They all laughed, including the much relieved Blue, grateful for his reprieve.

Both he and Irish may have worn the Skinhead uniform but only one of them had the heart of the genuine article.

The smiling Shirley lit another king size cigarette from the dying embers of her existing smoke then caught hold of Irish's blood stained right hand, "I enjoyed that... I mean *really* enjoyed it."

Tommy grinned broadly saying "There yer are then, that's an offer yer can't refuse. Shirley's gonna take yer both upstairs and look after yer."

Blue was bemused by Tommy's comments, Irish answered for them both, "No, yer alright, thanks Tommy, we're fine. As long as I know I've got the job that's good enough f'me, we'll be gettin' off."

Niall, the Gerard senior's expression changed once more, "Yer've got the job alright as long as yer tell me y'not a pair of queers, 'cause there's no fuckin' queers in this crew."

"No, we're defo not queers, honest, I've got two twin daughters." Blue blurted out defensively.

"Alright there stud, calm down, that's grand." Niall paused, finished his whiskey then added firmly, "Now gerrup stairs with Shirley and seal the deal."

Nothing more was said and both Crown players meekly followed the smiling Shirley up the back stairs to a small, one room, sparsely furnished apartment above the first floor parlour.

"Clean y'self up there in the kitchen sink, Patrick." Shirley instructed and turning to Blue continued, "You can help me with me zip, if yer hands are clean but don't fuckin' touch me clothes."

Again Irish and Blue followed their orders and while the 'fighter' cleaned his wounded face and blood stained hands, the 'bird bandit' carefully unzipped Shirley's clinging, red satin dress, after she had removed and hung up her hugely expensive, fur coat.

"Listen, don't take it personally but I don't think I can manage..." the injured Irish began.

Shirley looked directly at him and said, "*You* don't have to manage anything, now go and make yerself comfortable in that armchair and unfasten yer jeans."

Irish did as instructed watching as she stepped out of her dress then proceeded to fold it neatly, laying it on the old worn couch that matched his armchair seat. Shirley may have taken some hard punches to the face during her own 'career' but her voluptuous body had all the right curves in all the right places. Standing in front of them wearing only a figure-hugging, short, flesh-coloured slip over her lacy black bra and matching panties, with her long, shapely legs encased in the sheerest dark tights and her Italian black leather stilettos, she had their full attention, dismissing any further protests from Irish's mind.

Nature began to take over as she crossed the floor and knelt before Irish affording him a generous view of her deep cleavage and barely restrained breasts. He could feel his ardour rising, allowing his gaze to focus on her grown woman's form.

"Let me help you with that." she offered, easing the youth's growing erection from his restrictive Y-fronts.

Irish moaned involuntarily as she began to lick his throbbing member with her pink tongue, before enclosing the head in her ruby-red lipped mouth. Shirley set about her task with wild enthusiasm, her large rounded bottom quivering as she knelt at her work. Blue was holding his coat with one hand and his own excited manhood with the other, watching the erotic tableau before him, fixating on her inviting rear.

The obliging Shirley carefully removed Irish's glistening tool from her mouth and looking over her shoulder called to Blue, who was busily tugging at his own straining erection through his trousers, "What's the fuckin' matter with you lad, yer've just told Niall yer not queer haven't yer?"

"Yeah, that's right, I mean... no am not queer." Blue stammered, embarrassed to be caught in mid-masturbation.

"Well get over 'ere and get stuck in, or I'll tell them all yer a fuckin' shirt lifter."

Blue needed no second invitation, quickly crossing the floor, unzipping his uncomfortably tight, high-waist trousers, yanking them and his underwear down his thighs, before kneeling immediately behind her quivering, broad bottom. Shirley had already returned to her task, applying her experienced tongue and mouth with exquisite skill to the pulsating penis of the now delirious Irish. At her opposite end, with equal haste as when removing his own garments, Blue dragged Shirley's black panties and dark tights to her knees. After a moment of excited fumbling he found the correct orifice, nudged the head of his iron hard rod inside then forced its shaft onwards to the hilt. As he reached round to further stimulate her moist thatch with one hand, whilst stretching forward to grasp her large breasts with the other, Shirley took control.

She slammed herself hard against Blue's groin, trapping him in her warm firmness then drew him on with every stroke, all the while without altering her master-class fellatio performance on the ecstatic Irish. It was hard to tell who was riding who while Shirley pulled, pushed, licked and sucked to her own rhythm and pace, giving and extracting pleasure as she decided. Irish was the first to reach the finish line, exploding with a violent orgasm inside Shirley's cavernous mouth. Without altering her thrusting-drawing stroke, she quickly removed his still spurting member and spat his warm seed violently onto the floor.

"No offence lad, I never swaller." she managed to utter, her face running with perspiration.

"None taken." the much relieved, battered and bruised Irish gasped then sat back with a huge sigh of satisfaction, ready to encourage his purple faced team mate who was pounding as if his life depended upon it. "Go 'ed Blue, you're the bird bandit, ride her cowboy." Irish exhorted, his own face dripping with sweat.

Shirley sensed her remaining partner's approaching climax, reached between her thighs removed his clumsy hand and replaced it with her own expert, self-pleasure giving digits. Slamming back and forth whilst teasing herself, she climaxed almost simultaneously with the orgasmic Blue who was roaring with delight.

Both exhausted males put away their spent members, adjusted and fastened their clothing then waited for Shirley's next instruction. She washed herself briefly at the kitchen sink then dressed in silence.

"Okay, I think we're all finished here, so let's go down to the parlour, I could do with a stiff drink." she laughed.

A few moments later they joined the rest of the family, who had settled back into their cosy chamber.

"Feelin' better now lads are yer?" Niall asked as they sat down.

Irish smiled as he replied to the Gerard senior "Thanks Niall that was decent of yer t'send yer bird up there with us, nice one."

Niall raised his eyebrows and with a sly grin looked to Shirley for her comments.

"'Ey soft lad, I don't fuck because Niall or anyone else tells me to, I fuck when I like, with whoever I like because I love it, especially with two young bucks like yerselves." She laughed then lit a post coitus king size cigarette adding, "And one more thing, I'm not his fuckin' bird, I'm his sister and don't you forget it."

Everyone laughed and another round of drinks appeared before them.

"Slainte!" the Gerard Boys offered with Tommy adding, "Not a bad night after all hey fellers?"

Irish and Blue returned the salutation, looked to each other and wisely declined to comment further.

Chapter 3

Police and Thieves

Saturday 24th April 1976

After almost two months of regular delivery work for the Gerard Boys, Irish's finances had significantly improved and both he and his mother appreciated their new circumstances. Mrs O'Hare did initially ask awkward questions about the supposed courier firm, that her son was now employed by but eventually the relief of not having to worry about where their next rent payment, or domestic bill funds would be found, allowed her to accept his implausible tale of this sudden, fortuitous offer of lucrative work. There was one issue however, that she would not let rest, constantly referring to it at unexpected, random moments much to Irish's discomfort.

"I saw Mrs Chadwick in the shops today, God alone knows how that poor woman can even stand up, never mind go out shoppin' for food after what happened to her little Malcolm, knocked down and left for dead by some evil coward." she suddenly announced, whilst putting away her own supply of groceries, as Irish was preparing to leave, about to meet his cousins for a pre-match drink.

"Ma, he wasn't 'little' Malcolm, the sad prick was in his twenties, older than me." Irish responded curtly adding, "Anyway who knows what really happened? Maybe he ran out in front of some poor feller who hit him by accident."

Mrs O'Hare looked at her son quizzically for a few moments then said, "Don't be callin' him names like that, y'shouldn't speak ill of the dead, y'should be prayin' for his soul." She paused and stared directly into his face, "Listen t'me Patrick, if you know anythin' about this terrible thing, you had better go to the polis. There's nothin' worse than not knowin' the truth, that poor woman must be goin' out of her mind. D'yer hear me Patrick?"

Irish had slipped on his Levi's denim jacket, with bleached collar and pocket flaps and was giving his gleaming, cherry-red Airwair a vigorous buffing with the soft, polish-stained cloth that he now always carried. "Yeah okay ma, I hear yer, I don't know why yer sayin' all this t'me, I know nothin' about what happened to that weirdo, so leave it will yer."

He marched out of the kitchen, through the living room and slammed the front door behind him as he left. Striding rapidly along the street where he lived, Irish made his way to Blue's residence having uniquely agreed that he could accompany him and his relations to the match, affording his former team mate some brief respite from his arduous domestic duties.

"Alright Irish, nice one mate." Blue greeted his friend, departing from his own house with equal haste, "Everythin' ok? Y'look a bit pissed off there."

"Don't ask Blue, I'm not in the mood. Let's get down to the Blue House and drop a few fuckin' pints before kick-off." Irish responded in his usual dour manner.

Both youths joined the lengthy queue of people comprised mostly of other Everton supporters, who were waiting at the nearby bus stop all eager to do exactly as Irish was planning and then enjoy the final match of the season.

Shortly before three o'clock on that unusually warm spring afternoon, Irish, his two cousins, Andy and Callum and Blue, having rapidly downed several pints of intoxicating alcohol in the nearby Blue House pub, joined another tightly packed queue of supporters pushing their way through the turnstiles of the Toffee's hallowed ground, Goodison Park. Despite their team heading towards a disappointing eleventh place finish in this year's First Division race and their arch rivals across Stanley Park, Liverpool FC, assured of clinching the title with European glory beckoning, these loyal fans were far from being 'Bitter Blues'. The vast majority of that afternoon's local spectators were in good spirits, looking forward to a home win against their east London opponents, West Ham.

Apart from the chirpy Blue, Irish was accompanied by two of his cousins because that was his preferred arrangement, usually supplemented by his presently absent brother, Dermot and his now departed father. For Irish going to the match on a Saturday afternoon was strictly a family affair. Unlike his friend Jay Mac, who had supported the Red footballing maestros of Liverpool FC and always attended with a full crew of Crown Team Kopites, Irish was not looking for trouble with anyone; his enjoyment was in watching the match with his kinfolk. Andy and Callum were of similar age to their cousin but unlike him in any other respect. They had long dark feather-cut hair and were dressed in casual civilian clothes of tee-shirts, flared jeans and platform shoes, their only item of football related paraphernalia were their royal blue and white scarves, hanging loosely round their necks. Above all they did not fight, having only experience of school-yard scuffles they enjoyed the pre and post match drinking, the banter and the craic. Not only were they, like their cousin, not out for trouble but they were unprepared to deal with it if it found them.

Just under two hours after taking their positions in the stands, Irish's contingent was shuffling back out to the crowded streets happy with their team's two-nil defeat of their opponents. Mike Bernard's accurate penalty and Jim Pearson's rocket of a goal were sufficient to be considered *nil satis nisi optimum* for most Blues that day, most but not all.

That was not the case for the travelling claret and blue army of West Ham United. Having started with nine straight wins, they were hoping for something more than to come away empty handed, knowing it would inevitably lead to an eighteenth place finish, only six points from relegation. One dazzling moment was left to them when two weeks later, they would meet Anderlecht in the European Cup Winners Final, only then would their dreams 'fade and die,' beaten four-two on the night. That was yet to come, today their acknowledged firm of football hooligans demanded something much more tangible, something bloody to add to their violent trophy display.

Pouring out from the Bullens Road stands, a raging crew stormed round into Walton Lane, overwhelmed the inadequate police presence and charged directly into a tightly packed throng of unsuspecting, civilian 'dad and lad' Evertonians, including Irish, his cousins and Blue.

"Fackin' do these Scarse cunts" the youthful leader of a junior breakaway group shouted as they cut a bloody swathe into the surprised, unprepared Blues with their Stanley knives, lead shot filled coshes and knuckle dusters.

Irish's cousins raised their forearms across their faces ready to receive the attack, trying to plea for rationality, common sense, even at this juncture, "Lads we don't want any..." they both shouted before being gashed across their limbs, coshed and booted.

"Get those fackin' scarves," the same spotty young hooligan ordered his companions. Even as the blood stained scarves were being dragged from them, the enraged Irish came to their aid.

"Do my cousins will yer, you Cockney twat!" he roared, going straight into them using only his unaided fists, delivering hard accurate punches to all about. One powerful blow smashed into the nose and mouth of the crew leader, splitting both in one scarlet instant. Though not the equal of his former team mate, Blue did his best to assist Irish in making a stand; rallying a growing resistance around them.

Wild punches, kicks, slashes and strikes were exchanged by both sides, with Irish the lone Skinhead embodying the spirit of the 1969 Originals, standing his ground, trading blows grimly determined to be the victor at any cost. Despite his valiant efforts, the largely civilian Evertonians' lack of weaponry threatened to turn the tide against them as more armed West Ham Juniors joined the mêlée. Their backs to the railings, outnumbered and surrounded, both Irish and Blue, the seasoned scrappers, knew they could not sustain their present level of fighting for much longer and would soon be reduced to their knees, receiving a good kicking as their reward.

Suddenly Blue was culled from the group, despite Irish's best attempts to keep him close by. Dragged to the ground, every boot and fist within striking distance found its target, with painful efficacy. Irish reached out to his friend desperately trying to grasp the collar of his leather jacket, his hair or any other hold he could achieve. In so doing he too was wrenched from the relative security of the battered Evertonian fraternity. Sensing *he* was the leader of the swirling resistance, the southern crew laid into Irish with wild vigour, punching, kicking and striking their downed prey relentlessly.

Irish, like his late team mate and school friend, Jay Mac, had also survived five years in the brutal educational institution of the *Cardinals School for Catholic Boys* and knew the drill, quickly assuming the foetal position with his head tucked in and his knees drawn up. Whilst being repeatedly booted and struck he tried to mentally remove himself from his present situation, until a series of devastatingly painful blows returned him sharply to the here and now. Above all the din of excited yelling and agonised shouts, Irish suddenly heard a familiar voice, growing louder by each passing moment.

"I'm Weaver! I done this to yer! I'm Weaver!" Charging in at the head of a huge phalanx of Gwladys Street Boot Boys, the Crown Team psychopath smashed all around him with his famed toffee hammer, held in his right hand and slashed wildly with his razor sharp Stanley knife in his left. "C'mon you Cockney shits, make a fuckin' effort!" he jeered, setting about his work with a vicious delight. His equally crazed companions, comprised of a disparate mix drawn from teams from across the city, enjoyed their violent endeavours to a similar extent, cutting, slashing, striking and kicking the West Ham Juniors without mercy.

Jumping up and down on the bleeding, cracked head of a fallen southern youth was Weaver's unlikely fellow commander for the day, Danny (H) of the Kings Team. Ever since the warning Danny had arranged, under the auspices of the most senior Kings leader, the imprisoned Craig 'Crag' Griffiths, for Weaver on the Christmas morning following his ill-chosen painting expedition, Danny (H) had established a rapprochement of sorts, a temporary understanding with his former deadly enemy, often joining with him on match days to attack visiting football team's supporters.

The half gallon of petrol poured through the front door of Weaver's parents' council flat, followed by the burning rolled up *Liverpool Echo* newspaper and the narrow escape of himself and his family, due to his youngest brother raising the alarm after spotting the billowing smoke entering from the narrow lobby, had convinced Weaver not to pursue his personal vendetta against the Kings Team any further. With an accompanying message sprayed outside on the walls of his flat advising 'LET IT GO – KINGS TEAM' and the fact that if his young sibling had not risen early to open his presents, no one may have escaped, Weaver finally accepted he was out-gunned and could not possibly hope to realistically challenge the vast enemy estate arrayed against him.

"Fuck, I never thought I'd be 'appy t'see this mad bastard." Blue observed, rising stiffly to his feet.

"Nah, me neither, who'd fuckin' believe it... rescued by Weaver?" Irish replied, incorrectly; this was a temporary respite not a rescue.

While Weaver, Danny (H) and the rest of their crazy crew exacted a suitably bloody revenge on the West Ham Juniors, *their* own formidable saviours were about to upset the balance of power dramatically.

"Let's 'ave it you Scarse slags!" a massive late-twenties, cropped haired male wearing a dark leather jacket, flared trousers and a gleaming pair of cherry red, 1490s Dr Marten's, roared as he crashed into the rear of the Gwladys Street Boot Boys.

More than a dozen others of like size and age followed in his wake, with equally damaging effect. Apart from their roughly chronological and physical similarities there was no additional visible feature that would have suggested they were a unified crew. Their hair ranged from traditional number one crops with razored trenches, to long, unkempt manes of no specific style and they were dressed in an eclectic mix of leather jackets, checked shirts, v-neck jumpers, flares or Oxford bag trousers or denim jeans and original white Baker's trousers. Even their footwear was entirely individual, instead of primarily being the ubiquitous Dr Marten boot, they also wore platform shoes, white Converse 'Chuck Taylor' All Star basketball boots, or the new, increasingly popular training shoe in the form of blue Adidas Gazelles. They had been Mods, Original Skinheads, Suedeheads and Boot Boys but now they were a football hooligan firm with one unifying passion only, West Ham United.

"Fack awf you little cant!" the lead male shouted, violently thrusting his boot into Blue's gut, sending him sprawling backwards into his own crowd.

Irish leapt forward throwing punches wildly, only to receive a thundering head-butt to the right side of his face from a long haired, moustache wearing giant. Weaver, Danny (H) and the rest of their cohort turned to greet the new arrivals as warmly as possible, steaming in with their own assortment of Stanley knives, coshes and knuckle dusters, neither side prepared to give ground.

In the blur of the bloody chaos that ensued, Irish caught a brief sight of Weaver, jumping onto the back of the cropped-haired apparent leader of the West Ham Seniors and then repeatedly striking his skull with his already scarlet stained toffee hammer. It was a defining act, one which normally would have resulted in Weaver's victim falling to his knees to receive a furious kicking but it was to no avail in this instance. Even with his wounded head streaming red rivulets down his meaty face, the Cockney contender grabbed hold of his tormentor, flung him to the floor and began his own frenzied assault, booting Weaver's grim visage over and over until he too was drenched in scarlet.

Only the timely intervention of his unlikely ally, Danny (H), saved him from serious, permanent damage. Drawing his now preferred weapon of choice, a heavy black metal air pistol and using it as a club rather than its intended purpose, he battered the large male's face about the nose, brow and mouth, time and again.

"'Ave this you fuckin' big southern blurt!" he shouted, exhausting his arm with the force of his blows until finally the giant stumbled backwards a few paces, allowing Weaver just sufficient time to stagger to his feet.

All around the madness raged on, Boot Boys versus hooligans, with civilians caught between. Blood, snot and sweat stained the official colours of both teams, with the occasional tooth caught in the woollen fibres of a traditional scarf, making an unexpected, additional souvenir of the day.

A warm, sunny, English Saturday afternoon was filled with the exhortations and cries of rage and pain as one group of working class males clashed with another purely for the adrenalin rush, the buzz, confirming they were still alive whilst beating each other near to death. This was the Sceptered Isle in its rawest state and its angry citizens would become a regular feature of every football fixture across the land.

The 'fun' could not continue for much longer and the official referees would soon be calling full time.

"Its the bizzies, the fuckin' bizzies!" rang out the familiar, age-old cry of warning as a reinforced, dark uniformed army arrived en masse replete with barking, snarling, German shepherd dogs and a mounted cavalry wing. It was every man for himself, escape by any means, any route with the forces of law and order unleashing their own legally sanctioned violence upon the battling mob.

"C'mon Blue, run like fuck man!" Irish shouted, before darting into the crowd, his dazed cousins in hot pursuit.

"Don't leave me Irish, don't leave me." Blue pleaded, panicking at the possibility of capture, knowing his running ability was limited at best.

Irish raced for the entrance of Stanley Park, just across from where the wild skirmish had been occurring. His primary objective was to get Andy and Callum to safety, Blue would have to fend for himself, blood was after all, thicker than water. With the police all around tackling would-be escapees and closing on him rapidly, he reached the old iron railings that encircled the perimeter of the park. Knowing that he was out of time and could not make the open main gates, the frantic Irish spotted a gap in the ironworks, just sufficient to admit one person at a time, with a squeeze.

"Gerrin' Andy, move yerself", he demanded, forcing the first of his cousins through to the leafy interior, "Right you're next Callum, fuckin' gerrin' there now." He turned to look over his right shoulder as he pushed Callum into the narrow opening between the bent, distorted railings. Running towards him was a young, slim, uniformed constable intent on his arrest. Irish knew if he too passed into the park at this point, the officer would definitely follow and may even capture him, or one of his cousins; that was a risk he could not take.

"Patrick, what are yer doin', c'mon man get through!" Callum shouted from within, reaching out to him.

"Get the fuck out of 'ere, run and don't stop runnin'." Irish ordered, stepping away from his only means of escape.

"Come 'ed then bizzie let's fuckin' do it!" he roared and sprang forward to meet his nemesis.

Both Skinhead and constable crashed to the ground with the force of the collision and began a desperate grappling contest, rolling about on the aged pavement then into the road. Digging his fingers into the officer's eyes, Irish momentarily gained the upper hand but try as he might he could not extricate himself from the young man's determined grip.

"Let me go you fuckin' cunt." Irish warned, then swapped from eye-gouging to face battering, punching with all his strength. So intent was he on trying to free himself, that he did not notice the two burly constables almost upon him.

"You fuckin' little shit." the first to arrive called as he booted Irish hard in the ribs, following up with a vicious truncheon blow to his head.

His heavyweight colleague joined him moments later and immediately began kicking the downed youth as if he too were one of the hooligans. Their junior novice rose to his feet, collected his peaked cap from the pavement nearby were it had fallen then stood alongside the two more experienced officers whilst they amused themselves, battering their helpless victim. Finally the larger of the pair handcuffed Irish, formally arrested him and turned to the young constable, "Here y'go mate, we'll hold 'im while you give 'im a few digs." With a look of disbelief the younger officer replied, "No thanks, he's been nicked, that's good enough f'me." Both of the stocky pair laughed, with the arresting officer asking, "Fuckin' hell boy, you're in the wrong job, y'not queer are yer?"

The young PC declined to reply and helped the bloodied Irish to his feet before leading him to the large, dark blue police van, known colloquially as a 'meat wagon' or 'meaty', parked across the road from the football ground.

When the doors at the rear of the vehicle were opened, Irish was roughly pushed into the gloomy interior, joining its five existing occupants. As he adjusted his vision and looked about, he heard a loud bang on the outside of the van with an accompanying shout, "Right move off with these pricks, get them down to Cheapside." Scrambling from the cold metal floor onto the small bench, Irish was in part relieved to see his friend Blue seated in one corner with his head down, looking beaten but at least otherwise relatively uninjured. Apart from his former team mate, there was one other civilian Evertonian and three West Ham crew members, including the cropped haired giant senior of the original clash. His head wounds had been cleaned and dressed by one of the many St. John's ambulance men, who worked tirelessly throughout that afternoon to deal with the aftermath of the bloody battle.

"Blue, it's me, Irish, are yer alright mate?" Irish asked.

Blue finally raised his head having previously been too afraid to do so, not wishing to catch the evil eye of the massive cockney sitting opposite him.

"Thank fuck you're 'ere," Blue said nervously, "I thought I was a gonner, what a fuckin' scrap."

The elder male across from him laughed "Fackin' hell boy, if you thought that was a scrap, you should see Millwall when they go in." He spat some blood and phlegm onto the floor, continuing, "Go darn the Den if yer've got the bottle, meet the fackin' Treatment or worse F Troop and yer'll be lucky t'get out alive boy." He laughed again then asked, "Anyone got a fackin' ciggie, I'm gaspin' here?"

Irish replied, "Throw me one over if yer 'ave an I'll even smoke it for yer." They all laughed at the gallows humour bound as they were with their hands cuffed behind their backs. For the remainder of their short journey to the city centre, the reluctant passengers sat in the silence of their own thoughts.

Within twenty minutes they arrived at their destination, Liverpool's own Bastille, the main Bridewell in Cheapside. This grim, forbidding, archaic structure had seen generations of unfortunate captives pass through its heavy doors and enjoyed a sinister reputation for brutality and despair. The vehicle came to an abrupt stop and the doors were flung open, allowing the bright daylight to flood the gloomy, stuffy interior.

"Right, gerrout scum!" the driver and his fellow officer called.

Following in the footsteps of countless others all six detainees were led up the well-worn, sandstone stairs, through the entrance chamber and brought to a halt in front of the huge desk sergeant, ready to be processed. The heavy door to the outside world of the twentieth century clanged shut behind them and they were instantly transported back to mid-Victorian

England, as if time had stood still inside this antique relic of the prison system.

After a cursory search and with their handcuffs removed their details were established. The sergeant then stepped round from his old, weathered desk to study the new inmates.

"Well we've got a right collection of dickheads here, haven't we?" he asked rhetorically, whilst stroking his bristling grey moustache. His four guard companions and the two transport officers did not reply but smiled at his humorous observation.

"Watch who yer callin' a dickhead, granddad," the giant Cockney, who had given his details as 'Billy Smith of no fixed abode' warned.

"Eye, eye, trouble maker is it? Tough guy are yer?" the sergeant asked with a sly smile. "Cuff him again, we've got a live one here." he ordered.

This time Billy's hands were restrained to his front. Even as the cuffs were snapped shut he received a tremendous blow to his stomach from the elder male and was also struck twice in the kidneys by two of the warders standing to his rear.

"You fackin' slags." Billy called out, only to receive another powerful punch to his aching gut.

"We're gonna 'ave a really nice time, you and me, Billy Smith, while you're our guest. Open that fuckin' mouth again an I'll ram my truncheon right down you're fuckin' throat." the sergeant warned, not realising the double entendre of his words.

"There's an offer I can't refuse you arl cant." Billy replied with a grin.

This time all three of his attackers struck him repeatedly from the front and back, dropping him to his knees with two well-aimed truncheon strikes across his calves. Common sense finally prevailed and the kneeling man made no further response. A few moments later all six hooligans were forced into a narrow, cramped cell, initially designed for a maximum occupancy of two people. Billy slumped down on the single plank bench that was affixed to the aged white-washed walls, with one of his crew seated next to him, everyone else sat on the floor wherever they could wedge themselves into a space.

"You still wanna smoke?" Irish asked of Billy.

"Yeah, unless you've got them stashed up yer jacksey." Billy replied honestly.

"Nah, no need, I 'ardly got searched, the one who done me was too busy fiddlin' with me plumbs." Irish noted then produced a five pack of Senior Service containing three remaining cigarettes and a small book of matches that he had recently begun to carry for convenience. He lit one smoke then passed it to Billy, lit another for himself then offered "If anyone else fancies a drag, yer'll 'ave t'share this one." Only the civilian Evertonian and one of Billy's associates were smokers and they gladly accepted.

While they quietly enjoyed their nicotine fix, Blue and his fellow abstainer also sat silently, all contemplating their fate for a few minutes. As Billy neared the end of his cigarette his thoughts returned to the grim reality of their present surroundings, in particular his geographical location.

"What a fackin' result, West Ham loses two, nil t'some Scarse nonces and am banged up in this northern shit hole. Fack me somebody's havin' a larf." He flicked the still glowing butt of his smoke across at Blue then farted enthusiastically "That's better, that'll make this fackin' place smell sweeter." Laughing he turned to Irish and asked, "D'you boys do any scrappin' up 'ere in the norf, or do yer just wait for our little juniors to show before yer'll 'ave a go?"

Irish finished his cigarette before replying, "We do plenty of scrappin' round 'ere mate when we need to. Me and Blue 'ere are from the Crown Team, nobody fuck's with our crew."

Billy was less than impressed, "Well, if you two are anyfin' t'go by yers must be a shit team, yer wouldn't stand a fackin' chance darn London, boy."

Irish was becoming increasingly irritated and responded angrily, "You know fuck all mate, there's lads in our crew who'd take on anyone, who don't give a fuck about the odds, they're proper hard cases, thee don't just talk a good fight."

Again Billy laughed and advised, "It's a different world darn sarf, boy, we're fightin' a fackin' war darn there."

Irish interrupted sharply, "I'll stop yer right there mate. We don't go for all that racial shite up 'ere..."

Billy snapped back, "Who said anyfin' bout fackin' race, I never mentioned race, all of yer big London firms 'ave got yer black lads in their Top Boys. They're as English as jellied eels and pie and mash, they're 'ard cants, they get stuck right in in a ruck and they won't shit out." He paused then added, "No mate, you'll see, all yous Northern mugs'll see when it comes to yer, when it's too fackin' late. Yous'll mark my words then." He said no more and settled instead on pursing his lips and disconcertingly blowing random kisses at Blue, much to the Crown player's considerable alarm.

Irish was bemused by the Cockney sage's cryptic comments but did not reply, quickly dismissing them from his mind. Far more pressing matters were his immediate concern as he mulled over the charges he was accused of including; affray, aggravated assault, resisting arrest and assaulting a police officer. He knew it was unlikely that he would be walking away with just a fine and that a lengthy prison sentence was almost certain.

Several slow, mind-numbing hours passed with the tiny window, located in the upper area of the outward wall revealing the eventual passage of sunny afternoon to pale evening and ultimately dark night. They had not been fed or watered at any time since their arrival and the cramped, smelly conditions were also adding to the discomfort of their growing thirst and hunger pangs. Shortly the first of the evening's drunk and disorderly guests began to arrive, adding their shrieks, screams and violent protestations to the general disturbing ambience of their surroundings.

Billy had had enough and after pushing his way to the metal cell door, began pounding it with his cuffed hands while verbally registering his disappointment with the standard of accommodation, roaring at the top of his voice.

"Come on you fackin' cants, bring us some food and drink, I wouldn't keep my dogs like this, you Scarse queers!" Over and over he repeated his complaints, becoming louder and more enraged on each repetition.

Blue was growing increasingly anxious, fearful of what the handcuffed Cockney giant may still be capable of. "When d'yer think thee'll let us go Irish? I can't stand it much longer in 'ere with this fuckin' nutter." he said quietly to Irish.

"Yer'll be alright Blue, thee've only charged you with public disorder, you'll be out of 'ere anytime now." Irish replied reassuringly, if incorrectly.

Billy was now raging like a madman, booting the door and roaring, "Fackin' open this door before I murder one of these slags... don't blame me, I've fackin' warned yers."

Suddenly the loud fall of heavy boots could be heard echoing around the dank corridor, announcing the approach of one of the stocky warders. On hearing the iron key in the lock to the door of their cell, Billy calmed a little and stepped away a few paces, standing on the feet of a fellow inmate as he did "About fackin' time you got darn 'ere, I wanna make a phone call t'my solicitor, now!"

The vicious truncheon blow that struck him across the clavicle just below his throat, staggered the giant in his present weakened state, the follow-up powerful thrust into his gut sent him stumbling back across his companions.

"Sit down, you fuckin' Cockney tit or I will burst your fuckin' skull right 'ere and now."

Billy wisely remained where he had landed, whilst the warder planted himself firmly in the doorway.

"Which one of you fuckin' scum is Patrick O'Hare?" he asked.

Irish identified himself and was told to stand up, "Right c'mon Paddy, you're out of 'ere, yer brother's waiting for yer at the front desk."

"Me brother? How did he get 'ere from Northampton, how did he even know I was in 'ere?" Irish asked genuinely surprised.

"D'you wanna go or stay 'ere lad, 'cause am not arsed either way?" the surly warder asked with equal sincerity.

Irish stepped across his seated fellows as quickly as he could.

Blue called out in fear, "Irish! Yer not leavin' me in 'ere are yer?"

His former team mate answered pragmatically, "Sorry Blue I can't help yer, I'll tell yer arl feller what's happened when I get back to the Crown."

Blue was nearly in tears as he watched his friend exit the cell, followed by the heavy door being firmly slammed shut.

"Don't worry sweetheart, I'll take care of yer." Billy offered kindly.

Moments later a much relieved Irish was standing at the desk sergeant's counter receiving those personal items that had been confiscated, back from the duty officer. His obliging 'brother' was in fact Danny Boy, youngest of the Gerard siblings; it was he who now stood nearby smiling and chatting with the warders.

"Alright lad, off y'go, hope yer enjoyed y'stay with us." said the grey haired officer, carefully folding a small brown envelope before placing it in the breast pocket of his dark uniformed jacket.

"Sorry about that little misunderstandin' there Jack, I hope that's all sorted now." Danny enquired leading his 'brother' out of the grim building.

"Don't mention it Danny we all make mistakes, say 'ello t'the lads for me." the desk sergeant called after them as they disappeared back into the twentieth century.

Irish stood on the top sandstone step and breathed in deeply, filling his lungs with the cool night air. "Thanks for bailin' me out, I don't know how yers knew I was there but thanks..." he began but was quickly interrupted by Danny.

"Save it dickhead, gerrin the fuckin' car quick style."

Irish did as instructed entering into a dark blue Ford Cortina at the rear passenger door, Danny followed suit. Inside he found an angry Francis, one of the Gerard Seniors, waiting for him. "You fuckin' ejit, gettin' yerself nicked for fuck all." Francis prefaced the beginning of his lengthy criticism of Irish, before tapping the driver of the vehicle on the shoulder to signal their departure. "Y'lucky old Jack has been on the payroll f'years and keeps his eye's out for any of our boys." Francis advised.

"Right, but how did he know I was with yous?" Irish asked curiously.

"We keep 'im and a few other plods up to date with the names of our new lads," Francis replied, adding, "Yer've not long been added so y'touched lucky there, anyway never mind all that, what we wanna know is just how fuckin' stupid are yer, gettin' pulled in f'scrappin' in the street, at a football match, y'tit."

Irish tried to offer a response but Francis raised his hand and stopped him, "Save all that boy, y'gonna need t'do yer explainin' to Niall and he's fuckin' *really* pissed off with yer."

Not long after they arrived outside The Central public house on London Road and Irish was roughly bundled out of the vehicle before being led into the shabby building. Passing from bar to first floor lounge and beyond, Irish was brought once more to the second storey flat where he and Blue had previously been entertained by the obliging Shirley in a mutually satisfying, reciprocal arrangement. He doubted this evening's encounter would be as stimulating or quite so pleasant. Niall was sitting in the same comfortable armchair where Irish had sat while Shirley performed her expert oral service upon him. Flanked by Tommy and Danny the 'prisoner' stood silently in front of the scowling arbiter of his fate, awaiting his sentence.

"You fuckin' big gob shite." Niall began, "Not gripped for doin' a proper bit of business, not even for rollin' a cunt for a few bob, or scrappin' f'cash, no, not you, fightin' with yer little friends over a shitty game of football." Niall paused and poured himself a large measure of Jameson's Whiskey from a bottle standing on a small round table nearby and took a hefty swig from the glass tumbler he was holding before continuing, "You cost us money tonight boy, a lorra money to line the pockets of some bent coppers, helpin' them lose their memories. Yer gonna pay us back every fuckin' penny, with interest, d'yer understand that boy?"

Irish knew he was in a hopeless situation and acquiesced without argument. "Yeah of course Niall, I'll pay yers back, whatever it cost yer."

Niall smiled, took another drink then explained exactly what he had meant. "I don't think I've made myself clear, you belong to us, we fuckin' *own* you, anythin' we want you t'do, a*nythin'*, you're doin' it, no question, no argument."

Irish nodded his acceptance; he now finally understood fully why his friend Jay Mac had always warned him against having any contact with his dangerous cousins. His understanding came too late.

"Your luck must be runnin' good t'night Patrick because we happen t'have a vacancy that's just come up and you're gonna fuckin' fill it." Niall advised, his demeanour appearing slightly less threatening. "We set our John up with a really good job, doin' a bit of international business for us. 'Course he never got started because that Morgo cunt done him in and we had to use someone else. Anyway that opening is available again now, if yer get my drift."

Irish had an uneasy feeling about Niall's remarks and this particular offer of employment but made no comment.

"It's the States f'you boy, New York. Yer'll be deliverin' some packages for us and pickin' up some more t'bring back. That's it... simple. A bit of travel will do yer good, keep yer out of trouble, no more playin' with yer little Skinhead friends." Niall paused and poured himself another drink.

Irish used the opportunity to ask a few questions of his own. "No disrespect but I'd like t'know a couple of things like who am I meetin' over there, what's in the packages and what happens if there's any trouble?"

Niall placed his glass tumbler filled with whiskey back down onto the small table and replied, "Yer'll be meetin' whoever we tell yer at the time yer goin', you don't need t'know what's in the packages an if yer stupid enough t'get pinched, nothin' happens, y'keep yer fuckin' mouth shut and do yer time. Anythin' else, let's hear it now."

Irish thought for a moment then asked, "What happened to the lad who was doin' this job?"

Niall smiled and stared up directly at Irish, "He started askin' too many fuckin' questions."

The siblings laughed, Niall continued, "Right yer'll need t'sort out a passport f'yerself, yer've gorra few weeks then we'll be in touch. Before y'go yer'll probably have t'put in an appearance in front the magistrates but that'll just be a fine, you can take care of that yerself. Ok, that's all, yer can piss off now."

Irish turned to walk away and had just grasped the handle of the door, when Niall called after him, "One more thing Patrick... Shirley sends her regards, she says there might be a couple of things she'll need *your* help with, see yer." Again the brothers laughed, Irish shuddered. Francis noticed his reaction and called "Hey boy, just be glad none of us are arse bandits, it could've been a lot worse for yer." Once more the sibling laughter was spontaneous.

After leaving the Central public house, Irish quickly made his way down London Road and then passed the magnificent neo-classical buildings of the Walker Art Gallery, the City Museum and Central Library standing proud along the gentle slope of William Brown Street. Crossing into Dale Street at the base of the rise he soon came by Cheapside, location of the dreaded main Bridewell.

'God I hope old Blue's holdin' out in there, with that mad Cockney bastard.' he thought glancing momentarily towards the brooding, dark structure, lit from above by a pale moonlight. A short walk later he arrived at his destination, the Pier Head bus and ferry terminus, just in time to catch the midnight bus to the Crown Estate, the final one of the day.

Sitting upstairs on the rear seat of the vehicle he cadged a cigarette and a light from an inebriated fellow passenger and sat back to enjoy a smoke, whilst listening to a discordant selection of songs from some of the more animated drunks. Travelling through the dark night Irish began reflecting on the events of the day and their unexpected outcome. As he stubbed out the glowing butt of his cigarette, against the graffiti covered rear of the seat in front of him, he smiled on noticing the now barely discernible Crown Team logo accompanied by his name and those of several other crew, including the late Jay Mac. Irish smiled, the bitter paradoxical irony of the situation not lost on him.

His obsessive Americana friend had always dreamed of visiting the United States, even of migrating to that vast continent but had been murdered just on the eve of achieving his ambition. Whereas Irish had no desires or even thoughts about America, other than those he had acquired by osmosis from two polarised views; Jay Mac's egalitarian utopia, the land of endless possibility open to everyone, versus that of the estate's only Hippie, Oliver Furlong's antithetical capitalist empire of warmongers and opportunists, riddled with social and racial inequality. One thing he knew for certain was that he personally would very shortly be able to form his own first-hand opinion and draw his own conclusions.

Not far from the bleak Crown Estate whilst partially listening to a standing drunk soloist delivering a particularly lewd version of *Dirty Maggie May* and simultaneously urinating copiously, causing Irish and any other cognisant passengers to raise their feet to avoid the flood, the youth was suddenly snapped back to his present situation. Dozens of bricks, bottles and other projectiles struck the vehicle from every side as it slowed to a stop near the crossroads junction, close to the municipal cemetery.

"Ravens Crew, Ravens Crew!" their assailants shouted from without, launching another noisy salvo at the beleaguered, green Atlantean bus. Fortunately there was no attempt to storm the vehicle, the show of strength was merely this particular team announcing their presence and reminding everyone that they were passing through Ravens' territory.

Irish smiled, he was unconcerned either way having survived worse assaults. He raised two fingers in victory salute, not caring whether any of the Ravens crew members could see him or not. 'Fuck me that's something I won't miss when I get t'the States.' he told himself, convinced that anywhere must be better than his present, hostile environment.

June 1976

With more than a month passing since Irish's meeting with the Gerards and receiving no contact from them, even at his brief court appearance in front of the city magistrates, which resulted as Niall had correctly predicted, in the imposition of a monetary fine, he began to believe that perhaps they no longer required his services as a courier. This was until his mother received a telephone call from 'A very nice gentleman' requesting her son's attendance at 'their city office' to discuss a 'lucrative employment opportunity'. Irish did as instructed finding himself once more standing in the second floor flat above the shabby London Road public house, being told precise details of his travel and rendezvous arrangements.

"Don't forget Patrick you belong to us, you're our representative. You don't wanna make any mistakes or let us down, we wouldn't like that and neither would our friends over there." Niall warned unnecessarily. "Okay, yer'll be getttin' off in a few days so keep yer fuckin' head down, no trouble, don't go gettin' yerself stabbed t'death like our John, 'cause that would really piss us off."

"I'll do me best not to Niall, I'll see yer when I get back." Irish replied, placing his documents in the inside pocket of his denim jacket.

"Oh you will boy, don't you fuckin' doubt it." Niall promised, smiling as he rose from his chair then patted his employee firmly on the shoulder with his heavy hand, in a farewell gesture.

Saturday, 12 June 1976

It was an exceptionally warm Saturday evening and would prove to be the herald of many more to follow, as the hottest, sustained heat wave on record was about to scorch England's green and pleasant land for several weeks to come, leading to water shortages and the first ever hosepipe ban. Irish, Blue and for one last time, Glynn, were sitting with the rest of the former Eagle crew in the boiling lounge of that eponymous alehouse, quenching their considerable thirst with copious amounts of golden, amber fluid and dark stout accompanied by obligatory whiskey chasers.

A celebration of sorts was taking place with three separate causes at its root, not that any specific cause was actually needed for the team to enjoy an evening of excessive drinking and exaggerated story telling but a trio of reasons was too good to let pass. Two fond farewells, one of a temporary nature, the other permanent and a welcome return, found the ex-Eagle players both commiserating and congratulating in equal measure.

Irish had let it generally be known that he had obtained regular work, away from the Estate and the city, 'down south'. Glynn on the other hand had finally achieved his long held ambition and was relocating, with his family, to an undisclosed destination, for personal reasons which they all fully understood. These were minor events compared with the core célèbre of the evening, that of the return of their courageous former leader, Tommy (S), in good health and spirits. His near fatal beating that he had endured in a desperate bid to save his team from being overwhelmed and becoming tortured captives of their deadly rivals, the Kings Team, had necessitated an emergency life-saving operation, a protracted period of regular hospital visits for additional treatment and a lengthy convalescence. They all knew what Tommy's altruistic actions had spared them from and what it had cost him; he was universally admired. With Pluto's *Dat* playing on the juke box, the pint glasses clinking and the blue-grey nicotine haze swirling all about, the party was in full swing.

"It's fuckin' roastin' in 'ere t'night." Blue noted, stating the obvious, "You'll have to get use to this Irish, it'll be even hotter where you're goin'."

"Yer mean *down south*, do yer Blue, yeah?" Irish replied, reminding his garrulous friend that he had only revealed his true destination to him and Glynn, not wishing for anybody else to become aware of this.

"Oh yeah, down south, that's warra mean." Blue confirmed, for once understanding exactly what his former team mate was saying.

"Lookin' forward to gettin' off Irish?" Glynn asked, lighting a cigarette, which everyone knew he would only pretend to smoke, hardly inhaling at all.

"Sort of Glynn but probably not as much as you are. I haven't really got much choice, if y'know warra mean."

"I can't believe yer even workin' for those mad cunts." Glynn observed.

Irish smiled, "Well, like I said mate, it's hard t'turn *them* down when they 'offer' yer a job."

Tommy (S), who was positioned at the centre of the semi-circular seating arrangement, a few places to the left of Irish,

Blue and Glynn, flanked by his old guard lieutenants, called across to them, "Hey Irish, yer've put us all t'shame lad. You're the only one who still looks like a real fuckin' player, well in mate."

Irish laughed and called back, "Thanks Tommy, I do me best someone's gorra keep up the standards."

Their former leader who had been the quintessential Skinhead but now dressed in the contemporary style of leather jacket, high-waist Oxford bag trousers and platform shoes, was commenting on Irish's distinctive, original, now out-dated look. With his recently cropped number one length hair and obligatory razored trench, wearing his short-sleeved, checked Ben Sherman shirt, black half inch elasticated bracers, twenty-two inch blue-green two-tone parallels and gleaming cherry red Airwair, he had preserved a unique working class style that had otherwise almost totally disappeared.

"Come over 'ere Irish I wanna word with yer anyway." Tommy requested.

Irish complied without question and quickly changed places with Tommy's right hand ex-fellow commander, the recently released from prison brother of the late Heron crew leader, Yad, Dayo (G). Sitting next to each other team leader and player looked totally incongruous, as if representing two distinct periods in English youth fashion. Tommy's thick, dark hair had grown into a dense, coarse mane and with his large bushy sideburns surrounding his angular face, thin lipped mouth and tiny triangular, barely visible steel-grey eyes, he had a lionised appearance.

"So yer off down south 'ey?" he asked rhetorically, "Well do us proud when yer there Irish, never forget you were a Crown Team Skin."

"I'll do me best Tommy if I have any bother but t'be honest I'm not expectin' any trouble. Am just gonna keep me head down." Irish responded honestly.

Tommy placed his pint down on the small table in front of him and reached into the inside of his dark leather, broad lapelled jacket. "Yeah that's the way t'go mate but its funny how even when yer not lookin' for it, trouble's gorra way of findin' yer." He paused and passed Irish a heavy, solid brass object, "'Ere yer are Irish, a little present for yer just in case some fucker won't back off an needs a bit of persuadin'."

Irish looked down at his 'gift', recognising Tommy's own secondary weapon of choice, his well used knuckle duster which had cracked many an enemy's nose and dislocated an equal number of opponent's jaws.

"Thanks Tommy that's fuckin' ace mate, nice one." he replied.

Suddenly the leader's mood changed and the momentary smile he had worn disappeared from his grim countenance. Staring directly towards the lounge main door he observed in a low, cool tone, "Here's a fuckin' prick who can burst anyone's balloon."

With *Take it to the Limit* by the Eagles playing on the juke box near the entrance, Weaver the crazed psychopath had just arrived accompanied by two of his ever-dwindling crew of Heron Juniors.

"Alright lads, havin' a little party are yers but forgot to invite yer arl mate Weaver." he asked, smiling slyly.

"What is it yer wanted Weaver, we're just havin' a few drinks 'ere?" Dayo (G) asked, returning to his seat next to Tommy (S), with Irish also resuming his original position.

"That's very kind of yer Dayo, three pints of bitter if yer gettin' a round in." Weaver responded.

Dayo did not reply, ignoring the leader of his former crew.

Weaver pressed on, "Nah, yer ok Dayo lad, am only jokin' with yer, we pay for own drinks." Turning to his Juniors he ordered, "What are yer fuckin' waitin' for Stevo, go an get the ale in an you, Joey, find me a stool, quick style."

Of the two scruffy looking Juniors, Joey the younger brother of Peza the convicted rapist, one of Yad's accomplices in an horrendous attack a few years earlier, was the first to complete his quest, returning with the required stool. "'Ere yer are boss." he said, placing the item next to Weaver, before wiping his crusty nose with the sleeve of his grimy v-neck jumper.

Weaver quickly snatched the three legged seat and immediately placed it directly in front of Irish, Blue and Glynn,

"Now then Irish, me old mate, what's this about you gettin' off t'do a birra work down in London." he asked grinning.

Irish looked at his battered features, framed by his wild, unkempt bush of hair and into his small piercing steel-grey eyes, almost a perfect match of those of Tommy (S). Normally he would have flinched, or avoided the psychopath's gaze but recent events had hardened his heart and steeled his nerve.

"Am not goin' t'London, just workin' all round the south, and just so we're clear I'm not yer mate, Weaver."

"Fuck me, grown a little pair of balls 'ave yer, well good f'you, about fuckin' time I say." Weaver observed sarcastically.

Just then Stevo returned with three pints of bitter handing one to his leader. Both Juniors positioned themselves standing behind Weaver, drinking their ale, listening to his words of wisdom, watching how he operated.

"How are you gettin' on there Blue? All shacked up nice an cosy with Beryl the slag and *her* two little girls?" Weaver asked, turning his attention towards the corpulent, nervous youth.

"Am doin' alright... thanks... an I don't like yer callin' Beryl a slag." he stammered.

Once more Weaver was surprised by this uncharacteristically aggressive response.

"What the fuck 'ave you boys been on, is it the ale talkin' or 'ave yers 'ad a little taste of somethin'?" He took a deep draught of his pint then belched loudly in their direction, focusing his icy stare on the real reason for his unwelcome, uninvited appearance at the Eagle public house that night. "'Ello little Glynn, I didn't notice you there boy." he began then took another swig of his ale, "Now I've heard some story about you an yer ma runnin' away from the Estate. Is that right boy?"

Glynn did not answer but looked down into his half-empty pint glass.

"What's the matter with you 'ey, 'ave I said somethin' out of order? Fuckin' hell I'm only askin' cos I wouldn't want you or yer ma bein' too far away so I couldn't come round an visit... yer know how much she likes my visits." Weaver lowered his pint down onto their table, grinning at his victim, waiting for a response.

It was Blue who spoke first, even as Irish was slipping the knuckle duster onto his right fist, under that same table. "Why don't you just fuck off and leave 'im alone, nobody wants you 'ere."

Weaver kept his gaze on Glynn but replied to Blue, "Shut yer fuckin' mouth fat boy, before I knock every tooth out of it."

Irish closed his left hand firmly round his pint, ready to fling it in Weaver's face before striking him with his metal encased right.

The psychopath tried once more to elicit a response from Glynn. "Your ma *has* told yer about that night when me, Yad an Macca (G) banged 'er good an proper an she loved it... 'asn't she?

Before anyone else made a move or could reply, Tommy (S) rose from his seat, silencing the whole assembly and called out, "Say one more word you piece of shit an *I'll* take you outside an fuckin' open you right up." The leader waited a few pregnant seconds but received no response. "What d'jer think Weaver, me an you... now in the car park, y'can even use yer little hammer. Am not up t'full strength but I can promise yer *I'll* still fuckin' lay you out boy."

Weaver may have been insane but he was not stupid.

"No offence Tommy, am only havin' a laugh, I'll say no more, ok mate?"

Tommy stood perfectly still, silently watching Weaver allowing him to feel the full weight of his own unnerving stare. The Heron leader rose from his seat and moved away from Irish, Blue and Glynn with his two disappointed disciples.

For a few seconds only the sound of The Temptations' *Cloud Nine* could be heard and then as if nothing had occurred the crew members resumed their own conversations, their leader laughing and joking with his old guard.

Having replaced the heavy brass knuckle duster in his trouser pocket, Irish raised the thumb of his right hand as a gesture of gratitude, in the direction of Tommy (S).

"You alright Glynn? he asked.

"Yeah I will be, when I get me an me mum out of this fuckin' hell hole." Both of his companions acknowledged his comments, concurring with his sentiment.

Blue then stood up to go to the bar, "Same again lads?" he asked, adding "I'll get some packets of crisps and salted peanuts while am there 'ey?"

"There's a fuckin' surprise." Irish noted.

While their team mate was waiting to be served, wedged into the tightly packed throng shouting their orders, each urgently trying to catch the attention of the overworked bar staff, Glynn began to ask Irish about his forth coming trip and particularly his intended destination. "It's gonna be a fuckin' different world over there Irish, y'know what the Yanks are like for carryin' guns. If yer gerrin t'any bother, yer gonna be fucked without a shooter."

Irish finished the dregs of his existing pint and replied, "Thanks f'that Glynn but I think that's all shite, only what yer see on the telly."

Glynn was not convinced, "Nah mate, y'defo need somethin' an I might be able t'help yer out..." He paused and checked to ensure he could not be overheard then continued in a low voice "... I've got that 'thing' Jay Mac gave me just before..."

Irish interrupted him "No thanks Glynn, I thought that's what he might 'ave done with it. You keep it mate, Jay Mac intended you t'have it. Maybe one day the opportunity might come where you can put it t'good use." Irish paused threw back his whiskey chaser and continued, "Besides I've lived on this shit hole of an estate for twenty one years, what's gonna happen t'me over there in the States?" He said no more, his attention was now diverted towards Blue who was making his way back to their table precariously balancing a small metal tray containing two pints of bitter, one of Guinness and numerous bags of salted snacks. Blue had been stopped by Weaver who appeared to be delivering a serious message, prodding him firmly in the chest for emphasis. When he finally arrived at the table, Irish asked, "What did that knobhead want Blue, lookin' f'trouble again is he?"

After placing down the tray and passing each of them their pints he answered, "He said 'tell that fuckin' queer Glyn that Tommy (S) won't always be around t'watch his back, next time he's really gonna hurt yer'."

Weaver was watching as Blue spoke, he raised his pint towards them and smiled. Irish turned to Glynn and then looking directly across at the smiling psychopath said, "Like I said Glynn, when the chance comes put it to good use."

Chapter 4

All Gone to Look for America

Friday 25th June 1976

A golden sun dominated a pale blue morning sky, having already burned away an early low grey mist from the horizon, which had obscured the imposing skyline of the teeming metropolis the lurching vessel was rapidly approaching. Even with the cool sea breeze presently blowing the heat was barely dissipated; it was clear that this was going to be another scorching day on shore, within the stifling confines of the concrete and steel canyons.

Irish was stood on the spray-soaked metal deck of the Dutch merchant vessel *The Prince of Orange*, as it entered the mouth of the Hudson River, bound for the Manhattan Docks. The irony of a young Catholic male being transported on a vessel named after the famous leader of his traditional sectarian enemy, was not lost on Irish. It had, however, not occurred to him that if not for an aggressive takeover bid by the British in 1664 he would soon have been arriving in New Amsterdam rather than its anglicised successor, New York.

He would be glad to reach the harbour; it had been a long journey for the youth who had never travelled further than New Brighton on the Mersey Ferry, a twenty minute boat trip at most. After catching a train to London and then on to Southampton, where he had been given his 'luggage', Irish had been at sea for twelve days during his Atlantic crossing. It was not being out on the open waters of the dark ocean that had perturbed him, on the contrary he had found the steady, rhythmic rise and fall of the waves relaxing, almost soporific but the confinement below deck was another matter. As the majority of the crew, except for the officers, spoke only Dutch or French and with Irish's knowledge of the former being non-existent and his mastery of the latter extending to 'bonjour mademoiselle' and 'baise moi', a combination of both being of limited use, communication with his travelling companions had been difficult. He had almost wished that he had paid some attention to the struggling efforts of the increasingly desperate Mr 'wanker' Watts, his ill-fated teacher of French at the brutal *Cardinals School for Catholic Boys.*

"Not for you much longer I think."

Irish suddenly heard to his immediate rear on his right side. He glanced over his shoulder at the handsome smiling Chief Petty Officer in his immaculate uniform. Momentarily the youth was disconcerted at hearing his native tongue after almost a two week absence.

"Alright mate, how's it goin'?" Irish responded warmly.

The officer came alongside, studying Irish's unique style of dress in his dark blue Harrington jacket, twenty-four inch parallel, well-scrubbed Fleming's jeans with bleached half-inch turn ups and his obligatory gleaming cherry-red Airwair. With his number one cropped hair, it was entirely reasonable that the smartly dressed older male, would make a logical assumption.

"You are perhaps a soldier my friend?"

Irish laughed, "Yeah, sort of mate."

"You are keeping yourself very fit, I believe." the officer observed, moving closer.

"Fit enough." Irish answered honestly, beginning to suspect that there may be an ulterior motive to his new companion's friendliness.

"Your voyage could have been much more comfortable, yes?" he said placing his left hand upon Irish's right shoulder, squeezing it firmly.

The no longer smiling Skinhead stepped a few paces to his left replying, "Nah mate, am strictly portside not starboard, so I wouldn't 'ave been more comfortable but thanks anyway."

The officer's English was sufficient for him to understand Irish's meaning and he said no more for the time being.

Shortly they passed by the awe inspiring colossal Statue of Liberty standing majestically on her island of the same name. With Ellis Island the original gateway to the New World just visible beyond, the older male speculated, "How many thousands of poor, hopeful souls must have passed through the halls of that place, I wonder?"

Irish also wondered considering how many of his extended, widely distributed O'Hare clan may have had their details recorded within those halls, before beginning their American adventures. He recalled his father talking about his own father's brother who had left the family in Ireland to make his fortune in the United States but had never been heard from again. 'Imagine meetin' one of his people over here; now *that* really would be a small world.' Irish thought fancifully.

The *'Prince of Orange'* steered to the port and began its cautious approach to the dockside at one of the last remaining piers still in operation. In an absolute mirror of what had happened to the great maritime city of Liverpool and other such ports nationally and globally, the necessary, if unwelcome introduction of containerisation, had decimated existing traditional merchant fleets and all but annihilated the vast army of stevedores who had toiled for generations to service those ships. The docks of New York were now only a pale shadow of their former bustling self.

"Fuckin' hell, would y'look at the size of those two buildin's there?!" Irish exclaimed as they passed by the magnificent architectural achievement of the Twin Towers of the World Trade Centre. For a short time after their completion in 1972 they were the tallest structures in the world, until being eclipsed the following year by the Sear's Tower in another US rival, Chicago.

"There are many such wonderful things to see in this city; perhaps I could enjoy showing these to you?" Irish's admirer offered generously.

The youth stiffened and turned towards the Dutch officer, "Like I said mate, I don't play for *your* team. Whatever sights there is t'see here, I'll find them meself. Don't push y'luck any further, right?"

"As you please." the disappointed older male replied before walking away.

Almost two hours later, having docked, disembarked and been processed by the customs department at the port authority terminus, Irish was about to retrieve his luggage before exiting the building. On picking up the battered, grey checked suitcase and his old army rucksack containing his clothing, he was addressed directly by a stocky, dark uniformed officer standing close by.

"That your case is it sir?" the swarthy late forties male, sporting an impressive crew cut asked.

"Yeah mate it is." Irish replied trying to remain calm.

"Did you pack it yourself?" he continued.

Again Irish confirmed this was correct, leading to a further set of statutory questions concerning Irish's intended destination, duration of stay and purpose of visit.

Finally after scrutinising Irish's distinctive appearance, the officer concluded with the question, "Ex-military are yer buddy?"

"No, I'm not... it's just a style... I'm what thee call a 'Skinhead'." he answered genuinely.

Shaking his head, the officer observed, "Well it's a better look than my kids have, I wish they'd follow this 'Skinhead' style. Welcome to America, enjoy yer stay."

Relieved and now experiencing some unexpected feelings of excitement, Irish stepped out into the brilliant sunshine and ferocious heat of a New York summer's day.

Having successfully hailed a cab he set off on the next stage of his own adventure to a guest house on the lower East Side as prearranged by his 'tour operators' the Gerard Boys.

Peering out of the grimy side windows of the roomy, comfortable vehicle, Irish was increasingly in awe of the engineering tour de force and sheer audacity of the towering structures, vying for his attention all along the route to his destination. This was not, however, the glorious Technicolour, choreographed arrival in the city that never sleeps of Gene Kelly, Frank Sinatra and Jules Munschin from the opening of MGM's musical spectacular *'On the Town'*, those days, if they had ever existed were long gone.

In reality Irish had arrived at a time in the Big Apple's chequered history when it was rapidly plummeting to its nadir. This was a city haemorrhaging from a thousand financial wounds, apparently in irreversible, terminal decline, with no hope of a vital cash infusion from the Central Government, as perfectly encapsulated in the *Daily News* bitter headline 'Ford to City – Drop Dead'. The principal activities of the innumerable denizens that prowled its thousands of alleys and plagued its parks were murder, rape and drugs. Irish was about to be rapidly and painfully made aware that places far worse than the bleak Crown Estate did exist.

McCabe's Grande Hotel situated at the junction of Grand and Orchard Street, on the Lower East Side, was a perfect example of a somewhat misleading, outdated title being applied to an establishment whose brief moment of grandeur and respectability, had already passed several decades earlier, leaving only the name of the original as a lingering reminder.

When the taxi pulled up alongside the kerb immediately in front of the shabby, rundown building, Irish paid the driver, collected his bags and stepped out onto the litter-strewn pavement. The old brownstone had not been considered grand in living memory and could now more accurately be described as a 'flop house' than hotel. He climbed the worn stone stairs and entered a small, musty reception lobby.

An elderly male with a lengthy combed-over hairstyle plastered into place in the hope of obscuring his bald pate, acknowledged his presence.

"Yes young feller, come for y'room have yer? I've been expectin' you Mr O'Hare." He wiped his hands on his greasy black waistcoat that he wore over a badly creased off-white shirt, with a thin black tie hanging loosely at the open collar.

"Have y'now, well that's good t'hear." Irish replied smiling, pleased with this warm reception, before shaking the man's outstretched hand.

"Ben McCabe, nice t'meet yer." he offered.

"Patrick O'Hare, likewise." Irish replied then signed the guest register, noticing the marked absence of any other names and collected his key.

"Room number ninety, top of the shop." the desk clerk-owner replied, lapsing into English bingo parlance, to Irish's surprise.

"You been over t'England 'ave yer mate?" he asked curiously.

"Oh yes, back in WW2, just before we set off f'Normandy. Tell me Mr O'Hare what part of Ireland are you from?" the older male enquired, intrigued by Irish's accent.

"The capital part... Liverpool." Irish quipped."

Ben laughed. "Of course, I should have realised with y'being a friend of 'The Boys.' I'll show yer to yer room."

Irish made no comment and followed the man to his third floor bijou apartment.

"Here you are sir, lovely room with a view for yer. Now I do have some house rules and I'll expect you to follow them: No drunkenness; no fighting and no 'guests' in y'room after midnight, okay?"

It was Irish's turn to laugh, "Is that all three aren't allowed after midnight, so they're alright before then?"

"You know well enough what I mean young feller. My granddad bought this place from money he'd made workin' on the railroads, breakin' his back day and night. I run a respectable establishment here, not a house of ill repute, like the rest of them." he advised still smiling but clearly serious.

Irish entered his room and after placing a dollar bill tip in the owner's hand, said goodbye to him, closing the door after he had left. He put his case and rucksack onto the bed then opened the window to admit some warm fresh air into the damp smelly interior. It was much as he had expected; faded, peeling wallpaper masking a decaying structural fabric, with rotted skirting boards barely covered in flaking paint, a crazed grubby sink and a battered old dressing table-cum-chest of drawers, with matching wardrobe. Its one late twentieth century concession other than the single, shadeless electric light bulb hanging from a dusty ceiling cord, was a small black and white, pay slot TV with a circular wire indoor aerial. Irish was soon to find that he was not the only 'guest' occupying the room, as the smiling owner had forgotten to mention the other three principal tenants of the hotel, bed-bugs, fleas and cockroaches.

It was mid afternoon and the Crown Team player, who was a long way from home in an entirely unfamiliar environment, was both tired and hungry. He knew he could continue to ignore his tiredness for the time being but his hunger had to be addressed. After emptying his clothes from his rucksack onto the bed, he quickly changed his Ben Sherman shirt for a thin, short-sleeved, red, white and blue checked Jaytex then forced the old suitcase inside the creaky wardrobe, locking the door with its small metal key, placing this into the pocket of his Fleming's jeans. Once he was happy with his appearance, particularly his gleaming Airwair which had received a cursory wipe, Irish left the room securing it behind him and made his way back down to the reception desk in the entrance lobby.

"Alright boss, I'm goin' out for a bit t'get somethin' t'eat an have a look round." Irish advised the older male who was sitting in an armchair behind the counter, reading the *New York Times*.

"Ok son, you do that, there's plenty t'see and lots of places to eat." he advised.

"Listen, no disrespect but will me gear be safe while am out?" Irish asked.

The proud owner put down his paper and replied, "Let me tell you friend, no one gets by me at the door of my own place and secondly no fucker is stupid enough to try to steal from *this* hotel, they all know who my business partners are."

A reassured Irish said no more, exiting the building to pursue his urgent quest for sustenance. Once outside he was immediately aware of the tremendous heat and particularly the stifling humidity which was all enveloping. He may have left the UK while it was experiencing a unique heat wave of its own but this was nothing in comparison to the southern Mediterranean climate he had now entered. Apart from the uncomfortable temperature, Irish's senses were assailed by the sheer volume of traffic and pedestrian noise, the pungent, sulphurous smell of bad eggs escaping from the innumerable man-hole covers set at the inspection entrances above the vast subterranean sewage system and the piles of refuse stacked high on every corner.

Here he was the lone English Skinhead in the vastness of New York City being swept along by the tide of humanity, unnoticed and totally invisible. Irish soon realised this was a place of easy anonymity, nobody cared how he was dressed or who he was. From Liverpool, a city with a population of barely half a million to a megalopolis of over seven million, he felt as if he was Lemuel Gulliver crossing from the land of the Lilliputians to the kingdom of the giants. The other core difference Irish was actually happy to note was the abundance of choice. Whereas at home in north west England he was used to the attitude of 'you will have what you're given and like it', or 'Hobson's Choice' as it was euphemistically known, he soon found that in the US you could have anything you liked and as much as you wanted.

His first port of call was a street vendor with a mobile eatery packed with burgers and hot dogs. "Alright mate, two of yer all beef, foot-long dogs with all the trimmin's, when y'ready." Irish asked expectantly. He was soon tucking into a huge meat and bread snack, smothered in onions, mustard and sauerkraut. His thirst was next to be quenched as he shortly stopped at a nearby news stand, again packed with every kind of reading material from paperback novels to comic books and a vast array of sweets, most of which he had never heard of before, including Hershey bars and Tootsie Rolls. Equipped with a generous selection of candies tucked into the crook of his left arm whilst drinking a cold bottle of Pepsi held in his right hand, he mused at his present situation.

'Fuck me, its lucky Blue's not here he'd eat himself t'death.' he observed then smiled as he recalled Jay Mac's obsession with all things Americana, in particular super hero comics. 'Pity y'never made it mate, this *is* the fuckin' place for you."

He wandered on continuing his aimless meandering and as he did he speculated on how long he may actually be there. Niall, the elder of the Gerard Crew, had given him no clue as to the duration of his stay, merely telling him that he must meet his contact at midday on Saturday 26th June at Grand Central Station, adding specifics of what he must wear and say at the rendezvous. Irish did have a basic street map but this gave no indication of scale or distance between blocks and he was soon to find that it was a lengthy trek from where he was lodged, to the famous Midtown railway station.

By the time he had reached the unique architectural gem known as the 'Flat Iron' building, located on the windy corner of 23rd Street and 5th Avenue, that had given rise to the expression '23 Skidoo', he was drenched in sweat and sat down on a nearby park bench to enjoy another refreshing soft drink with an accompanying large ice cream of various flavours, purchased from one more conveniently located vendor.

"Can you spare a few cents buddy for a cup of Joe?" a long haired, bearded, bedraggled tramp asked, shuffling alongside his bench unable to stand still for a few moments. Normally Irish would have refused and responded with an expletive instruction, being well used to the beggars and tramps of his native city but as he looked at this sorry individual he realised he was not much older than himself and was wearing the threadbare torn fatigues of a military uniform.

"'Ere y'go mate." he said, passing some mixed coin into the man's filthy, bandaged hand.

"God bless ya brother, God bless America." the grateful Vietnam veteran declared as he took the meagre hand-out.

Irish finished his snack and moved on along Fifth Avenue pausing once more, briefly to marvel at the iconic Empire State building at West 34th before continuing eight more blocks to West 42nd Street, turning right towards the equally splendid Chrysler building and his destination immediately beyond, Grand Central Station. On entering the cavernous interior of this magnificent structure, with its stellar decorated spectacular vaulted ceiling, Irish looked about for a suitable place where he may loiter the following day without arousing suspicion and yet still remain conspicuous. As he was scrutinising the vast concourse packed with its teaming multitude of hasty travellers hurrying in every direction, yet somehow managing to avoid violent collision, Irish also noted the police presence at different junctures. His attention was drawn in particular to the dark wooden night sticks and clearly visible fire arms secured at their waists. These were not the same police as those officers he was used to dealing with on the Crown Estate or in the City Centre, who could at worst administer a good kicking, here they presented a potentially lethal response.

Satisfied with his reconnoitre, Irish decided to return to his lodgings to freshen up and make plans for the evening. Choosing to catch a downtown bus rather than repeat his lengthy walk, he was soon travelling in relative comfort back towards the lower East Side and McCabe's Grande Hotel. Sitting at the rear of the vehicle he lit a cigarette from a packet of Marlborough's from his original well supplied news stand and began to let his mind drift away, considering what he had already seen that day and what may lay ahead. The youth had viewed many fine examples of ambitious, costly, well-maintained building projects throughout his brief excursion but he had also come across even more dilapidated, unfit for purpose properties that were either derelict or worse, still occupied.

Like most great cities around the world, New York was a place of stark contrast with fabulous wealth existing incongruously parallel alongside grinding poverty, inequality and excess hand-in-grubby-hand. The abundance and cornucopia on display particularly along the city's grand commercial avenues and some of its more renowned side streets, was a glittering façade masking the deprivation and violent crime of its crumbling, public housing projects and the genuine, ever-present dangers that lurked in its maze of filthy, dark alleys.

Irish reflected on Glynn's offer of a weapon and wondered if perhaps he should have accepted. 'If their bizzies are armed like that, I'd hate t'see what *their* gangs go round with.' he thought. In a country where the second amendment to the national constitution enshrined its citizens' right to bear arms, he was correct to be circumspect.

"Had a good stroll young feller?" Mr McCabe asked when Irish entered once more into his establishment.

"Yeah, definitely some interestin' sights t'see alright." Irish replied, adding "Am gonna chill for a bit then get off for a meal. Is thee anywhere decent round 'ere for a good scran?"

"Am not sure what yer sayin' friend but I think you're lookin' for somewhere good t'eat, so am gonna recommend Uncle Sam's Diner, two blocks from here." the older man advised, passing Irish his newspaper, "Here, read this it'll help ya sleep." he offered, smiling.

As soon as he had returned to his room, Irish stripped to his underpants, threw some cold water over himself from the grimy sink and lay back on the bed trying to cool down, unsuccessfully, whilst gathering his thoughts. A sharp nip from one of his fellow, uninvited bed companions caused him to quickly sit back up, reminding him this was a shared facility. He casually scanned the loaned copy of the *New York Times*, becoming more perturbed as he did so, reading the latest statistics for murder, rape and other violent crime including a category he was not familiar with, under the alien heading 'Muggings'. He took this to be some sort of attack similar to being 'rolled', as it was known locally in Liverpool. Either way it was clear that despite the desperate efforts of the city's mayor, Abraham Beame, to obtain vital financial assistance needed to shore up failing public services, including policing, no external relief would be forthcoming allowing the crime wave to spiral out of control, with residents' personal safety seriously compromised.

'I'm defo takin' that fuckin' duster with me when I go out t'night.' he told himself before finally drifting off into a brief period of much needed sleep.

At half past eight that same evening Irish had located the recommended Uncle Sam's Diner and was standing at the counter in this busy eatery suitably attired in his white short-sleeved Ben Sherman shirt, cream twenty-two inch parallel trousers with half-inch turn ups, supported by his black elasticated braces of similar width and his gleaming cherry red Airwair. He was also carrying his dark blue Harrington jacket, draped over his left arm, even though he did not really require this item due to the continuing warmth of the night, which had barely dissipated from the scorching day. In its pockets, however, apart from his room key and some loose change, was the heavy brass knuckle duster.

"Hi feller, you eatin' in or takin' out?" a hard faced female in her early fifties asked."

Irish replied that he was intending to have an evening meal on the premises.

"Okay then take a seat in a booth, when y'can and someone will be right over to take your order sir."

Within minutes of sitting in one of the comfortably upholstered dark leather furnished booths, that had just become vacant, Irish was about to experience a Damascene moment. As he was casually looking through the large single-pane window out to the still bustling sidewalk, he heard a pleasant voice say, "Hi honey, I'm Rosita, I'll be your waitress tonight can I get you something to drink while you are looking at the menu?" He turned to answer but was momentarily struck dumb as he gazed at the beautiful, dark eyed girl with shoulder length, raven black hair standing beside his table, dressed in a figure revealing, candy stripe short-sleeved uniform with open white collar, hat and apron.

"You ok honey? D'ya need more time, should I come back?" Rosita asked smiling sweetly.

"No, don't... I mean don't go... I mean I'll have a beer please." Irish finally managed to stammer.

Rosita continued to smile as she reeled off an impressive list of alcoholic beverages on offer, ending with "... and we do have a local ale, from a Brooklyn brewery that's very popular."

"I'll have that then, thanks." the stunned youth replied.

Finally for Irish, who had only ever experienced the briefest of relationships and casual sexual encounters, usually bartered for in exchange of cash, goods, or services, he was smitten, unable to take his gaze from the lovely Rosita. It was a Monkees, *I'm a Believer* instant, *when he saw her face there was no trace of doubt in his mind*, he had to get to know her.

When Rosita returned with his drink he was delighted to see her again, even though she had only been gone for a short while. "Ready to order honey?" she asked.

He answered that he was even though he had barely looked at the menu, "I'll have that Uncle Sam's special, please."

"Okay, good choice, that's an eighteen ounce sirloin with your choice of sides, how would ya like it done?"

Irish did not know what 'sides' were, so replied diplomatically "I'll have it well done please and you can choose those sides for me, if yer don't mind."

Rosita laughed "Ya not from round here are ya?"

"No I'm from Liverpool, England." he answered.

"Oh yeah, I know, like the Beatles. Have ya just come out the forces, or..." she stopped short of naming the only other institution that demanded such a uniform haircut.

It was Irish's turn to laugh, "Nah, I haven't just got out the army, or any other place. I'm a Skinhead, it's a style thing, if y'know what I mean? I used to hang around with lots of other lads who looked like this but that's all finished now."

Rosita suddenly stopped smiling, "Ya mean a gang, that's a pity, I know *all* about gangs." she said coldly, adding, "I'll get ya order."

With that Rosita turned and walked away much to Irish's dismay. He knew he had said the wrong thing, as usual.

When his meal was ready and Rosita had brought it to him, Irish tried to redeem himself, "Listen Rosita, I think I've given yer the wrong idea, we was just lads hangin' round together who happened to like the same things, nothin' more."

Rosita smiled once more passing him a plate containing the biggest steak he had ever seen in his life. "Enjoy ya meal." she said before leaving.

'Fuckin' hell, I could feed a family of five for a week on this,' he mentally conjectured.

Much later as Irish collapsed back in his comfortable seating barely able to breathe, Rosita returned once more enquiring if his meal was acceptable and if he required any dessert, offering a local speciality, cheesecake.

"What sort of a cake is that... made of cheese? God I've never heard of such a thing... trust the Yanks to have thought of that." Irish responded, opting for the safe choice of a recognisable classic American staple, blueberry pie with fresh cream.

Finally at the end of the night as he was enjoying a strong coffee and some mints, the desperate young Skinhead summoned up the courage to ask his dreamgirl if he could see her home. "I was wonderin'... when y'shift ends... if I could maybe..."

The lovely Rosita stopped him short, "Sorry honey, its not gonna happen, I never date customers."

"What if I go out and pretend I've never been in here, could I see yer home then? I mean, it doesn't look too safe round here and from what I've read in the papers..." He tried in vain only to be stopped once more in mid plea.

"Like I said, it'll never happen and if you think its lively round here, believe me where I come from wouldn't be a good place for *you* to go. I'll get ya check." Rosita replied firmly, ending the matter.

For the moment Irish resigned to failure, paid his bill, said goodnight and strolled disconsolately back to his grubby, 'shared' lodgings. Sometime later as he sat on the bed with his back against the damp wall having placed sufficient coinage in the pay TV, he watched continuous episodes of *I Love Lucy*, *The Dick Van Dyke Show* and *Gilligan's Island*, switching channels as required. Finally, settling on Bella Lugosi's classic *Dracula*, he turned up the volume, trying to drown out the sounds of the boiling night outside. Screams and angry shouts were matched with the constant wail of police sirens and the more ominous, distinctive loud bangs, which he tried to convince himself were no more than cars regularly backfiring.

Sitting alone, bathed in the flickering light of the black and white television in his tiny room, he knew he was a long way from home and also not a little afraid. Only the illuminating thought of seeing the lovely Rosita again, sustained him through the long hours of darkness.

Saturday 26th June 1976

A blazing sun had already made its ascent into the clear blue, morning sky ready for another day of baking heat, when Irish set off in hope of encountering Rosita, whilst ordering his breakfast at Uncle Sam's. It had been a hot, sticky, uncomfortable night and he had acquired several itchy souvenirs from his equally restless bed fellows.

"Looking for Rosita are ya feller?" asked the older waitress who had directed him to his booth the previous evening.

Irish admitted that he was hoping to see her if she happened to be there.

"Well you're outa luck, she only works the evenin' shift, she's a good Catholic girl, she'll probably be in confession right now." she laughed adding, "waffles, eggs and bacon that's the usual most folks like, how does that sound?"

Once again Irish had no idea what waffles might be but decided to console himself with a generous portion of this breakfast dish, though he found the usual difficulty when trying to order his eggs, which seemed to be available in a confusing variety of cooking styles. One thing was clear George Bernard Shaw's often quoted observation that Britain and America "Were two nations divided by a common language" was still as apt as it had ever been.

Several hours later Irish was casually walking about amongst the hectic throng, teeming across the great concourse of Grand Central Station, trying to be noticed whilst avoiding official, law enforcement attention. Apart from his usual kit of thin, checked Jaytex, cream parallel trousers and cherry red Airwair, he was wearing an incongruous, unseasonal woollen blue and white Everton FC scarf, loosely hanging around his neck. He gripped the handle of the battered, grey checked suitcase firmly with his left hand, whilst slipping the heavy brass knuckle-duster on and off his right, inside the pocket of his trousers. Niall, the senior Gerard Boy, had told him to be there by midday; he had arrived early at a quarter to and it was now almost twelve thirty. The longer he waited the more anxious he became, watching every entrance for an obvious contact.

"Look out there mac." a heavy set mid-forties male, wearing a well cut pale grey suit and matching trilby warned, almost colliding with the younger man.

"Yeah, you wanna look where yer goin' mate." Irish snapped in reply.

"From England are ya buddy, or is it Ireland, I can't quite make out that accent?" the suit wearer asked, stopping alongside the agitated Skinhead.

"It's Liverpool, England, okay?" he replied still looking about for his anticipated liaison.

About to walk away, Irish turned as the man called "Up the Toffees!"

Recognising the first of his key identification phrases, Irish responded accordingly, "Up the Blues!"

"Evertonian are ya?" his contact continued then added "That Dixie Dean was the best player yous ever had. Eighty goals in one season, what a record, when was that?"

Now Irish knew this was his man and answered "It was eighty-five goals, in the 1927-28 season."

The contact smiled, "Give me the case."

Irish was about to pass it to him but paused asking "Haven't you got somethin' for me?"

Firmly gripping Irish's wrist, the older man stopped smiling and advised, "Change of plans... we'll be in touch... in about a week."

"A week, what the fuck am I s'possed t'do till then?" Irish asked angrily.

"Yer in New York, ya fuckin' dip shit, go figure." he replied, adding, "Now let go of the case or I'll take ya fuckin' arm with it." He leaned forward allowing his jacket to fall open revealing the dark grips of his weapon in its leather holster.

Irish did as instructed passing the case to him, receiving a small brown envelope in return.

"Here's a little float for ya, we thought ya might be runnin' short."

The youth took the envelope and watched as the older man strode away, turning momentarily to call over his shoulder, "Hey kid, don't ask too many questions, it ain't good f'ya health, ya gotta nice thing goin' here." With that final piece of advice he was gone, merged into the hurrying mass of commuters, racing in every direction.

That evening having supplemented his depleted funds with the twenty dollar donation from his American 'friends' Irish decided to follow the advice that accompanied the cash and make the most of his enforced stay in the US. Washed and dressed in his freshly aired smartest kit, which had been hanging out of the rear window of his room throughout the scorching day and, having polished his Airwair to their gleaming best, he made his way once more to Uncle Sam's determined to pursue the object of his desire.

"Hey Rosita, ya boyfriend's back again, it must be love, why can't I get the cute ones?" the senior waitress shouted to her colleague, much to her embarrassment when he entered the diner.

"Leave it Marge nobody thinks ya funny." Rosita called back then turning to Irish asked, "Okay honey what's it gonna be tonight?"

He smiled and said, "Well that's up t'you Rosita and by the way me name's Patrick, maybe you could help me choose."

"Patrick, that's a nice name; okay, if y'like, I'll help ya pick something really good." she replied obligingly then sat alongside him in the comfortable booth looking through the menu, explaining some of the less familiar dishes.

Irish did not care what she chose; he was captivated by her very presence, her closeness, her warmth. For the rest of that pleasant evening he tried his best to convince Rosita that they could be more than just customer and waitress. Finally towards closing time Rosita succumbed to his never-before-used charm offensive, at least in part.

"Okay Patrick am gonna take a chance and break my own rules, ya can walk with me to my subway station but no further... deal?"

Irish was delighted and agreed at once. "Deal; thanks Rosita."

When the lights were dimmed and the owner was locking up for the night, before counting his takings, the young couple left the diner and set off for the subway just two blocks away. Rosita did most of the talking as they strolled along, with Irish just happy to be in her company, listening to her every word, totally under her spell.

"... so although I was born in Puerto Rico I've never actually seen the country, my mum and dad brought me over here when I was a baby twenty years ago... I've got five brothers; Diego, Luis, Victor, Alejandro and Eduardo, three of them are older than me and the other two are younger... I live up town in El Barrio with my family..." She told him how she had been working in the diner for almost a year and was studying during the day at college, hoping to become a primary school teacher. "...y'see Patrick everyone says there are only two ways out of the ghetto, sport or crime but I don't agree, I think there is another way, education. If we educate our young ones we can change their hopes and dreams, their world."

As they drew parallel to a group of four young men across the street from them, standing outside a small corner bar, one of them, a tall African-American called over "Hey brother, you *are* one lucky man!"

Irish smiled raising the thumb of his right hand and replied, "Nice one mate!"

"Semper Fi, mac" he called over once more.

Irish had no understanding of what he meant but smiled.

Rosita also smiled but warned, "Don't go gettin' any ideas; this is a walk to the subway, nothin' more."

Though slightly crest fallen Irish remained hopeful and carried on listening to her talk, thrilling to the sound of her voice. If he had not been so enraptured he may not have allowed his usual, instinctive, streetwise radar to switch off and have become aware of the two menacing characters who had been following the couple for at least a block. Rosita, who had walked that route regularly for nearly a year and also possessed similar well-honed, potential danger intuitiveness, would later feel bitter personal recriminations at letting her own guard drop, momentarily.

Suddenly both Irish and Rosita felt the presence of two other bodies immediately behind them and the sharp points of the knives they were carrying, pressed into their backs.

"Gerrin that fuckin' alley now the pair of yer." a sinister voice ordered, indicating a broad dark opening that had been created by the demolition of a small shop previously standing in that row of retail outlets.

Even as they entered the alley the captive couple were struck by the overpowering, eye-watering stench emanating from the collection of refuse bins lining its sides and, mountain of garbage bags stacked at its rear, well above head height, blocking any hope of escape by that route. Three other companions of their captors were waiting for them positioned midway between them and the reeking refuse stockpile. Their apparent leader was standing in the centre of the grinning trio, dressed in a filthy, once-white capped sleeved tee-shirt, patchwork denim flares and stack-heeled, dark tan cowboy boots. Round his neck hung a leather cord, displaying a disturbing collection of human teeth. His grimy pale skin was covered in a dazzling array of tattoos extending up his throat to his jaw line.

"Well what have we got ourselves here tonight?" he asked rhetorically, continuing "Some sort of bald-headed army boy and a hot Latino whore, lookin' for five real men t'give it to her hard." As he spoke he moved his dirty strings of hair away from his pock-marked face, revealing a large nose and a gapped-tooth grin.

"Hey shit head, you even think about touchin' this lady an yer'll be addin' the rest of y'rotten teeth to yer fancy necklace." Irish warned angrily.

The leader of the evil quintet was stunned, "I don't know where ya from ya little fuck but after we've jumped y'girlfriend, am really gonna enjoy cuttin' you. Get a good grip on that prick, he's gonna watch the whole thing."

Irish was suitably restrained by the two nearest thugs.

"He's not my boyfriend, he was just walkin' me to the subway, so why not let him go, no need for any trouble, then we can all party." Rosita offered in desperation.

"Now ya talkin' bitch but there ain't gonna be no trouble, just you bring that hot ass over to me and let me feel the goods."

Irish struggled but could not free himself from the restraining grip of his 'guards'. Rosita stepped towards the grinning leader, while he rubbed his crotch with his right hand. She kept her head down and her hands dug deep into the pockets of the cream coloured, thin woollen cardigan that she was wearing over her candy striped waitress uniform. Even in the limited light of the stinking alley her radiant beauty was undimmed and her curvaceous figure presented an alluring silhouette. When she reached the leering leader, he quickly grabbed her by the hips and spun her round, pulling her close to him.

"Hmm, smells good, like that home cookin' ma momma never used to make." His cronies laughed; Irish's stomach churned, he felt sick, impotent and totally helpless.

The leader slipped his arms between Rosita's and wrapped them round her pulling her even closer, pressing himself firmly against her soft contours. "Feels good too, real good." he said, keeping one arm tightly round her slim waist allowing his right hand to grope her firm breasts. "Not bad, not as big as I'd like but good enough."

Rosita said nothing but turned her head away from his fetid breath.

Now his exploring hand travelled down to her smooth upper thigh and began massaging that area, raising the hem of her short dress.

"Fuckin' leave her alone you piece of shit, I swear to God I will kill yer!" Irish shouted.

"Shut that fool boy up will ya, he's disturbin' my fun." the leader ordered.

The henchman to his left strolled over to the furious youth to carry out his commands, grasping him firmly round the throat. As the groping leader continued his assault, moving Rosita's hem even higher, he revealed a distinctive tattoo just below her panty line; a colourful, snarling jaguar's head clearly visible. They all saw it except the groper.

"Fuck this, this bitch is with the 'Jaguars' man." the male who was squeezing Irish's throat, warned.

"Is that right bitch, are you one of them punk Jaguars?" the leader asked, moving his hand between her legs holding her firmly over her panties.

"My brother Diego is Jaguar war chief." she replied coldly, waiting for her moment.

"No fuckin' way, am not fuckin' messin' with the sister of the Jag's war chief." the youngest of the group, standing to the right of the now fully aroused leader announced.

The trio that held Irish also expressed their concerns but their leader was beyond caring, rubbing himself back and forth rhythmically against Rosita's well-rounded bottom.

"All you wimps can fuck off if ya want, am gonna ride this bitch's ass then waste the pair of them." he warned.

Rosita could feel his erection pushing firmly against her, through the thin material of her panties. Her right hand that had remained in her pocket all the while, had already deftly opened the lock-knife that her brothers insisted she always carry for her own protection. She felt the man's urgency, knew he was distracted, knew the others were worried no longer fully committed and that the moment had arrived. In a lightning fast, single movement she brought the knife out from her pocket, in a rising arc directly overhead and backwards thrusting it into the right eye of the unsuspecting groper.

"Aghh, she's blinded me, the fuckin' bitch has blinded me!" he screamed in agony.

A brief moment of inertia occurred as his followers were uncertain of what action to take. Irish needed nothing more, sensing their collective grip slacking, the heavy brass knuckleduster that he too had already slipped onto his fist now struck the male immediately in front of him with a force accelerated by primal rage. He may be held captive and a long way from the bleak estate but he was still a Crown Team Skinhead, whose righteous fury was awesome. His devastating punch to the jaw sent the recipient sprawling backwards across the alley. Breaking free from the two remaining gang members on either side of him and dodging to his left he quickly snatched up a metal lid from one of the nearby trashcans, by its handle. Armed with this improvised shield and his knuckle-duster Irish went berserk, attacking both nearest males who had now redrawn their own knives.

"C'mon you cunts, let's 'ave it!" he roared, taking the fight to them, lashing out with his metal assisted fist whilst parrying their wild slashes with his metal disc. His closest adversary lunged forward only to receive a sickening boot to his groin, which dropped him to his knees, the perfect position for Irish to smash in his face with a ferocious straight right. While the other more cautious knife-wielder circled about him keeping out of range of both his fist and 'shield', Irish crouched ready to pounce at any second, seething with anger.

At that same time the blinded leader staggered about in excruciating agony, holding his sightless eye socket trying to stem the bleeding with his right hand, whilst frantically reaching behind him with his left to the Smith and Wesson .38 special revolver, he kept tucked in his trouser waistband.

The nervous youth to Rosita's right, who had previously expressed his concerns, tried to redeem himself by attempting to catch hold of the female Jaguar, whose wrath was even more terrifying than that of Irish.

"Come 'ere ya fuckin' bitch", he shouted, foolishly reaching for the wild cat.

Rosita's knife-slash arced across his face, opening him from just under his left eye, down below his nose, through his upper lip, separating his features into two diagonal halves. Blood spurted from the deep wound and he stepped a few paces to the rear before collapsing into the stinking garbage mountain, howling in unbearable pain.

"Hey you, whore!" Rosita heard from behind before turning round to see the blind leader almost upon her. Too late to dodge, she was punched hard in the left side of the face and stumbled, falling down to the filthy floor. Instantly the one-eyed leader snatched hold of her raven black hair with his right hand, forcing the hard cold tip of the gun's barrel against her temple with his left. Triumphant he called to Irish, "You there, army boy, give it up now, if you want this whore to go on livin'."

Irish immediately dropped his shield, lowered his fists and stood perfectly still. "Please don't hurt her, I'll do anything you say."

"I know you fuckin' will boy." the leader replied, pressing the gun firmly into Rosita's temple, "I don't know which one of you two fucks to do first, you or this little bitch." He winced in pain, clutching his burst eye as another agonising wave passed over him, helping him to decide, "Yep, I think its gorra be you bitch, ya cost me an eye." He cocked the weapon.

"Please, am beggin' yer, don't do this. Do what yer want with me but let her go." Irish pleaded in desperation.

"Okay boy, you've convinced me, you first and then it's the whore." the leader announced now turning the gun in the direction of Irish. Even as he did Rosita let out an ear-piercing scream, though she had not done so once throughout her ordeal. She broke free of the gunman's grip, turning her head opening her mouth wide, before clamping her teeth deep into the flesh of his left wrist. The trigger was pulled, the shot fired but his blurred monocular vision and the searing pain in both his head and punctured wrist misguided his aim, sending the bullet through the right shoulder of one of his accomplices, standing close to Irish, tearing flesh and breaking bone, throwing him against the wall to his side. No second shot was fired.

Suddenly a huge figure ran into the alley, charged directly at the gunman tackling him to the filthy ground. His solid brick fists pounded over and over into the already damaged face of the crazed leader, until he no longer moved. The nearest henchman to the alley's opening made to run away but the powerful right upper-cut from Irish to his jaw rocked him backwards, with the follow up blow to his gut doubling him over. Irish grabbed hold of him by his dirty, stained tee-shirt and slammed him violently into the line of trashcans, where he wisely lay unmoving.

Their courageous, giant rescuer leapt onto the remaining standing henchman, as he was about to stab Irish in the back. "No ya don't ya chicken-shit." he declared, quickly disarming the man then lifting him from the ground with his strong hands around his throat. Moments later choked senseless he was allowed to slump to the floor.

Irish looked about him at the scene of devastation; one male lay on his back with blood pouring from the exit wound of his ruined shoulder, making a growing dark pool around him, two others were unconscious or appeared so, another sat where he had fell at the rear of the alley, trying to hold the two scarlet-drenched halves of his face together. The one-eyed leader murmured something and tried to crawl to where his gun had landed.

Rosita stepped towards him kicking the weapon away underneath the stack of refuse. She leaned over the whimpering, blinded man and pushed him onto his back. In an instant she had plunged her knife deep into his no-longer excited groin. He screamed an agonised more piercing scream than any other that night. Rosita knelt down on one knee and said, "If you don't die from this pig, kill yourself before my brothers find you." She stood up and slowly walked back toward Irish and their anonymous rescuer. They both tried to thank him but he waved them away with a smile.

"Evenin' folks... Gabriel Stone, United States Marine Corps, happy to help." he advised, continuing, "Much as I'd like t'stick around for formal introductions, I think we'd better split. The cops don't usually turn up for a while for a little event like this but it's probably best if we're not here when they do."

The trio quickly departed from that foul place, without looking back. Whilst walking the short remaining distance to Rosita's subway destination, both Irish and she briefly introduced themselves then Rosita spoke directly to Gabriel.

"Listen I know I've only just met you but would ya do me a real favour?"

"I don't think any man would refuse *you* Rosita." he replied smiling.

"Please look after Patrick for me, he's a stranger here, he don't know this City." she asked.

"Looks like Patrick can take care of his self just fine but if that's what ya want..." Gabriel offered.

Irish ignored them both, he was determined to accompany Rosita to her home. "But Rosita can't I see you back to where yer live, especially with what's just happened?"

"No Patrick, not now, I just wanna go home. It wouldn't be good f'ya to come with me." Rosita replied, as they arrived at the subway entrance. She leaned into him, kissing him on the cheek before departing, descending the subway steps. "Bye Patrick, be careful."

Irish made to follow her but Gabriel caught him by the arm. "Let her go man, she's right, you wouldn't be welcome where Rosita's goin'."

Irish did not understand what he meant and called after her, "Rosita, I'll see yer again t'morrer at the diner, okay?" It was too late, she was gone, he turned to Gabriel and said, "Any chance of us gettin' a drink mate, 'cause I could really do with one?"

Gabriel smiled, "Patrick, this is New York 'the City that never sleeps.' Come with me brother, I know just what you need right now." He looked about then added, "First we need to get out of this area, we'll get a cab, ya better call one over, they don't usually stop round here f'me, for some reason."

Irish looked at the smiling six foot three African American, whose handsome features appeared as if they had been hand-chiselled, with the heavy musculature of an Olympic gymnast and took his comments regarding local taxi drivers' reluctance to mean this was due to his size and physique.

"How come you came runnin' in like that t'help us, even though that bastard had a gun?" he asked.

"When I saw ya walkin' by with Rosita, I knew you was another military brother from ya haircut to ya polished boots, I couldn't let another G.I. down, its not my way, and as for his little pop-gun, well after two tours in 'Nam' it didn't look that impressive." Gabriel replied honestly.

Irish laughed, "Am not a soldier mate, am a Skinhead but it doesn't matter, I really appreciate what yer done, yer've got balls man."

"Whatever brother, now try and catch this cab before he sees me." Gabriel answered.

A short time later after a taxi ride up and across town, they arrived at their destination pulling up outside a small bar just off Broadway close to Times Square. Once inside the dimly lit hostelry, Irish was surprised to find it was crowded and drinks were still being served even though it was past midnight.

"Don't thee have last orders round 'ere Gabriel?"

"Like I said Patrick, this City is always buzzin', if someone started puttin' times on that, they wouldn't be in business much longer."

The two men took their places at the bar, sitting on high stools. Irish ordered their drinks and then lit a cigarette, offering one to his new friend.

"No thanks man, whiskey and women is my pleasure, those things'll kill ya." Gabriel replied.

Irish laughed, "Nice one mate, I used to 'ave a friend who thought like that, he wouldn't never smoke."

"Oh yeah, really and how's he doin'?" Gabriel enquired.

"He's gone, murdered, stabbed t'death in some filthy shit house in Liverpool city centre." Irish replied grimly.

"Sorry to hear that man, I lost some good friends in the war; it leaves a pain that never goes away."

Irish reached out and shook hands with his giant companion, "Patrick O'Hare, me friends call me 'Irish' pleased to meet yer."

Gabriel shook his hand firmly and replied, "Gabriel Nathan Stone, likewise, my friends call me Gabe, everyone else calls me Trouble, with a capital T."

Both men laughed, their drinks having now arrived, they raised their glasses.

"Cheers brother." Gabe offered.

"Sliante." Irish replied.

After throwing back their whiskeys they followed with a round of beers, Irish trying a cold Budweiser for the first time instead of his usual Guinness.

"I think I could get into this, at least durin' the hot weather." he observed then asked, "Can yer explain t'me Gabe why both you an Rosita, said it wouldn't be good f'me to go with her to where she lives?"

"Irish my man, there's a lot ya don't know about this place, or this country." Gabe replied cryptically.

"She said somethin' about livin' in the 'Barrier' or somethin', if am right." Irish offered naively.

Gabe laughed, "No man, not the Barriers but Los Barrios, Spanish Harlem to you and me. It's a place uptown beyond Central Park, to the north east side of the City. Not many of you white folks round there unless they're original Italian Americans. The way you're dressed and look might make people think yer an undercover cop an that wouldn't be cool."

Irish continued drinking then announced, "Fuck me, yer right Gabe I don't know this place. I don't read the papers much, my mate was more into that but I do watch the news, I thought yer had all these marches and protests an a civil rights movement back in the '60s to sort all this prejudice shite out?"

Gabe stared blankly into the immediate distance, squeezing his glass with his strong hand, "No offence brother but you really are a dumb hick fresh off the boat, y'gonna get picked clean in this city if ya don't wise up, quick. We *all* heard the words of the great Dr King but not everyone was listenin'. Real freedom is waitin' at the end of a long hard road; we've only just stepped onto it."

Irish did not pursue the issue further, ordering another round of drinks instead. The powerful Gabriel, who was dressed in a pale grey cap-sleeved tee-shirt, straight cut Levi's

501 blue jeans and a pair of Chuck Taylor Converse All Star basketball boots, sat quietly for a few moments as if contemplating the enormity of his wise words. He knew that sadly he was correct.

America was still a divided nation of anything but united states. It would take more than an emancipation proclamation, constitutional amendments, a bloody civil war and civil rights campaign to redress the obscenity of the founding fathers, declaring all men to be created equal but allowing some to be considered less so and included in the inalienable property rights of their more equal fellows. The poisoned, distorted mind-set that this encouraged to take root at the very beginning of a new society, would flourish and bear bitter fruit for generations to come; even taking an almighty axe to it would never fully eradicate its hateful seed.

Irish suddenly intruded on Gabriel's reflective state. "How did y'come t'be in the Marines, did yer get called up like?"

Gabe smiled, "No man the draft wasn't for me. I wanted t'make my own choice but like they say ya don't choose the corps, the corps chooses you." He took a swig of his beer then continued, "I was born in south Bronx in 1951 an all I can ever remember wantin' t'be was a pro football star, I had no other plans. When I was in high school I was the number one runnin' back an I tried out for the Jets. Everythin' was goin' good but I kept seein' my brothers goin' away to Nam and most of them came back in body bags. Somethin' a great man once said kept playin' over in my mind 'ask not what your country can do for you but what you can do for your country.' So when the time came I joined the greatest brotherhood of them all, the United States Marine Corps." Gabriel said no more and apart from the noise of the crowd, for a few moments all they could hear was the sound of War's *Me and Baby Brother* on the juke box.

Irish had to ask the vital question, "Was it all worth it Gabe, y'know all those years of fightin' and dyin', the young fellers lost or ruined?"

"Irish, that's a fuckin' helluva question man, it's worth more than sixty-four thousand dollars to know the answer to that one. Many nights am lyin' there, eyes closed tight but there ain't no escape from those faces, those things that were done. I know one thing f'sure, I was proud t'serve my country and do my duty."

Again Gabriel was right, the troops had done their duty, followed their orders faithful to the commands of their faithless commander in chief. Courageous in combat yet cursed in civilian life by a growing army of dissenters, some of whom were veterans from within their ranks. This was a war for hearts and minds; it could not be won by bullets and bombs. Chemical agent defoliants scarring the landscapes and napalm strikes burning the innocent populous, would only serve to strengthen the resolve of their implacable enemy, catalysing world condemnation at the same time. Even as the conflict hastened towards its ugly ending, it was still capable of inflicting monumental damage. President Nixon having made the egregious error, not of lying to the public, he was a politician after all, but of being caught in the act and finally realising too late that in the words of his most illustrious predecessor, 'you cannot fool all of the people all of the time.' That was a wound so deep it would never completely heal.

"Enough of this sad shit brother, I know exactly what you need tonight and so do I come to think of it... some hot female action." Gabe announced.

Irish was not entirely convinced, "I don't know about that Gabe, am not really in the mood, I can't stop thinkin' about Rosita t'be honest."

His friend put down his beer and looked about "Well I can't see no Rosita in here an y'know what they say, if ya can't be with the one ya love, love the one ya with."

Irish laughed.

Gabe continued, "Anyway, ya can't come t'New York without tryin' some local pussy... that would just be plain rude man."

Faced with such indisputable logic Irish conceded, "Ok Gabe, you win man, just tell me how we're supposed t'find a couple of pros round here, at this time?"

"Brother, are ya from another planet or somethin'? This is Times Square, if ya wanna get laid ya just ask, c'mon man, let's go." Gabe advised.

With Silver Convention's *Get Up and Boogie* just beginning to play on the juke box, the two hopeful companions went looking for love. Shortly after leaving the bar, they strolled along to Seventh Avenue and entered into the neon wonderland of Times Square. Irish looked all around in awe at the bewildering, eye-catching, eclectic displays adorning the façades of every building, reaching into the dark sky above, funnelling a portion of its heated excitement upwards to the heavens. The litter-strewn, grimy sidewalks were as crowded as during the scorching day, if not more so.

Dominating all the advertised delights on offer was sex; the majority of visitors both tourists and local having been drawn to this place by its undeniable, primal allure. Live shows, topless dancers and adult shops, triple, quadruple and quintuple 'X' rated films were showing at every cinema, all officially licensed. Paradoxically it was the existence of this plethora of perversion, which had enjoyed an exponential rate of growth during the past decade, that would prove to be this area's seedy saviour, preserving it from arson and abandonment that had plagued so many of its surrounding districts. Were other commercial enterprises may have failed due to exorbitant rents and rising overheads, this industry more than paid its way, holding its own comfortably, sex sold as always.

Despite this abundance of legitimate availability it was unsanctioned entertainment that Gabriel and his guest, Irish, were in search of; there was no shortage of this commodity either.

"Fuckin' hell Gabe, some of these birds are stunnin' are yer sure they're on the game?" Irish asked genuinely.

"Put ya tongue back in man, yer'll need it later." Gabe advised, already mentally making his selection from the long-legged females shaking their tail feathers, strutting their stuff on Broadway.

"Alright sisters, what's happenin'?" he said, stopping alongside two tall African American ladies, whose natural height was artificially aided by their knee-high platform boots.

One of the females, who was wearing a pair of satin shorts that clung revealingly to her well-rounded bottom and were so small they could easily have been mistaken for the panties she had clearly forgotten to put on that particular evening, smiled looking directly at Gabe and replied, "Hi handsome, what's on *your* mind tonight." The loose transparent blouse that she was almost wearing revealed her ample bosom and deep cleavage, prompting his response. "Just two things right now sugar." Both women laughed and the shorts wearer's equally provocatively attired colleague, in her see-through, clinging, white lace dress, which barely covered her dignity, put her hand on Irish's shoulder asking, "What's the matter honey, shy? I can tell y'like what y'see."

Before Irish could reply, Gabe offered, "This is ma friend Patrick, come all the way from Liverpool town, England just t'make your acquaintance."

"Well it's a pleasure t'meet ya Patrick." said the lady in the white dress.

All was proceeding as planned and a financial deal was about to be brokered, when suddenly a tall black male wearing a lilac Fedora at a rakish angle, a tight-fitting, heavily patterned silk shirt and high-waist purple, wide flared trousers reaching down to his dark blue leather, high platform shoes, appeared at their side.

"Well, well, lookie here, two of New York's finest lookin' f'some action. Can you two nice young police officers stop harrasin' my girls, they ain't doin' no wrong?" He unwisely placed his hand on Gabriel's shoulder whilst talking.

"Y'wanna keep that hand man, cos if ya don't move it right now, ya'll never use it again." Gabe warned, bristling with anger. The man removed his hand and Gabe continued, "Listen brother, we ain't cops so watch who ya bad mouthin', an one more thing, don't ya fuckin' ever come up on me like that again."

Now taking a good look at the powerful ex-marine, the Fedora wearer replied, "Okay man, chill, no need f'any aggravation. Do what ya gotta do but don't think *I* don't know whats goin' down." he smiled revealing two gold eye-teeth.

Gabe ignored him as if he was not there. "Ladies, you gotta place nearby where we can have some fun?"

The females exchanged glances then looked towards their employer, who shrugged his shoulders saying "Your call ladies."

The dress wearer took the initiative, replying to Gabe "Yeah sure, why not sugar we're fun girls, okay Cisco?"

Cisco the pimp tipped his hat towards them and acquiesced though still not entirely convinced. "Okay Crystal, okay Tammy, any problems ya on ya own, have a good night 'gents'."

Both women linked arms with their prospective partners and teetered off away from the bright lights of Times Square, into the less dazzling side streets. Within fifty yards they stopped by a battered old front door wedged in the narrow space between two shops, which displayed a wide selection of pornographic magazines and sex toys, some of which looked better designed to inflict pain rather than induce pleasure.

After Crystal unlocked the door they entered into the building and ascended a creaky, wooden staircase that was barely shoulder width. A pungent mixture of rising damp and stale urine permeated the limited air within this cramped space, making them glad to reach the women's apartment located at the end of the equally narrow, first floor landing as they stepped into this small one room flat, they were engulfed in a more heady aroma of cheap scent and joss-sticks, both of which were being employed to mask other more natural, lingering odours.

Having switched on the low-watt lighting Crystal took charge of the serious business, "Okay boys its money up front, before y'sample the goods."

Irish reached into the pocket of his trousers but Gabe stopped him, "No Patrick, this is on me brother, ya money's no good here."

After a brief half-hearted show of resistance, Irish accepted, allowing the festivities to commence.

"Bed or couch?" Gabe asked Irish with a smile.

"I don't mind either." he replied honestly though feeling a little uncomfortable at the prospect of having to perform before an audience.

Gabe tossed a coin inviting Irish to call.

"Heads."

"You win, the bed it is, f'you and Tammy." Gabe responded then quickly pulled off his tee-shirt, revealing the well defined musculature of his torso.

Crystal had already unzipped her platform boots and removed her negligible, transparent blouse allowing her magnificent breasts to be fully seen, without even the pretence of a covering. She began to peel down her clinging, miniscule shorts, with Gabe eagerly assisting her, even as he unbuttoned the fly of his Levi's jeans with his other hand.

"Help me with my zip honey." Tammy called to Irish, who had removed his Airwair boots and his shirt and was standing at the foot of the bed unfastening his trousers. He did as requested, assisting Tammy to pull her indecently short dress up and over her head, freeing her own large breasts in a single quivering, erotic movement.

Unlike her partner, the knickerless Crystal, Tammy had actually been wearing some semblance of underwear in the form of a tiny g-string, which was rolled down and quickly dispensed with.

"Here ya go honey, slip one of these on and I'll join ya on the bed in a second." she said, passing Irish a prophylactic in its foil wrapper then placed her clothes on a small, whicker chair nearby. Again Irish did as instructed lying on his back on the sagging, single bed, rolling the rubber sheath down his determined erection which had rapidly grown on watching Tammy's brief striptease. Whether or not his friend had also been provided with this primary protection he did not know but a cursory glance in Gabe's direction, revealed that he had already assumed the position and was vigorously plunging into the recumbent Crystal.

"Need a little help there feller?" Tammy asked obligingly, before reaching for Irish's erect member then tugging it firmly several times, bringing it to full strength and rigidity. "That's better sugar," Tammy observed joining him on the bed, straddling his groin preparing to lower herself onto his throbbing penis. She tossed her head back, opened her mouth, licking her teeth with her tongue, playing with her own shapely breasts. Irish grasped her hips trying to pull her onto him but she resisted, teasing him further until she was ready to ride. Slowly she pushed herself down onto his shaft until fully engaged and then began a slow rhythmic rocking to and fro. Irish reached up to her breasts mounding and squeezing them firmly, adding to his own pleasure. Tammy began increasing her pace, pushing down firmly then rising slightly before repeating the process.

The sounds of the two couples lost in carnal passion were all that could be heard in the tiny room, drowning even the wailing sirens of the police patrol cars that raced from one deadly incident to another, in the heat of yet one more violent night.

Crystal shrieked and moaned as Gabe continued to pound her, bringing his tremendous strength and athletic vigour fully into play. Tammy repeated these same noises massaging Irish's ego, spuring him on to greater efforts, whether they were genuine or merely part of a well-rehearsed performance.

It was not long until Irish, who was exquisitely trapped beneath the expert gyrations of his capable partner, could sense a tremendous orgasm rapidly approaching. He looked up into the ecstatic face of his glistening, dark skinned partner now close to climax herself and unintentionally, involuntarily superimposed it with that of the lovely Rosita. "You're the only one for me!" he called out as he finally exploded deep inside her.

"Course I am sugar and ya the only one for me too." Tammy replied, as she had done so many times before to an army of previous lovers, happy to indulge their fantasies.

Chapter 5

Across 110th Street

Sunday 27th June 1976

It was past noon when Irish awoke the next day with a start, courtesy of one of his minute bedfellows, back in his own unsanitary lodgings at McCabe's establishment on the Lower East Side. He lay down once more, soaked in sweat, the room already filled with stifling heat. Irish was completely exhausted and spent; placing his hand on his now flaccid member, recalling the energetic events of the previous night. 'No wonder me cock's sore,' he thought, smiling.

After their initial session with the expert Crystal and Tammy had reached its natural, satisfying conclusion, Gabe suggested that, allowing for a brief respite, they should change partners, return to the fray and try to exceed their previous efforts. Not wishing to let his personal and national honour be compromised, Irish accepted the pleasurable challenge and was soon ploughing into the seemingly inexhaustible Crystal, whilst Gabriel bent Tammy over the back of the couch before hammering her from behind. It proved to be a long night.

Sometime just before dawn the two males and females parted company and Irish finally left his entertaining 'tour guide' in Times Square, catching a cab back to his dingy hotel.

By the evening of that day having idled away another scorching hot afternoon, Irish set off once more to the local diner, hoping to see Rosita. All the things he planned to say and questions he was wanting to ask, had to be put on hold when her older colleague Marge announced, "Ya outa luck fella, she rang in sick earlier, so ya'll have t'settle f'me tonight if ya still eatin' in."

Irish's appetite departed almost as rapidly as his expectations and he spent the rest of the evening wandering about the neighbourhood, finally returning to his stuffy, uncomfortable room to watch television until he eventually drifted into sleep. Unfortunately for the dismayed youth

Monday followed a similar pattern, the only difference being that Marge was not in good spirits stating "I tell ya what if Rosita don't get that cute little touche of hers back here tomorrer, she won't have no job to go to no more."

Tuesday 29th June 1976

Sitting in Uncle Sam's diner on a warm evening eating his massive New York version of a Philly cheese steak, drinking a chilled Budweiser and gazing at the object of his affections, the lovely Rosita, Irish's persistence had been rewarded. Rosita had returned to work before the deadline for her termination of employment expired and was busily hurrying from customer to customer ensuring their orders were served promptly and with a smile.

"I can't talk to ya now Patrick but I'll see ya when I finish, okay?" she offered, much to his delight.

Apart from everything else that was racing about in his excited mind, he wondered if the noticeable bruising to her face, which was clearly visible even through her attempts to mask it with make up, had something to do with her two day absence.

Later after the diner was closed and Rosita had agreed that Irish could walk with her to the nearby subway but no further, he decided to ask her about this.

"So was thee a bit of trouble when y'got home the other night... I mean when thee saw yer face?"

"Patrick ya don't know the half of it, my brothers wanted t'come down here, find those guys and kill them an that's 'cause I only said they tried to steal my purse." Rosita replied.

"Thee sound like good lads. I know if anyone went near my sisters I'd feel the same." Irish observed.

"Really? And would you stop ya sisters from goin' out the house f'two days, nearly causin' them t'loose their jobs?" Rosita asked angrily.

Irish wisely tried to change the subject, "Listen I don't know how much longer am gonna be here so I'd like to really get t'know yer and meet y'family?"

Rosita suddenly came to an abrupt stop, "You're a nice boy Patrick and I do like ya but that can never happen, never." Irish tried to protest but Rosita continued, "Me an you are from different worlds, I wouldn't fit in yours and you can't ever go into mine, it just wouldn't work."

"I don't know about where you live but you'd have no problem comin' home t'Liverpool with me."

"Is that right? I thought England was all about fish and chips, havin' cups of tea, talkin' like the Queen, people wearin' bowler hats an it rainin' all the time." Rosita answered part in jest.

"Well y'right about the rain, the fish and chips and the tea but nobody goes round wearin' a bowler hat or speakin' like the Queen, not unless they're twats." Irish stopped short waiting for Rosita's reaction to this colloquial obscenity.

"I don't know what a 'twat' is but whatever it is it don't make no difference to what I've already told ya, ya heard what I said the other night, I wasn't lyin'. Diego is Jaguar's war chief but he's not the only one of my brother's who's a Jaguar, they're all gang members." she answered.

"Well I know a bit about gangs meself, so I'll take me chances." Irish replied.

"Patrick, why have ya got t'be so stubborn?" Rosita asked.

"Because you're worth the effort." he answered genuinely, just as they reached Rosita's subway stop.

She kissed him on the cheek before quickly descending the steps, "I'll see ya tomorrow Patrick, if ya want. Don't go causin' any trouble."

Irish looked down into the darkened stairwell long after she was gone. He knew he could not deny the fact that he was well and truly smitten.

Saturday, 3rd July 1976

"Wake up ya lazy bum!" The well-dressed mid-forties male shouted, acting as an unwelcome alarm call for the soundly sleeping Irish.

"What the fuck... who are you... an how did yer get in 'ere?" Irish responded angrily, having been woken from a particularly passionate dream involving him and the lovely Rosita.

After tipping some of Irish's clothes, which were piled onto the room's one wooden chair, onto the floor, the alarming male sat upon this rickety piece of furniture leaning across its back with his arms folded, staring at the recumbent youth. "Is this all you've done with ya time in New York... ya prick?"

Irish did not immediately answer but instead lazily got out of bed, dressed only in his underpants, inadvertently revealing his recent state of arousal.

"If that's f'my benefit ya wastin' ya time, am strictly a tits an ass guy." his unwelcome visitor declared with a wry smile.

"Yeah, very funny, I was havin' a really good dream until you ruined it, an yer still haven't told me who yer are and what the fuck yer want." Irish replied angrily, opening the threadbare curtains officially allowing the brilliant sunlight to enter the room, ending the weak resistance they had offered to its powerful rays.

"You know who I am, an ya know why am here, so fuckin' put ya pants on" the seated male answered.

Irish pulled on his Fleming's twenty-four inch parallel jeans, stepped into his boots and put on a plain white tee-shirt then leaned with his back against the windowsill, turning to face his guest, whom he now realised looked vaguely familiar.

"Okay, say what yer've got t'say then am goin' out for some breakfast."

The man smiled as he lit a cigarette replying, "I'm Alfie Mack, a cousin of the Boys, originally from Ireland by way of Liverpool, came over here a long time ago, decided t'stay. I set up the business end here, made all the right connections so-to-speak." He paused and took a long drag of his cigarette then continued, "Ya luggage is over there, ya better take good care of it. Make the most of ya last day an a half, 'cause at six a. m. Monday ya gonna be sailin' away across the ocean, back home." Alfie stopped once more, rose from the wooden chair and approached Irish, "Just before ya leave this place old Ben is gonna give ya another package. *Whatever* happens ya don't let go of that package at any time, don't hand it to anyone but Niall Mack, right?"

Irish replied half heartedly that he would do as instructed, much to Alfie's annoyance. He crossed to the youth and prodded him in the chest warning "Listen boyo so far ya done okay, kept ya head down not got into any bother, not been pinched but you fuck this up an it'll be the last thing you ever do." Slapping Irish sharply on the face with his heavy open hand he advised, "Yer a good kid, come from good stock, I know all about you but *you* don't wanna get t'know about me. This is a family business an our friends like doin' business with other families, it's their way, you're only in because of ya old man and ya friendship with our cousin John, loyalty is what it's all about, capisce?"

Irish understood his meaning well enough but was curious about his closing comment. "Did yer know Jay Mac... I mean John?"

Alfie stubbed out his cigarette, flicking the still glowing butt through the half open window, "Yeah y'could say I sort of knew him. I was at his Christenin' back in '55, had a good time at the party after but then somethin' happened and I had to leave Liverpool in a hurry, I can't never go back, which is a pity I would've liked to have gone to the boy's funeral outa' respect."

Irish interrupted, "You know about that, you know how it came about?"

Alfie looked directly at him, "Yeah, I know what happened alright, an who dunnit, it cuts me up every time I see that sick bastard Morgo, knowin' there's nothin I can do about it."

For a few moments Irish was dumbstruck as he fully grasped what Alfie had said then he blurted out "Yer just said every time you *see* that cunt but that must mean he's here in New York, 'cause you haven't been back to England, am I right?"

"Listen Patrick, Morgo is here in this city and that's as far as it goes. After he'd done young John, he got himself t'the States, t'Boston, where he had some friends in a crew there. Since then he's got himself well connected with the Celtic 'family' and does jobs for them here and back in Boston. He can't be touched by no one." Alfie warned in deadly earnest.

"No fuckin' way, so Niall an the rest of them knew that fuckin' piece of shit was here all the time and they did nothin' about it? I promise yer I'm gonna find that fucker an..."

Before he could continue Alfie caught him round the throat in a lightning fast movement with is left hand and with equal speed brought the barrel of his snub nosed Colt Python hard up against Irish's temple. "Ya fuckin' dumb ass punk, I just told yer he can't be touched by *no one*. Even if ya was t'see him strollin' down Fifth Avenue, or ridin' the subway, ya can't do nothin'... nothin'. Do I make myself clear?" he asked almost forcing the steel hard tip through Irish's skin. He released the seething youth, holstered his weapon and stepped away a few paces waiting for Irish's reply.

"I get the fuckin' message, let's leave it at that." he finally responded.

Alfie walked towards the door, flinging some loose dollar bills onto the lively bed. "Okay kid, here's a few extra bucks for ya, I won't see ya before ya go, so happy Fourth of July for tomorrer, be lucky."

Irish picked up the cash, stuffed it into his jeans pocket then spun round enraged punching the filthy mirror, shattering it in the process, roaring "Bastard!"

By the time Uncle Sam's Diner was closing for the night an agitated Irish could hardly wait to tell Rosita his news. With barely two days left before his departure he was determined to let her know how he felt and equally to accompany her to her home in El Barrio. Walking together towards her subway station, the anxious youth could contain himself no longer.

"I had a visitor this morning... from the people I work for... anyway I'll be gettin' off early on Monday mornin' so... I wanted t'tell yer... like... I mean... I really..."

Rosita interrupted his awkward declaration, "Patrick, don't say nomore, I know how ya feel because I've got to admit I've got feelings for you too... but nothin' can ever come of it, like I've already told ya." Irish would not be deterred but for the moment he said no more. "Okay Patrick, I'll have t'go now, come in an see me before ya leave, please." Rosita asked before kissing him softly on the cheek, about to depart.

"Am comin' with yer Rosita an I won't take no for an answer" he announced, following her doggedly, even as she descended the stone stairwell.

"Patrick please don't do this." Rosita pleaded futilely.

"Just tell me where we're goin' so I can gerra ticket." Irish responded.

She could see his absolute determination and finally acquiesced, giving him the necessary destination details.

Moments later having obtained his ticket and passing through the turnstiles behind Rosita, the couple walked down another flight of stairs to the platform, which was relatively empty at that time of night, with only a few random fellow travellers waiting for trains. Having been to London a number of times as part of Everton FC's army of travelling supporters to watch clashes with various southern rivals, Irish had some familiarity with the underground transport of that capital city. As he was not very comfortable with the deep subterranean system, finding it claustrophobic and confusing, Irish was happy to note that this network felt as if it were not too far beneath the street above.

After a preceding gust of warm air burst out from the nearest tunnel to their left, the first carriage of an elaborately decorated train soon followed. Irish was again surprised by the extensive graffiti that covered every available area of the vehicle's outside surface, even though he was used to contributing to similar if less grand works back home.

"Thee take their sprayin' serious round 'ere don't thee?" he asked rhetorically, adding "That's some piece of graffiti."

They entered the train and took their seats in the equally decorative interior, with Rosita advising, "They call it 'writing' not graffiti, the guys and girls who do it."

Soon they were hurtling along through dark tunnels that were temporarily illuminated by the occasional flash of blue-white electric sparks.

"Just tell me again Patrick, why do ya wanna do this?" Rosita asked.

"Like I told yer Rosita, I want t'get to know yer, I want t'be part of your world and at least see where yer live." Irish replied honestly.

Rosita decided to accept the situation for the moment; she had her game-plan planned.

It was not very long before the natural Skinhead reverted to form. Surrounded by dozens of individual scrawls, gang names and symbols, obscene sketches and pithy observations, Irish had to make his own contribution.

"'Ave yer got anythin' t'write with?" he casually asked Rosita.

After searching in her bag she produced a pen and a black felt-tip marker.

"Jackpot!" Irish exclaimed taking the marker from her, before reaching down to the one vacant space close to the doors, a few inches above the floor, 'Crown Skins Rule OK! Irish' he wrote in a bold font then added their Boot Boy logo of a capital C in the centre of a chevron with a capital B on either side. Looking back at Rosita who was shaking her head, though smiling, he decided to add a romantic gesture, quickly drawing an outlined stylised heart, he wrote 'Patrick L Rosita' finishing with an arrow passing horizontally through its centre.

Rosita laughed and blushed saying "Boys, they never grow up."

The few other passengers stared blankly in front of them, read their newspapers or in the case of one clearly inebriated traveller, lay partially straddling several seats with his left arm and hand trailing on the floor, cursing and mumbling to himself incoherently. No one wished to make eye contact with anyone else. 'It must be the same the world over.' Irish thought philosophically.

Once they had passed 42nd Street and began leaving the Midtown region, their carriage emptied with now only a few remaining fellow travellers. Shortly, on completing the long stretch that spanned the length of Central Park from 59th Street to 110th Street, Rosita announced "This is our stop." signalling their departure from the train. On exiting the station Rosita led them in a due east direction across Lexington and Third Avenue then began to turn north, passing 111th and 112th Street. She was deliberately avoiding taking Irish to her actual home, believing that he would be satisfied being in this approximate vicinity of it.

Irish, for his part, had been observing their surroundings as they journeyed through the bleak, forbidding landscape of rundown tenements, dark alleys, derelict buildings and rubble-strewn open spaces. What struck him most amidst the obvious dilapidation and deprivation was an even greater abundance of graffiti than on their subway train. It reminded him of the Crown Estate but on a gigantic scale with generations of gang names overlaying each other, in a confusing claim for their ownership of this turf. A number stood out as predominant, particularly: The Black Spades; The Savage Skulls; The Young Lords and The Latin Kings.

"Gorra few crews round 'ere then Rosita?" he asked.

"Yeah, one or two." she replied then, as they passed a small bodega close to East 113th Street she added, "Almost there now so I'll leave ya just here an run on, thanks for walkin' me home Patrick."

Irish was not to be so easily dismissed, not being entirely convinced that they were actually at her home. "Yer ok Rosita, I've come this far so I might as well take yer t'yer front door."

They walked on a dozen or so yards, Rosita becoming increasingly agitated with each step. There were now groups of youths gathered in shop doorways and loitering on the street corners, all of them eyeing the couple as they passed, particularly the incongruous, uniquely dressed Skinhead, some of them calling or wolf-whistling in derision.

"You *really* have got to go now Patrick, please." Rosita pleaded, stopping by an abandoned tenement covered in graffiti, almost all of which warned that this was the territory of the Jaguars. "The boss has said we can close a bit earlier tomorrow, so we can go and watch the celebrations down by the river. I'll see ya then and we can go together, make the most of ya last night, okay?" Rosita offered, intending on walking away from him.

"Rosita hang on!" Irish called, trying to catch hold of her arm.

Rosita broke away, running on along the darkened street. Irish knew enough to let her go, watching as she disappeared into the night. He turned to walk away, almost making the corner of the block before the car screeched to a halt alongside him. A pulsating, midnight blue, 1972 Dodge Charger mounted the kerb, its two doors flinging open allowing its four occupants to rapidly emerge. Irish knew running was not an option, quickly slipping the heavy brass knuckle-duster onto his right fist ready for the inevitable.

"Yo fuckin' dead white boy!" shouted the lead male wearing a deep red bandana on his head, dressed in his sleeveless Levi's denim jacket, blue vest, flared jeans and Adidas gazelle trainers, lashing Irish hard across the face with his thick leather belt.

Irish threw a powerful punch to his assailant's iron-hard stomach, to no effect; it was the only blow he would land before being overwhelmed by all four attackers. The experienced Crown Team player quickly assumed the position, five years tutelage at the Cardinals' brutal educational establishment had taught him well in that respect. Punched, kicked, lashed and stomped, he bore the beating in stoic silence, not wishing to add to their pleasure.

"You put yo fuckin' hand on one of our ladies, you piece of shit." he heard another of his excited assailants shout, as he rolled about in foetal form.

"Please, no Diego, please leave him alone!" Rosita screamed, frantically running back toward the scene.

"Stay the fuck back Rosita, I'll stop when I've killed this pig who touched you." Diego advised, continuing his wild lashing of the bloodied Irish.

"No, no, Diego, ya've got it wrong, Patrick saved me when I was bein' attacked, please!" Rosita called out to no avail, all four Jaguars carrying on with their assault. "Please Diego there was five of them, they were gonna rape me, Patrick took them all on... even blinded one of them." Rosita tried once more.

"Stop amigos!" Diego ordered, immediately ending their combined exertions, "Ya tryin' t'shame me, bitch?" he asked, snatching hold of her raven black hair, pulling her to him.

"Let go of me Diego or I'll tell mama." Rosita warned angrily.

This seemed to prove a sufficient threat for the ferocious war chief to release her.

"Okay, let's hear what ya've got t'say." Diego ordered, leading Rosita to give a brief account of the events of the previous Saturday evening, exaggerating Irish's role in the proceedings, making only a brief, passing reference to her own efforts and completely omitting even the presence of their rescuer, Gabriel. Her elder sibling listened intently then after a few moments of consideration gave his opinion.

"They must've been total wimps if this boy done all five of them alone, he didn't do so good against the four of us." His accomplices laughed at this observation.

Rosita was forced to admit that she had 'pricked' one of them, with her own knife but also to insist "Their leader had a gun and Patrick got it away from him, shot one of them and then all the others ran off."

Diego appeared more inclined to accept this version of the tale and turned his attention towards Irish, who had now regained his feet and was wiping the blood from several facial cuts, with a handkerchief that Rosita had passed to him.

"Yo just got out the army or somethin' boy?" Diego asked curiously.

"No, am a Skinhead, its a style. I was part of a team, a gang of Skinheads, back home in Liverpool." Irish replied honestly.

"Liverpool, where the fuck's that, I've never heard of it?" Diego responded with a sneer, lying.

One of his crew added, "Skinheads? We've got Baldheads here but you don't look like one of them. Ya more like a farm boy, a dumb red neck." Again they laughed at this witty comment. Irish remained silent, studying his tormentors, particularly their leader Diego, brother of his love interest, Rosita.

At six foot two with a lean, athletic musculature, golden brown skin, dark eyes, a thin pencil moustache and short goatee and displaying the proud bearing of a warrior, in any walk of life he would have been an impressive figure. Irish was no stranger to physical violence and its permanent markings, recognising Diego's multiple scars, particularly one that ran across the bridge of his nose down below his left eye, across his cheek, as visible evidence of some of the deadly, close range encounters he had been involved in. Ignoring everyone other than Diego he spoke directly to him.

"Listen, Diego, there's been a misunderstandin', so let's start over, okay? I'm Patrick O'Hare from Liverpool, England; most people call me 'Irish'." he advised, offering his hand to Diego to shake.

The stern war chief eyed the youth coldly, refused the gesture and spat forcefully onto the floor, "Fuck you Patrick O'Hare, I don't care what they call ya, so you can fuck off back to Liverpool, England." Nobody else spoke; Rosita looked down with tears in her dark eyes. "Go on boy, ya gettin' a free pass tonight, don't ever come back here and never even think about my sister again, or ya balls are mine." There was no court of appeal, no argument, Diego had given his judgement and passed his sentence.

Irish the lone Skinhead kept his head held high, stared directly at Diego for a few tense moments then turned and walked away along the litter strewn pavement, without another word. He did not look back but was now utterly determined to be with Rosita, whatever the consequences.

Sunday 4th July 1976

It was the dawn of yet another American blue sky day, and it was the Fourth of July. This was not just any Fourth of July but that of America's Bicentennial, the two hundredth anniversary of the fledgling nation's brave declaration of independence from its eighteenth century, global super-power masters, Great Britain. Choosing freedom, for some, rather than vassalage for all, it would take equally audacious courage and several years of bitter, if sporadic, fighting until finally with Lord Cornwallis' surrender at Yorktown on 19th October 1781, that liberty was secured and eventually ratified at the Treaty of Paris two years later. This year's momentous anniversary of the original declaration would be a day of national celebration with festivities and fireworks, tall ships and towering parades marking the occasion and perhaps in part acting as a salve to the terrible wounds of recent years, both those inflicted by a foreign foe with the dreadful debacle of Vietnam and the deeper self-inflicted hurt of Watergate, providing some small degree of closure, the end of a beginning of a new America. Not that Irish was aware of any of this as he lay soundly snoring in his active bed, after yet another uncomfortable night wrestling with his emotional dilemma and his biting, stinging companions.

By the time he arose, close to midday, President Ford had already sailed down the Hudson River inspecting an international fleet of sail-powered schooners and representative convoys from the world's navies. Soon the president would be breaking bread and taking tea with the First Lady and the not quite direct descendents of their original Hanoverian overlords, the British monarchy, in the form of Queen Elizabeth II and his Royal Highness, Prince Philip, The Duke of Edinburgh. Gerald and Betty would sit down with Liz and Phil in The White House, one hundred and sixty two years since the British had burned down the original building, all very civilised.

Irish wiped the sleep from his eyes and tried to focus on his new selection of angry bites, in the dirty, cracked mirror as he stood by the grimy sink, splashing water onto his face and body.

"I won't miss these little fuckers when I go." he said out loud. In truth though, he knew that was all he was glad to be leaving behind, everything else, the warmth, the blue skies, and the wide choice of food all had contrived to begin his reluctant conversion into an Americanophile. He had to admit that his new perception was critically coloured by his meeting with and feelings for the lovely Rosita, no one had ever had this confusing emotional impact on him before, he could not wait to see her that evening and could hardly bear the thought of leaving her the following day.

"Great day for the Irish." a smiling Mr McCabe announced as his sole guest finally made an appearance in the narrow lobby of the small hotel, causing the youth to look at him blankly. "...and all the other hard workin' people who built this great country." he added, still failing to draw a response from Irish other than, "Yeah, whatever y'say Ben."

The Crown Team player suddenly remembered Alfie Mack's words to him the previous day, asking "Hey have you got somethin' there for me? Me 'visitor' said y'might."

"No, not yet that'll be just before y'go, that's the way *they* like to operate." the older man replied.

Irish was busily scratching some of his itchy souvenirs as he stood by the reception counter, prompting him to ask, "Any chance yer could change the beddin' in me room? I think some of those fleas have got fleas of their own, thee've been there that long."

The proud proprietor was unhappy with this unsanitary slur, "Well ya cheeky pup. I change those sheets once a week I'll have you know, whether they need it or not." he advised.

"Ben, I've been 'ere since last Friday an they're still the same sheets, I think the fuckin' fleas'll start complainin' if y'dont change them soon."

"I tell y'what y'Lordship, I'll do them now, while ya out, just f'you, how's that?" Ben offered reluctantly.

Irish strolled off towards the front entrance intent on spending his last afternoon as a tourist; see some more sights, buying souvenirs for his mother and siblings and something special for Rosita.

Ben called after him "Don't get into any *more* trouble will ya, yer've only got one night before yer off."

Irish laughed dismissively, stepping out into the bright sunlight of a transformed red, white and blue landscape. 'Shit, someone's been busy while I've been sleepin'.' he thought, observing the elaborate displays of bunting, rosettes and 'Old Glory' flags of all sizes, including a large out of date, pre-1959 version containing only forty eight stars hanging proudly from his present lodgings. Everywhere he would travel on that day would be the same, completely altered from drab, utilitarian decor to a blaze of colourful national fervour.

Before setting off on his mementoes mission, Irish decided to visit Uncle Sam's for a late breakfast. As usual once he had taken his seat in the comfortable booth he was presented with an abundance of choice. Irish decided to avail himself of an Uncle Sam's 'Bicentennial Breakfast Special', which was basically the same mountainous meal as usual only this now came with a small stars and stripes flag as a nod to the occasion and a hefty price hike, acknowledging the benefits of capitalism as an integral part of the American way. Irish was not complaining however, as he tucked into his fried eggs, bacon, sausages, hash browns and tomatoes with a side order of pancakes and maple syrup, plus fresh orange juice, not the watery, diluted type he was used to at home, and as much black coffee as his bladder could hold.

Having satisfied his urgent hunger pangs with his late breakfast and feeling reasonably confident in his ability to navigate the subway system, Irish headed for the shops of Midtown to obtain presents for his family and Rosita. By the early evening he had purchased an eclectic selection of New York themed goods from the varied disparate stores along 5th Avenue and was standing in the gift shop of the magnificent Roman Catholic cathedral of his patron saint, St Patrick, looking for something appropriate for his mother. Finally after much deliberation, he settled for a deep ruby red set of Rosary beads replete with a silver Gothic crucifix, 'That's me ma sorted, now for somethin' special for Rosita.' he thought, conscious of the time drawing close to when he would actually see her again.

Several hours later dressed in his usual petrol blue, twenty-two inch parallel trousers, with red half-inch elasticated braces and gleaming, parade ground finish Airwair, Irish added one new item of kit to his evening attire as a personal observation of the occasion, a new white tee-shirt bearing a superb bald-headed eagle, proudly flying wings outstretched over the slogan 'Sprit of '76'.

"Wow! Yer've really gone for the red, white'n'blue look haven't yer feller?" Rosita's older female colleague observed when he arrived at Uncle Sam's Diner.

"Hey leave him alone Marge, I think he looks cute." Rosita warned, smiling sweetly. Irish was delighted and settled into his booth ready for his final meal at the diner, for the present at least.

Just after ten o'clock following another culinary satisfying evening, Irish paid his bill and was preparing to leave with Rosita, the owner of the diner having kept to his word, allowing his staff to close early.

"Where are we goin' Rosita?" Irish asked.

"Let's go down to Battery Park, to get the best view." she advised.

A short time later after catching a cab to the very base of Lower Manhattan, they joined a huge crowd of enthusiastic spectators already gathered in this key vantage point.

"Sorry about last night Rosita, I didn't mean t'cause yer any trouble." Irish offered apologetically.

"Patrick, I should be apologisin' t'you, I'm so sorry about Diego..." she began, only to be quickly interrupted by him.

"Rosita, forget it, y'warned me not t'come to yer area and I still wanted to go... it was worth it just t'be with yer for that bit longer."

Rosita smiled, placing her hand in his then kissed him on the cheek.

For the next few hours they enjoyed the extravagant celebrations, watching the illuminated international flotilla of ships sail by, all accompanied throughout by thrilling fireworks, thundering above them. This was the coming together of the people in the face of adversity, determined to mark the two-hundredth anniversary of their nation's birth. It was undoubtedly the worst of times, yet paradoxically there remained glittering moments of the very best. A tale of two cities but in this instance both were contained within the one, inextricably wound about each other, New York's glorious bicentennial celebrations found the indefatigable human spirit soaring higher than the spectacular pyrotechnics that burst into the blue velvet summer night sky.

"Wow! Look at the Statue of Liberty; don't she look great with all those fireworks goin' off around her?" Rosita called out like an excited child.

The world famous icon of Liberty was surrounded by dozens of thunderous, brilliant, airborne explosions, standing resolutely defiant to "the rockets red glare, the bombs bursting in air" guarding the gateway to "the land of the free and the home of the brave." Irish enjoyed every minute of the show, lost to its full significance yet unavoidably aware that this was a momentous night, his happiness was unbounded and growing exponentially the longer he was in the presence of the lovely Rosita.

Towards the end of the night he turned to her and said "Don't take offence Rosita but I got yer somethin' up at St Patrick's Cathedral, earlier today." He passed her a small, square black box, which she then opened, "Oh Patrick ya shouldn't have done this!" Rosita exclaimed as she removed the fine silver necklace with gleaming blue enamel and silver Miraculous Medal, displaying an exquisite bas-relief image of Our Lady.

"I've got the receipt if yer don't like it but you'll have t'take it back yerself, 'cause I won't be here." he offered, misunderstanding her comment.

"No, not at all Patrick, it's lovely... I don't know what t'say." she replied.

"Then don't say anythin'." he answered.

Rosita took him at his word, said no more leaning into him as he fastened the necklace about her slim neck then kissed him fully on the lips. It was a long, lingering kiss. For Irish it was as if it were his first, all the sordid experiences he had had before were gone, dissipated like tawdry phantoms, he was renewed, reborn. They embraced silent, wrapped in each other's arms for several magical moments, until Irish finally spoke.

"I know I only met yer just over a week ago, and this is gonna sound mad but I really..."

Rosita put her finger to his lips saying "Don't say anymore Patrick, lets just enjoy the moment, its gettin' late an I'll have t'go home soon."

Once more they kissed then stood looking out over the calm, silver waters of the Hudson River towards the distant Statue of Liberty, all now bathed in the natural radiance of a large full moon. They both knew that they must part, Rosita to her home in Los Barrios and Irish back to his lodgings, before commencing his dawn voyage across the wide Atlantic Ocean and eventually his own home in Liverpool.

Finally Irish hailed a cab and passed Rosita the last of his US currency, to more than cover the fare.

"I'll be gone in the mornin', Rosita but I'll be back as soon as I can... honest." he promised, adding "I'll come lookin' for yer in the diner, straight off the boat."

Rosita smiled then kissed him softly on the lips before she departed in the taxi, "I'll look for ya there every night until then, safe journey Patrick."

Long after the vehicle sped into the night and the glow of its red tail lights had disappeared from view, he stood and stared into the darkness. Eventually he trudged away, for one final restless night at McCabe's Grande Hotel.

A pale sun had barely risen into a water colour blue sky, announcing the dawn of one more New York day as Irish, standing in the stern of the merchant vessel, *Prince of Orange*, recently returned from a brief sojourn further up the New England coast in Boston, gazed back towards the teeming city. Only when the ship was increasing knot speed full steam ahead into open waters did Irish finally turn away from his vigil. Walking across the spray lashed metal deck, with a cool salt sea breeze making its refreshing presence felt, he saw the handsome officer standing close by, smiling.

"I believe you may have found what you where looking for in that city, yes?" he asked.

Irish laughed and replied, "Yeah, yer right mate, only I didn't even know I was lookin' for it until I found it." then asked, "What about yerself, did y'have any luck?"

The smiling officer nodded, "My friend, I can always find what *I* want in any port, around the world."

"Am sure y'can; well next stop Southampton, see yer." Irish replied, passing by the older male, staring directly ahead without making eye contact, intent on reaching his own small cabin.

"Are you certain that I cannot offer you something more comfortable than your cramped quarters?" the officer asked once more, hopefully.

Irish ignored his proposal and continued on, entering the ship's interior to his designated lodgings, locking the door securely once inside. He had no further contact with his merchant marine admirer for the remainder of the voyage.

Friday 16th July 1976

After twelve days at sea, a long train journey from Southampton to London and an even longer one from Euston to Lime Street Station, Irish arrived back in Liverpool late evening on a scorching July Friday, the unusual protracted heatwave still ongoing. Carrying his suitcase in one hand and with the securely wrapped, large square box, that old Ben McCabe had given him immediately prior to his departure, tucked under his left arm, Irish briskly walked from the famed nineteenth century railway terminus up to London Road and the senior Gerard Boys' main hostelry headquarters, The Central public house.

Entering into the smoky, stifling ground floor bar with Dean Martin's *Ain't that a Kick in the Head* playing on the juke box, he pushed through the crowd of drinkers and shouted to the surly bar tender, "Hey mate, I've gorra delivery for Niall from his Uncle Sam." the exact words he had been instructed to say by his employer on his return.

The portly male quickly left his busy position and climbed the few wooden steps to the lounge above, where a cosy side room served as the inner-sanctum for the Mack siblings. Returning swiftly, the bar tender called to Irish "Alright lad, go straight up."

Irish did as instructed, strolling into the packed anti-chamber, still keeping a firm hold on both items of luggage.

"Well here he is, back from Yankee Land all in one piece." Niall shouted, immediately ordering his youngest brother Danny to relieve Irish of his suitcase. "Take that straight upstairs Danny and check everythin's as it should be, let me know if there's fuckin' anythin' missin'." Smiling broadly Niall put down his pint of Guinness motioning with his index finger for Irish to approach. "Yer've got somethin' else there for my attention only, haven't yer? Well pass it over; let's have a look at what our 'friends' have sent us."

Irish passed him the extensively taped box glad to be rid of it, having been worried about losing this apparently precious item his entire journey. Niall produced a shiny black handled flick knife, opening it in one deft movement then sliced through the tape bindings. Dropping the wooden lid to the floor Niall tilted the box towards himself, Tommy and Francis, who were sitting on either side of him. All three laughed loudly, clearly pleased with the contents.

"Here y'go Patrick, shake hands with the lad who done the job before you." Niall called, tossing a well preserved, severed right hand, wearing a heavy gold ring set with an emerald shamrock on its broad face, out from its crushed salt packaging, across to the startled Skinhead.

"Fuck that!" Irish exclaimed, batting the grisly paw away from him, unintentionally knocking it onto the small table in front of the laughing trio.

In an instant Niall's mood completely changed, "This is what happens when yer don't use family." he observed, continuing, "We gave this lad a chance, after we lost young John. He did good, real good for a while but then he started stickin' his fuckin' nose in where he shouldn't have and asking too many questions, well he won't be askin' any more."

Irish looked down at the pale, bloodless hand, roughly hacked off at the wrist then directly at Niall. "I already understood what yer meant, no need for this." he said.

"Did yer now, well this will help yer fuckin' remember. Now pick it up, take off that ring and put it on yer own finger." Niall ordered.

Irish hesitated, reluctant to even touch the macabre dismembered paw.

Niall grew angry, "Pick it up now, I won't fuckin' tell yer again!" he roared.

Finally after a further few tense moments, Irish complied, taking the ring from the cold, stiff hand and placing it onto the little finger of his own right hand.

"Good, that's more fuckin' like it, you *belong* to us, there's only one way out, don't ever forget it. Now throw that piece of shit on the deck and kick it away from this table." Again the youth did as ordered kicking the hand away to the furthest corner of the room.

Just at that moment Danny Boy returned and spoke to Niall, "It's all good Niall, nothin' missin'."

The elder Gerard Boy smiled once more, "Alright Patrick, take a seat an have a drink on us." he offered, motioning for an underling to bring Irish a stool and get him a pint. A few moments later Niall addressed a seated Irish who had been supplied with a dark pint of Guinness and a lighted cigarette, "Right that's all behind us now, is there anythin' yer wanted t'ask before y'get off?"

Irish took a lengthy swallow from his drink before answering "Yeah, when am I goin' back?"

The three Seniors laughed and Niall observed, "Got a taste f'New York did yer, or was it somethin' else that took y'fancy?"

Irish did not have the opportunity to reply, as Francis noted, "We've heard all about yer sexy Latino bird, y'dirty cunt."

The Crown Player was taken by surprise and blurted out "How the fuck did yers know about Rosita..."

Niall explained, "Yer've been in the States, dickhead, not the dark side of the fuckin' moon. Thee have these things called telephones, yeah? Alfie's been keepin' an eye on yer, he soon filled us in." Irish said no more for the moment, allowing Niall to continue, "That's good, that yer've got a bird on the go over there, more motivation for yer an if yer do ever step out of line, she gets a little slap."

"No one better ever go near her, no one, or it'll be the last thing thee ever do!" Irish warned firmly, without caring how they reacted.

Niall appeared delighted, "Even better, y'must really like this bird, that's good all round, anythin' else yer wanna say?"

Irish had the burning question ready to ask from the moment he arrived and now put it to them, "Yer seem t'know everythin' so yer must know that shit house Morgo is in the States, in New York City?" Niall waited to hear what Irish would say next. "What I want t'know is... what the fuck yers are doin' about it... when is *he* gettin' sorted?" Irish asked angrily.

Niall leaned forward onto the table and replied, "Never; he's outa bounds, can't be touched. Anyone makes that move an it's all over, it'll start a fuckin' war that no one's gonna win. You stay the fuck away from Morgo... right?"

Irish got the message loud and clear but kept his own thoughts silent.

A grim smile returned to Niall's battered visage, "Here's some cash for yer; we'll be in touch. Now fuck off back t'yer shitty estate an yer little Skinhead mates."

Irish picked up his wages from the table, turned away, walked down the wooden steps and left the heaving public house without another word.

Saturday 17th July 1976

Having had a hot bath, a good night's sleep and distributed his American presents to his family, including his older brother Dermot, who had also only recently returned home after successfully completing his studies at Northampton university and was temporarily working in the off-licence of The Bear public house, Irish spent the bulk of that Saturday relaxing in his home.

By the evening, after a sizeable meal of Scouse, followed by apple pie and custard, he was eager to meet up with his ex-Crown Team player friends in their former base of operations, The Eagle.

Wearing a pair of cream, twenty-two inch parallel trousers, black half-inch elasticated braces and his gleaming cherry red Airwair, he chose his 'Spirit of 76' bald headed eagle tee-shirt to complete his ensemble and as a likely controversial talking point. As he was about to leave for the pub, his long-haired, ex-hippy brother called to him, "Since I've been back I've been gettin' around on your Lambretta, so d'yer mind if I use it tonight, t'get t'work?"

"Yeah, go 'ed, 'elp yerself, am not gonna be usin' it, am gonna drop a few pints with the lads tonight, see yer later." Irish replied, exiting the house into the street, on his way to 'knock' for Blue as his first port of call.

"Alright mate, back from the States, not been shot or stabbed or murdered?" Blue asked excitedly, on opening the neatly painted front door to Irish, a few moments later.

"No Blue, I haven't been shot or stabbed and I think I'd know about it if I'd been murdered." Irish answered with a wry smile.

"I'll get me denim and some dosh and be right with yer." Blue shouted, above the background noise of the television blaring loudly in a futile attempt to drown out the howling of his infant twin daughters. "It's all been kickin' off 'ere since you've been away mate." Blue advised as they turned the corner and approached the dilapidated library with its continuous concrete sill where the crew used to regularly gather.

"What the fuck!" Irish exclaimed on seeing the shattered windows and extensive graffiti display covering the semi-circular frontage of the tired building. 'RAVEN'S CREW RULE OK!' and 'CROWN TEAM SHIT HOUSES!' he read with disbelief then asked, "I've only been away just over a fuckin' month, what's been goin' on?"

Whilst walking on towards The Eagle, Blue briefly explained, "The Raven's Crew have gone fuckin' massive, thee've even got back-up from the Barley's, so nobody wants t'fuck with them. Anyway, whoever's supplyin' their gear, wants them to run this estate as well and thee've started doin' raids down 'ere, thee say they're gonna take The Eagle any time now."

Irish could hardly believe what he was hearing but said no more for the time being, as they entered the eponymous alehouse. Once inside the packed lounge he was further surprised to find only a handful of the old crew present and that their usual places in the semi-circular seating area, were occupied by a younger crowd, most of whom were the siblings of the original team.

"It's all fuckin' changed in 'ere Blue," Irish observed as they were waiting to be served.

"Yeah mate, these kids are takin' over the place now an most of them are fuckin' junkies." Blue advised, before shouting their order of a pint of Guinness, a pint of lager and several packets of salted snacks. They casually listened to Gladys Knight's *Midnight Train To Georgia* which was currently playing on the juke box in the corner, as they waited at the bar. After they had obtained their drinks, they wove their way between the seated revellers surrounding the small circular tables and squeezed in along the external wall seating, between Johno and Terry (H) on one side and Brain and Tank on the other.

"Alright Irish, back in the land of the livin', hey?" Johno noted, with Terry (H) asking "What was it like down there with all those Southern blurts?"

Irish quickly remembered his cover story and replied accordingly, "It was alright, thee didn't bother me but yer can't beat bein' back in the Pool, y'know warra mean?"

They all concurred with this traditional view, raising their pint glasses in accord.

"What's with the crazy tee-shirt, where's y'usual Benny or Jaytex?" Tank asked.

"Yeah, an what the fuck does that mean 'Spirit of 76', is that some southern ponce sayin'?" Brain added provocatively.

Irish smiled and responded suitably, "'Ave either of yers ever 'eard of that big country thee call America?" he began.

"Yeah, of course we 'ave." Tank answered for the pair.

"Good, an can yers tell me what year it is Brain?" Irish asked the slow-witted, ex-team player directly.

"'Course I can, I'm not fuckin' thick, its 1976."

"You said it Brain." Irish replied, adding, "Two hundred years ago, that's 1776, ok, the Americans were sick of bein' fucked over by the rich bastard toffs from this country, so thee had a revolution an spewed the cunts off." He waited whilst they absorbed his colourful, concise history lesson. "Right, so this year they're havin' loads of parties and the like, t'celebrate two hundred years since that 'appened." Irish concluded his explanation and took a lengthy draught of his Guinness.

Tank was not quite satisfied, "So why are yer wearin' a Yank's tee-shirt, what's the connection?"

Irish realised his ruse about working in the south of England was almost compromised and quickly answered, "There is no connection, I liked the look of it and bought it in some shop down in London that sells American gear, alright?" He was beginning to regret his choice of clothing that evening, changing the subject to a more pressing issue, "Anyway, what's the fuckin' score with all this Ravens Crew shite painted on the library?"

Terry (H) their senior ex-player answered, "There gettin' t'be cheeky bastards since the Barley's started t'back them up. What we need is a fuckin' good scrap with them now, remind them who we are an who they're messin' with."

As Johno the immensely strong farm labourer stood up to get in another round, he observed, "Yeah, that's what's needed but whose gonna jump in, Terry? We're not a Skinhead team no more and look at these younger lads, they're all fuckin' dope heads, thee couldn't give a shit."

With The Rolling Stones' *Fool To Cry* now playing on the juke box, Johno strolled over to the bar, Brain following him to assist with the ale for the sextet of old Skinheads.

"Fuck me, this is depressin'." Irish noted, "What a way f'the Crown Team to end up, turned over by a second division crew of wankers." He decided it was going to take a lot of Guinness that night to help him put recent developments into perspective.

Several hours and numerous pints later, Irish and Blue, having left the Eagle at closing time, where standing somewhat unsteadily outside Mr Li's Golden Diner, tearing into their meals of golden battered cod and thick cut soggy chips, liberally sprinkled with salt and doused in vinegar. Terry (H) and their other chronological peers had remained in the pub, determined to force the management to agree an after hours 'lock in', so they could carry on drinking.

Irish continued to express his incredulity at the present change of fortunes for their once famed team, "D'yer know what Blue, I've just been in the Land of the Gangs," he began, slurring his words, "I mean real fuckin' gangs, not shit heads. Thee use knives an guns like its nothin' to them, thee'll just blow some cunt away." He stopped talking for a few moments to push yet another handful of steaming white fish and hot chips into his mouth.

"Oh yeah, I know what yer mean, definitely." Blue answered drunkenly, in between swallows, not really following his friend's comments.

"These Ravens pricks need teachin' a lesson, put them in their place, y'know worram sayin'?" Irish continued, his alcohol induced bravado rising apace with the increasing volume of his inebriated voice.

"Oh yeah, an who's gonna fuckin' teach them that lesson, *you*?" they heard being called to them from nearby. Weaver now appeared with several of his Junior Heron Crew.

Irish turned angrily towards him, released from any sense of sober caution. "Who's askin' you to butt in? This is a private conversation!"

Weaver laughed, amused by the condition of them both. "The fuckin' state of yers, yer pair of drunks," he laughed again continuing, "Irish you'll have a go but yer no match for a crew of Ravens boys, an Blue, well, you couldn't punch yer way out of a fuckin' paper bag."

His juniors joined in the merriment, much to Irish's annoyance, "Fuck you Weaver! I'll have a go at any of those shits. I've already done half a dozen of them, no fuckin' problem."

Weaver, the crazed psychopath was intrigued, "When was this then? I've never heard any talk about this, from anyone."

"Yeah, well yer wouldn't would yer, thee was too fuckin' embarrassed t'tell anyone." Irish continued, his anger also growing by the moment.

"Really, is that fuckin' right? An when was this supposed to have happened? 'Cause I don't fuckin' believe yer." Weaver asked again, enjoying goading the intoxicated Irish.

"The same night I done Mal the Pig..." Irish blurted out, before realising too late what he had said.

They all heard his incriminating, accidental confession and fell silent.

Blue was the first to react, "Okay, well we've got t'be goin' now, he's pissed, doesn't even know what he's fuckin' sayin'."

"He knows what he's sayin' alright, an now we all know who done Mal the Pig." Weaver announced, adding, "But who cares? Nobody liked that fuckin' weirdo an none of my lads are gonna grass yer up, right?"

His crew all voiced their agreement and Blue made to lead his friend away from the shop front, before any other compromising comments where let slip.

Weaver called to the departing ex-Eagle players, "'Ey, Irish, if yer really serious about doin' some of those fuckin' Ravens Crew just give me a shout, I'm yer man. I know where those shitbags hang out, an I'll be happy t'go with yer.

Not long after, as they were part way up their Central Road route, back to their sector of the estate, Irish stopped suddenly and brought forth a violent, Technicolor yawn, spewing most of the contents of his evening meal mixed with several pints worth of Guinness, steaming out onto the already filthy pavement.

"Feelin' better mate?" Blue asked prematurely, just as Irish roared another foul-smelling stream, into the still, warm night.

"Fuckin' hell, what 'ave I said?" Irish asked, now fully cognisant of his recent remarks.

"Fuck it, like Weaver said no one give a shit about Looney Tunes and no fucker is gonna grass." Blue offered reassuringly.

They turned the corner of the street in which they both lived and Blue announced, "Seein' as yer alright 'am gettin' in while I can. If 'am any later Beryl will probably lock me out, the fuckin' bitch. You okay from 'ere on yer own?"

"Yeah I'm sound, thanks Blue, an if yer do get locked out give us a knock, y'can crash in ours, it'll probably be quieter, see yer." Irish replied then walked on slowly to the opposite end of the street, where his house was located.

As soon as he turned his key in the door he knew something was wrong, "Patrick, Patrick, oh thank God yer back, I've been lookin' for yer everywhere, even been bangin on the door of the Eagle but gettin' no answer." his mother called out, rushing towards him, tears filling her eyes.

"What the... I mean, what's happened?" he asked, totally bewildered, catching hold of the distraught woman.

"It's our Dermot... thee've nearly killed him... the polis were here... thee've only just gone..." she garbled.

"Ma, what are yer sayin', calm down will yer." Irish pleaded, growing increasingly alarmed.

"Thee said a gang of these lads dragged him out of the Off-licence and battered him with their fists and boots and God knows what else. No one would stop it, even though there were lots of people around... Dermot's been rushed to hospital and the polis say he's in a bad way, he might not make it... we've gotta go now, d'yer hear me? The girls can see to our Sean."

Irish was dumbfounded for a few seconds then replied "Okay ma, I'll ring for a taxi, don't you worry no more... did thee say who these lads might be?"

His tearful mother stood sobbing, trying to recall the details then said, "Yes, thee did, thee called themselves after some birds... Ravens, that's it."

Irish asked nothing else and telephoned for a taxi.

Chapter 6

Mona Lisas and Mad Hatters

July-August 1976

It was just before closing time at The Bear public house and off-licence when an unkindness of angry Ravens arrived in the forlorn litter-strewn car park of the dilapidated hostelry on that fateful, warm July night. Following reports from some of their own Juniors, who had been tasked with locating a particular Lambretta LI175, the crew had decided to investigate for themselves whether this was the vehicle they sought.

"What d'you think Smidge, is this the one that Crown cunt rode into us with?" the long haired second-in-command asked his team leader, as they carefully examined Irish's altered and repaired scooter, standing immediately outside the off-licence entrance.

"Y'can see where he's done a bit a work on it an where he's took off the letters for Crown Team but this is *defo* that fucker's bike alright." Jimmy 'Smidge' Smith or, Smi(J) as he often styled himself, was the younger brother of the famed Ravens Hall Skinhead Ronnie 'Smigger' Smith and, as with many of his chronological peers who also had had Senior siblings in this original team, he wanted to establish a reputation of his own. These were the young bloods of Ravens Hall Estate, tired of living under the shadow of their elder brothers and cousins. Even though the Skinhead, Suedehead and Boot Boy youth cults had now passed, they too wanted to be known as 'somebodies', prepared to sacrifice a fragile peace that had existed between their estate and their nearest rivals The Crown for the past two years, to achieve that status.

"Alright Franny, spread everyone out so when this prick comes out we're ready for 'im and he can't run off." Smidge began outlining his plan then when everyone was in place continued, "Okay, send in a couple of Juniors askin' for ale and ciggies, wind the prick behind the counter up. He won't serve them, so they snatch some stuff then leg it, he'll come after them and we'll do the rest."

Franny, Smidge's lieutenant did as instructed, deploying the troops and sending in the bait. Within minutes the trap was sprung, the young decoys racing from the off-licence armed with packets of cigarettes, crisps and salted peanuts. The innocent, unsuspecting Dermot was in hot pursuit, stopping short when he saw the dozen-strong crew accompanied by some of their giggling female admirers, ready and eager for the show.

"What d'you kids want, hangin' round outside here?" he asked naively, brushing his long, straggly hair away from his face, standing in front of the sinister, smiling crowd, in his skinny-rib, short-sleeved jumper, wide flares and 'desert wellie' suede boots. His distinctive Liverpool-Irish brogue was all the proof Smidge and co. needed, removing any doubt from their minds.

"Remember us, yer Irish tit, not so fuckin' tough now are yer wirrout yer fuckin' shit scooter." Smidge called to him, flexing his muscles and cracking his knuckles.

"Listen young feller, I don't know what yer talkin' about but I don't want any trouble, so just get yer boys t'give back those fags and we'll leave it at that." Dermot offered generously, though doubting there was little chance of them accepting his sporting gesture.

Smidge laughed ordering his Juniors into action, "Young lads, in y'go, do that fuckin' bike, wreck it."

Immediately they ran towards the immaculate Lambretta and began booting it from every angle.

"Hey! Leave that alone, yer wee fuckers!" Dermot shouted.

"Do this cunt, everyone in!" Smidge roared, unleashing his salivating pack onto their helpless victim.

"Come on then, let's have it." Dermot called back defiantly, raising his fists ready to fight for his life. He was no coward, it took a brave man to be a committed pacifist in these violent times, he already bore the scars of his conviction to prove it.

Franny took a hard fist to the mouth on coming into range of Dermot's lengthy reach; two others of the pack suffered the same fate as Irish's older brother used every move his gentle giant of a father had taught him as a boy, just for such an occasion.

"Get that cunt down!" Smidge roared as the pack swarmed round the tall, determined medical graduate, who was about to start his career in a junior capacity after convocation. Kicked, punched and head butted, Dermot was eventually caught by his hair and dragged about like a ragdoll, being struck from all sides, until he fell to his knees. Now the beating could begin in earnest.

"Cripple this shit, fuck 'im up good." Smidge demanded, unnecessarily his frenzied crew fully possessed by blood lust, determined to inflict maximum, permanent damage.

Some of the older, local Bear regulars spilled out from the ale house and stood casually watching, from a safe distance as the vicious assault raged on. There were some half-hearted calls for the young thugs to stop but as one old curmudgeon pointed out, "He's not one of our lads, he's only been workin' in the offie for a few days." Another sage agreed, "Aye yer right, he should've known better than t'take a job round 'ere, if he couldn't 'andle 'imself."

Several of the Bear team's former players also considered intervening but decided it was best to mind their own business, after all who was this long-haired stranger being beaten to death in their car park, nobody they knew. By the time the giggling Ravens girls got their opportunity to kick and scratch the blood drenched, unconscious Dermot, he had long since ceased to move. Finally, exhausted by their efforts, raging anger spent and drenched in the sweat of those efforts, the combined crew stood back and admired their work.

"Fuckin' job done, nice one." Smidge acknowledged, breathing heavily, "You girls are in for some hard shaggin' now, get them lads." he ordered laughing.

With collective screams of mock fear, the equally excited females ran from the scene towards the old municipal cemetery that straddled the border of their territory and that of the Crown Estate.

"Eee, no! Yers'll after catch us first, y'dirty bastards." they called expectantly, their male pursuers aroused and ready for further physical exertions.

A brave, elderly, local resident in the nearby grey concrete, high-rise tower blocks, who actually had a telephone, rang for the emergency services now that it appeared safe to do so. She did not wish to be identified for fear of reprisals but her action meant the difference between life and death for the broken Dermot.

Sunday 18th July 1976
Irish stood silently at the side of his elder brother's hospital bed in the intensive care unit, looking at the confusing collection of wires, tubes and cannulas that harnessed the battered young man to vital life-saving supplies and an array of monitors. Mrs O'Hare knelt weeping by the bed of her first-born, clasping her worn, reddened hands together in prayer, with her new deep ruby red Rosary beads between them.

"God spare him please, take me instead, no parent should outlive their child." she repeated over and over in between decades of the Rosary's litany.

It was the early hours of Sunday morning, those that are darkest just before dawn, Irish and his mother had been in this dread location since the taxi had dropped them off at the hospital, just after midnight. Irish was cold, cold to everything, including the Almighty. He left his mother to her prayers to the divine; he had no room for anything else other than all consuming hate and a burning anger that roared for revenge, immolating his soul with a fire that could only be quenched by one terrible course of action.

"Our Dermot will be okay ma, he's made of strong stuff, he'll pull through, don't you worry, I'll take care of everythin' I promise yer." Irish offered as reassurance to his distraught mother and as a sworn oath to his destroyed brother.

◇◇◇

For almost a week Irish had done nothing other than concentrate on how, he would exact his righteous revenge. Only twice had his thoughts been disturbed by receiving the exact same warning, from two totally disparate sources, during one day. The first of the two occurred in the afternoon of the Monday following the vicious assault on his brother, who remained unconscious, in a critical condition. A keen eyed young police officer, who arrived to take details from Mrs O'Hare at the hospital, noticed Irish's distinctive Skinhead attire and decided to report this to his superior, the detective assigned to investigate the incident.

"Patrick O'Hare, brother of Dermot O'Hare, is it?" the heavy set, overweight, early forties male asked, after knocking on the door of Irish's small end terraced home. Irish confirmed who he was and waited for the invitation that he knew was about to be made.

"I'm DC Banks, would y'mind answerin' a few questions, we can do it here or down the station if y'prefer." the sweating detective offered.

"I'll get me coat, me sisters are mindin' me little brother an me ma will be back from the hospital soon, so its probably better if I come with yer, I don't want her upsettin' any more." Irish replied, before momentarily disappearing back into the living room to advise his sisters as to what was happening and pick up his dark blue Harrington jacket. "I'm just goin' down the cop shop t'see if I can be of any help, okay? Tell me ma not t'worry, I won't be long." he shouted, pulling the front door shut.

A quarter of an hour later, without being formally arrested or charged, Irish was sat in the small, claustrophobic interrogation room of The Lanes police station, assisting them 'voluntarily' with their enquiries. He did not know then that this was where his friend Jay Mac had already been questioned a few years earlier and this was one of the brutal detectives present on that occassion, or that he had a personal, long standing hatred of the gangs of the Crown Estate.

"So, y'like the old Skinhead gear, do yer?" the detective began, pushing his greasy quiff away from his round face, allowing the stark fluorescent light of the buzzing tube set in the ceiling above, to fully reveal his scarred countenance.

"Yer I do, why who are you the fashion police, it's not a crime is it?" Irish asked in response.

"Alright, calm down, you're a bit defensive aren't yer, on edge like... got somethin' t'hide 'ave yer?" the flabby officer replied, adding, "Like I told yer, *I'm* DC Banks, yer've probably 'eard all about me."

Irish recognised the name but not the man, replying, "No, I've never heard of yer an I've got nothin' t'hide either."

Adjusting his garish patterned, broad kipper tie the somewhat crestfallen detective pressed on, "Had a little touch yerself couple of months ago, causin' trouble at the match. Funny that cos from what I've read it was causin' an affray, offensive weapon and resistin' arrest, yet yer only got a fine, not six months, not even a fuckin' suspended sentence. What does that tell yer?"

Irish stared blankly at the DC. "British legal system best in the world, is what it tells me." he offered with a grin.

Officer Banks was not happy, "Don't fuck with me dickhead, I know your sort, I've put plenty of them away. I think you're 'connected' somehow, got friends with a little bit of influence, so am gonna look into you, do some diggin' see what I can find."

"Help y'self, like I said, I've got nothin' t'hide, can I go now, is that it?" Irish replied coolly.

DC Banks snapped, his thin patience already exhausted, "Look boy, I know those Ravens Hall toolbags, they're all mouth and no trousers. They wouldn't have just jumped yer brother an nearly killed him over a few packs of ciggies, no fuckin' way. This is down to you, there's somethin' that puts you in the frame, an am gonna find it. You're not squeaky clean like yer arl ma thinks, you're a fuckin' player."

Irish made no response for a few moments then asked again, "Finished detective, anythin' else, or am I free t'go?"

The older male leaned across the table at which they were seated, allowing Irish to fully appreciate the mixed aroma of his overpowering body odour and ferocious halitosis breath. "Get it right boy, am onto yer. I'll be watchin' your every fuckin' move, so just in case yer thinkin' of takin' things further with the Ravens Crew, remember that." he paused then added, "Is that clear enough for yer, Skinhead?"

Irish stood up ready to leave and replied, "I've got yer DC Banks. Now if yer don't mind, I'll be off an leave yer t'gerron with yer work, like tryin' t'find the cunts who done me brother."

The detective also rose, "Go 'ed Mr O'Hare, thanks for your co-operation. See yer again, *soon*."

In the unsurprising abscence of an offer of a return ride to the Crown Estate, Irish briskly marched from The Lanes police station, along the road that ran immediately below the outer edge of the ten foot high perimeter walls that enclosed the Ravens Hall housing development. Fortunately for him, dressed in his full Skinhead kit as he was, none of the eponymous crew were in the vicinity, most of them being located in the Raven alehouse, celebrating the hospitalisation and critical status of their victim, which had become common knowledge and could only add to their growing reputation.

A short time later, after a brief, uneventful bus journey, Irish was entering his home when his mother, having returned from the hospital, called to him "Patrick one of yer friends called round before, yer've not long missed him. Come and look at the beautiful flowers thee brought for me."

Irish walked into the living room and was immediately engulfed by the powerful, sweet scent of fresh-cut flowers.

"They're decent ma, who did yer say brought them?" he asked, casually glancing in the direction of the extensive mixed boquet, which his mother had placed in her best glass vase and stood on the small hearth in front of the two-bar electric fire, not presently in use due to the protracted heatwave.

"He didnt give his name, he was a big feller, in his early forties I'd say, had a real boxer's nose on him."

Irish began to feel uneasy with this description and his disquiet was confirmed a few moments later when his mother advised, "There's two cards with the flowers, one addressed t'me an one f'you."

He quickly opened the small envelope bearing his first name only, after briefly reading the general encouraging salutation to his mother, signed by the Mack brothers. Irish's card was not quiet so warm. 'To Patrick, Sorry to hear about your brother. Don't do anything fuckin' stupid, let it go.' Signed Niall and the Boys.

"Shall we put both cards on the mantlepiece Patrick?" his mother asked.

"No ma, you just put yours there, I'll keep hold of mine as a sort of reminder, if y'know what I mean?" he replied, stuffing the warning note into his jean's pocket.

"Okay son, suit yerself. Its good t'know yer've got genuine friends at times like this, don't y'think?"

Irish left the room without replying.

Friday 23rd July 1976

Sitting in the crowded lounge of The Eagle on another warm Friday evening, Irish was receiving drinks and well-meant commisserations from his former team mates.

"How's yer brother gettin' on Irish, any improvement?" Terry (H) asked, genuinely interested.

"Well, he hasn't got any worse, thank God but he's still in a coma and they're still tellin' us he's critical." Irish replied truthfully.

"'Ave the bizzies gripped any of those Ravens shitbags yet?" Johno asked.

"Nah, thee haven't not yet, there too busy fuckin' playin' with themselves, the useless bastards." Irish answered angrily, reflecting on his own recent encounter with DC Banks.

With *Silver Star* by The Four Seasons playing on the ever popular juke box, Blue returned from the bar carrying a tray of whiskeys and his usual supply of salted snacks. When they all had a shot glass in their hands containing a measure of the mellow amber spirit, they raised a toast to Irish's brother.

"Cheers and good luck t'Dermot!" Blue called out, acting as toastmaster.

Everyone threw back their warming drinks in one gulp, slamming their glasses back down upon the small circular tables at which they sat.

Brain was the first to speak while Irish lit a cigarette, one of an increasing number he was now resorting to each day, 'to calm his rage' he told himself in excuse. "Those Ravens Crew fuckers need teachin' a lesson. Weaver said the same ages ago an we should've listened to 'im then."

"Yeah, yer fuckin' dead right Brain." Tank agreed, adding, "A crew is gonna have t'go into their ground and give them a fuckin' good kickin', y'know warra mean?"

Similar views were expressed all round, which was exactly what Irish was hoping to hear, personally encouraging this sentiment as much as possible. As the evening progressed, their drinking keeping apace, the general consensus appeared to be confirmed as accepting urgent, violent repraisals by the old crew, was the only acceptable course of action. Just as 10CC's *I'm Mandy Fly Me* began to play on the juke box, Irish decided the time was right for him to recruit his friends to his planned enterprise, putting their alcohol fuelled verbal bravado to the test.

"So listen lads, we only need a small crew, no more than eight of us." he began, continuing, "We get tooled up good style, yeah, do maximum damage to these cunts right where thee live."

Terry (H) suddenly interrupted, "'Ang on Irish, are you sayin' we go into Ravens Hall, behind their fuckin' big walls?"

"Yeah I am, we put Brain 'ere keepin' dixie by the entrance then the rest of us grab some of their boys and really fuck them up, do a bit of cuttin'."

They all knew this was uncharacteristic for Irish to suggest such brutal action but equally they understood his motivation.

Terry (H) was the first to voice concerns about his plan, "'Ave yer thought this through, Irish? All it'll do is lead to their whole fuckin' team comin' onto the Crown lookin' for revenge, how are we gonna deal with that?"

Irish was a little phased by his old school friend's negativity but pressed on "Yeah that's right Terry, from what I've been hearin' and seein' it looks like Weaver was fuckin' spot on. Bring these cunts onto our ground, get the old team together again from The Bear, The Hounds, The Unicorn and The Heron and finish these no-marks f'good, end it in one last game." He took a lengthy draught of his Guinness and waited for their approbation. Sadly for Irish his suggested course of action was out of line with current thinking.

The diminutive boxing brothers known respectively as Ant One and Ant Two, who were usually the least vocal of the crew were now the first to raise objections and decline, Bobby Anton spoke for the pair, "Sorry Irish we'll 'ave t'let this one go. We've both got bouts comin' up an t'be honest mate, we don't need a fuckin' gang war kickin' off right now."

Irish nodded accepting his comments, "Okay, so that leaves us six, that's still enough to pull this off, yeah?"

Brain was not so sure, "Er... I don't think that's gonna work Irish. My eyesights fucked so I wouldn't be much use on dixie an am not really up for riskin' me other eye, yer understand?"

Tank quickly followed, "There yer are mate, five of us defo can't do this stunt, so yer best lettin' it go, until y'can come up with somethin' better."

Irish turned to Terry (H) and Johno seated on his left, "Any views lads, go or no go?"

"I'll have t'say no go, we've gorra load of work on at the farm I couldn't take a chance on gettin' injured at this time of year, y'know I only get paid by the day." Johno answered pragmatically.

Terry (H) cast the final vote, "Patrick, 'ave known yer all these years an I've gorra tell yer t'leave it, its not gonna 'appen. The days of The Eagle Crew leadin' the whole Crown Team into action are gone. Yer can't do this on yer own, so let it go. The bizzies are shit but give them a chance, thee might just do the business for once and grip these Ravens shitbags."

Irish did not respond and for a short interval none of the former companions spoke, listening to the sound of The Sensational Alex Harvey's *Boston Tea Party* on the juke box, enjoying their pints in silence. Blue's possible contribution seemed to be overlooked, or viewed as irrelevent.

Irish now turned to him, saying quietly, "Well at least I know you're with me Blue. Me an you can take on a few of those shit heads and leave them in a bad way, yeah?"

His corupulent friend stared down at his pint as if an appropriate answer could be found there. "Listen... er... am sorry like but... I've got t'think of Beryl and the twins y'see... if anythin' happened t'me... sorry Irish."

Irish finished his cigarette then drained the remaining third of his pint in a single swallow. He said nothing as he rose to his feet, put on his Harrington jacket and left the ale house.

Stepping out from the stifling pub into the warm night air of that unique British summer heatwave, Irish was confronted by the sight of Weaver directing his Juniors busily overpainting the inflammatory statements of the Ravens Crew, presently covering the library's façade.

"Alright Irish!" Weaver called to him, in an unusually friendly manner.

Irish crossed the road, walking towards the Heron Crew leader but intending to ignore him.

Weaver stepped into his path, "Didn't yer fuckin' hear me, I just let on to yer?"

Irish stopped and looked directly at the smiling psychopath, "Yeah, nice one Weaver, I've got things on me mind like, so no disrespect but I don't need any shit from you just now."

Weaver stopped smiling, "Alright, cunt, I was only gonna ask how yer brother's gettin' on in the hosie."

Irish was surprised by this seemingly normal behaviour from the hammer-wielding madman. "Sorry about that lad; he's not doin' too good, still wired up to all these fuckin' machines tryin' t'keep him alive but thanks for askin'." He paused then quickly changed the subject, "What are you boys up to anyway?"

Weaver answered his question first, "We're doin' what you Eagle wankers should've done, gettin' rid of this Ravens bollocks." Returning to his original question he continued, "Am sorry to hear about your Dermot, I've seen him about an I know he's not a player, just an ordinary lad. I've got brothers meself an they're not into the 'game' either, so I'd be really fucked off if some cunts jumped any one of them."

This was the most Irish had ever heard from Weaver and again he was uncertain how to respond, "Okay, well... er... thanks f'that. I'll see yer," he replied then made to walk on.

Weaver caught hold of his arm as he did asking, "So when are we goin' up there t'fuck these shitbags?"

A stunned Irish stopped in his tracks, turning back to fully face Weaver, "No one's goin' anywhere, I've just tried askin' that same fuckin' question in The Eagle but no one's up for it."

Weaver ran his hand down across his battered face, equally surprised, "Fuck them. I told yer before, I know where thee hang out an am yer man, whenever yer ready to do somethin' about it."

Irish was now looking at Weaver with increasing incredulity, "Did you hear what I said? Nobody else is interested, it'd be just you an me goin' into Ravens Hall on our own."

Weaver laughed loudly, "Like I said, whenever y'ready, let's do it."

Irish could not help but be impressed by the bravery of his words and taking them on face value replied, "Alright, thanks, how d' yer feel about tomorrer night?"

Again Weaver seemed delighted, "Fuckin' suits me fine, I've got nothin' else planned, an by the way we don't need t'go into Ravens Hall, I done a bit of that a couple of years ago with Jay Mac an Macca (G) an I wouldn't fancy doin' it again."

Irish appeared puzzled and Weaver enlightened him accordingly, "Listen I've got connections with The Bear Crew an I've been askin' them a few questions. Thee tell me the cunts who done your Dermot were led by Smidge, he's the kid brother of Smigger, a nasty little shit who's tryin t'build a rep. Anyway him an his crew hang around in the arl cemetery with some of their slags, there's probably no more than ten of them. If we do the job right me an you could 'ave them off, what d'yer say?"

Irish's fog of confussion was completely dispersed, instead a brilliant light of crystal clarity illuminated his seething brain, Weaver had presented him with a simple, obvious solution. "Weaver, everyone knows you're a mad bastard and an evil cunt, I can't think of anyone else I'd rather have with me. Tomorrer night it is."

The crazed psychopath grinned slyly, pleased with Irish's assessment of his vicious character, "See yer here tomorrer around eight, make sure yer tooled up, 'cause I'm looking forward to bleedin' some Ravens."

Irish strolled off entering the road behind the shops heading towards his home, smiling with wicked delight.

Saturday 24th July 1976
Standing once again by his comotose brother's hospital bedside, watching his assisted breathing rise and fall, Irish was resolute in his chosen course of action, whatever may result from this. He squeezed his silent sibling's hand as a farewell gesture before leaving.

"Thee'll all be sorry tonight Dermot, don't you worry." Irish promised, though he knew in reality, violence was something that his elder brother totally abhorred.

By the early afternoon, Irish, having returned to the Crown Estate, paid a brief visit to his neighbouring ex-team mate Blue. After walking the short distance to the opposite end of the street where they both lived, he rang the bell on the neatly painted front door of Blue's parents' council house.

"Alright Irish, everythin' okay mate?" Blue asked.

"Yeah I'm sound mate. I just wanna quick word with yer." Irish replied.

"'Ave yer given up yer mad idea of goin' after the Ravens Crew?" Blue enquired hopefully.

"Not really Blue that's why I'm 'ere talkin' to you now." Irish answered cryptically, much to his friend's alarm.

"Er... y'did hear what I was sayin' last night didn't yer... 'cause I really can't go with yer..." Blue announced nervously.

Irish laughed, "No need t'shit yer kecks Blue. Am talkin' to you now because I'm goin' *without* yer. I just wanna ask yer t'keep an eye on me ma, in case anything goes pear-shaped t'night."

"Fuck, Irish, don't do this mate, yer can't go on yer own, yer'll be joinin' your Dermot in the fuckin' hosie." Blue advised, genuinelly concerned.

"That's alright then 'cause am not goin' alone, Weaver's comin' with me." Irish advised with a grin.

"Tell me yer fuckin' jokin', that's like takin' a friggin' mad dog with yer." Blue warned.

"Good, I fuckin' hope so,'cause that's just what I'm gonna need t'take this crew in the cemetery tonight."

Blue tried again to warn Irish against his seemingly insane plan. "No one can control that crazy cunt, once he kick's off he fuckin' loses it." His warning had the opposite effect.

"Blue, quit while yer ahead, the more y'say, the more I'm certain Weaver, the Mad Hatter is just the *right* cunt t'take. See yer." Irish advised finally then turned and walked away to his home, to prepare himself for the coming action.

With barely quarter of an hour remaining before his eight o'clock library rendezvous, Irish was making the final adjustments to his chosen kit for the night. After applying a finishing top coat of Kiwi oxblood polish to his cherry red Airwair, he was rapidly buffing them with a soft rag, bringing them to their gleaming best, while listening to Simaryp's *Skinhead Moonstomp* playing on the record player in his bedroom. He stood up and moved in front of the wall hung rectangular mirror, checking his appearance in his Levi's denim jacket, which still bore his Crown Team emblem of a hollow crown outline containing the word Skins at its centre, drawn with a black marker pen across its shoulders, just below the collar. His twenty-four inch parallel Fleming's jeans, with bleached half-inch turn up, supported by black clasticated braces of the same width, were set at just the right height to almost fully reveal his Dr Marten's 1460 classics. A plain white tee-shirt worn under his braces and denim jacket completed his uniform. Satisfied with his look he reviewed his choice of primary and secondary weapons, as he had done numerous times already that evening. The heavy brass knuckle-duster, given to him by Tommy (S) was in his left-hand inside pocket and his old wooden-handled craft knife was in his right. Both were close-range 'tools' and to supplement these he had rummaged about in his late father's small garden shed for something that would possibly extend his striking capacity, without being too obtrusive when hidden within his clothing.

"This'll do just fine." he announced on finding a two-foot length of old lead pipe replete with a sweat-jointed, brass 'T' fitting, amongst a pile of miscellaneous plumbing odds and ends, making a perfect improvised mace or war-hammer. 'Some Ravens skulls are gettin' cracked with this tonight.' he thought, pushing the weapon inside the back of his jeans, securing it lengthwise with his braces, completely obscured beneath his denim jacket.

"See yers!" he called to his two sisters, whom he had charged with minding their youngest brother Sean, "When ma gets in from the hosie, tell 'er I probably won't be back t'night, am gonna be stayin' over at one of me mates."

Shortly, after passing by Blue's residence, he turned into the central road heading towards the library. Weaver had not yet arrived and Irish sat alone on the coninuous concrete windowsill, lighting a cigarette, staring blankly into the middle distance, clearing his mind in readiness.

"Hey lad, giz a ciggie." he heard a female voice calling to him from his right. Without turning his head or acknowledging her presence in any way, other than a cursory reply of "Piss off," Irish took a long drag of his cigarette and then blew two consecutive smoke rings.

"Go 'ed lad, giz a ciggie, don't be fuckin' sly." another voice of the same gender and similar age called in response.

Irish casually turned and looked in their direction. Both speakers were girls younger than his own sisters, 'The next generation of Molly Brown's or even Little Jane's' he thought, dismayed. Dressed in high waisted Oxford bags with large turn ups that reached down over their stilt-like platform shoes and wearing colourful open necked, deep collared satin blouses, they looked as if they were on their way to a school disco, rather than preparing for an evening's scrounging session, bartering favours for tobacco and alcohol. Their excessive, plastered on make up of dark brown eye shadow, thick mascara and ruby red lipstick gave them a garish clown-like appearance, the exact opposite of the grown up sophisticated look they had been hoping to achieve.

"Girls, go home will yers, its gettin' late, yer shouldn't even be out at this time." Irish warned genuinely concerned for their safety.

They ignored his well-meant advice and the original cigarette seeker asked, "Are yer gonna give us a fuckin' ciggie or what?"

"No I'm not, now go home, there's all kinds of fuckin' wierdos round 'ere and thee'll be comin' out t'play soon." Irish tried once more in vain.

"Fuck you arl man, keep yer ciggies, like y'said there'll be plenty of other fellers we can ask." the second girl responded angrily.

It was a clear case of the old addage of 'speak of the devil and he's sure to appear.' Even as they completed their exchanges, Weaver arrived at the scene.

"Alright Irish, very nice too, good of yer t'lay on a bit of entertainment before we gerroff." Clothed in an almost mirror image of Irish, except for a dark blue and white checked, short-sleeved Ben Sherman under his denim jacket and his personal preference of a pair of black Airwair, rather than the ubiquitous cherry red variety, Weaver was primed and ready for action in any form. He quickly slipped his arms around the narrow waists of both girls, slyly groping their bottoms in the process with his wandering hands and pulled them both to him. "Right girls, yer'll have t'fight over me an then the loser gets grumpy arse Irish. Am sorry but I need t'save some energy, otherwise I'd fuck the arses off the pair of yer." the crazed psychopath announced grinning broadly.

Both girls struggled free from him, horrified at the prospect, "Eee, fuck off yer dirty git, we know you Weaver, yer a pig." one of them called.

"Oink, oink." he replied, much amused then bent down, making as if to sniff their bottoms like a randy swine. Both girls shrieked and ran away from the scene as fast as they could manage on their disabling platform footwear.

Irish laughed, "Fuck me Weaver, yer've deffo got a way with the birds. I rememeber Jay Mac tellin' us about a wild night out in town that he had with yer, one summer and yer fuckin' mad antics. Well at least yer done better than me in scarin' those two off, I don't think they'll be hangin' round 'ere cadgin' ciggies for a while."

Weaver was nonplussed, "Their fuckin' loss, if I hadn't have been lookin' forward t'this night and bleedin' a few Ravens, I'd 'ave knobbed the pair of them in the alley, whether they wanted it or not."

Irish stared at the mad man in disbelief, Weaver remained an unfathomable enigma of ever changing mood, his one constant being his unpredictability.

"Ready for the game, tooled up are yer?" he asked Irish.

"Yeah, I've got me knuckle duster, me blade and a nice little surprise, tucked behind me braces that should do a bit of fuckin' damage." Irish advised.

"Nice one Irish, that's what I like t'hear, I've brought me Stanley for a bit of slashin', 'Thor' for hammerin' their teeth an' noses and an extra family tool from me arl feller, his lead cosh. Should be a good result." Weaver observed.

"I didn't know y'called yer toffee hammer 'Thor', when did yer start doin' that?" Irish asked curiously.

"Well t'be honest it was down to Devo (S) an Jay Mac, when I heard that Devo called his blade 'Fritz', I thought I'd have a decent name for me own weapon, anyway y'know what Jay Mac was like for those fuckin' Yank comics, he showed me some about this really strong cunt called Thor, that fucked everyone with his hammer, so I went for that." Weaver advised with his usual sly smile, adding, "Let's gerrup there, am really fuckin' buzzin f'this one."

The old municipal cemetery entered Crown Estate territory at its most south westerly point, just a distance of three bus stops from the Eagle public house. It had been there long before any of its surrounding, grim, utilitarian, overspill housing developments had ever been considered by the worthy luminaries of the city's planning office. Originally serving only the sparse rural farming community, then as an increasingly busy final resting place for the exponentially growing Victorian population, whose spectacular infant mortality figures could only be negated by the phenomenal numbers of surviving children born to the fashionably large families of the era; during the second half of the twentieth century it had begun to experience a decline in business and material upkeep. Consequently ancient simple rustic headstones competed for space amidst elaborate mausoleums, displaying appropriately mournful statuary, principally in the form of stone angels weeping for lost souls, evidencing the Victorian obsession with death.

Since the gangs decided to choose this eerie setting for sporadic encounters, both violent and sexual, the entire wall enclosed hallowed grounds were subject to extensive vandalism. Everywhere were signs of the different teams' occassional presence from graffiti to broken grave stones and the scattered mixed detritus of a throw-away society. Most people, unless they had specific business, such as attending a funeral or a loved ones grave, wisely kept away from the place and never entered there.

It was dusk when Irish and Weaver climbed over the moss covered walls, accessing the cemetery as the late July sun disappeared below the western horizon. A low thin mist hung between the weeping willows and tall yews, partially veiling their movement as they crept towards the centre, crouching down, and passing between the headstones.

"There thee are, the cunts." Weaver advised on spotting their enemy's position revealed by the glowing tips of their cigarettes and herbal joints, even though they were still many yards distant. Creeping nearer, the sounds of their excited conversations drifted on a light breeze that was now blowing, confirming to the hunter duo that this was their prey. As yet only partial snippets of conversation could be heard though clearly their general mood was one of celebration; clinking glass bottles further suggested a relaxed party mood. Within twenty yards of the Raven revellers, Irish and Weaver came to a halt to assess the situation.

"Are you any good with numbers Weaver?" Irish asked sarcastically in a low voice, adding "'Cause if that's your idea of 'no more than ten,' yer've gorra real fuckin' problem."

At least two dozen of their enemy crew were present for this night's graveside gathering, changing the odds against the Crown pair dramatically.

"Fuck you, who cares how many there is after what thee done t'yer brother. Anyway a good few of them are birds, so don't shit out." Weaver whispered in angry reply.

Suitably admonished Irish said no more for a few moments, trying to formulate a plan of attack in these altered circumstances.

Weaver was growing impatient asking, "Come on, how d'yer wanna fuckin' play this?"

"Well, I think surroundin' them's not gonna fuckin' work." Irish replied.

Both Crown players slowly moved forward a few yards until they could clearly hear what was being said.

Franny, Smidge's lieutenant was standing alongside his leader on a raised ornamental grave site, surrounded by funery decoration; he was currently holding court... "Yeah, did yer see the way that Irish prick's head popped when Smidge stamped on it? Fuckin' hell, talk about blood, it was fuckin' ace."

A smiling Smidge took over M.C. duties, "Nice one Franny but I can't take all the fuckin' credit. You cut 'im good style while we was holdin' him down. I tell yer what, some of you girls couldn't 'ave screamed louder, what a fuckin' blast."

There was an outbreak of spontaneous cheering then the conversation returned to crediting a catalogue of the teams' individual assaults upon Irish's brother. All thoughts of strategy fled from Irish's raging brain. He was about to leap from their concealed position, ready to attack the entire crew single handed, when Weaver caught his arm, "Wait a fuckin' minute, crazy arse, look who's comin' our way," he whispered, watching as Franny casually strolled towards them unzipping his jeans.

Stopping just in front of the headstone behind which Weaver was crouching, Franny pulled out his member and began a lengthy urination on the grave of the resting deceased. Not caring whether this was someone's mother, father, sister, brother or child, totally lacking any respect he pissed upon their aged memorial and beloved memory until, with a start, mid-stream he spied the wicked glint of Weaver's evil eye.

"What the fuck...?" he began then was instantly silenced by Irish's strong knuckle-duster encased right hand clamping around his mouth, with the razor sharp blade of his craft knife pressed painfully into his trachea.

"Shut your fuckin' mouth you piece of shit or I'll slit yer throat and slice off yer tiny prick."

Franny wisely did as instructed, allowing himself to be dragged to the ground then pulled behind the broad trunk of an ancient yew. Irish's fevered brain had formulated a plan, even while executing it.

"Weaver, you circle over t'the opposite side from me then when y'get me signal start lashin' stones at the shits, make a load of noise like there's a good few of us, yeah?" he ordered now fully in control.

"How will I know when t'start?" Weaver asked.

"Just listen out, yer'll fuckin' know alright." Irish advised with a sinister grin.

Keeping low, Weaver quickly scrambled away on his circuitous route around the edge of the celebrating Ravens Crew, whilst they continued imbibing and indulging their other passions.

After waiting several minutes for Weaver to reach his position, Irish began his painful revenge. "Cut my fuckin' brother did yer, had *him* callin' out for yer t'stop, is that right? Well bitch yer gonna be doin' a bit of that screamin' yerself when I take me hand away."

Instantly he slashed the terrified youth downward across his exposed penis, causing him to shriek in excruciating agony. Again Irish whisked his craft knife across Franny's privates and groin then once more until that area was a bloody, mutilated mess. With each biting stroke the Ravens player let out horrific cries of pain, completely freezing the rest of his crew into a static tableau of fear.

"What the fuckin' hell's going on." Smidge called out.

Irish encouraged Franny to reply, scripting his exact words. "Please help me Smidge, please. Thee've got me over 'ere, loads of them, they're cuttin' me dick off."

Even as that blood curdling message was being absorbed, Weaver, realising that this was his signal, began throwing stones and gravel from his position roaring, "Crown Team! Let's get these shits!"

As soon as he had delivered his threat he moved to another location and repeated his performance.

No longer having any use for the sobbing Franny, Irish decided to silence him, for the foreseeable future. "Okay dickless, yer can shut yer screamin' now." he advised before repeatedly pounding the agonised youth's jaw bone until it fractured with a sickening crack. "Lie there and bleed, yer little fuck." Irish said coldly then called "Crown Team! Do these Ravens queers!"

The icy grip of fear had produced two distinctly opposite effects on Smidge and his crew. Most of the females, none of whom were or had ever been Skinhead Girls and some of the younger males, ran about in blind panic wanting only to flee the scene and escape. Smidge and his inner coterie of chronological peers remained frozen, impotent, unable to decide on a course of action.

Finally Smidge revealed some leadership quality, choosing to send a sortie in Irish's direction to investigate, "Micky (B), Robbo and Jamesy in y'go. Find Franny and see how many Crown cunts thee really is over there."

Reluctantly at first the trio accepted their orders, sprinting forward to where the unfortunate Franny had chosen to relieve himself. The blood crazed Irish lay in wait for them craft knife in his left hand, knuckle duster on his right whilst also clutching his lead and brass war hammer with that scarlet paw.

"Fuckin' hell, look what the sick bastards 'ave done t'Franny." Jamsie announced horror struck as the trio stared down at their bloody, barely conscious crew mate.

"Can yer speak... Franny? How many of them was thee?" Robbo asked, leaning forward, straining to hear a reply.

"Just me!" Irish roared, leaping out from behind the broad, rough bark enclosed yew, cracking the questioner across the forehead with two rapid, powerful strokes. Jamsie drew his own Stanley knife, slashing wildly in panic, barely missing Irish's left upper arm. In one lightning fast movement Irish closed the distance between them, coming inside his opponents range deliberately, booting him in the testicles and smashing him hard in the mouth with his metal-assisted fist.

Mickey (B) did not have the stomach for the fight, unwisely turning his back on the furious Irish, running a few paces forward, shouting "Smidge! Over 'ere, there's only one of them...!"

Before he made another step, Irish's warhammer had already struck him on the back of his skull, dropping him to his knees to receive a wild battering about his head and shoulders.

A thin sickle moon provided the only illumination within the cemetery's dark confines, revealing the menacing, motionless silhouette of the vengeful Irish, glaring with burning eyes towards Smidge and his stunned crew.

"There's only one of them, only fuckin' *one*?" Smidge called out in disbelief still unable to trust his ears at the sheer audacity of this daring assault.

The element of surprise was gone, Weaver knew the moment had arrived that he had been anticipating with an almost sexual yearning, "'Ey bollock'ed, make that only two of them." he roared, then formally announced his presence, "I'm Weaver an am gonna fuckin' do yer, I'm Weaver!"

Both he and Irish came running from their opposite positions directly towards the Ravens Crew, taking the fight to them. Smidge felt fear's debilitating icy grip close even tighter about his spine, calling out, "Get round me, make a fuckin' circle, their comin' for me."

A spell of inertia appeared to be cast upon the Ravens players, once they had formed a defensive ring about their cowardly leader, gifting the advantage once more to Irish and Weaver, who crashed into their circular wall almost simultaneously from two opposing sides. Impelled by the dynamic of murderous rage, Irish wreaked havoc amongst these largely unarmed youths, who had been expecting an evening of drinking, drug-taking and casual sex in their home ground, anything but that which was now occurring.

Whilst Irish hammered and punched a bloody swathe through their ranks, all the while with one goal only in mind to reach Smidge at the circle's centre, Weaver unleashed his own inner demon, though with no other objective than to revel in the mayhem and blood letting.

Smidge called out in panic, "Don't let them get t'me, for fuck's sake stop them!"

Irish was struck with a dark brown glass ale bottle across the forehead, opening a jagged scarlet gash but this did little to slow his momentum. Some of the injured defenders fell away from the action, wanting to take no more part in the violence.

Smidge shouted to one of them, "Degsy, fuckin' run over to Ravens Hall, get our Smigger out the ale house with his boys!"

Degsy was the Ravens crews' equivalent of Jay Mac or Johno, the acknowledged top runners of the Crown Team and was gone in an instant, leaping over headstones as if competing in a hurdles athletic event.

"Come 'ed, there's only fuckin' two of them, gerra fuckin' grip on them." Smidge ordered. His confidence beginning to return, as he watched his despatch runner disappear into the night, heading for his home estate to summon their elite relief. Stood in the heart of the mêlée Smidge was finding that giving an order and having it achieved, were two entirely different entities. Though both Irish and Weaver were now bloodied from several facial wounds, no one had yet managed to deliver a decisive blow, or sieze hold of the wild pair.

Weaver had been as good as his word, breaking noses and cracking teeth wherever he struck with his toffee hammer or cosh; Irish thumped faces, torsos and limbs both with his metal encased fist and metalic 'mace.' It was the difference between pitting raw recruits against battle-hardened troops.

Both Crown players were veterans of many bloody combat encounters, these Ravens novices, three or four years their junior, were fodder to their experienced martial prowess. Though undeserving of their loyalty, Smidge's own officer corps, however, held firm bearing the brunt of Irish and Weaver's relentless, almost mechanical assault, encouraging some of the walking wounded to return to their aid. Irish was finally siezed around the waist and neck as several Ravens Juniors struggled to restrain him; Weaver proved a more difficult beast to harness, breaking free numerous times until eventually, almost upon Smidge, he too was overcome by sheer weight of numbers.

It had been a glorious effort, evidenced by more than a dozen bloody casualties lying in their wake but the Crown team mates had failed to secure their primary target, their mission objective was unachieved as yet.

"Get your fuckin' hands off me, I'm Weaver." the downed mad man warned, restrained as he was with considerable difficulty by six struggling Ravens Juniors.

Irish was similarly secured with one of his half dozen captors, choking him in a determined headlock.

Smidge now felt confident enough to leave the safety of the living pallisade, formed by his personal bodyguard. "Gripped 'ey? On your fuckin' knees, yer pair of shits." he began, smirking, "You cheeky bastards, comin' in 'ere to our ground, thinkin' yers could 'ave us off? Well yers are fucked now."

Irish stared up at the grinning youth with his long feather-cut hair, his sly, weasely features and cruel mouth. "You're the one who's gonna be fucked before this night's over." he warned.

Smidge lashed out, booting Irish's already scarlet-stained face, drawing a spray of blood and sweat from him. "You're that fuckin' Irish prick, it's you, you're the one we was lookin' for!" Smidge exclaimed astonished, asking, "Who was that other poor cunt that we jumped then?"

Irish glared directly at him with an intense gaze of pure hatred "It was me brother, you little shit and yer gonna fuckin' pay t'night f'what yous have done t'him."

Again Smidge booted Irish in the face, following up with two straight punches, "Fuck me this is even better, two thick Irish cunts for the price of one, brilliant." he announced triumphantly.

Just at that moment the Ravens Crew's elation was disturbed by their own Senior Team leader, Smigger and four of his closest companions. They pushed their way to the front of the assembly so that Smigger may view their Crown captives and address the crowd.

At six foot tall and of stocky build, also with shoulder length, feather cut, dark hair, similar to his brother, apart from his flattened nose, received as a result of being struck by a petrified tree branch, used as an impromptu club by Jay Mac whilst he was being pursued through the old cemetery, one frozen winter's night several years earlier, there was nothing particularly noticeable either in appearance or ability about Smidge's elder sibling. He was a capable scrapper and had been rising through the ranks of Ravens command under his own merits but achieved sole leadership status by default when his two preceeding Seniors were arrested for violent assault and imprisoned. Smigger quickly established a reputation for sickening brutality, which helped maintain his position, deterring would-be challengers and inspiring his younger brother to emulate him. Dressed in a dark brown, three-quarter length leather jacket, over a two-coloured patchwork jumper, wide flared jeans and wearing a pair of black 1460's Airwair, he now stood before the two subdued Crown 'prisoners', with his four grinning subordinates.

"Fuck me, the mighty Weaver brought down by a crew of Ravens Juniors, wait till this gets round the ale houses." Smigger announced delighted. "You fuckin' Crown Team pricks 'ave been a pain in the arse f'years but that's all over. Yers need t'get wise, it's our time now, the Ravens are on top, you're fuckin' finished." He smiled slyly reaching into his brown leather jacket and produced a simple unadorned, dark green handled kitchen knife, "See I've gorra blade meself, only we don't give our weapons names like you Crown queers but d'yer know what shit heads, it cuts really good just the same."

The Ravens cheered their Senior team leader and jeered their helpless captives, Smigger was jubilant leaning forward, snatching hold of Weaver's wild mane, pulling his head upwards, "Right mad arse, am gonna start with you first. I'll just take *one* of yer eyes so y'can watch me workin' on you an yer dumb fuckin' mate. What is it you always say... oh yeah I know, well let's change that a bit... I'm Smigger an I done this to yer... I'm Smigger." he called out plagerising Weaver's own dread proclaimation, about to plunge the tip of his glistening blade into the crazed psychopath's right eye.

The perfectly thrown duck egg sized spherical stone that struck him fully in the centre of his forehead, like a piece of grape shot fired from a cannon, dropped him unconscious to the damp earth at his feet.

"Crown Team!" Tommy (S) bellowed, bursting forth from out of the thin grey mist, like a terrifying apparition, swirling his short, heavy-metal shank dog leash as a medieval flail, charging into the very centre of the stunned Ravens crew. It was time for one last throw of the dice, as the heroic, former Crown Team leader entered the arena, alone, outnumbered, against the odds. Wearing his full kit of Levi's denim jacket, Fleming's twenty-four inch parallel jeans and gleaming cherry red Airwair, the original Skinhead was back in his environment at the bloody hub of a savage encounter.

"It's that fuckin' Tommy Southern, I thought he was dead." one of the fallen Smigger's retinue observed, in almost reverential recognition. All four came at him at once, hoping against established wisdom that they may have a slim chance of overcoming the legendary fighter. It was a naive hope, Tommy moved with the grace of a panther, possessed the strength of a bear and the heart of a lion, every shot was on target, every strike hit home. The first of Smigger's crew lunged with his flick-knife, whisking past Tommy's head to the right, only to receive two powerfully acurate blows from the solid steel clasp at the end of the flailing chain. One caught him fully in the open mouth breaking his two front teeth; the second struck his right eye, filling the blinded orb with blood.

Whilst that casualty staggered about clutching at his face, hindering rather than helping his three companions, the former Crown Team leader launched into two of them. Both were lashed, punched and kicked in rapid sequence, with Tommy employing his usual economy of effort to achieve maximum damage, yet using minimal movement to avoid being hit himself. Only one tactical difference was glaringly obvious by its omission from his usual arsenal, he was not bringing his famous, devestating head butt into play. The fourth of Smigger's peers noticed this reluctance and, remembering the reports of this Crown Team Senior's terrible head injuries, received in a final monumental battle with the Kings Team, decided to strike at that weakened, vulnerable region with the short wooden club that he carried as his primary weapon, shaped like a marlin spike, personally crafted on a school centre lathe some years prior.

"'Ave that y'Crown bastard!" he shouted, thumping Tommy (S) across his previously fractured cranium.

Momentarily it appeared that the 'war machine' had been struck a decisive blow but a temporary reduction in the pace of his relentless attack, was all that resulted. Swinging his metal flail above his head Tommy leapt forward lashing the steel leash whip-like in front of him, bringing it to coil tightly about his adversary's throat. Yanking the choking, ensnared male towards him, Tommy projected his own brick of a fist hard into his face, bursting his nose and splitting his lip on impact.

With the Crown leader delivering a master-class in martial prowess, the concentration and focus of Irish and Weaver's guards wandered, leading to a slackening of their grip. Sensing the time had arrived for them to return to the fray both Crown captives broke free, regained their weapons and renewed their assault on Smidge's crew.

"Let's 'ave it you fuckin' queers!" Weaver roared, charging once more into the breach, with Irish alongside, lashing out at all within range to devastating effect.

Their Seniors were downed and their ranks broken, the Ravens spirit soon followed suit, flying from the remaining combatants, swifter than their namesakes nesting in the treetops high above. A terrified Smidge watched the decimation of his own crew and the Ravens Seniors, with one thought only growing in his squirming brain, self-preservation, he must escape. Pushing his injured team mates out of his way and into the path of Weaver and Irish, he fled from the scene, racing for the ancient perimeter walls, hoping to reach the main road and the safety of Ravens Hall beyond.

Irish had just despatched his last foe with a skull splitting crack of his 'warhammer' as he spied the fleeing Smidge. Blood boiling with rage at the prospect of losing his prey when he was almost within his grasp, Irish set off in reckless pursuit.

"Am comin' for yer, you shitbag!" he called, foolishly wasting vital breath that he would need for the chase.

Leaping headstones, ducking under branches, running for his life, Smidge sprinted on along the familiar route, through the mist-shrouded cemetery, desperate to reach its outer edge. Irish came on with lungs bursting, regretting with each stride his recent increase in nicotine intake as he saw the younger, fitter man widening the gap between them. He was spurred on to one final effort but it was too late, Smidge was already scrambling over the low wall and about to escape. As a dismayed Irish reached that same spot he let out an agonised roar of deep pained frustration.

Smidge turned and laughed, racing out across the dual carriageway, raising two fingers to Irish, calling back "Yer too slow, yer fucker...!" He was cut off mid-sentence by the huge, inbound articulated vehicle that ploughed into him with its full accelerated weight.

The speeding truck that had to make its delivery deadline at the Liverpool Docks was unable to stop, despite the desperate driver's best efforts. With one almighty thump Smidge was struck and thrown into the air, landing remade in broken, spastic form many yards distant. The sadistic youth would soon be rushed to the same critical emergency unit as his kindly victim had been taken the previous Saturday night and still remained seven days later. For a few moments Irish stayed perfectly still where he was standing, just inside the aged moss-covered walls, staring dispationately at the bleeding wreck of his enemy's body then turned and strolled away from the ugly tableau.

Irish did not have his revenge but his brother had been avenged, the blood feud was satisfied, the blood lust sated. As the veil of red mist that had hung before his eyes for almost a week, clouding his brain began to dissipate a serene state of calmness washed over him, restoring rational thought. He walked back towards the centre of the cemetery, threading his way through the headstones he had so recently leapt over without regard.

Even as Irish approached the cemetery's centre, he could hear the moans and groans of the walking wounded, occasionally interspersed with agonised shrieks of pain as Weaver continued to torment the vanquished Ravens, repeatedly reminding them, unnecessarily, that he was the one who had inflicted this retribution upon them.

"'Aven't you had enough for one night?" Irish asked as he watched the Heron leader striking out teeth from the fallen Smigger who had barely regained consciousness before Weaver was upon him with his trusty hammer, performing his cruel dentistry. Smigger's lieutenants had continued to endure the wrath of Tommy (S) after Irish had raced off in pursuit of

Smidge and they had made their own escape shortly after, abandoning their leader to his fate.

Weaver glanced momentarily towards Irish without deviating from the task in hand, warning, "Don't ever fuckin' disturb me when I'm enjoyin' meself, 'ave told yer about that before."

Looking about at the bloody carnage that had resulted from this night's clash, although Irish expected to feel some grim satisfaction from this, in stark contrast he was surprised to find an unpleasant nausea beginning to crawl into the pit of his stomach. He was experiencing a paradoxical disquiet at achieving such an ugly victory; Irish now wanted to be gone from this place. Scanning the immediate area he searched for any sign of the illustrious Crown Team leader, Tommy (S) so as to thank him personally.

"Where's Tommy got to Weaver, I can't see' im anywhere around?" he asked.

"Y'too late, he's already fucked off. Y'missed out there, yer should've seen 'im go, once he battered Smigger's boys he went into the whole Ravens Crew, until any of them still standin' legged it.., fuckin' ace." Weaver advised smiling slyly, finally allowing the dentally challenged Smigger to collapse back to the damp earth, with some few teeth remaining. "Am finished 'ere so we might as well gerroff, unless yer wanna do a bit of torturin' yerself." Weaver added as a generous gesture.

"Nah, am alright thanks Weaver, am not a sick fuck like you but thanks anyway." Irish replied, anxious to leave without further delay.

Weaver laughed, pleased with the 'compliment.' "Alright soft shite, suit yerself, don't say I didn't offer yer the chance, come 'ed."

Both Crown players strolled away into the thickening mist without a backward glance.

The Ravens reputation was in tatters, soon the lightning fast bush telegraph system would transmit its Chinese whispers exaggerating exponentially the nature of this Crown trio's victory, pouring scorn on their vastly numerically superior enemys' pathetic efforts, effectively removing them from the list of serious contenders for the elusive, prestigious title of Top Team.

After exiting the cemetery Irish and Weaver strolled down towards their own sector of the Crown Estate. As they did Irish asked "I wonder how the fuck Tommy knew about us goin' up t'do the Ravens Crew tonight. Did he say anythin' before he gorroff?"

Weaver thought for a few moments then answered, "Yeah, he said, thanks for the exercise and to thank yer mate Blue for the invite."

Irish laughed, "Blue! The sneaky fuck, he was the only one who knew where we were goin' and that it was just us two. He must've give Tommy the word." He paused then added, "Thank fuck f'that or we'd have been shafted."

Weaver turned sharply towards him, "What the fuck are you talkin' about yer cheeky cunt? I was just waitin' for the right moment then I was gonna take that blade off Smigger and shove it right up his arse, I didn't need Tommy's help, I don't fuckin' need anyone." After a few minutes and, on calming down to some extent, Weaver asked, "Did yer manage t'catch that Smidge shit house, when yer ran after 'im?"

"Nah, he got over the wall an out into the road." Irish replied honestly.

"So the little turd got away after all?" Weaver exclaimed dismayed.

"No, I didn't say he gorraway, not from the fuckin' big lorry that twatted into 'im and spread 'im all over the road, he didn't." Irish replied with a bitter smile.

"Fuck, that's a shame, I'd really liked to 'ave seen that meself." Weaver observed, disappointedly.

Irish did not respond.

For the remainder of their journey neither of them spoke. Finally, as they arrived at the central library, Irish broke the uncomfortable silence, "Listen Weaver... I, er... really appreciate what yer've done... so... er... thanks."

Weaver glanced at him with his usual grim expression, responding, "Forget it, if yer hadn't of asked me, I probably would've gone on me own. Those Ravens shit bags needed bringin' down, see yer."

With that he turned and strolled away, heading onward to the lower part of the bleak estate, to the rundown tenement block where he lived.

It was close to midnight when Irish entered his own street and passed by Blue's residence. Noticing a low light was still turned on in the living room Irish decided to knock, thank his friend for what he had done and ask him for one more favour.

Blue answered the door almost as soon as Irish had pressed the bell, "Thank God f'that, yer still 'ere. I was worried I'd 'ave t'tell yer ma y'was in the fuckin' hosie with your Dermot." he announced clearly relieved.

"Alright Blue, I know what yer did goin' an tellin' Tommy (S) about t'night. I just wanna say thanks; we'd have been well and truly fucked without him turnin' up when he did." Irish advised in spite of Weaver's earlier objections.

"No problem mate, I ran up to The Unicorn after yer left here an found Tommy (S) in there. When I told 'im what you was plannin' to do, he just gorrup an left, wirrout sayin' anythin'. For a minute I thought he was pissed off an was gonna jib it." Blue informed.

Irish laughed, "Fuckin' hell that must've been some sight, you runnin' up t'The Unicorn."

Blue also laughed, then noticing Irish's still weeping head wound, said "Irish yer not lookin' too good mate, that fuckin' cut needs seein' to, probably needs a few stitches, I think we'd better be gettin' yer off down the hosie after all."

"Alright Florence Nightingale, whatever you say. I only called t'thank yer an ask if I could kip in yours tonight, I don't want me ma seein' me like this." Irish answered with a grin.

"Yeah, that'll be okay but we better get y'head sorted first. I can't have yer fuckin' bleedin' all over the furniture, Beryl would burst the pair of us, even Tommy (S) couldn't help there."

Irish smiled, acknowledging that Blue was speaking only part in jest.

Chapter 7

Them Never Love Poor Marcus

July-August 1976

Joe Shultz was sitting reading the sports pages of his *New York Times* newspaper, smoking a cigarette and relaxing, as best he could on the cramped subway train conveying him to his home in the Bronx. 'At least I've gotta seat.' he thought smugly, exhaling a cloud of blue-grey smoke, casually glancing up at the ever-changing strap-hangers, who stood uncomfortably waiting to reach their own destinations.

He returned his mind to analysing the performance of the Yankees in the World Series and, studying the football pre-season free agent acquisitions of both his team, the Jets and their same city rivals, the Giants. At forty-four years of age, built like a Sherman tank and possessing a bristling silver-grey crew cut, he was a solid citizen, both physically and morally, having served his country in Korea and Vietnam, determined to confront the Red Menace wherever it raised its Bolshevik head.

Beyond 125th Street the carriage began to empty to some extent and when Joe next looked up to check his bearings, five new travelling companions had joined him. Aged in their early to mid-twenties, uniformly dressed in sleeveless, black leather waistcoats over grey or white capped sleeved tee-shirts, tight fitting, leather, flared trousers and heavy biker boots bearing chain straps across the instep, they all were bedecked in a glittering selection of silver or gold chains, rings and other individual items of jewellery. They were unshaven, displaying a variety of facial hair fashions, from several days stubble to full beards, all were bald headed either by stylistic choice or natural design. Shouting, swearing, pushing each other about, they smelled of alcohol, drugs and sex. Four of them had local New York accents but one, the tallest and apparent leader, spoke with a distinctly different tonality, enunciation and inflection.

Joe and the other civilian pasengers wisely ignored their increasingly boisterous antics, either by choosing to study their papers and magazines, or some fascinating spot on the grimy floor.

"C'mon boyo, give it up." the non-native New Yorker demanded, in the middle of a heated wrestling contest with the owner of a dark, drooping moustache and lengthy goatee. Catching hold of the younger man by the back of his head, he began to forcefully kiss him open mouthed, using his intrusive tongue enthusiastically, whilst groping his bottom and groin with equal vigour.

Joe cleared his throat noisily, shuffling his broadsheet newspaper at the same time. The amorous leader ceased his passionate embrace; the deliberate gesture of uncomfortable embarrassement catching his attention. He leaned across to the source of objection, asking, "Are you alright there granddad, did yer have somethin' yer wanted t'say?"

Joe ignored him, continuing to read his newspaper, much to the questioner's annoyance, "I asked you a fuckin' question, was it that yer fancied a bit yerself, yer randy arl git." he asked angrily, knocking Joe's paper away from his face.

The older man looked up directly at him, replying "I don't want fuckin' anythin' from you faggot, so get outa my face."

His fellow passengers stiffened, moving away on either side, maintaining their focus on their chosen distractions.

Smiling slyly the bald leader turned away as if to take no further action then instantly spun around on his left leg, kicking out with his right boot into the centre of Joe's *New York Times*, catching him fully in the mid section.

"Have that yer arl cunt!" he shouted, ready to follow up with a series of punches. He was thrwarted in his intent and mistaken in his choice of target.

Joe moved with surprising alacrity, springing to his feet, launching a rock hard right fist up and under the jaw of his attacker, snapping his head back violently. A left-right combination to the body followed by a straight left to the face were delivered within moments all with devastating accuracy, by the former GI boxer.

Dropping to the floor, senses reeling, the stunned younger man lay where he fell, trying to regain his bearings. As he did he spied some very specific graffiti amongst that which covered the lower section of the interior wall, close to the doors.

Shouting from his downed position he ordered, "Get into that fucker all of yers!"

Joe kept his fists raised ready for action, a survivor of the Frozen Choisin, these 'boys' did not even register as a threat to the brave veteran, "Come and get it ladies!" he called gamely.

All four set about him as one punching, kicking, using their knees and the weapons they had drawn.

Born and raised in the mean streets of New York City, Joe instantly diverted to the intuitive brawler that he was, abandoning Marquis of Queensbury boxing etiquette for raw, savage scrapping. It was a ferocious bout that raged for several spectacular minutes with Joe bleeding the youths even as their knives, coshes and studded belts wounded him. If only one other passenger would have come to his aid, he may have had a sporting chance. As it was, every other occupant of that carriage acted as if nothing extraordinary was occurring and remained entirely detached from the violent struggle taking place in their midst.

"Hold that arl bastard still will yers, for fuck's sake." their leader ordered on regaining his feet, reaching behind to a specially made leather scabbard, to draw the distinctive knife secured there. Finally with Joe momentarly restrained by the leader's four accomplices, the tall male stepped towards their bloodied captive, knife in hand. Glancing down at the M1918 combat weapon, with its dull, stained, five-inch blade reading the intention of its holder, Joe observed defiantly, "Fuck you Tinkerbell, ya haven't got the balls, so put it away before ya cut y'self."

The younger man smiled, replying "I like you granddad, you're my type of guy.., pity." In one swift, powerful thrust he drove the knife into Joe's abdomen up to the hilt and its knuckle-duster hand-grip.

The stalwart patriot's heart was burst, killing him were he stood. By the time the scarlet blade was withdrawn his soul had already departed, leaving another New York crime statistic to bleed out on the City's dangerous subway system.

"This is our stop." the grinning murderer announced as they arrived at 135th Street, even though this was not their intended destination. When the doors opened all five left in haste, quickly exiting the station, running off into the night. At last one of Joe's fellow passengers now came and knelt by his lifeless body, saying a brief prayer, wishing he could have found some small vestage of the courage the deceased veteran had displayed and helped him before it was too late.

A short time after, sitting in a rundown bar, several blocks on from the subway, one of the killer's companions asked, "Why the fuck do ya have t'take it too far every time man?"

Morgan 'Morgo' Jones smiled, "Because it gives me a fuckin' hard dick, okay?"

Another of his crew asked curiously "What were ya starin' at on that train wall, ya looked like ya'd seen a fuckin' ghost?"

Again Morgo smiled, "I had mate, I saw somethin' I thought I'd never see again, not here in the States. Now I know some cunt is here that I've got unfinished business with, am gonna do some askin' round and then am gonna sort things for good."

Irish's proud proclamation of his own name that of the Crown Team and its distinctive emblem, written on that same subway train, along with his declaration of affection for Rosita, had inadvertently alerted his deadly enemy Morgo to his presence. Worse still Irish had revealed that he had a local love interest, who could perhaps be traced and subjected to some sickening torture.

Sunday 25th July 1976

Three thousand miles away, across the other side of the dark Atlantic Ocean, Irish was unsurprisingly unaware that his simple action would have such potentially deadly consequences and expose the girl of his dreams to the attention of Morgo the sadist.

It was Sunday evening and against his better judgement, Irish had allowed Blue to persuade him to return to The Eagle for an evening's drinking in celebration of The Crown triumvirate's triumph, which had already become an instant ledgend. Even as he entered the lounge with Blue, Irish was greeted by the cheers of his former team mates.

"Nice one, Irish," "Good effort mate," "Crown Team rule!" they shouted.

Taking his seat at the centre of the semi-circular arrangement, at the far end of the long, rectangular room, Irish was not quite so vocal or ebulient in his response, remembering their previous attitude to his proposed attack on the Ravens Team.

"Fuckin' great result for the team." Terry (H) observed with pride.

Irish did not reply but picked up the pint of Guinness that Johno had just placed before him.

"You really fuckin' caned those Ravens queers, Irish." Johno, the immensely strong farm labourer announced.

"Yeah mate what a fuckin' beatin' they won't fuck with the Crown Team again," Brain added.

Irish was being feted as the hero and his destruction of the Ravens Crew the cause célèbre. With KC and The Sunshine Band's *Shake, Shake, Shake Your Booty* playing on the juke box he sat back taking a lengthy draught of his pint, listening to his Eagle crew mates as they continued to praise his efforts, exaggerating his role in the conflict as they saw fit.

After several minutes of receiving their plaudits, he decided to put the record straight. "Listen lads, this is all great stuff an I'm happy t'let yers get the ale in all night but yer need t'get yer facts right." He paused to refuse a cigarette from Tank, much to his surprise, then continued, "First of all it was me *and* Weaver who went up to the Ravens ground, 'cause if yers remember the rest of yers had other important stuff to do." He paused again waiting for their reaction, which was generally one of surprise as if they had totally forgotten their previous responses. "Anyway, apart from it bein' me an Weaver, I tell yers straight if Tommy (S) hadn't 'ave shown up when he did, we both would've been well and truly fucked. He came in like a fuckin' one-man-army, took out Smigger and his top boys then laid into the rest of them, while I went after Smidge the shit house. When I got back it was all over, Tommy had got off and Weaver was goin' round doin' his usual torture shit."

Irish's honest summary of the event did little to dent the Crew's elation."

"Yeah but if you hadn't 'ave had the fuckin' balls t'go up there in the first place, none of this would've 'appened." Terry (H) observed accurately, leaving Johno to announce, "Irish, yer a fuckin' hero."

The Crew roared their appreciation at this, raising their glasses shouting "Irish, Irish!"

Faced with this degree of undetered adulation, Irish acquiesced, relaxing into his role of reluctant hero. The beer and whiskey flowed freely, everyone in a celebratory mood, with random outbreaks of communal singing adding to the positive ambience.

Mid way through the evening with Champs Boys disco version of *Tubular Bells* just beginning to play on the juke box, the lounge door opened to admit a distinctly unwelcome visitor, with the warm summer's breeze.

DC Banks dabbed his sweating forehead with a grubby handkerchief as he pushed his way through the throng of drinkers seated around the small circular tables, arriving directly in front of Irish.

"I've got you now O'Hare, y'little shit." he announced triumphantly.

"Evenin' officer, did yer fancy a pint while yer here, or is it a Babycham you'd prefer?" Terry (H) asked with a grin.

"Shut your fuckin' mouth boy or I'll have you as an accessory." the detective warned angrily.

"An accessory to what?" Irish asked casually.

"I warned you t'keep away from those Ravens lads didn't I but last night a dozen or more of their boys took a kickin' in the cemetery and your fuckin' names in the frame." DC Banks shouted, flecks of spittle settling in the corners of his mouth.

"So you're sayin' you think I'm up to takin' on twelve of the Ravens Crew on me own an kickin' the shit out of them? Fuck, I know they're a crap team but even they're not that far down that one Skin could take that many out, thanks for the compliment all the same." Irish replied with a smile. The rest of the crew laughed also amused at his comments.

The detective leaned forward and pressed his chubby index finger along the jagged line of Irish's recently stitched scar. "Looks nasty, I bet its fuckin' painful." he observed, pressing firmly along its length, asking "And how did yer get that O'Hare?"

Irish pulled his injured head away from the tubby officer's offending digit then stared directly at him replying "I cut meself shavin' the mirrors in our house aren't that good, d'yer know warra mean?"

DC Banks smiled, "You little tit, I've got witnesses that describe you and two other Crown dickheads as the one's who done them. Yer banged t'rights boy."

Terry (H) interrupted once more, "Sorry officer but when did yer say this 'appened?"

"Last night between twenty-one hundred and twenty-three hundred hours... that's nine to eleven o'clock to you boy... anythin' else you want to say, 'cause I'm ready to take statements off the lot of yer."

Terry now laughed, "Yeah, I'll give yer a statement no problem, so will the rest of the lads. Patrick O'Hare was in this alehouse, sittin' next t'me from eight o'clock till chuckin' out time around half eleven, that's twenty hundred to twenty-three-thirty hours to you, isn't that right lads?"

Every member of the crew shouted their agreement, each adding they were prepared to sign statements to that effect now, or at any other time.

The frustrated DC asked "Are you all fuckin' sure you want to do this?"

Again they called back their total agreement, leaving officer Banks to turn to the management, "Hey you there, behind the bar." he called to the late forties male landlord, who had only recently replaced the previous incumbent.

"Mate, all I can tell yer is these fellers are in 'ere every evenin' and thee was *all* 'ere last night."

DC Banks pressed on "I'm askin' yer about this cunt 'ere, the one who still goes round lookin' like a fuckin' Skinhead, was *he* here, yes or no."

The landlord stared directly at Irish, scrutinising his distinctive appearance. He may have been new to this particular alehouse but he had been in the licensee trade for most of his working life and knew where his own best interest lay, "Oh yeah, him, *he* was definitely 'ere, I remember him alright with his cropped head, braces and boots, I thought I'd seen the last of his kind, that's what made me remember him."

The detective acknowledged defeat but left with a parting shot, "Yer off the hook for the minute O'Hare but don't get too cozy with yer little boyfriends, because I'll keep diggin' and when I've got enough shit on you, I'll be right back for you and them." He left the pub to the derisory sound of the crew whistling the Laurel and Hardy signature tune.

Everyone laughed, with Terry (H) shouting, "Hey mate, same round again when yer ready and whatever yer havin' yerself, nice one!"

They were a crew once more, at least for the moment, unified by their hatred of a common enemy, the police.

Friday, 30th July 1976

During the week following The Eagle celebration two significant developments occurred that would impact on Irish's relationship with the Gerard Boys and his membership of the Crown Team. The first of these came about as a result of good news received from the hospital where Irish's brother, Dermot was being treated in the Intensive Care Unit. Late on Thursday evening the battered, unconscious, young man suddenly woke from his coma and within a short time his condition was down-graded from critical to severe, a small distinction in words but a major transition in medical terms, one which finally returned a smile to Mrs O'Hare's care-worn face.

Rushing to the hospital with Irish she knelt and prayed in grateful thanksgiving to a merciful God, for her son's return from the brink of death. Tears of relief and gratitude ran down her face as she listened to the doctors explain what the current status meant and what the prognosis may hold, should Dermot's condition improve further.

On their way home in a taxi, she turned to Irish and said, "Thank God Patrick for your brother's safe keeping. I've told yer all this time prayers move mountains, never forget that son, always keep yer faith, it's all yer've really got when bad times come."

Irish smiled humouring his mother, even though he remained his usual religiously sceptical self. "Oh yeah ma, I'll always keep me faith, y'can be sure of that."

The next day after enjoying a much less restless night's sleep and fully absorbing the implictions of what the hospital specialists had told her, Mrs O'Hare was ready to move on to the next stage of her life and by extension that of her children. While Irish was eating a late breakfast of fried eggs, fried bacon and fried bread, draining the entire contents of an accompanying pot of stewed tea, his mother gave her considered opinion.

"Well Patrick, I've been doin' a lot of thinkin' and prayin' to the Holy Ghost f'guidance. Y'heard what those doctors said last night about Dermot, how he's unlikely to ever walk again, or be able to use his private parts for goin' the toilet, or anythin' else. He's goin' to need constant care night and day. So I've decided enough's enough, I'm leavin' Liverpool, gettin' out of this God forsaken country of heathens and goin' back home, to Ireland."

She paused for a few moments to receive his expected objections but was pleasantly surprised to find that he did not, as yet, raise any.

"I'm takin' Dermot and Sean back to Kerry, to Kilarney, t'live with me sister Roisin and her husband. Y'know thee never had any children of their own and thee've got that big house with loads of land around them. It'll be just what Dermot needs, away from this devil's playground of an estate. He'll get plenty of good, clean, fresh air down at the Dingle, lookin' out onto the Atlantic. Yer sisters are off t'college and university in September so thee'll be livin' away and young Sean can get a proper Catholic education from the Brothers..."

This time Irish interrupted her mid-sentence, "Ma, I agree with everythin' yer've said, it all makes sense but yer've got t'promise me, yer'll never let our Sean fall into the clutches of those evil bastards."

"Now Patrick yer've got no call t'be sayin' things like that, sure didn't you go to one of the Brothers' schools here yerself?" she observed.

"Exactly... and *that's* why am sayin' me little brother must never end up in one of *their* places, not over my dead body." Irish responded vehemently.

"Alright Patrick let's leave that f'now but you should be thinkin' about movin' on yerself, that crowd of hooligans yer runnin' round with will be the death of yer."

Again Irish interrupted as if bemused by her allegation, "I don't know what yer talkin' about ma, what crowd?"

Mrs O'Hare laughed, "Oh behave yerself Patrick, I'm yer mother and a mother knows these things. D'yer think I haven't known about you and yer Skinhead gang all these years? Just look at what happened to poor young John Mack, stabbed t'death in some filthy toilet; it was all over the newspapers at the time. God knows what his aunt and uncle must've gone through, I don't want the same happenin' to you."

Irish protested, feigning indignation but his wise parent continued.

"And don't keep tellin' me that gash on yer head came from fallin' over in the Eagle car park, d'yer really believe I came down with the last shower?" She paused, changing her smiling expression to one of genuine, frustration-fuelled anger, "I'll tell yer one thing that I do *know* f'certain, I've found all the time that I've lived here from bein' a young woman, a Catholic will only ever be a second-class citizen, nothin' more. Keep that in mind when yer makin' yer own decision."

His mother stopped talking and left the room, anxious to begin her preparations, hoping for the earliest possible departure. She had given her honest opinion and judgement, there was nothing more to say.

Irish finished his breakfast in silence, considering the implications for his own future. He did not have long to reflect on how his mother's departure from the Crown Estate, Liverpool and England may effect him personally. Just as he was entering the living room with his old, stained mug containing the dregs of a cup of tea in his hand, the telephone rang.

"Alright, who's this?" he asked on answering the phone, thinking that it may be someone from the hospital.

"Hello, is that you Patrick?" a male voice enquired.

Irish confirmed that it was he who was speaking, leaving the caller to state, "Well get your fuckin' arse down to The Central alehouse now, we want a word with you."

Their brief conversation ended abruptly, Irish experiencing a deep foreboding but recognising that he had no option other than to comply.

Quickly getting dressed into his dark blue Harrington jacket over a blue checked, short-sleeved Ben Sherman shirt, cream twenty-two inch parallel trousers and gleaming Airwair, he set off to catch the next bus bound for the city centre.

Within three-quarters of an hour he had entered The Central pub and was being ushered into the presence of the Gerard Boy seniors and their younger sibling Danny Boy. All four were seated in the snug, first floor parlour, with pints of beer and tumblers of whiskey filling the small circular tables in front of them. They had clearly been drinking for some time, even though it was not long past midday and officially the hostelry had only been open for just over an hour. Instead of their usual smart tailored suits, the brothers were casually dressed in open necked, short-sleeved fitted shirts, similar to that which Irish was wearing.

The Crown player could now clearly see the heavy musculature of the three older brothers and some of their more colourful tattoos, which included blue-black swallows, dark green shamrocks and bleeding red hearts pierced by silver daggers. The sinister siblings all displayed black capital letters G and B in a Gothic font in the centre of their inner forearms.

Niall Mack began the interview with a seemingly innocuous observation, "Been busy have yer Patrick since we last saw yer, had a bit of an accident by the looks of it?"

Irish traced the jagged line of his forehead scar with his index finger, replying, "Oh this, yeah, I'd had a few drinks too many and fell over in the alehouse car park but other than that, things 'ave been pretty quiet."

For several uncomfortable moments there was no sound other than Bobby Darin's *Somewhere Beyond the Sea* playing on the juke box in the bar a few short, wooden steps below, as the seated Gerard Boys hosts studied their standing Skinhead guest.

"Is that right?" Francis asked, continuing "Its got nothin' t'do with a dozen Ravens Boys gettin' fucked up, one of them with his cock sliced through and another thrown under a fuckin' articulated lorry, is that what yer tellin' us?"

Irish shuffled nervously but replied clearly "I heard somethin' about that but I don't know what exactly happened to those lads."

Francis leaned on the table in front of him, put down his pint and cracked his knuckles, displaying his large, well-developed biceps. "Whatever y'do Patrick, don't take up playin' poker, yer've got an awful 'tell' there. When y'fuckin' lyin' yer raise y'right eyebrow, it's a dead giveaway."

Again Irish tried to persist in his fabrication, "Like I said, I don't know anythin' about that business with the Ravens Crew."

Niall rose to his feet with a furious expression on his battered face, "We sent y'ma some flowers with a card for her an one f'you. Did you fuckin' read that card or what?" he demanded.

"Yeah I did Niall." Irish answered honestly.

"And what did we tell yer t'do about those fuckers who done yer brother, just tell me that, yer fuckin' ejit?"

"Yers said t'leave it, let it go." Irish replied.

"But yer didn't leave it did yer, tell us what yer *really* did." Niall insisted.

After a brief pause Irish offered his version of events, concluding "... so I did fuck them up a bit, with some help but the cunt who ended up gettin' splattered by the truck was down to 'imself." He waited for a few moments ready to receive Niall's judgement.

The elder Gerard Boy leaned forward grasping Irish by the shoulders with his strong, ring-encrusted paws.

"You went after those lads that done yer brother, yer didn't care what anyone said, how many of them there was or what the consequences might be. Y'got stuck into those bastards and fucked them up good an proper. Well in boy, yer done good!"

Niall kissed him on his injured forehead, announcing, "You *are* one of us Patrick, yer've got balls and yer understand there's nothing more important than family. If some cunt hurts one of your family, y'find them no matter what anyone else says and yer put them in a world of pain." Resuming his seat Niall shouted, "Will someone get this man a drink, before I come down t'that bar meself."

Within moments Irish had a pint of Guinness in his hand and the brothers raised their glasses to salute him.

"Sliante!" they called. He returned their salutation then sat down on the stool that was offered to him, confused and much relieved.

"Right, that's enough frivolity, let's get down t'business." Niall ordered, instantly transforming to his usual dour self. "You'll be gettin' off back t'the States on Monday, yer train t'London's gonna be leavin' Lime Street on Sunday mornin' and yer better not miss yer connection t'Southampton, so no more fuckin' about between now and then, right?" he warned, continuing, "This time yer'll be takin' a bit more luggage and comin' back fully loaded. We've got t'get as much shifted while we can."

Irish interrupted to ask the seemingly obvious, "Why's that Niall, is there some problem?"

Niall and his brothers laughed, with the elder replying, "Yer might say that Patrick. We all know the bizzies are stupid cunts but even they eventually get onto what's happenin' right under their snouts, if thee start gettin' too close we'll have t'change yer route, up to Boston or Chicago if need be."

Once more Irish interrupted, this time for a different reason, "I'd rather not Niall... I mean... am happy t'keep the arrangements the way thee are, stayin' with New York. 'Am not worried about the bizzies."

They all laughed, Tommy observing, "We know you'd rather keep things the way thee are, y'randy little bugger, can't wait t'get back t'yer sexy bird, is that it?"

Irish smiled, admitting "Yer've got me there Tommy, I can't say that she's not been on me mind but I'll still do me job, don't you worry."

Niall quickly caught hold of his wrist, warning with a grin, "We fuckin' know yer will Patrick, you're on the ball that's why we offered yer the work in the first place."

"And the fact that yer understand not t'fuck with us." Francis added, smiling slyly.

Another round of drinks appeared, supplemented with the obligatory whiskey chasers. The spirits were downed first in one gulp then as they drank their pints with Roy Orbison's *Dream Baby* playing in the background, Niall issued one final warning.

"Remember what we've told yer Patrick, yer've gorra good thing goin' here, don't fuck it up. When you're over *there* don't forget yer've still got people back *here* who'd have t'face the consequences of you doin' somethin' stupid, are yer with me?"

Irish looked directly at Niall and replied, "I'm with yer Niall, I won't *ever* forget what you've said about my family, that's for sure."

Even as he spoke he smiled inside, knowing that in reality his beloved family would soon be beyond the reach of the Gerard Boys, surrounded and protected by his mother's relatives, who everybody quietly acknowledged were 'connected' themselves, to much more deadly Republican kinsmen. He was careful not to let his errant right eyebrow betray him.

Friday 13th August 1976

It was Friday the thirteenth, unlucky for some perhaps but for Irish, newly returned to New York City, having docked in the Hudson harbour that morning, this was the beginning of what he hoped would prove to be a fortuitous day. His journey from Liverpool to New York, particularly his time at sea, had afforded him a much needed opportunity to reflect on his choice of lifestyle, a period of relative isolation suspended between the beloved city of his home and the home city of his beloved.

At just twenty one years of age he had the look of a veteran contender. It seemed to him all that he could remember, in the decade since entering the brutal educational institution known as the *The Cardinals School for Catholic Boys,* was violence. When the Skinhead youth culture had first emerged in 1969, Irish, like most of his chronological peers, including his best friend Jay Mac, had embraced every aspect of its unique ethos and distinctive look. In the past seven years his membership of the Crown Team had dominated his life, leading him to be involved in every possible action from individual scraps to wholesale gang warfare. Perhaps it was time to bring it all to a close, he speculated and start anew, reinvented.

The lovely Rosita featured strongly in his considerations, coupled with the fact that his urgent need for employment with the Gerard Boys, principally to support his mother and younger siblings, had effectively been removed.

By mid-afternoon Irish, having passed through customs with his 'extra' luggage, once again without any difficulty, had checked into old Ben McCabe's Grande Hotel in the Lower East Side and was unpacking his choice of clothing, for his much anticipated evening reunion with Rosita at Uncle Sam's Diner. Shortly after six o'clock, dressed in his smartest kit of white short sleeved Ben Sherman, blue-green two-tone, twenty-two inch parallels, black half inch braces, dark blue Harrington jacket and gleaming cherry red Airwair, Irish was about to set off for the diner. As he passed by the reception counter in the narrow front lobby, the proud owner called to him.

"Alright y'lordship, hope ya happy with ya room, everything in order?"

Irish smiled, replying, "Yeah, so far so good, no signs of any uninvited guests."

"Ya cheeky pup and t'think I even changed the sheets after the last guy left." Ben advised, leading Irish to ask, "Last guy? I thought only people who worked for the Macks stayed here?"

"Yeah, that's right but ya didn't think you was the only one did yer?" Ben asked, adding, "The Boys have got guys workin' all over for them."

"Do thee ever get t'meet up?" Irish asked niavely.

"No fuckin' chance, that'll never happen. They go by 'need to know' and you guys don't qualify. Anyway it's for y'own good, if the cops pinched one of ya, y'couldn't tell 'em nothin' about anyone but yerself." his host informed, before quickly changing the subject. "Been keepin' y'self busy back in Liverpool by the looks a things," he said, indicating Irish's forehead scar.

"Yeah, I had t'sort out some family business of me own."

Ben nodded, observing, "Maybe you'd be safer stayin' here in The States."

Irish said nothing in reply, not wishing to even hint at the plan he had already been formulating.

"See ya later young feller, have a good evenin'." the older male called as the Skinhead strolled down the stairs and into the golden sunlit street outside.

Two blocks on from his sparce lodgings, Irish entered the comfortably furnished local diner, to receive a warm welcome.

"Head's up Rosita, Loverman's back in town!" Marge, the senior waitress, called on recognising the distinctly dressed customer.

Rosita was serving at a nearby table when she heard the news she had been waiting for. Finishing her order she quickly crossed to the smiling young man and kissed him softly on the lips.

Irish beamed with delight, 'She looks gorgeous' he thought. "Any chance of gettin' a table, miss?" he asked.

"I'll see what I can do handsome stranger, would a booth by the window be okay, sir?"

"That'll be fine miss, with service like this I might just come here again." Irish replied, taking a seat in the well-upholstered, limousine-style leather covered, cosy dining station. "I've really missed you Rosita." he said as she leaned forward handing him his menu, revealing the Miraculous Medal that he had given her, hanging around her golden brown neck, on its fine chain.

"Likewise." she replied, adding "We're busy tonight Patrick so I'll speak t'ya later, if that's alright."

"I'll hold yer to that, I'll see yer later." he answered smiling.

For the rest of the evening until close of business, Irish sat captivated by fleeting glimpses of his love interest, whilst enjoying his mountainous meal of sirloin steak with all the trimmings.

Several hours later, with her shift almost done Rosita began to clear away the crockery and cutlery when Marge called to her, "That's okay honey, we'll finish up you run along with your guy. Hell, I think if he waits another second to see ya he's gonna burst."

Rosita quickly removed her apron hurrying to join Irish, who was standing patiently just outside the entrance, enjoying the warm night air. As soon as the couple were reunited they kissed, a long passionate kiss then strolled arm in arm away towards the beckoning subway.

"Tell me all ya news Patrick, I can't wait t'hear what you've been gettin' up to back home in Liverpool." she asked excitedly.

"Not much t'tell really, it was pretty quiet to be honest." he lied.

"Really, is that right, so how'd ya explain that little nick on ya forehead?" she asked knowingly.

Irish accepted honesty was the best policy and provided the briefest possible summary, "Some bad guys hurt me big brother, so I hurt them worse."

She leaned into him and kissed him tenderly saying "I understand, family is all there is, ya don't need t'say anythin' more."

Irish was just happy to have found her, he knew that she meant what she said and that he never need be afraid to tell her the truth, about anything.

They walked on, deep in conversation, with Rosita reluctantly agreeing that he could accompany her on the subway to her stop but no further. Irish accepted the logic of her ruling, remembering what had occurred on the previous occasion when he had ventured into her home territory.

"No problem Rosita, I'll just gerron the next train back here, at least I can see yer for a bit longer that way." he advised. Once they had entered the subway and boarded her train Irish asked, "Yer haven't told me what's been happenin' round 'ere, what been goin' on like?"

"Well if y'mean what's been happenin' in New York, it's been quiet here too, except for a visit we got from Hurricane Belle. That caused some damage in Jersey and Long Island but nothin' that couldn't be put right." the hard-nosed native New Yorker replied, displaying a typical American spirit of defiance in the face of adversity.

"What about where you live, up in Los Barrios?" he asked, trying to impress her with his use of the coloquially correct name.

"Hey not bad, you remembered. What can I say, life goes on day by day, what it is, is what it is." she replied, once again with a pragmatism born of the ghetto.

As with his previous 'business trip' Irish did not know the duration of his stay, only that his contact would advise him of this, when they met. He wanted to make the most of his time in the city, seeing Rosita at every possible opportunity. As they travelled through the dark subterranean tunnels, the couple made what speculative plans they could. Finally with only a few stops remaining until they reached Rosita's, she remembered a disturbing piece of news that had slipped her mind.

"Oh yeah, sorry Patrick, I forgot somethin' I've gorra tell ya."

"Nothin' bad I hope?" he answered, slightly perturbed.

"I don't know really. About two weeks ago some guys came into the diner and one of them was askin' about you. He said he was a friend of yours but he wasn't dressed like you in ya 'Skinhead' style, they looked more like a biker gang, and none of them seemed that friendly. Four of them sounded like they was from here but the one who said he was ya friend had an accent a bit like yours, only different."

Irish was growing increasingly concerned, asking, "What did he look like, the one with the different accent?"

"He was tall, heavy built and had a bald head, not shaved, or cropped like yours. Oh yeah and when he left he walked with a stiff leg, sort of a limp."

The Crown Team player's blood ran cold and he asked one more question, "What did he have t'say for 'imself, this bald-headed, lame, character?"

Rosita thought for a moment then replied, "He said he'd got your message that you were here and to tell ya that he'd be in touch soon."

Irish cursed himself, realising that his simple graffiti scrawl, on an already enthusiastically decorated subway train, had alerted his deadly enemy to his presence in New York. Morgo knew he was here and worse still had made the connection between him and the lovely Rosita. There could be only one resolution, no matter what anyone else warned.

"You okay Patrick? You've gone really pale, is everythin' alright?" Rosita asked, genuinely worried.

"Yeah, everythin's fine and I can promise yer Rosita, *you've* got nothin' t'worry about. C'mon, this is your stop isn't it?"

They left the carriage together at 110th Street, said their goodbyes and kissed before going their separate ways. Irish caught the next train back to the Lower East Side and his lodgings. He knew he would not get much sleep that night with or without the presence of the bed bugs.

At ten o'clock the following morning after a restless night, Irish met his contact, a smartly dressed male in his early sixties, this time at Penn Station. The handover of luggage went without any complication and Irish was pleased to be informed that he should expect to stay in the city, for at least a week or more. Satisfied that his business committment had been dealt with for the moment, Irish determined to make the most of his time, seeing Rosita at every possible opportunity. For the next few days with Rosita's college studies on hold for the summer recess, except for her evening waitress duties at the diner, the couple were inseperable enjoying together the sights and sounds of the sleepless city.

On Sunday morning having already travelled to and from Staten Island on the free, huge multi-decked, eponymous ferry, they decided next to visit Liberty Island and view up close the magnificent Lady standing on her lofty vantage point. From there they caught a smaller ferry to Ellis Island, the original entrance processing point for all those beginning their lives anew in the New World. Irish in particular used the opportunity to research some of the numerous O'Hare clan that had passed this way before him.

For four idylic days the love-struck pair could indulge in their joint fantasy, that they were tourists on holiday just like any other couple, both denying the existence of their grim home realities.

As they strolled about arm-in-arm, eating hot dogs and popcorn, drinking chilled sodas, experiencing some of the hottest New York City summer temperatures for almost sixty years, Irish, the visitor from overseas, felt as if the bleak Crown Estate could actually be escaped and consigned to a dark corner of his memory. He was naive in thinking however, that he could out distance his nemesis, wherever he may run to. The hopeful youth may believe that he had forsaken a life of violence but violence was not yet ready to be forsook.

Wednesday 18th August 1976
On a stifling Wednesday night, after Rosita's shift at Uncle Sam's had ended, both she and Irish were slowly meandering towards her subway station. As they passed by the bar on the opposite side of the street where they had previously encountered Gabe and just before they reached the alleyway where he had come to their rescue, a shabby 1966 Oldsmobile Toronado in need of some urgent body work and a full respray over its dull, worn, once black paint, pulled in a few feet ahead of them. Its occupants exited the car with some sense of urgency, as if anxious not to let the couple pass and quickly encircled them. All five males were dressed uniformly in capped-sleeved tee-shirts of grey, black or white, black leather waistcoats and flared trousers of the same material, with heavy biker boots on their feet. Irish had his right arm around Rosita and he pulled her closer to him.

"Can I help you lads with somethin', are yer lost, needin' directions?" Irish asked, studying their appearance, unnecessarily looking for clues as to who they were, already knowing full well their leader's identity.

Morgo stood directly in front of the pair, smiling with wicked delight. He seemed bigger than Irish remembered, as if he had been regularly working out with heavy weights and his previously grey skin had lost its just-released from prison pallor, after several years' exposure to the bronzing American sun. The sadist's chillingly sinister countenance and expression though, had not altered to the slightest degree; an ice cold shiver ran down Irish's spine as he stared into his pitiless eyes.

"Alright O'Hare, come back for another taste hey, liked it that much did yer? Well I can't say I blame yer, once yer've been done by Morgo, nothin' else will do; isn't that right boys?" he asked his crew with a cruel smile on his evil face.

"Fuck you, yer sick bastard!" Irish replied angrily.

"No O'Hare, it's gonna be the other way round, you're the one what's gonna be gettin fucked... hard." He glanced at Rosita letting his gaze pass over her pretty face, slim figure and long legs. "Goin' for a bit of the dark meat are yer, O'Hare?" Morgo asked, leering, "I don't blame yer, I hear that these Latino birds are real goers. If I was that way inclined I might just try a piece of that meself."

"Shut your filthy mouth!" Irish shouted.

Morgo turned to Rosita, "What are you supposed to be anyway, Mexican; Spanish; Peurto Rican?"

Rosita smiled replying succinctly, "I'm an American, you douche bag."

Morgo raised his right hand as if about to slap Rosita across her face.

Irish snapped, interrupting before anything else was said or done, "Listen Morgo you piece of shit, this is between you and me. Don't even speak t'this lady or I'll..."

"Or you'll what O'Hare, you're not in any position to do fuck all, gerrin that fuckin' car now, you're comin' with us." Morgo ordered.

Suddenly a familiar deep voice called to them from close by "Holy shit, is that my best buddy Irish O'Hare back in New York city, out with his foxy lady Rosita?" The tall powerfully built former US Marine, Gabriel Stone, strolled across to join the group, a broad smile on his face, "Good t'see ya brother, an its always a pleasure t'see you Rosita." he said, totally ignoring Morgo and his crew, much to the sexual sadist's annoyance.

"Hey *boy*, no one called for you so fuck off back to where y'came from, y'not wanted here." Morgo stated angrily.

Gabe stopped smiling and looked directly at Morgo, "You tired of livin', freak? 'Cause if you call me *boy* again, I'll tear ya ugly head clean off and kick it so hard ya folks back in the circus is gonna feel ya pain."

A stunned Morgo was uncertain how to react for a few moments then blurted out, "Didn't thee ever teach you t'count, there's five of us, only two of you an this bitch."

"Now that's just plain rude, ya gonna have t'aplogise t'the lady before I can let ya go." Gabe ordered casually raising his right hand, open palm and signalling to his friends to his rear, gathered by the door of the bar, to join them.

A group of four equally large sized males, two of them wearing olive drab combat jackets, bearing numerous Vietnam Veteran insignia, including MIA and POW patches, arrived alongside their African American commrade.

"D'we have a problem here Gabe?" one of them, who wore an impressive handlebar moustache, asked.

An almost palpable smell of fear now emanated from Morgo and his crew, as they looked into the cold, dead eyes of men, not much older than themselves, who had witnessed untold horrors.

Gabe smiled once more, "No, we aint gorra problem, these *boys* are just leavin' before they start cryin'." He looked in their direction again, flicking his hand forward in a dismissive gesture, as if brushing away trash, "Before ya go, Ugly, don't forget y'apology t'the lady."

Morgo was approaching a paroxysm of rage but knew better than to allow it to vent. He turned towards Rosita keeping his angry gaze lowered, saying "Sorry miss, so, so, sorry."

"Ok, move on, ya makin' the area look bad." Gabe ordered.

Morgo and crew returned to their shabby vehicle ready to leave. As they did, Morgo, now feeling a lot more safe, called back, "It'll keep f'now O'Hare but I'll see yer again and y'slut, there's a lorra pain comin' your way... both of yer." The car pulled away from the kerb with a roar.

Another member of Gabe's veteran commrades launched an empty beer bottle with the accuracy of a quarter-back throwing a 'Hail Mary' pass close to full time. It struck the rear windscreen perfectly in the centre, shattering it on impact. "Touchdown!" he shouted as they all cheered.

Irish shook hands with Gabe, "Thanks man, for jumpin' in again, this is embarassin' its gettin' t'be a habit." he observed smiling.

"No problem Irish, ya welcome, anyway that's what I'm here for, to 'protect and serve,' isn't that right guys?" Gabe called to his friends, who were strolling back towards the bar across the street.

"Yeah Gabe, yer a regular superhero, y'just need the badge t'prove it." the beer bottle thrower shouted in reply.

The veterans all laughed sharing some joke that as yet only they were privy to.

"Catch you guys in a while, I just wanna few words with ma main man here." Gabe advised, before his commrades re-entered the noisy bar.

Irish explained to Gabe that he was back in the US for another few days at least, on business.

His friend smiled saying, "I better not ask ya what kinda business, just don't tell me *that* guy is in the same line of work."

"Nah, that bastard an me have got history, I just didn't expect it to find me here." Irish answered cryptically.

Gabe did not press the issue, changing the topic to something more positive, "Look guys we're havin' a bit of a celebration in the bar, ya welcome t'join us, both of ya, if ya fancy it."

"I'll have t'get home but thanks all the same Gabe." Rosita replied, adding, "Patrick why don't ya go and enjoy yaself, ya could do with a few beers after meetin' that freak."

Irish thought for a few moments, deciding, "Okay Rosita, I might just do that but only if yer let me get yer a taxi back home, straight t'yer door, is that a deal?"

Rosita reluctantly agreed on seeing how determined Irish was, knowing he was concerned for her safety.

Several minutes later after hailing a cab and saying farewell to Rosita, Irish crossed the street and entered the noisy bar with its narrow, shabby frontage. Once inside the appropriately named 'Old Glory' ex-serviceman's watering hole, he could just about see through the thick blue-grey smoke haze that it was deceptively bigger than its external appearance suggested, being a long, extended room with its rear exit continuing into the street behind. It was decorated from the dado rail to its low ceiling with military penants, insignia and emblems, including those of PIR units, Air Cavalry, Rifle Regiments and, a strong showing of USMC paraphenalia. Owning a magnificent juke box stacked with an eclectic mix of Rolling Stones, Hendrix, Elvis, Sinatra and Country and Western classics, two pool tables and a small colour TV, permanently set to sports coverage, Irish could immediately understand why it was packed to capacity and a popular venue with these veterans.

"This is Patrick O'Hare, a.k.a, Irish, from Liverpool Town, England and he's a stand-up guy." Gabe announced providing the briefest of introductions.

Quickly supplied with a glass of Jim Beam and an obligitory cigar, Irish was then given cursory introductions to Gabe's ex-Marine, Vietnam crew. For the next few hours the Crown Team Skinhead relaxed in the testosterone fuelled atmosphere, similar to that of The Eagle though taken to the nth degree, listening to inspiring stories of altruism, patriotism and above all commradeship. He felt as if he were in a Valhalla of heroic warriors. As they all recounted their individual tales of life 'in country' in the Mekong Delta, it became clear to Irish that the modest Gabe had played a significant role in saving each of them from certain death.

"Yeah, Irish, I tell ya man, it was one mother-fucker of a tight spot, we was all pinned down by Gook crossfire." the huge, proud owner of an impressive, thick, ginger beard, who was known to them all simply as 'Red', began outlining one of Gabe's adventures. "Anyway, this crazy S.O.B. breaks from cover, runnin' a zig-zag route right at them with his M-16 and an armful of grenades. Next thing is he's right in amongst them shootin' from the hip an lobbin' grenades all round... man it was a sight t'see, fuckin' Gook blood'n'guts flyin' everywhere. Got the Silver Star f'that one didn't ya Gabe?" Red asked.

Gabe smiled and waved his hand dismissively, "Red, anyone of you guys would've done the same. I just saw an openin' and went for it. Let's move on man, like why we're celebratin' tonight."

"What is it, yer birthday or somethin'?" Irish asked, becoming increasingly inebriated as the drinks arrived in rapid succession.

"No man, better than that. I've just passed a medical for the NYPD, I've had one interview an I've only got one more t'go then I'm in." Gabe advised, with a beaming smile.

"Look out New York city!" Red exclaimed.

"Never mind them, he's only doin' it for the uniform, it's a fuckin' babe magnet, lock up ya daughters." another huge veteran warned.

Irish laughed along with everyone else but inside he knew that he and his smiling host would soon be on opposite sides of the law.

"Fuckin' hell! What's happenin' t'me head, somebody shoot me please." Irish called out, finally waking past midday, following his extended, extensive drinking session with Gabe and the veterans the previous night. As he lay there in the boiling room drenched in his sweat, with head pounding relentlessly, he tried to recall some of what had occurred during the aclohol and spirit soaked celebration in the Old Glory bar.

Irish could see a kaleidoscopic montage in his mind's own cinema, of arm wrestling bouts, dart throwing aimed at human targets, press-up contests off the slippery floor and an ongoing drinking marathon, were each competitor was determined to be the last-man-standing. He briefly smiled to himself before leaping out of bed and vomiting violently into the small grimy sink. Voiding his stomach somehow seemed to restore a degree of lucidity to his memory, as, on lying down once again on the crumpled, damp bedding, he began to fixate about a particular incident that he started to remember with increasingly clarity.

"What *is* ya line of work anyhow Irish?" Gabe had asked several times and on receiving Irish's deliberately vague reply of "Transportin' stuff, from 'ere t'there." had become more insistent.

"Well I just hope that the 'stuff' ya movin' round don't have any bad consequences f'those people who gets it in the end, on either side of the Atlantic." Gabe had observed, before offering Irish a unique opportunity. "Hey brother, here's an idea for ya, why don't ya come see where I live, be my guest, get a guided tour?"

Irish had been just about drunk enough to accept but asked cautiously, "I thought yer said that was a no-go area, too dangerous like?"

"C'mon man, ya no pussy, life's fulla danger but ya've just gorra grab that son of a bitch by the throat an take ya chances, besides ya'll be with me brother, in *my* neighbourhood... deal?" Gabe persisted, pressing his offer.

Irish accepted and agreed he would accompany his friend to his home ground. "When d'yer wanna do this, 'cause I don't know when I'll be goin' back t'Liverpool?" he asked.

"No problem Irish, I'll be here at the weekend on Saturday and Sunday night, so whichever suits you brother." Gabe advised.

"Okay mate, if nothin' changes between now an then I'll meet yer here on Sunday night, after Rosita's shift finishes." Irish responded, believing that Sunday would perhaps be the quieter of the two days available.

By the evening of his hangover day, Irish was beginning to feel more like himself and, after getting cleaned up, he set off for Uncle Sam's. During his meal, whenever the opportunity arose and later as he was walking Rosita to her subway station he discussed the matter with her. As if Rosita had some inspired divination of what purpose lay behind Gabe's proposal, she advised, "I think ya should go Patrick, see f'ya self what its like f'people who are already down but then get exploited by others for their own gain."

Irish partially understood her meaning and acquiesced. "Sunday night it is then, after I've seen yer to yer train."

Rosita smiled sweetly, saying "Ya'll be fine, what could possibly happen t'ya with Gabe lookin' out for ya?"

Sunday 22nd August 1976

Dressed in his dark blue Harrington jacket over a white Fred Perry tee-shirt with royal blue piping to collar and sleeves, his black half inch braces, twenty-four inch parallel Flemings jeans and obligatory 1460s Airwair, Irish was sitting between

Rosita on his left and the powerful, ex-Marine, Gabe on his right as the subway train approached their mutual destination, 110th Street and Lexington Avenue.

With business being fairly quiet in the diner, Rosita had been allowed to leave earlier than usual and consequently they had collected Gabe from outside the Old Glory bar just before ten thirty. Half an hour later Irish was saying goodbye to Rosita as he and Gabe departed to go on their own route, which deviated from hers to Los Barrios.

She kissed Irish softly on the lips and warned, "Gabe, ya better take good care of my man or ya'll have me to answer to, d'ya hear?"

Gabe smiled then sprang to attention in mock salute, replying, "Ma'am, yes ma'am, received loud and clear."

Wearing one of his tight fitting cap sleeved tee-shirts, in this instance bearing a magnificent flowing Stars and Stripes, with the slogan "God Bless America" below, Gabe's heavy musculature was clearly visible and with his six foot three inch height, Rosita had arguably left 'her man' with the best possible personal bodyguard. The Vietnam veteran strolled on in a general north, north-west direction, though every so often diverting obliquely to some other path. Irish felt as with Rosita's previous 'guiding' he was being deliberately led on a confusing route, so that he could not find his way to this same location at some future time. They passed rows of boarded shops, where every so often, a random retailer would still be open, the premises lit by a single electric bulb or flourescent tube. Delapidated, formerly grand brownstones, juxtaposed with more modern developments and large open spaces in between, filled with nothing other than a mixed detritus of burned out cars, one wheeled prams, no longer functioning white goods or dead television sets and general filthy refuse. Young children played on these disease-ridden sites, as children would the world over. Even at this late hour it appeared no one was calling them to come home and to all intents and purposes they were ferrel, without constraint.

Gabe spoke once only at this disturbing sight, "There's the next generation brother, the dealers will be gettin' their evil claws into them soon enough."

Irish did not reply, he was beginning to understand the purpose of Gabe's insisted upon visit by him to this area. Dead-eyed males of varying ages wandered about aimlessly or sat soaked in their urine on the hard sidewalk, or on stone stoops, or lay in shop doorways no longer in this world but not yet fully departed. The same self-inflicted malaise held them in thrall, an ingested, inhaled, injected mind-obliterating, soul-destroying poison. Irish was finding his edifying meander growing increasingly disturbing. Still they wandered on.

Other than returning the greetings of some of his soul sisters and brothers, Gabe did not speak or make any comment, escorting Irish through his neighbourhood like a silent version of the phantom Spirit of Christmas Present, that had accompanied a reluctant Ebeneezer Scrooge on his tour of old London Town, allowing the Skinhead to form his own opinion and make his own judgement.

Eventually they reached the venue that Gabe had chosen, a small rundown bar, with a single frosted plate-glass window next to the narrow, wooden entrance door and the flickering neon sign declaring 'Marvin's Sports' Bar.'

Just as they entered the smoke-filled interior Bo Diddley's *Hey Bo Diddley* began to play on the juke box. Irish looked about, deciding that there may have been an over ambitious use of the word 'sports' in the naming of this bijou establishment as, apart from one small pool table, there was little other than an eclectic collection of baseball memorabilia displayed all about the faded magnolia coloured walls.

"What ya fetched in there Gabe? A little spook white boy, lost his way?" one old cumudgeon displaying a snowy white, short afro hairstyle called, with another adding "What is this neighbourhood comin' too? I tell ya, I is gonna have to look for some place mo respectable if these white boys is gonna start movin' in round here."

Gabe laughed calling back, "No need for ya to worry old timer, this here is ma friend Irish, all the way from Liverpool Town, England."

"Never heard of it, where the fuck's that?" the first speaker observed, before taking a sip of his Bourbon.

Gabe provided some useful background information, "'Course ya heard of it, that's where those Beatles came from, yeah?"

"Who the fuck is the Beatles? Is they another white band whose been stealin' black folks' music an passin' it off as they own?" the original questioner continued.

"No fool, that's them Rollin' Stones faggots, all their music is black folks' music, am I right?" the second elderly speaker announced, much to the amusement of his friends who all laughed giving this sage a variety of handshakes in acknowldgement of his extensive popular musical knowledge.

Gabe left them to continue their fascinating discussion and took Irish to the bar, where he introduced him to his friend, the eponymous owner, Marvin J. Wilson, a local sports celebrity, usually referred to as 'Marvin' or 'MJ'.

"What'll it be gents?" Marvin asked.

"Two beers'll do t'start MJ." Gabe replied.

As in the Old Glory bar, Irish soon began to feel at home and settled easily into these familiar if different surroundings. "What was on y'mind Gabe, did y'have somethin' y'wanted t'say, like?" Irish asked, swigging his chilled beer.

Gabe finished his swallow then said, "Ya seen the neighbourhood yeah, what did ya think of what ya saw?"

"Well it looked pretty rough t'be honest, a bit like Liverpool only on a bigger scale, so-to-speak." Irish replied honestly.

"Yeah, is that right, well I don't know about Liverpool but I do know that less than ten years ago this place didn't look nothin' like it does now. Since those mother fuckin' dealers have taken over bit by bit, floodin' the streets with their shit, no one's safe no more, young or old." Gabe advised with a growing tone of anger in his voice, continuing, "When I joined the Corps, I took an oath to defend my country from all enemies foreign and domestic, and that's what I intend to do until my last breath."

Irish smiled, "Well that's grand, now yer in the bizzies... I mean cops, yer'll be able t'do just that all the time."

Gabe caught hold of his wrist with his powerful hand saying, "I love my country and I will do anything to keep her safe, no matter if it's an enemy or a 'friend' of mine who puts her in danger. Ya with me brother?"

Irish blanched feeling uneasy, he now fully understood why he was there, "Gabe, I'm with yer, no need t'worry on my account, honest."

Gabe smiled and released his friend's forearm from his vice-like grip. "That's good Irish, real good. I like you an Rosita, ya'll make a nice couple, don't let nothin' fuck up what ya've got there, or ya'll regret it for the rest of ya days."

Muddy Waters outstanding *Im a Man* now began to play, encouraging Gabe and several other drinkers to join in, cheering, banging down their glasses or bottles rhythmically on the tables, or bar, shouting, "Is right brother, is right!"

With several more rounds of drinks following in quick succession both Veteran and Skinhead relaxed enjoying the chilled atmosphere. Sitting in the small bar, drinking their beers, listening to great tunes on the juke box, they had no idea that a storm was coming their way and it was travelling fast.

Two blocks over from their hostelry location, a teenage African American boy was about to try his hand at obtaining some easy money. Threatening the young, spotty faced, male cashier, who was not much older than himself, in a dimly lit late night drug store, he drew his black, shiny, starting pistol and demanded the night's takings. His counterpart fancied he was something of a dime-store cowboy, drawing his own fully loaded, genuine article ready to return fire. The boy saw the weapon, panicked and threw his own 'gun' directly at the cashier, causing him to discharge his. Staggering back a few paces the teenager was fatally wounded, already dead before his body hit the greasy linolium-covered floor.

Rooky police officer Jacob Wazinski was first on the scene, having already been sitting with his partner in their vehicle parked nearby. Instinctively responding to the sound of the shot, he drew his Colt Python, running into the store. Officer Wazinski found the dead perpetrator where he lay, in a pool of blood and knelt down in the desperate hope of locating some faint sign of life, that he may be able to resuscitate the boy.

Other members of the community burst into the store while Wazinski's partner rang for backup from any other units in the area. Horror and rage filled the locals as they saw the grim indicting tableau before them. A black youth had been shot down and a young white police officer was stained with his blood, still holding his unholstered gun in his hand, nothing needed to be said, the picture was self evident. When the word hit the street it broke into a sprint, racing for the Projects. Now it no longer mattered who fired the fatal bullet, the fuse had been lit and the powder keg was about to explode.

"Lorra noise from those punk kids t'night." Marvin, the elderly bar owner observed, while he poured two shots of Bourbon for Gabe and Irish, commenting on the growing clamour from the street outside, rising even above the sound of the juke box currently playing Howlin' Wolf's *Smoke Stack Lightnin'*.

"Whats the matter, gettin' jittery in ya old age are ya Marvin?" Gabe asked with a grin.

"Maybe I is, these kids nowadays ain't got no respect. What we need is more cops on the beat, give them a good slap when they step outa line." Marvin concluded.

"I think we got plenty of those already man." Gabe replied.

Even as he finished speaking a bloodied, battered police officer staggered into the bar though the front door. "F'God's sake give me some help!" he called.

Gabe leapt from his bar stool, immediately taking control of the situation, giving orders while running to the wounded man's aid.

"Some of you guys get a couple of tables over here now, block this doorway. MJ, call the cops an if ya've still got 'home run Rube' under the counter, let me have 'im."

Marvin, who had been an all conquering baseball hero in the days of the 'Negro Leagues,' did as instructed, dialling the number of the local precinct with one hand whilst tossing his trophy winning bat to Gabe with the other. 'Never Struck Out!' was lightly carved and inked along the grain of the hickory wood shaft. Gabe was determined to put it to good use if need be.

Irish had as yet remained seated, reluctant to assist, viewing all police not just those of the Crown Estate and Liverpool, as his natural enemy. Several of the other drinkers shared a similar feeling, having no particular love of the largely white comprised New York City police force.

Instinctively sensing the reason for their lack of assistance and annoyed by their initial inertia, Gabe demanded "What the fuck's goin' on here, this is a human being who's been hurt and needs our help, gerroff ya butts and lend a hand, or hang up ya cocks in the bathroom." Galvanised by his stinging criticism they all followed his orders without objection.

The attack was imminent and within moments of barricading the door, the mob, who had split into two factions, those baying for the police officer's blood and those who felt stealing a twenty-six inch colour TV and other electrical appliances was righteous compensation, directed their attentions to battering down the wooden obstruction and hurling bricks at the bar's single plate-glass window.

With the wounded man safely secured in Marvin's back room, Gabe gave the order to remove the stacked tables from the entrance, preparing to take the fight to the mob.

"Ya'll stay in here, close the door behind me; don't let no fucker in no matter what happens." he warned then sprang out into the raging storm that awaited him. "Move the fuck away from this place, ain't none of ya gettin' past me." the ex-Marine instructed.

"Gerrout of our way you mother fuckin' Uncle Tom bitch." a huge, muscular, African American roared in reply.

"Give us that cracker pig before we cut ya down boy!" another member of the raging crowd shouted.

"None of you fools is gonna lay a hand on that man, not while am standin', so step off before the cops arrive." Gabe called back defiantly, preparing to swing his bat over his left shoulder.

Knowing from bitter experience in these desperate situations that attack was the best form of defence, even as the giant came at him, Gabe swung with all his might, bursting the man's nose wide open and cracking his skull with an equally powerful second stroke. His next challenger was quickly dismissed with similar efficacy, stumbling about with a broken face after receiving two devastating blows from 'Rube'. Gabe had stepped up to the plate and was delivering a tour de force in striking out all comers, either using his sporting weapon with both hands or by transferring it to one only, deploying his piledriver punch with the same awesome effect. Soon his hands and the shaft of the bat were covered in blood, snot and gore. His attackers wisely moved out of striking range, resorting to hurling projectiles at the lone ex-Marine, bat-wielding fury, instead.

Inside the bar, Irish was becoming increasingly agitated. He was no stranger to this type of action and disliked being unable to gauge the size of the enemy, preferring the decisive moment of actual contact to the agonising period of uncertainty that preceded it. The single plate-glass window was finally shattered into thousands of glittering fragments as a mixed volley struck the bar and its determined defender. Irish could bear the inactivity no longer and, disobeying the veteran's orders, moved the table barricade to one side, pulled the door open and leapt out to join Gabe, armed with a pool cue that he had snatched from one of the tables.

"There's another fuckin' snowflake." one of the mob shouted, leading a companion to question "How many white boys you hidin' in there mother fucker?"

Even as Gabe turned to look towards Irish, he was struck by a flying bottle on the top of his head, which immediately opened a series of bloodied cuts. Irish came to his side, swinging his own improvised weapon in a wild arc, keeping their attackers at pool cue length.

"I told ya t'stay inside man!" Gabe shouted angrily.

Irish did not reply, as, at that moment two homemade incendiary devices were thrown through the shattered window, exploding into balls of flame on impact. The small bar, stacked with spirits, was ablaze in a matter of seconds with an accompanying thick, black smoke billowing out of the open doorway, shortly after. All the other occupants including Marvin the owner rapidly vacated the building, leaving only the wounded police officer in the back room.

The crowd were ecstatic. "Let the fuckin' pig roast!" one of them called, raising a chorus of approving cheers.

With no thought for his own safety Gabe darted back through the dense choking smoke; there was a man down and that was all that mattered. 'Never leave a man behind' was his life's motto, he was not about to change now.

"Gabe, leave the fuckin bizzie, forget him, he's gone!" Irish called after him, convincing himself that it was his natural hatred of the police that was causing him not to act, rather than an overriding desire for self-preservation.

"Clear this area! Clear this area now!" the commanding officer called over the loud hailer, as his crew of riot police forced their way through the mob and took up their positions.

Irish was roughly pushed into the crowd while a perimeter cordon of black- uniformed males was formed. Acrid smoke, blinding search lights, wild screams and the sound of boots crunching glass underfoot, created a surreal scene all about as Gabe emerged from the firey hell-hole, dragging the wounded cop, still holding 'Home Run Rube' in his mighty hand. Turning in their direction a group of riot officers were horrified by the sight before them. A huge, muscular black male was standing with his arm around a bloodied NYPD colleague of theirs, whilst grasping a blood-stained baseball bat. In an exact paradoxical opposite image to that which had unleashed this night of madness, it was equally self-evident to them what had occurred. Seeing with unreasoning eyes formed by generations of bigotry and racial hatred, the rational ego totally subsumed by the unrestrained id, they could draw only one conclusion and pursue only one course of action.

"Freeze, you black son of a bitch!" one officer called as a preliminary warning, raising his gun ready to shoot at the slightest perceived resistance. Gabe crouched a little further, lowering his weapon as he did. It was all the provocation the officer required, firing at once, without hesitation. The bullet struck the veteran high to his right side, shattering his collar bone, causing him to stagger forward a few paces. Faced with this seemingly deadly threat, the officer and his colleagues immediately surrounded the wounded veteran, pounding him from every possible angle with their batons. Even after Gabe had collapsed to his knees, blow after blow rained down upon him.

Irish broke free from the crowd, roaring "No! For Christ's sake no!" But Christ was not to be found amongst that unholy assembly. As Irish reached the baton wielding uniformed gang, two of them turned their attention towards him, lashing out at his head, chest and abdomen.

"Stay the fuck outa this!" one of them warned, his baton striking Irish across the bridge of the nose.

The Crown Player lost his footing and fell close to where Gabe's relentless beating raged on.

Finally they tired of their sport, concentrating instead on moving the crowd out of the vicinity. Irish the Skinhead crawled to his battered, unconscious friend, cursing the evil that had been set upon him, praying for his life.

Gabe's hoped for police career of service to the public, was rapidly disappearing along with his scarlet blood as it flowed along the sidewalk and down into the gutter. The recipient of two Purple Hearts, a Silver Star and countless citations for bravery, he would eventually recover from his injuries but never sufficiently to be allowed to lay his life on the line again. His dream ended on the filthy pavement of his beloved city, protecting and serving to the last. Gabe was just another innocent victim of being in the right skin in his rightful place, at a time of wrong.

When the police eventually managed to disperse the mob and restore some semblance of order, there were many casualties, with varying degrees of injury. Shortly after the FDNY and emergency services arrived, the ambulances began ferrying away first those who the paramedics assessed as critical or serious, dealing with the walking wounded on site.

The unconscious Gabe was among those urgent patients who were raced to hospitals across the city. Irish insisted on accompanying his battered friend to provide whatever details he could about his identity. Fortunately the veteran always wore his service dog tags and when his blood soaked 'God Bless America' tee-shirt was cut from him, these were uncovered, requiring Irish to give only the briefest of additional information. Wounds cleaned and dressed, the Crown Team player was soon discharged, leaving his friend to the care of the professionals.

In the early hours of Monday morning he caught a cab back to the lower East Side and McCabe's Grande Hotel. Irish had a lot to reflect upon as he lay in his restless bed in the boiling room. He knew he would be returning to Liverpool and the Crown Estate shortly, conveying another consignment of the contageon that had already ravaged Gabe's community and must surely do the same to his.

When he eventually said farewell to Rosita two days later on a sultry Tuesday night, they embraced and kissed passionately, both declaring their deep feelings for each other.

"Don't be gone too long Patrick, I really miss you." Rosita announced with tears in her dark eyes.

"I'll be back as soon as I can, I promise." Irish replied with genuine intent.

"Maybe you could stay a bit longer next time... or even get a job here... then you wouldn't have t'go back... ever." Rosita suggested hopefully.

Irish was already planning his exit strategy from his employment with the Gerard Boys but accepted that his timing for this bold move would entirely depend on his brother's discharge from hospital and then his mother's relocation back home to Ireland with him and the young Sean. Once he knew they were safe he intended to put his game-plan into effect but not before that moment.

"Rosita, believe me there's nothin' I want more. When the time comes there'll be no more Atlantic crossin's for me, I'll be stayin 'ere, with you, for as long as y'want me."

Rosita kissed him again then nestled her head onto his shoulder, holding the Miraculous Medal that he had given her between her forefinger and thumb, saying "That's what I've been prayin' for Patrick, let's not let anythin' get in our way."

Though her prayers were devout, cruel fate still waited in the wings to torment them both further, before they could be answered.

CHAPTER 8

Jeremiah Johnson

Monday 6th September 1976

Late on a cold, wet September night, Irish arrived back in Liverpool at Lime Street Station. The long hot summer and the unprecedented heatwave had ended during the time he had been away, when, in the second week of August the heavens had opened quickly restoring England's parched, yellowed grasses and scorched heaths, to their former verdant glory.

Struggling with his excessively heavy baggage, Irish trudged uphill, the short distance from the famed nineteenth century station to the infamous Victorian alehouse. With *Big River* by Johnny Cash playing on the juke box in the smoky saloon bar he crashed in through the swing door, spraying rain all about, anxious to be rid of his lethal load.

"Alright lad, back in the Pool hey, I bet y'fuckin' glad t'be home." Niall observed, in his usual sardonic manner, when Irish was ushered into his presence in the first floor parlour.

Danny Boy was quickly despatched with Irish's battered cases, to the Gerard Boy's private quarters above, charged with inspecting the goods and checking all was as listed in their own detailed manifest. While this audit was being conducted Irish was provided with a pint of Guinness and two packets of cheese and onion crisps, by way of a suitable snack and invited to sit in front of the three senior brothers.

"Been gettin' around in New York have yer Patrick, broadening yer horizon's is it?" Niall asked knowingly.

"I'm not sure what yer mean Niall but I did 'ave a bit of a look round while I was there." Irish replied.

"I'll bet it was a bit fuckin' lively up in Harlem when yer was 'lookin' round' there, was it?" Francis observed.

Irish took a lengthy draught of his pint, replying, "No more lively than the Crown Estate on a Saturday night, bizzies are cunts wherever y'meet them, here or in the States."

Niall laughed, "How's it goin' with yer Seniorita, gettin' a bit heavy is is?"

"Nah, I wouldn't say that, it's nothin' I couldn't walk away from." Irish lied.

"Fuckin' good 'cause that's just what yer gonna be doin' boy." Niall announced, continuing "Yer've probably got another couple of trips left goin' t'New York, three at most and then yer'll be changin' yer route."

"Why's that, why 'ave I gorra change, what about the other lads...?" Irish blurted out without thinking.

Niall instantly transformed from his genial façade, demanding, "What other fuckin' lads; who've you been talkin' to?"

Irish realised he had revealed too much and tried to retrieve the situation.

"No one... I just thought y'might have some other fellers doin' the same line of work for yer, that's all."

Niall was unconvinced, "It's that fuckin' arl fool McCabe, isn't it? I bet he's been flappin' his gums, the soft arl git. He'll be gettin' a slap if he opens his fuckin' trap again."

"Niall it was nothin'... honest. He's harmless... arl Ben, no need t'go hurtin' him on my account..." Irish offered but was interrupted by a livid Niall.

"Don't you fuckin' tell *me* what t'do, yer gobshite. If that arl tit becomes a liability a lot of people could go down, so he's gonna be after gettin' a visit from our Alfie, just t'remind him."

At that moment Danny returned and once again confirmed that everything in this delivery was as it should be which restored Niall to a seemingly more pleasant demeanour. "Yer remember that little scrap yer had with those Ravens pricks in the cemetery?" he began, "It turns out those fuckers didn't take their kickin' too good and thee was thinkin' of grassin' t'the bizzies about you."

Irish was astounded as this proposed action would be a breech of all established protocol. "Y'fuckin' jokin' Niall, not even those cunts are that low that thee'd rat t'the bizzies, about a fuckin' kickin'."

Niall smiled, "Is that yer Skinhead code is it? Y'fuckin' ejit, thee weren't gonna grass about that, the law wouldn't give two fucks about a gang of bitches havin' a lover's tiff in the cemetery. Some of their boys reckon thee was hangin' round there one night earlier in the year, when a total fuckin' wierdo got twatted by a certain scooter-ridin' Skinhead that fits your description."

Irish realised he was in a difficult predicament, asking, "They're not gonna grass me up are thee, f'fuck's sake?"

"Not *now* they're not." Niall advised, continuing, "Thee've been put wise, so they're gonna forget all about it."

"Thank fuck f'that. Thanks Niall f'sortin' it out." a relieved Irish replied.

Niall's smile broadened even as his grip on the Crown Team player tightened further. "Loss of memory costs, Patrick, d'yer follow what I'm sayin'?" he asked.

"Yeah of course Niall, I understand." Irish replied.

"Good, 'cause you keep that in mind, we've got enough on you to let yer go down for a long stretch. We're keepin' you out the nick 'cause it suits us, for now, but fuck us about in any way, get some smart arse ideas in yer cropped head and those Ravens pricks are gonna be gettin' their memories back, just like that." He clicked the fingers of his right hand to signify their instantaneous recovery.

Irish continued drinking his pint, trying not to let his expression, or errant eyebrow, betray him, conscious that Francis was studying him closely.

"I'm just happy to be doin' me job and be gettin' paid Niall, so no need t'worry about *me*." he replied as calmly and straight-faced as he could.

It appeared that he had passed Francis's scrutiny as he made no comment.

Niall reached into the pocket of his tailored suit jacket and passed Irish his wages, "That's good Patrick, real good." he said, unknowingly mimicking the words of Gabe when Irish had made a similar promise to him, though for an entirely different purpose. "Relax and have another bevvie, before y'get off." he offered, now the generous host, "Yer'll be keen t'see yer ma when yer get home no doubt, give her my regards, tell her I was askin' about her health and, yer brother."

Irish sat uncomfortably in their presence, listening to the juke box and swallowing his second pint as rapidly as he could, without appearing to be in haste to leave their company.

Thoughts of his mother and his elder brother's condition were uppermost in his mind also.

When he finally reached his home on the bleak Crown Estate, Irish was both happy to see his mother and sad to find her still in residence. Although his brother's condition had been downgraded to stable, the hospital doctors had, as yet, given no indication of when he may be considered fit for discharge. Irish would have to put his plans on hold; he could make no move that might betray his hand, until his family were completely safe, out of harm's way. Forced to play the waiting game Irish followed the routine he had now established, settling back into his life on the estate, ready to receive the next summons to return to the USA and the lovely Rosita.

Time moved on with only the mundane filling the shortening Autumnal days and his yearning desire to see Rosita once more, tormenting the lengthening darkness of each passing night. Those days became weeks and eventually, just as that dreary, wet September drew to a close Irish was again despatched to New York City.

Friday 8th October 1976
Arriving on a bright, crisp, 'Fall' day in early October, Irish sought out the girl of his dreams as soon as her evening shift at Uncle Sam's began. For the two reunited lovers it was as if that same time had stood still, resuming their romance anew, happy just to be in each other's company.

Apart from exchanging their news on what had occurred on either side of the Atlantic, Irish was anxious to hear if Rosita had any word on the condition of Gabe.

"Oh yeah Patrick, it was all in the papers... sayin' what a great guy he is... what he'd done for his country... and that it was a disgrace what had happened to him. Anyway the cop you said Gabe rescued from the burning bar gave a full statement sayin' how if Gabe hadnt've been there, he would've been murdered or burned t'death. He said Gabe was a genuine American hero."

Irish was delighted, "Thank God, 'cause that's just what he is. I'll have t'go an see 'im before I go back t'Liverpool but it might not be a good idea to go into his neighbourhood again, without him."

"Y'don't need to, he's been taken care of in some place overlooking Central Park, I'll get the details for ya, out the newspaper. Some rich guy, whose son was in the army but got killed, is sortin' everythin' out for him, medical expenses, a place to live, the whole thing." Rosita added, making Irish even happier and restoring his faith that perhaps some prayers *are* answered.

Wednesday 13th October 1976

Several days later, before his latest stay in New York drew to an enforced close, Irish made his way to the up-market, Upper East Side, Fifth Avenue apartment address, that Rosita had provided him with. The snooty uniformed consierge was at first reluctant to admit Mr Stone's uninvited, peculiarly dressed guest, particularly as he clearly did not have an appointment, or failed to produce an appropriate card of introduction. Fortunately it transpired that Mr Stone was at home and receiving company, especially when he was informed that his caller was a certain Mr Patrick O'Hare of Liverpool Town, England.

"What's happenin' brother?" Gabe asked with a beaming smile, opening the door of his penthouse appartment using his left hand, the other still strapped up in a sling bound diagonally across his wounded clavicle and admitting Irish, before wheeling himself back into the spacious room, in his chair.

Momentarily Irish was downhearted at seeing the disabled condition of his mighty friend but the irrepressible Gabe would have none of it. "Don't get down about this chair man, its only temporary I've got some nerve problems with my legs but I'll be up runnin' my usual routes soon. Besides, the chicks dig it, I can't tell yer how much sympathy sex I've been gettin'." he said, lying.

Irish looked about the airy, bright apartment, taking in the expensive, hand-crafted furniture, juxtaposed antique and modern ornamentation, the huge television set and an impressive hi-fi system, currently playing the title track from Kool and the Gang's *Wild and Peaceful* album. His attention was drawn to a portrait study of a handsome man in his mid-twenties, dressed in a United States Marine Corps officer's uniform. Immediately below where this oil painting hung in its embossed gilt frame, was a triangular, folded Stars and Stripes flag, proudly displayed in a glass case. The Crown Team player began to understand why Gabe's benefactor had been so generous, though did not broach the subject in his observations.

"Fuckin' hell Gabe, yer a jammy bastard. I've taken some bad beatin's meself but no cunt ever set me up with a shag nest like this."

Gabe laughed, "Well ya probably never had a Pulitzer prize winning journalist writin' a piece about you afterwards, did ya?"

"No, I suppose not, there's probably not many of them workin' for the *Liverpool Echo* anyway."

"Help y'self to whatever ya fancy t'drink then take a seat man, it's really good t'see ya. I know what ya did for me Irish." Gabe advised.

Irish poured a whiskey for himself, offering one to Gabe, who declined on medical grounds. "Those bizzies who went for yer were real bastards, I hope thee've all lost their fuckin' jobs." Irish said angrily.

Gabe waved away his comments in his typical philosophical manner, "No need t'go bad-mouthin' the cops, they just done what anyone else woulda done in their position."

"What about that cunt who started it all off, the one who shot yer?" Irish insisted.

"Look Irish, it was a hairy situation man, I've been in plenty of those myself, the guy had to make a judgement call an that's what he did, end of story." Gabe responded firmly, closing their discussion. "Anyway brother, as y'can see am doin' fine now, old man Peterson who set me up here is a real A1 guy; that's his son, Chris in that paintin'. He was in Nam until '69 but his luck ran out, he didn't make it home." Gabe paused for a few moments before continuing, "Turns out Mr Peterson is the owner of a multi-million dollar publishing company and does a lot of work for the Vets. He's got me writin' a book about my life in the Corps and back here, says it's gonna be a best seller, can ya believe it?"

Irish laughed, genuinely pleased with the news of his friend's good fortune, "Sliante!" he said raising his cut-glass tumbler, filled with a good measure of expensive, aged whiskey.

For the remainder of that afternoon they sat relaxing, swapping anecdotes and amusing tales whilst listening to Gabe's collection of cool tunes, including almost the entire catalogue of Mr Marvin Gaye. As dusk was falling and a myriad pinpoint lights came into life down in the streets below and here and there about the huge public park opposite, giving it a misleading fairy-tale appearance which belied the reality of its deadly nature, Gabe turned their conversation to Irish's own future.

"You're back here brother and ya've said ya'll be gettin' off soon, t'Liverpool, so am takin' it ya still in the same business of 'transportin' stuff from one country to another, am I right?"

Irish knew there was nothing to be gained in lying and replied, "Gabe its complicated mate. I'm gonna get out as soon as I can but that's not possible at this time."

Gabe was unconvinced, "Just tell me one good reason why you can't walk away from these people right now. Ya've already told me it's pretty grim where ya come from, so why not start a new life here with Rosita?"

Irish sighed, replying to his friend's questions in reverse order, "That's *all* I wanna do Gabe, believe me. I don't wanna go back but I've got to for one good reason, me family. These people I'm involved with will really hurt them bad, if I don't do what thee want an am not gonna risk that."

Gabe listened, nodding his head now fully understanding Irish's dilemma, saying "You ain't got but one choice, get ya family t'some place safe."

Again Irish confirmed that this was what he was hoping to do in the near future. Gabe looked directly at his friend saying, "You're a good man Patrick, ya'll is just stuck between a rock and a hard place right now but things'll come good for ya, I just know it. Keep ya mind positive brother, that's what always got me through tight spots."

Irish thanked his friend and rose to leave, "I'll let yer get some rest mate an I'll see yer next time I'm back, hopefully f'good."

Gabe laughed, "I don't know about rest brother, I've got me this fine young nurse comin' over shortly t'raise my spirits... y'know what am sayin? Anyway, you just think on what we've been talkin' bout 'cause I sure as hell don't wanna be readin' bout you in the newspapers for all the wrong reasons. C'mon I'll 'walk' ya out." With those words of warning Gabe wheeled himself towards the door of his appartment and pressed the switch close to the intercom, attached to the adjoining wall to allow it to open. "Catch ya later man!" he called finally.

"See ya Gabe!" Irish replied, making his way to the elevator in the hall.

On reaching the ground floor and about to exit, Irish noticed a heavily built, late forties female in a nurse's uniform, standing at the reception intercom saying "I'm here Mr Stone, are you ready for me now?" He smiled on hearing Gabe's dulcet tones replying "Ready'n'waitin' sugar, c'mon up."

Following his visit with Gabe, Irish spent as much as possible of his remaining time in New York with Rosita, when she was not engaged either with her studies or waitress duties. On a cool Autumnal Sunday night, after receiving his luggage earlier that day, he said goodbye once more to his lover, this time promising, with a necessary caveat, that it would be their last parting.

"As soon as I know me family are safe, there'll be no goin' back, me and you will be together, whatever it takes."

Rosita understood what he was saying; totally in agreement with his sentiment, "Patrick we've both got our families and would never let anyone harm them. So don't you worry about time, just make sure they're safe. I'll be here waitin' for ya, as long as it takes."

Early the next morning before the sun had risen, in the cold, pre-dawn darkness, Irish embarked on his return journey across the Atlantic. He hoped that his next voyage to New

York would be his last, determined more than ever to escape from the Gerard Boys, the Crown Estate and his present life.

Friday 5th November 1976

Irish had been back on the Crown Estate for barely a week, having been away for almost the entire month of October, either at sea or in New York. It was the fifth of November, Bonfire Night and he and Blue had just left The Eagle public house, unusually before closing time, after an evening's drinking and tall-story telling with other ex-members of their team. Irish the Skinhead turned up the collar of his well-cut Crombie, with Blue the henpecked husband doing the same with the broad collar of his long, double-breasted, black leather overcoat.

Directly across the road from them a group of teenage boys and girls were gathered around the semi-circular façade of the dilapidated library building. Dressed in loose leather jackets of a biker style, or denim alternatives, drainpipe jeans with a mixed selection of footwear, including dirty training shoes or scuffed old army boots, their hair was cut in a tufted, unkempt, scruffy style. Their appearance and manner was aggressive but without the sharpness of their Skinhead forebears, more as if they did not care how they looked. In many ways they could be seen as parodies or caricatures of previous youth street-fashion.

As Irish and Blue approached, the group began jumping about, slamming into each other, shouting, spitting and generally jostling themselves, spreading out across the pavement. One tall, skinny male with a stark, peroxide blond, spiky haircut, crashed into Blue.

"Watch where yer goin' there lad." Blue advised.

"Fuck off arl man." the youth replied angrily.

Irish had already punched him in the mouth, sending him sprawling into his friends, while Blue was deciding what action to take.

"Don't talk to us like that, y'cheeky fucker. *We* were the Crown Team Skins!" Irish announced.

The whole group stood still, with one of the females answering "Yeah, were yer, well that was fuckin' years ago and this is *now*! We're Crown Punks an yer better not fuck with us!"

Irish and Blue both laughed and turned to walk on, intent as they were in strolling down to Mr Li's Golden Diner for their suppers. A stocky, dark haired male with a number of facial piercings, competing for limited space with his own natural angry yellow and red spots, some of which were threatening to spontaneously errupt imminently, reached into his leather jacket as if about to draw a weapon, "Ey, you two shit heads, don't yous walk off from us, or I'll blow yers away, the pair of yer." he warned.

The former Crown Team players stopped and turned about, with Irish replying "Whatever yer've got there prick, yer'd better leave it 'cause if yous are really tryin' to threaten *us*, you must be soft in the fuckin' head." Irish waited a few silent moments then continued, "Make y'move boy but am warnin' yer if yer do pull a weapon outa that jacket, y'better know how t'use it, 'cause I'm gonna come over there and ram it right up your fuckin' arse, whatever it is."

The spotty youth kept his hand inside his jacket, saying nothing at first, then laughed, replying "We'll leave it f'now, let it go but remember who we are. We run this fuckin' estate and don't *you* forget it."

Irish and Blue turned away once more and resumed their journey; as they did the boy brought out his empty hand, mimicking the shape of a gun, raising his thumb and pointing his index finger in their direction, "Bang, bang, yers are both dead!" he called after them, grining slyly.

"What the fuck was all that about, why did that soft bitch call them all 'punks' I could see for meself that's all thee were, without her havin' to admit it?" Irish asked, bemused by the use of what had previously been considered as a derogatory term on both sides of the Atlantic, for any young aspiring, if unconvincing, street gang member or would-be tough guy.

"Irish, yer've been back'n'forth between 'ere and the States all these months but yer've totally missed what's been goin' on 'ere and there, by the sounds of it." Blue began then advised, "These kids wanna be called punks, thee think its somethin' cool, like us when we was Skins or Suedes, or even Boot Boys, this is their thing, our game's well and truly over. I mean, look around mate, you're the only fucker who still wears all the Skinhead gear, that's well dead, no disrespect like."

Irish remained mystified by what this latest youth fashion departure was meant to symbolise and dismissed it as a passing fad that would probably be gone before the year was out. "Fuck them, the little punks, that'll go nowhere whose gonna be arsed dressin' like a fuckin' scuffy wierdo, it'll never catch on. Come 'ed let's get some decent scran from Mr Li's."

Though he had spent some time in the city that arguably spawned this latest youth cult, New York, with bands like the Ramones, New York Dolls, Televison and others taking Rock'n'Roll back to basics, re-establishing its raw energy and rescuing it from mainstream moguls who had all but sucked the raging life out of a people's music and replaced it with a saccharin sweet, pop muzak, Irish had been totally oblivious to the momentous events that were occurring around him, that would reshape and redefine popular culture for a new generation. Once this embryonic punk movement crossed the Atlantic with the aid of entrepeneurs like Malcom McLaren and was filtered through a specifically English art school medium to give it a distinctive, unique look, it would rapidly spread out across that country and ultimately re-export itself back to the USA, to morph into its Americanised form that would last well into the following decade.

Irish was wrong to dismiss these particular punks as a fleeting fad and in failing to consider them as anything of a threat. Both time and trial would conspire to teach him otherwise.

Following a brief stroll they arrived at the Golden Diner and Irish concluded the tale he had been telling Blue during their brief journey "...so that's it really Blue, Rosita is somethin' special and as soon as the chance comes, I'm gonna be spendin' all me time with her, y'know worra mean?"

Blue laughed "Fuckin' right mate, it's about time, yer can't go on enjoyin' yerself forever."

They ambled into Mr Li's brightly lit, welcoming establishment, savouring the enticing fragrance of fried comfort food. Once they had purchased their meals of golden battered cod, thick cut soggy chips and an additional sausage dinner with extra chips and gravy for Blue, the pair left the shop and wandered past The Heron ale house standing nearby in the centre of its ever empty car park.

"What the fuck's been goin' on here?" Irish asked, even more surprised than his encounter with the Crown Punks. The rundown, utilitarian, purpose-built building that was The Heron pub and unofficial headquarters of the eponymous crew, who gathered there, was completely boarded across its windows and entrance porch, with its simple name sign removed. Its entire frontage was covered in black painted graffiti announcing 'Crown Punx' and 'Fuck You!' repeated several times for emphasis, with a list of 'names' added to aid identification.

Irish could barely believe what he was seeing, repeating, "Fuckin' hell Blue, yer better fill me in mate, some major shit's been happenin' while I've been away, that's f'sure."

"It started gettin' really bad 'bout a month ago, yer already know there's been loads of drugs comin' onto the estate for ages but now the whole fuckin' place is gettin' swamped with them." Blue began his tale, in between shovelling large handfulls of steaming white cod and greasy chips into his mouth. "Yeah so anyway, like I say, some of these punk characters started takin' over in The Heron, makin' it their place and then was dealin' from there. Next thing is there's a fuckin' big kick off, the manager got blinded by some cunt with a bottle and then the bizzies raided the place." Blue stopped once again to force the last of his fish supper into his mouth, before commencing on his sausage based second course. "A couple of days after that the place was closed down and thee started puttin' up these boards. Thee say its just gettin' redecorated but I think that's all me arse. I tell yer what Irish somebody's gorra sort out these drugs bastards, before its too fuckin' late."

Irish was unable to reply as the grim realisation that he had now become the instrument of destruction of his own home, had been painfully dawning upon him even as Blue spoke.

While Blue had been eating-talking-eating, they had been meandering in the direction of the old uncultivated farmers field situated at the rear of the Heron pub. They could already smell the acrid smoke from the traditional bonfire that was roaring ablaze, with huge tongues of orange-red flame lapping the bitterly cold, black night sky, even before they arrived at the overgrown abandoned field, which had been the site of many of the Crown Team's battles with their former bitter rivals from the Kings Estate.

Apart from a small crew of young males sitting on the damp grass, passing a hefty herbal joint amongst them, there was one dark figure standing alone, seemingly staring vacantly into the distance beyond; Weaver, the crazed hammer-wielding psychopath. Wearing his old black Crombie with its collar turned up and his wild hair blowing across his craggy features in the stiffening breeze, he could have been viewed by some as a tormented figure from any number of nineteenth century romantic novels but to those who knew him *he* was the figure responsible for the tormenting.

To Irish, however, having recently been in violent combat alongside him, he now presented something of an enigma appearing in this instance as a sad, pathetic character no longer with any real purpose.

"Alright Weaver, have a chip lad!" Irish shouted, startling the mad man who turned, reached over to the remains of Irish's newspaper wrapped meal and grabbed a handful of cold chips greedily.

Blue decided not to make a similar offer, quickly stuffing as much of his sausage dinner into his gaping mouth as possible. "What are yer doin' Weaver, watchin' the fireworks?" he asked choking down his food.

"Thee is no fuckin' fireworks, soft arse." Weaver advised in his usual surly manner, adding "Am lookin' at those cheeky Kings bastards over there, tryin' to wind me up."

Irish and Blue looked across the main aterial road to where, several hundred yards away, a group of Kings youths had lit a huge bonfire of their own.

"What is it they're doin' to wind *you* up Weaver?" Irish asked.

"Fuckin' hell are yer blind, Irish? Can't yer see the size of that fire? They're takin' the fuckin' piss lad. I've gorra good mind t'go over there and do the fuckin' lorra them." Weaver replied, his voice rising in anger.

"What's stoppin' yer? Yer don't usually give a fuck about how many there is, what about these boys 'ere, have yer asked them?" Irish persisted.

"Yeah, course I'ave but these pricks are total pot heads, they're fuckin' stoned, no use t'me, an as for goin' on me own, its too risky nowadays, no one wants t'stand and scrap any more, thee've all got fuckin' shooters."

Irish was stunned for a second time that night, asking naively, "How d'yer mean like?"

Weaver stared at him quizically, "'Ave you been on the fuckin' moon or somethin'? Guns are all over the place now; some cunt must be makin' a fortune. First thee sell their drugs everywhere an then thee sell the guns to the same fuckers. I don't know where they're comin' from but its gettin' like the Wild West round 'ere."

It finally dawned on Irish the true nature of what he had been transporting from the US and why his cases had been becoming increasingly heavy. He carried the ultimate contagion *and* the means of assisting its deadly outbreak. Feeling nauseous, Irish turned to walk away with Blue but Weaver caught hold of his arm.

"'Ere, have a look at this beaut." he said opening his Crombie so that they could see the latest acquisition to his own arsenal.

There tucked into the waistband of his jeans was a gleaming, nickel-plated, M1911 Colt.45.

"What d'yer want that for, got tired of usin' yer toffee hammer?" Irish asked.

"Nah, I still use Thor whenever I get the chance but even *he's* not gonna be much use, if I come up against some cunt armed with one of these. You know the score Irish, its kill or be killed and am not about t'be shot dead by some sneaky bastard with a grudge." he answered with a wicked grin. His relationship with his new 'best friend' would only be temporary however, when shortly after depleted funds led him to trade the lethal weapon for hard cash, a decision the madman would ultimately live to regret.

Irish did not reply but pulled his arm free from Weaver's grip and walked off with Blue in tow.

A short time later as they reached the street where they both lived, Blue asked a knowing question, "It's *you*, isn't it? You're the one bringin' this shite 'ere for the Gerard Boys?" Irish did not deny it and Blue continued angrily, "The drugs, the guns it's all you, yer cunt. I've got two little daughters; we've got to live here. Do us all a favour, fuck off back to the States and stay there, don't bother sayin' goodbye, just fuck off."

Irish did not sleep well that night. Racked with guilt he tossed and turned arguing with himself but was unable to escape from the cold, irrefutable truth that he was at the root of all the present misfortunes that were overtaking the estate, where he had lived since a child and which previously he had always tried to defend from any threat. Irish had brought misery and death to his own doorstep.

Two days later that dreadful message would be further underscored, by an incident that shocked even the most hardened residents of that bleak, post-war, overspill housing development. At close of business just before midnight, on a bitterly cold, rainy night a group of punks burst into Mr Li's famed Golden Diner and demanded the contents of his cash till from him. With his usual calm stoicism, the much respected Chinese proprietor refused, telling them all to leave his shop. A certain spotty-faced youth reached into his loose leather jacket and this time drew the genuine article, rather than his imitation 'fist' gun, aiming it at Mr Li as he stood perfectly still behind his spotless counter.

Even before the punk could squeeze the trigger of his deadly weapon, in a blur of lightning fast movement the Oriental warrior threw his own, the meat cleaver with razor sharp edge that usually appeared to be permanently attached to his right hand, with unerring accuracy. Struck hard in the dead centre of his sternum at pectoral height, the youth crashed to the ground, blood pouring from his deep chest wound. His accomplices panicked and fled the scene but not before one of them picked up the unfired gun, from where his wounded friend had dropped it.

Mr Li called to his wife who very rarely emerged from the back room of the premises, to telephone the emergency services at once then leapt over the counter to administer first aid to the would-be robber. When the police arrived they found a Caucasian youth, unarmed, with life-threatening injuries and the apologetic Chinese gentleman kneeling over his blood-drenched body trying desperately to revive him; the equally blood-stained cleaver lay nearby.

In the absence of any trace of the gun that Mr Li referred to, he was arrested, formally charged with attempted murder and taken away to face the full rigours of English law, even while the unsuccessful perpetrator was being conveyed to a nearby hospital by the ambulance service. For the first time in the memory of even the oldest original tenants of the bleak council estate, Mr Li's Golden Diner was closed. Like The Heron alehouse next door but for entirely different reasons, it would never re-open.

Subsequently at Mr Li's trial for his deadly charge, the prosecution barrister presented a highly emotive performance, worthy of Victorian theatre, proving beyond any possibility of reasonable doubt, despite innumerable glowing testimonials from locals past and present, that this 'inscrutable fiend' had over-reacted to the poor, innocent boy's request for a fish supper, after business had concluded for the day. If hanging would still have been an option, despite the fact that the youth survived his wound, this righteous legal eagle would have demanded it as the only just and proper punishment. Instead he was prepared to accept on behalf of the Crown, a lengthy term of imprisonment for the murderous Mr Li.

Tuesday 9th November 1976

When news of what had really occurred in the chip shop that fateful night reached him, Irish was distraught almost considering approaching the police and admitting his part in the supplying of both the poisonous drugs and the weapons by which some saught to obtain the funds to purchase them.

So obsessed was he in wallowing in his own self-inflicted misery, that he declined an offer from his mother to visit his brother Dermot in hospital that evening.

"No thanks ma, I'll give it a miss, the way am feelin' right now I'd only depress the life out of our Dermot, not cheer him up." he advised.

"Alright son, if that's how y'feel, hopefully it'll be good news tonight. I've done all me Novenas and had another Mass said for him today by Fr. Finnegan." his mother replied, adding, "and by the way if it's a girl that's gettin' yer down, don't worry there's always more fish in the sea."

"Brilliant ma, thanks f'that, I feel better already." her son answered, putting on his Crombie, preparing to leave for The Eagle.

Irish's destination for this evening's drinking session was not the slightly more salubrious, noisy lounge with its lively juke box and even livelier crowd of regulars. For him there was now only one place that suited his present mood, the bare floorboarded, spit and sawdust, undecorated gloomy bar of that same alehouse, the last resort of the depressed and life weary serious drinker. Having been served his double measure of whiskey and two pints of Guinness, Irish joined the ranks of other lost souls sitting at the small circular tables, each individually contributing to the melancholic milieu, some desperately searching for a solution, others too far removed from reality to even remember the cause of their driving need for liquid solace.

For Irish, even as the hours passed and time lost any meaning, the more he drank the less comforted he felt, no answers were to be found at the bottom of his glass, a frustrating outcome that any of his fellow hardened imbibers could have warned him of, if they had been capable of communicating coherently. Yet more annoying was the paradoxical conundrum of his inability to become drunk.

'Fuckin' hell, I can't even get that right' he thought, laughing loudly in an inane manner, without realising that he was.

Eventually, once again unusually for Irish before last orders had been called, he finished the last dregs of his final pint, threw back his whiskey and staggered out into the bitterly cold night air. Almost instantly he realised that he was woefully mistaken about his lack of intoxication as the freezing chill assailed his senses, while he lurched from alehouse door to its low perimeter walls. Before he had even passed the row of dilapidated, graffiti covered shops, Irish had to stop and void his churning stomach, violently.

Only yards from his own home the desperate need to relieve himself led to a lengthy al fresco urination, onto the unsuspecting head of the one remaining garden gnome who toiled heroically on the tiny patch of grass, immediately outside Irish's neighbour's house, situated directly opposite his.

When the strangely resistant lock on his front door finally stayed still long enough for Irish to insert his key, he stumbled inside and collapsed onto the floor of the living room.

"Back are yer, arsehole, and pissed by the look of it?" he heard a familiar, if shaky voice call.

Looking up from his position on the floor, Irish was overjoyed to see his brother Dermot in the extended room, even though he was seated in a wheelchair and appearing thin and frail, a shadow of his former self. For a short while Irish could hardly speak, tears of relief and gratitude welling up in his eyes.

"What's brought you back soft lad, got tired of lazin' round in that hospital did yer?" he asked, trying to raise himself from the floor.

Their mother entered the room with two steaming mugs of stewed tea.

"Will yer look at the state of yer, on the night yer poor brother comes home from his sick bed. Drink this and sort yersef out, we've got a lot of talkin' to do."

Just like that Irish's dilemma was resolved; the wait was over now his exit strategy could begin, the end of his nightmare was in sight.

Friday 12th November 1976

On another cold, damp morning with a thin fog rolling in off the sea and along the choppy brown waters of the Mersey, Irish said a last farewell to his departing mother and two brothers, before they embarked on their own brief voyage out to the West.

"Alright ma, you take care now, let me know when yer arrive at aunty Roisin's." he said, embracing her one final time.

"Its you who needs t'take care son, get yerself out of whatever business it is that yer caught up in then come and join us, back home." his tearful mother advised then turned and walked up the gangway, holding young Sean by the hand, who was excited at the prospect of 'riding on the big boat'.

Irish wheeled his elder brother on board then kissed him on the forehead saying "It'll all be sorted now, you'll be fine. All those Colleens will be fallin' over themselves to wheel yer round in yer chair, y'know what they're like." he said, paraphrasing Gabe's own words to some lesser extent.

Dermot looked up at his younger sibling and warned, "Look after yerself wee man and for fuck's sake drop all that Skinhead shite, it's done yer no good. And don't be comin' to visit us in aunty Roisin's wearin' those big red boots; we'll never hear the last of it."

Irish smiled, happy to see that, at least in spirit, his brother was fully recovered.

Sometime later he waved to them as their ship loosed its moorings, weighed anchor and moved out into the broad, deep channels of the world famous river. He followed the vessel's progress until it had exited the yawning mouth and joined the dark Celtic sea, bound for Dublin.

Like countless other sons and daughters of Erin who had made the journey out from their homeland in the great famine and blight driven diaspora of the nineteenth century and their descendents, Mrs O'Hare was amongst many who longed for a return to the land of their birth in songs, poetry and lamentations. Now finally for Irish's mother, the tale had come full circle and was ended.

Saturday 13th November 1976

Sitting relaxing on the old comfortable couch in the living room, Irish was enjoying a huge bowl of Rice Krispies, whilst listening to one of his latest reggae aquisitions, *Front Line*, a compilation album sampler, with the volume of the stereogramme turned to its maximum. He was lord of the manor, king of the castle. As the LP reached the I-Roy track *Don't Touch I Man Locks*, he became aware of a loud persistent knocking on his front door.

"For God's sake turn that bloody awful racket down!" his raging next door neighbour demanded. "Yer've been playin' those fuckin' records all mornin', have some thought for other people will yer!"

Irish stood up, stretched lazily then scratched his backside before walking towards the single-pane front window, lifting the net curtain he saw Mr Murray, a heavily built, early sixties male and recently retired docker from the Port of Liverpool.

"Sorry Mr Murray, I didn't realise you could hear it mate." Irish offered sarcastically then let the curtain drop and raised two fingers in victory salute to his no longer visible neighbour. On lowering the volume of the stereogramme he realised the telephone was ringing and quickly grabbed hold of the receiver.

"Who's that?" the caller asked in an angry, familiar voice.

"It's me, Patrick." Irish replied casually.

"Where the fuck have you been? I've been ringin' this phone all fuckin' mornin'."

Irish did not want to reveal even the slightest hint that his family had departed for Ireland the previous day and that he was temporarily enjoying the freedom of having the entire house to himself, replying simply, "I had a few too many bevvies last night so I slept in, that's all."

"Well get your arse down to The Central *now*. Yer off tomorrer so wake yerself up quick style, we don't want no fuckin' mistakes."

Irish was delighted, everything was falling into place. He quickly dressed, left his home and ran for the next bus bound for the city centre.

Later that day as the freezing cold darkness lay across the estate, having almost completed his packing and preparations, Irish smiled recalling Niall's final instructions. "This *is* yer last trip t'New York, seems there's been a lorra talkin' goin' on by some fuckin' rat, whose tryin' t'save his own skin. Don't you do nothin' stupid and everythin' will go just fine, we'll change yer route in the New Year when things have quietened down, okay?" Irish had nodded his acceptance leaving Niall to warn, "So say goodbye to yer senorita, give her a good hard fuck from me. Yer'll soon find another bird in Boston or Chicago and believe me *she'll* have forgotten all about you and be gettin' humped by some other fucker even before y'get back to Liverpool."

Later in the evening following his meeting at The Central public house, Irish was preparing for one other final matter that he had to attend to. After putting on his Crombie over his Levi's denim jacket and Fleming's jeans, he gave his Airwair a cursory buffing with the soft, polish-stained cloth that he always carried and exited his house, leaving the door on the latch only, ready for the short walk to the home of Blue.

Once he had rung the bell on the neatly painted front door, he waited for his ex-team mate's anticipated angry response.

"Yeah, what is it? We don't need no drugs or guns right now thanks, so fuck off before I call the bizzies." Blue snarled, about to close the door.

Irish shoved his highly polished boot in the way saying, "Just give me a couple of minutes Blue... for old time's sake, yeah?"

His corpulent, long time friend kept the door part closed and said, "Say what yer've got t'say but make it quick, me tea's gettin' cold."

"Alright Blue, I'm off in the mornin' t'the States, I won't be comin' back, me ma and me brothers have already gone 'home' and me sisters are safe out of here. I've paid the rent until the end of the month, so all I'm askin' is you keep an eye on the place until then and drop the keys off with the Corpy landlord." He paused and waited for Blue's response.

"Alright, I'll do that for yer." Blue said after a few moments of silence.

"Listen Blue I'm sorry the way things worked out, I'm gonna do me best to put it *all* right. There won't be no more poison or weapons comin', not by my hand or anyone else's if everythin' goes to plan. I've gorra few bob here that I've saved, you can have it to help out with..."

Blue quickly interrupted, "Keep yer blood money, I don't want none of it. I'll watch out f'yer ma's place an I'll give the Corpy back yer keys, that's it. I won't say see yer, 'cause hopefully yer won't ever come back 'ere." With that he took the keys from Irish, who withdrew his foot from the door, allowing Blue to slam it shut.

Irish strolled back to his own house for one last time to complete his preparations before leaving the bleak Crown Estate, his home for twenty one years, forever.

Friday 26th November 1976

"Happy Thanksgiving!" Rosita called, delighted, with a beaming smile as Irish entered Uncle Sam's diner on that freezing Friday evening a day after the traditional American family celebration. Quickly weaving her way through the crowded eatery, she embraced him warmly, kissing him on the lips then saying, "I knew you'd be back tonight, I just knew it."

Irish smiled, advising "Well I'm here t'stay, so yer'd better get used to it."

Rosita could hardly contain her excitement but said pragmatically, "Listen I can't talk now, as ya can see we're run off our feet but I'll be right over as soon as I get a chance."

"No worries, I'll speak t'yer later." Irish replied then took a seat in a space that had just become vacant at the counter, his usual booth and all the others being fully occupied.

He ordered an Uncle Sam's 'Thanksgiving Special' consisting of two half pound turkey burgers, smothered in cranberry jelly, served between two halves of a huge sesame seed bun and with a side order of steaming mixed vegetables, setting about it as if he had not eaten for a week.

Several hours later, when Rosita's shift had ended and the busy diner was finally closed for the night, the couple walked arm-in-arm towards her subway station, telling each other their news. When Irish had concluded outlining his speculative plans, Rosita advised, "I'm free on Sunday night, the manager is lettin' me have time off, rather than pay us for workin' over Thanksgiving. So we can spend the whole day and evening together if ya like and maybe we could go somewhere and *really* get to know each other."

Irish was at first a little bemused by her amorous suggestion, "I'm not sure what yer mean by *really* get to know each other, I think I've told yer everythin' there is to know." he replied naively.

Rosita smiled sweetly shaking her head, "Oh Patrick, you really don't know a damn thing about women; I'll show ya what I mean on Sunday."

Sunday 28th November 1976

A bitterly cold easterly breeze was ushering in the first light dusting of snow of the season, on that rapidly darkening late November afternoon as the love-struck couple strolled along Fifth Avenue, lost in each other's company, bathed in the warming light of the numerous shops vying for custom that lined the bustling thoroughfare. The lofty skyscrapers thrust their own brilliant luminescence into the heavily laden clouds that closed about their manufactured high peaks. Thanksgiving was over and Christmas was beckoning, with less than a month before that festive holiday would be upon the multitude of shoppers who scrambled from one brightly decorated retail outlet to another.

At West 34th Street, Irish and Rosita turned left passing below the magnificent, towering Empire State building and walked on in the direction of the biggest and possibly most famous department store in the world, Macey's. After amusing themselves in this mega emporium for a while, making a few actual purchases, whilst adding many fanciful ones to their joint wishlist, they left the store and moved on to their much anticipated final destination of the day.

Within walking a few hundred yards they arrived outside the attractive, well maintained façade of the Jefferson Hotel, a three star establishment, with a cheery, welcoming ambience that extended out from its spacious lobby to its waiting door staff. Dressed in his tailored black Crombie, petrol blue twenty-two inch parallels and highly polished Airwair, accompanied by Rosita wearing an equally smart wrap around beige, calf length coat with faux fur collar and dark brown platform boots, carrying their Macey's bags, the couple looked as if they were affluent tourists on a shopping trip, or mini-break.

"Luggage to follow is it sir?" the consierge asked as a formality.

"Misplaced at the airport, actually." Irish lied, adding "Not a problem is it, we can always stay somewhere else, it is only for the one night after all?" He was forgetting that this was America, where the customer was always right and *nothing* was too much trouble for the staff in any venue, were only the colour of the customer's money mattered.

"Not at all sir, here's your key, room 2015, the elevator is to your right. Enjoy your stay sir." the tall, immaculately dressed desk clerk advised handing Irish his key.

Twenty floors later the pair entered the small, comfortably furnished room which most importantly, unlike Irish's lodgings at McCabe's, was scrupulously clean, containing a double bed that only they would be sharing. After removing their coats and hanging them on the dark wooden stand, they stood together wrapped in each other's arms, kissing passionately. No words were spoken as they embraced, bathed in the warm glow of several lamps that were set about the room.

When Rosita moved away and began to disrobe, removing her loose fitting dress and revealing her slim figure in her clinging chemise, Irish froze as if the sudden realisation of where he was and who he was with had rendered him immobile.

"What's the matter honey; you're not disappointed are ya?" Rosita asked coyly, before peeling her chemise up and over her head, now wearing only a white bra and panties, complimenting her dark, golden skin.

"No... it's not you... it's me... I mean it is you... you're so beautiful." he declared nervously.

Rosita smiled, unclipping her bra, allowing him to see her perfect breasts fully revealed then slowly took down her panties, exposing her dark thatch to his growing delight. She slipped between the white cotton sheets and rested her head on one raised hand, watching whilst he quickly divested himself of his clothing. For Irish this was a unique experience. Here he was alone with the lovely Rosita about to lay with her in these surroundings, not in a filthy back alley on the grim estate with one of the unfortunate girls, who bartered sexual favours for cigarettes, booze or a handful of change, not giving in to the desires of an older woman purely for her own pleasure, nor even paying for the experiences of a lady of the night. This was the girl of his dreams in a moment that he could only have dreamed of.

Unsure at first, nature soon took control as the couple entwined with Irish transferring his lips from hers down to her slender neck and then her exquisite breasts. As he brought his throbbing member into her most intimate of places she moaned softly, whispering into his ear, encouraging him onward.

Soon there was no conversation; words were redundant only the primal sounds of a man and a woman moving together in a delicious, synchronised rythm, as old as humankind itself. A slow, tender pace increased in tempo and intensity as their mutual pleasure grew exponentionally with each exciting movement, until they were lost in an ecstasy that only true lovers may bring to each other. That intense degree of sensual delight could be sustained for just so long, before the innevitable explosive orgasm overtook them both.

They lay in each other's arms for a long, silent time, post coitus, with only the sound of their heartbeats to be heard, the soft light of the low lamps playing on their glistening bodies, the sheets thrown back in the heat of their passion.

"Are you okay Patrick, is anything wrong?" Rosita asked the first to break the spell of silence.

"Rosita, nothing's wrong in fact everything's perfect." Irish replied genuinely, adding "I just don't want this moment to end."

She smiled and laid her head close to his saying, "Neither do I Patrick but we'll have all the time in the world, now that you're here for good."

They resumed their sensual kissing once more, exploring each other's bodies with stimulating hands as they did. When sufficient re-energising time had passed, the amorous couple began again their mutually desirous liaison and soon were lost in their enjoyable quest to give and receive pleasure. After this second extended, exhausting love-making session, they both collapsed back into the comfortable bed and drifted into a deep, dreamless sleep.

Sometime later waking first from their relaxing repose, Rosita was anxious to know the hour.

"Patrick, wake up, what time is it? How long have we been asleep?"

Irish now woke and lazily answered "I don't know, does it matter, we've got all night."

"No Patrick we haven't. I've told ya before, I can't stay out overnight, I just can't." she replied, leaping out of the bed and frantically looking for a timepiece of any kind.

"Rosita, calm down will yer, there's a clock on the wall by the door." Irish advised, trying to reassure her.

"It's nearly 10.30! I'll have to be goin' soon t'get home near my usual time." she said putting her underwear on, getting back into the bed but sitting up resting against the padded headboard, rather than lying down.

Irish sat up also asking "Are yer alright, y'seem worried, it's not y'brother Diego is it? Is he the one yer'll have t'answer to if yer late?"

"Ya don't understand Patrick, Diego is lookin' out for me the way he always has done." she replied, intending to close the conversation.

"Really? Well I've got two younger sisters meself but now that they're eighteen thee wouldn't be too happy with me tryin' to control *their* lives." he persisted with an unwelcome honesty.

Rosita had been becoming annoyed with his questioning and advised, "Maybe if somethin' bad had happened to one of them when they were younger, ya might feel differently."

Irish had not yet understood fully what she meant and replied insensitively "I don't know about that Rosita, we all make mistakes, sometimes it's the only way t'learn, so unless it was somethin' *really* bad I'd mind me own business and let them got on with their lives."

Rosita turned and stared directly at him, "Is that right, how bad would ya call bein' raped when y'was thirteen years old by a dirty old pervert who followed ya from school?" she asked angrily.

Irish was dumbstruck now not knowing how to respond.

Rosita continued, "He was a guy who'd been hangin' round the neighbourhood, givin' candy to some of the kids, everyone thought he was just a harmless old man but he came after me one day and I couldn't get away."

"What happened to him?" Irish asked, finally speaking.

"Diego was a young Jaguar at the time, he went all over until he found him... then he cut off his balls and fed them to him. Later, after the cops arrested Diego, he got sent down for five years. Before he went away he insisted that I have my own Jaguar's tattoo, so that everyone would know not to mess with me ever again. Maybe now ya can understand why he is the way he is about me." Rosita concluded her terrible tale.

Irish caught hold of her in his arms and she began to weep. "I'm so sorry Rosita, sorry for what happened to yer and for makin' yer go over it again by tellin' me, can yer ever forgive me?"

For some time she sobbed without replying then dried her tears, saying, "That's all in the past and can't be changed. Bad things happen to good people, ya've just gorra move on or it'll ruin the rest of ya life, d'ya know what am sayin'?"

Irish desperately wanted to tell her about his brutal nightmare experience at the hands of Morgo but could not bring himself to do so. For Irish it was not yet possible to move on as Rosita had done, for him only one resolution would free him from the tormenting demons of his past.

Half an hour later, both fully dressed, they left the hotel, carrying their few whimsical purchases in their major department store bags. One of these was a handsome teddy bear wearing a plastic heart shaped pendant around his chubby neck, saying simply 'I love you'; Rosita's momento from Irish of the happy day and passionate evening they had spent together. It would prove to be not the only souvenir of that time, several months hence.

For now the couple said their goodbyes, agreeing to meet the following evening at the diner. Irish put Rosita into a cab then made his way through the swirling gusts of snow as they increased in intensity, heading back down to the lower East Side and his not quite so grand lodgings. He could have chosen to return to the much more comfortable Jefferson Hotel, as he had paid for the night but somehow his heart was not in it.

Monday 29th & Tuesday 30th November 1976

Shortly before seven thirty, Irish was completing his preparations to meet Rosita at Uncle Sam's. Once he had buffed his gleaming cherry red Airwair to a parade ground finish, he put on his black Crombie over his Levi's denim jacket, ready to face the biting cold outside and set off for the diner, only a few blocks distant. Wearing his Prince of Wales checked twenty-inch parallels, he looked particularly sharp that evening, striding purposefully towards the popular eatery, collar turned up, head down and hands dug deep into the pockets of his Crombie.

The mercury had been steadily moving down in thermometers across the city all through that day, as the temperature plummeted. Irish who had experienced many harsh winters in his native Liverpool, particularly those of the early sixties as a child, was beginning to suspect that perhaps a New York winter could be just as severe, or possibly even worse. Sporadic flurries of snow had also been blowing about throughout that day, gathering in drifts against the sides of buildings and in the alleys between. As Irish marched on this changed to a steady, continuous, heavy fall, making him even more glad to reach the welcoming, warm diner.

He knew Rosita's shift began at seven and that she liked to get herself settled into her duties before he got there, consequently he felt arriving at around eight o'clock was about right and expected to find her busily working when he entered the premises.

"Hi loverman, lookin' for Rosita are ya?" Marge called to him as he stepped inside, a white dusting clinging to the front of his dark overcoat. "Ya outa luck honey, she's not arrived yet, she must be runnin' late." Rosita's mature colleague advised.

Irish took a seat at the counter and ordered a burger, fries and a beer, preparing to wait for his beloved.

By the time he had finished his meal and the several additional beers he had washed it down with, Rosita had still not arrived and Irish was beginning to feel anxious about her failure to appear. 'Has she got into trouble at home, has Diego done somethin', or is it just the weather causin' problems?' he asked himself speculatively, providing innocent explanations for something he hoped would not prove to be of sinister reason.

As the evening drew to a close, Marge asked "What is it with you two; every time *you* show up she goes off? Are ya makin' her love-sick or somethin'?"

Irish tried to raise a smile to mask his fears "I hope y'right Marge and that's all it is, see yer."

He left the warmth of the diner and stepped into the frigid night where all around lay a deepening blanket of snow, with more still falling. Irish trudged on to Rosita's subway station as if he may find some trace of her presence, or maybe a clue to her absence, en route. Eventually abandoning his futile quest he made his way back to McCabe's establishment.

"Havin' an early night are yer, young feller?" Ben asked as the disconsolate Irish entered the lobby, shaking the thick covering of snow from his outer clothing and stamping his boots on the rough matting by the door.

"Yeah, thought I might as well." Irish replied, passing by without looking in the proprieters direction.

"Good idea, y'need a proper night's sleep, yer'll be gettin' off early day after tomorrow, remember?" the elder man advised.

"As if I could forget Ben with you around, see yer in the mornin." Irish replied, doubting very much if he would get any sleep that night.

After a long restless session, turning back and forth, constantly replaying all that had recently occurred between him and Rosita, particularly their final conversation; he did eventually slip into a troubled slumber. Irish was not asleep for long as just after one a.m. he awoke with a start, after hearing a loud bang from somewhere below his room, sounding like a small explosion. The accompanying shouting and yelling warned him that a serious altercation was taking place and he quickly pulled on his Fleming's jeans, drawing his black elasticated braces up over his plain white tee-shirt and stepped into his boots. Slipping his heavy brass knuckle-duster onto his right fist, he ran along the corridor then leapt down the flights of stairs.

Even as he was approaching the front reception desk in the narrow lobby, he could see a swirling cloud of smoke and plaster debris all about, in the midst of which old Ben was standing perfectly still holding his double-barrel sawn-off shot gun, levelled at the head of a tall male with striking features, wearing a bandana on his head and distinctive clothing; instantly he recognised Diego, Rosita's brother, warchief of the Jaguars.

Diego was holding a gleaming pistol of his own and pointing it directly at the head of the hotel owner. Four similarly dressed individuals all wearing leather jackets bearing the snarling Jaguar crest of that eponymous crew, were close by between the reception counter and the entrance.

"What the fuck is goin' on?" Irish demanded ready to intervene, though realising that his own weapon may be of little use in this situation.

Ben was first to reply, "Its okay Patrick, you just go on back to your room, I've got this covered."

Diego immediately turned in Irish's direction "It's you, you fuckin' son of a bitch, *Patrick*, you're the one she talks about; you're the one *he* wants." He called to his companions, who on this occasion were his brothers; Louis, Victor, Alejandro and Eduardo. "Get that fucker, bring him to me!"

Ben stepped into their path, having already discharged one barrel into his plaster and lath ceiling as a warning shot, he prepared to empty his second into Diego's angry face. "Make one move against this young feller and scarface here gets his fuckin' head blown off."

"I swear to God I will kill you right here, right now old man if you don't step the fuck outa my way." Diego warned, equally adamantly.

"Hold on the fuckin' lorra yer, will some cunt tell me what's goin on here?" Irish demanded more insensed than afraid.

Diego the Jaguar stared at the Crown Team Skinhead with a look of burning hatred, shouting, "Rosita has been taken by some sick fuck who calls himself 'Morgo'. He wants you in exchange for her and he's gonna get you *now*!"

Irish was stunned with horror, feeling like he wanted to vomit but replying firmly, "You don't need to come f'me like this Diego, with a fuckin' gun as if I need to be persuaded, for fuck's sake. I love Rosita, I'd do anythin' to keep her from harm." He paused for a second, allowing his words to be absorbed. "Just take me straight to him now, or tell me where he is an I'll go fuckin' runnin' to him on me own, to save Rosita."

Diego appeared bemused by Irish's strident, direct response and considered his comments before replying, "Okay, ya come with us now, we have a number to call once we have you and he says he will tell us where they have our sister."

"Alright, I'll get me gear on, y'can come up t'me room if yers don't fuckin' trust me, I'll only be a minute." Irish advised genuinely.

"Louis, Victor, Eduardo stay here, Alejandro you come with me. If we're not back in two minutes kill this old fool." Diego ordered.

With those words ringing in his ears Irish sprinted back to his room, Diego and Alejandro immediately behind him and quickly pulled on his denim jacket and Crombie then paused only to tie his boots properly. Grabbing his wallet and passport off the top of his dressing table, he ran back with Rosita's two brothers down the stairs and into the lobby.

"Patrick ya dont have to do this, I've heard about this Morgo bastard, he'll kill yer but real slow." Ben warned.

"I'll take me chances but thanks anyway Ben, yer the only decent one of the whole fuckin' lorra them. See yer." Irish replied, hurriedly passing by the anxious older male.

"The 'Boy's' won't like it when thee find out, what'll I tell them!" he called as Irish exited the building.

"Tell them to go fuck themselves!" he shouted in reply.

Once outside in the frozen, snowbound street, Irish found Diego's impressive Dodge Charger waiting at the barely visible kerb, with another equally spectacular vehicle containing five more Jaguars, parked behind. He was roughly bundled into the Charger and surrounded by the brothers, with Diego starting the powerful engine. He turned as they were about to pull away into the road, warning, "You fuck this up in any way bitch an I promise ya I won't kill ya, I'll keep ya alive in so much pain you will beg me to let you die!"

Irish could not care less for Diego's threat, he had lived with threats for most of his life, all that concerned him was saving Rosita from the clutches of the evil sadist, Morgo.

"Less talkin' more drivin' an put yer fuckin' foot down!" he snapped back in reply.

Both vehicles roared off into the white blizzard of that black night, spraying jets of grey tainted snow from their sports wheels as they struggled to gain sufficient purchase on the frozen road.

They made one brief stop only at the nearest payphone, where Diego rang the number Morgo had provided, delivering the simple message, "We have him!"

After he had been given the necessary directions the crew set off for their deadly destination.

It was not a long journey from Irish's Lower East Side lodgings to Morgo's lair on the Upper West Side beyond Pier 99 at the abandoned Conrail Piers. The brutal sexual sadist waited excitedly, almost salivating with anticipation of the horrendous tortures that he would inflict upon his helpless victim, Irish, when he was delivered to him.

Only recently released from prison on bail after accepting a deal to divulge all that he knew, about the business activities of a certain local crime family and their English partners, the Gerard Boys, in exchange for having his lewd behaviour charge dropped and threatened illegal alien deportation rescinded, Morgo knew in reality that his life expectancy would now be brief at best.

He had nothing to lose but had no desire to be caught up in a gang war with the fearsome Jaguars, whose reputation preceded them and that he was well aware of. When they had snatched Rosita on her way to work at Uncle Sam's, Morgo and his crew had no idea whose sister she was, kidnapping her only as disposable bait to ensnare Irish. As one of his sexually ambivalent associates decided to 'sample' the goods, he soon uncovered Rosita's unmistakable permanent identification marking, which quickly dampned his ardour.

Once Morgo was made aware of who their captive was, sister of the Jaguar's warchief an exchange was hastily arranged. Soon Irish would be in his clutches once more and Rosita would be returned, relatively unharmed to her family. Morgo watched from the dilapidated nineteenth century warehouse, peering into the blizzard, counting the passing minutes impatiently.

The powerful headlights of Diego's lead vehicle punctured two dazzling holes in the steadily falling white veil, announcing the imminent arrival of the Jaguars with Morgo's prey.

Smiling triumphantly, Morgo turned from his vantage point and called to his crew, "They're here, get the whore ready, clean it up a bit and bring her to the door!"

One of his associates who named himself Snake, being the proud owner of a much vaunted, slightly larger than average sized male member, did as instructed, roughly dragging Rosita to her feet, still with her hands tied behind her, from the filthy floor littered with industrial debris of a bygone age.

Their unofficial headquarters was a decaying former warehouse, constructed mostly of timber, lit by old, still functioning, rusty kerosene lamps with an equally aged wood burning stove providing some slight degree of warmth. All about lay the discarded implements and tools of a once-thriving labour intensive world of work, bearing testament to New York's blue collar heritage, a city built by the back breaking toil of hard men and women.

Snake led Rosita over to where Morgo stood, just inside the rickety front door of the rotten wooden façade, "I'll be glad t'get outa this place, its fuckin' freezin' worse than usual." Snake announced.

"All in good time Snake, we hand over the slut and then have some real fun with her boyfriend. We'll go when we've finished with him, not before; I've waited a fuckin' long time for this." Morgo replied then pulled Rosita to him. He leaned forward into her, bending down and passed his right hand behind her, reaching up under her short waitress uniform and groped her rounded bottom, saying "Nice, I can almost see why this fuckin' Irish prick is on heat for yer but it's not for me. I'll be ridin' *his* arse soon enough."

Rosita looked up at his evil, leering face and spat a mouthful of phlegm into it. "You filthy pig, I pray to God you will die this night!" she cursed.

Morgo removed his offending hand from her bottom and slapped her violently across the left side of her face, splitting the corner of her mouth and leaving a huge red imprint of his heavy paw as evidence. "Maybe I will bitch but not by *His* hand and not before yer little boyfriend bleeds out in agony after we've *all* finished with him." he replied much amused, unbolting the door preparing to make the exchange.

When the Jaguars arrived with Irish, they parked their cars a hundred yards or so from the building, as previously agreed. Diego flashed the headlights several times then stepped out of the Charger, Irish joining him without needing any persuasion.

"Don't try to run boy or I'll put a bullet through the back of ya head." Diego warned unnecessarily.

Irish did not reply to him but called out "Come on Morgo you shit house, show yerself."

When the door creaked open it was not Morgo who stepped out but Snake, pushing Rosita in front of him as a shield, his gun pressed into the back of her head, her hands now untied.

Irish moved forward to the mid-point between the Jaguar's cars and the warehouse, Diego to his rear, totally redundant in the process. The Skinhead studied the scene while waiting for Snake to approach with Rosita. He noticed two vehicles were parked nearby, one the familiar shabby Oldsmobile Toronado that he had previously seen and an equally unloved Ford pickup. Clearly there were more than just four of Morgo's crew within the building, he speculated.

Finally Rosita arrived alongside him looking dishevelled and bruised, having been subjected to some rough handling. Irish looked at her beautiful face, her tearful dark eyes, her damaged mouth and the glowing red handprint on her left cheek.

Enraged, he roared, "You fuckin' bastard Morgo, you're gonna pay for this!"

Morgo was standing just inside the doorway laughing and called in reply, "It's you whose gonna be fuckin' payin' boy, once we get yer in here."

Rosita flung her arms about her lover, tears now streaming down her face, they kissed and then, as she was about to move on with Diego, she squeezed Irish's hand saying "I love you."

Snake quickly pulled his captive away, placing his gun firmly into the front of Irish's head and making him stand before him as another shield, preferring to walk backwards rather than risk being shot in the back by any of the other Jaguars.

"Please Diego, do something, don't let this happen... please." Rosita pleaded, sobbing.

"Get in the fuckin' car Rosita. You've caused enough problems already, you and this Patrick." Diego answered firmly.

They walked towards the Jaguar's vehicles, her elder brother keeping his gun trained on the warehouse entrance looking over his shoulder, waiting for any deception, watching until Irish was eagerly dragged inside by the lurking Morgo.

Once he was in the gloomy, damp-smelling building, Irish blinked his eyes to adjust to the hazy light of the kerosene lamps then looked about him. Apart from Morgo he could see nine other gang members all similarly attired in black leather jackets and trousers with heavy biker's boots. As before each had a bald head, either by nature or design and they wore a varied selection of chains, rings and facial piercings.

"Get his fuckin' coat off then search the cunt, properly." Morgo ordered, remembering his former lover, Devo's reprimand, when he had failed to frisk Jay Mac sufficiently, nearly allowing him to bring the fatal Colt Python into their presence undetected. Irish's Crombie was almost torn from him and thrown to the filthy floor, while he was thoroughly searched, standing perfectly still with fists clenched.

"He's clean!" another of Morgo's henchmen called on completing his enthusiastic pat-down.

Irish was now brought in front of his beaming captor, whose growing excitement was already becoming visible in his tight trousers.

"Fuck, this is a turn up for the books, you comin' t'me lookin' for a good, hard shag." He paused on hearing a particular tune beginning to play on the small transistor radio that they had brought with them. "Turn that up, I like a bit of mood music." he ordered.

With Led Zeppelin's *Immigrant Song* blaring in the background Morgo began to rub his crotch, putting his face so close to Irish that the Crown player could smell his fetid breath.

"Yer always were a stinkin' cunt, with breath like shit, too much lickin' out arses I suppose." Irish observed.

Morgo's powerful fist pounded into Irish's stomach doubling him up, almost making him wretch. His tormentor was ecstatic, "I fuckin' love it when thee talk dirty."

Irish straightened up and stared coldly at his sadistic enemy.

Morgo continued, "You cost me a nut you little cunt, when you stuck Devo's blade into my ball sack. 'Ivor Bollockoff' thee all call me now 'cause of you but d'yer know what Skinhead, I can still get it up and before I kill yer, I'm really gonna split that arse of yours, again." He began to unfasten his trousers saying, "Alright, enough of the foreplay, get his kecks down and bend him over that table, ready for some real cock."

Even as two of Morgo's grinning accomplices went to lay their hands on him, Irish lashed out with the small folding blade that Rosita had furtively passed him. He slashed the nearest male across the face with a wild strike then moved further back into the room, while the whole crew sought to encircle him. Some were about to draw their firearms but Morgo ordered, "No fucker is to shoot this cunt, use yer blades, cut him enough to hurt but don't kill him, not yet."

Whooping and cheering they closed about their trapped victim, keeping out of range of his small knife but close enough to deliver painful slashes with their selection of full-sized versions.

Irish knew he was in a hopeless position and would soon be overcome. He dug deep into his Skinhead resolve, refusing to cry out in the biting pain of their bloody assault. Eventually he collapsed to his knees, leading Morgo's crew to change tactics going in with their heavy boots instead. Kicked almost unconscious Irish assumed the classic foetal position, allowing them to use him as a human football but denying them the pleasure of hearing him call for mercy, revealing his agony.

"Alright that's enough, pack it in." Morgo ordered. "I don't want him completely out of it, he's got to *feel* the pain. Pick him up and get him ready for me."

Suddenly there was a tremendous crash as the hot-wired pick up truck smashed through the rotten wooden façade, driven by one of the Jaguars with Diego leading the rest of his crew in its wake, like crack assault troops following a tank.

"No, no, not now!" Morgo called out in disbelief, hurriedly putting away his rapidly deflating member.

Random shots were fired by both sides but knives, coshes and chains were the order of the day as the two crews closed in hand-to-hand combat, with Deep Purple's *Black Night* playing on the small radio and pandemonium occurring all around.

Diego leapt upon Snake and the pair fell to the floor grappling, slashing with knives in their right fists whilst trying to get a choke-hold on each other with their left hands. Similar desperate bouts were taking place all about the poorly lit room. Skulls were cracked, ribs and limbs broken, vital organs punctured, a blood lust fury having descended upon both gangs, no one would escape unscathed.

In the whirling tumultuous madness a number of lamps were overturned, quickly leading to the wooden constructed warehouse catching light. Flames licked the frozen night sky outside and scorched the bloodied, determined combatants within; black acrid smoke choking them as they fought on.

Irish had dropped Rosita's small knife and was scrambling about on the debris strewn floor trying to locate it by touch. He peered towards where he had last seen Morgo, horrified as he spotted the evil sadist about to flee from the carnage, escaping through the destroyed frontage. The dazed Skinhead grasped the nearest implement he could find to use as a weapon, rose to his feet and went in pursuit of his brutal enemy.

Once outside in the wild, snowy night Morgo planned to use his unloved Oldsmobile to drive away from the pier to safety but found that the Jaguars had already slashed all four tyres. He turned towards the pier hoping to find some alternative means of transport moored there, so desperate was his desire.

"Morgo, you fuckin' shitty bastard, stand yer ground, let's finish it here, now!" Irish demanded.

Morgo momentarily glanced over his shoulder on hearing Irish's voice realising it was he alone chasing him, in his weakened condition, apparently unarmed. He stopped where he was close to the edge of the crumbling pier and turned to face the Skinhead.

"Come and get it boy, 'we're' waitin' for yer." he roared, drawing Fritz from his specially made leather sheath.

Wearing his slashed and tattered denim jacket and jeans, with his industrial boots Irish appeared as one of the hard labouring stevedores of days gone by. Brandishing his wooden-handled, iron 'docker's hook,' the image was complete.

Slowly coming towards the smiling, debauched, leather-clad Morgo, Irish the prolateriat warrior winced in the pain of his injuries ignoring all in his grim determination for vengence.

They circled each other looking for that tell-tale opening, vision hampered by the snow which had lessened in intensity but reverted to swiriling about in blinding gusts once more. Morgo struck first slashing Irish across the chest, though causing only superficial, material damage. Irish changed his stance, dropped low and gashed Morgo behind his left knee. The sadist was no stranger to pain either, enjoying receiving it almost as much as giving it. He stumbled only to grasp a handful of snow to throw in Irish's face, before cutting him across the front of his thigh. Irish was wounded but again revealed no outward sign, swinging with the rusty iron hook and impaling Morgo's left shoulder, bursting through his leather jacket deep into his well developed deltoid. This time the sadist cried out in agony, trying to extricate himself even as Irish's left fist smashed into his face. Morgo's swift response was a rising knee to his opponent's groin, followed immediately by a hard boot to Irish's sternum which sent him sprawling some feet away, his hook still protruding from Morgo's shoulder.

Sitting all this time in silence, less than twenty yards from the scene was Rosita, watching the life or death struggle from within Diego's Charger. The car was facing almost fully in their direction and just as Morgo raised his deadly knife to bring it down upon the weaponless Irish, she turned the headlights to full beam, momentarily dazzling the torturer in their brilliant intensity. Morgo shielded his eyes with his left hand, hoping to finish his foe but Irish leapt upon him, tackling him around the waist, bringing him thudding down into the compacted snow. Instantly retrieving his hook, Irish swung it again, this time connecting with Morgo's throat. Blood spurted from the wound, Morgo gurgled a scarlet fluid from his mouth, still smiling he slashed at Irish's head, succeeding in slicing the lower part of his left ear clean through. Both were soon bathed in each other's blood as they set about grappling, rolling over and over in the deep, red stained snow.

Once more Morgo struck, driving Fritz through Irish's denim jacket on his left side, piercing the flesh passing out the rear barely missing his kidney. Irish fell away onto his back holding his punctured side, trying to stem the flow of vital fluid.

Slowly Morgo rose, crawled towards him and then straddled the supine Skinhead. "End of the game for you Skin." he said in between spurts of blood running from his mouth.

Fritz was poised for his final plunge, Irish struck with every ounce of his remaining strength bringing the docker's hook in one powerful horizontal slash across Morgo's midriff, literally gutting him from left to right. Morgo stayed perfectly still for some moments then fell forward onto Irish, with the infamous knife held firmly in his dying grasp.

Breathing as if his heart would burst Irish made one supreme effort and rolled Morgo from him onto his back. The evil sadist's eyes were still open, staring directly up at Irish, his scarlet mouth moving like a fish out of water gasping for breath.

"See you... in hell..." he said in a barely audible hiss.

"I'll be lookin' out for yer, when I get there." Irish replied, prizing Fritz from Morgo's death-grip before plunging the blade into the sadist's groin then proceeding to slice him from there to the base of his sternum. Steam, blood and guts erupted from within as the light of life was finally extinguished from him.

Staggering to his feet, now drenched in vital fluids, stained with the gore of entrails, looking like an overworked butcher or an abattoir labourer, Irish caught hold of Morgo's wrist and dragged him to the edge of the pier. "In y'go, yer piece of shit." he said quietly, rolling his almost quartered corpse over the side to fall down into the dark waters of the Hudson below.

Picking up the knife that he had temporarily 'sheathed' standing in the snow, in one arcing throw he flung it out into the fast flowing river. "Thank God that's the end of that cursed thing." Irish called out in sheer relief. At last Fritz had returned to the land of his 'birth', he had come home to his final resting place.

Irish turned to find Rosita running through the snow towards him. The warehouse was ablaze, Morgo's crew had been defeated, those who could still run, or at least walk, fled from the scene, Diego and his Jaguars had emerged triumphant. He now called to Rosita and Irish, "Come on you two we've gotta leave this place before the cops get here."

Just as Irish was about to get into the second vehicle Diego held out his hand, "You are an honourable man, I would be proud to call *you* brother." Irish shook his hand firmly and smiled. He had left one family in his old home and found another in his new one.

EPILOGUE

It was the 23rd of December, the night before Christmas Eve and Irish was a long way from New York City. The driver of the Greyhound bus on which he was travelling, faced with the blinding 'whiteout' conditions, had no alternative other than to make an unscheduled pit-stop at a small diner and bar facility, located on the outskirts of St Paul, Minnesota.

"Sorry folks, we're gonna have to stay over until this storm rides itself out." he announced, opening the front doors with a hiss of the hydraulic mechanism.

Irish was only too pleased to leave his seat and stretch his legs. It seemed an eternity since he had boarded the vehicle over twenty four hours earlier and more than a thousand miles away, at the company's Midtown depot after saying goodbye to the lovely Rosita the previous evening, with the sincere promise of returning for her when he was certain that it would be safe to do so and no harm could befall her.

The lengthy journey, had given him ample opportunity to consider his recent actions and their likely outcome. Having killed Morgo he had inadvertently deprived the New York District Attorney, who was in the process of building his case against the local organised crime syndicate and their English partners, of his principal material witness. Morgo's sworn written statements would be of little use if not validated by his personal appearance, at any future trial. The evil sadist, however, could hardly have his day in court now that his virtually dismembered corpse, had become so much fish food for the aquatic occupants of the Hudson River. Irish hoped that his own signed confession, which *he* was willing to testify to if required, together with the detailed dossiers containing names, times, dates and locations he had prepared, would be sufficient supplementary corroboration to bring down the whole rotten house of cards.

Sitting in the small, comfortable diner eating a warming, hearty meal, Irish smiled as he thought of the series of dawn raids that would result from the receipt of those same dossiers by the authorities, on both sides of the Atlantic. Not trusting the police of his native city to pursue the Gerard Boys and bring them to trial, Irish had posted, via USPS Airmail, one of his large manilla envelopes containing all the incriminating evidence he could provide to the Chief Commissioner of the Metropolitan Police in London. The other duplicate report, sealed in a similar envelope, he had personally delivered to the 'sniffy' conscierge of a certain prestigious apartment building on Fifth Avenue, opposite Central Park, marked for the confidential attention of the once aspiring NYPD candidate, Mr Gabriel Nathan Stone. Both documents should at the very least, stop the deadly trade in narcotics and guns by the 'families' he had identified.

Irish had done his best to keep his word to Blue when he had promised, nothing else of that nature would be brought to the Crown Estate by his hand. Only one name had been excluded, that of the elderly Ben McCabe, proud owner of the Grande Hotel. Irish viewed him as an innocent pawn caught up in events that he had no real understanding of and as a genuinely decent man. No reference would be made to Ben or his establishment, he would walk away unscathed, Irish hoped.

After finishing his meal he strolled the short distance to the lively bar conveniently located next to the diner. On entering the one room hostelry he removed a necessary new addition to his kit, a close fitting, navy blue woollen hat and in doing so revealed his recent number one crop with obligatory razored trench. Irish had also managed to replace almost all the items of clothing that had been damaged beyond repair, either during his deadly duel with Morgo or, in the case of his tailored Crombie, reduced to a pile of ash in the blazing warehouse. His twenty four inch parallel Fleming's jeans, which were exclusively manufactured in Liverpool, could not be replaced like-for-like and instead he substituted the most suitable alternative, a pair of Levi's 501, eighteen inch straight cut jeans. Attired in this unique ensemble, with his particular haircut and highly polished, cherry red Airwair, Irish looked once again like an original Skinhead embodying the Spirit of '69.

In a bar filled mostly with local residents, sporting long hair and beards, wearing baseball caps, thick padded checked shirts, jeans and work boots, he was bound to attract some degree of curiosity. Irish strolled over to the bar, ordered a couple of beers then took a seat at a small round table close to the lively juke box, currently playing Jim Reeves' *Silver Bells*. His attention though was drawn to the small television, fixed to a shelf close to the opposite end of the bar from where he was sitting. Robert Redford's stellar portayal of the legendary mountain man *Jeremiah Johnson*, in the film of that name, was being shown, currently at the famous Indian fighting montage. Once again he smiled recalling seeing this classic tale of rugged adventure with his late friend Jay Mac, several years previous.

"Evenin' buddy, what unit are ya with?" a huge, stocky male wearing an impressive set of dark brown, bushy sideburns asked in a seemingly friendly manner, on approaching from the pool table just beyond where Irish sat.

"Alright mate, I'm not in the forces." Irish replied with his now usual response to this frequently asked question but without adding any further detail. His distinctive Liverpool-Irish accent caught the stranger's ear, as if it were familiar to him.

"Where y'from friend, I know that accent I'm sure?"

The male's three companions had finished their game and now also came over to where Irish and their friend were having their brief conversation. At first Irish almost replied in the form that Gabriel often introduced him, designating the *city* of Liverpool as a *town* in England but said simply "Am from Liverpool."

"Well aint that just great." the first questioner announced, adding, "My grandpa is from Liverpool, he's a 'Scouser', used to work the boats for the Cunard Line, sailin' between there and New York. Liked it so much over here, jumped ship and never went back."

It seemed this tenuous connection was sufficient excuse for a round of drinks to be ordered and soon all five males were sitting together, bonding over masculine trivia, sharing tall tales and crude jokes. Irish relaxed in this convivial atmosphere and forgot about time, or even completing the remainder of his journey. The storm outside had subsided and after several calls for his passengers to rejoin his bus, the driver moved off.

Though his ticket had been for New York to Montanna Irish was unconcerned, beginning to consider travelling even further afield in this magnificient territory.

One of his new found friends asked, "I hear they've got this punk thing goin' on over there in England, is that why you're dressed like that, are you one of these new 'Punks'?"

Irish put down his bottle of beer and announced proudly, "No, am not. I'm the last of the Skinheads."

Suitably impressed by this intriguing statement the first questioner, who had introduced himself as Magnus replied, "That sounds interestin', what's that all about?"

Finishing his drink Irish answered with a smile, "Well if you're buyin' am talkin'. Listen while I tell the story of 'Jay Mac and the Crown Team Skinheads'..."

Several hours later when Irish had finished his tale and the last of his drinks, he left the bar and his 'buddies', stepping out into the frozen Minesota night, with its crystal clear, blue velvet sky lit by a million, brilliant stars. Hitching a lift from an obliging big-rig truck driver, who was making an early start on his long-haul trek up to the 49th State, Alaska, after enjoying a much needed pit stop in St Paul, the former Crown Team player set off on his own journey of discovery.

Irish the last Skinhead disappeared into America's vast wilderness, finally free, at home in God's own country "...and some folk say he's out there still."

THE END

MUSIC

Chapter 1 – Spirit in the Sky (Norman Greenbaum)
I'm the Leader (Gary Glitter)
Natural Sinner (Fairweather)
Blockbuster (The Sweet)
Paint it Black (The Rolling Stones)

Chapter 2 – Whiskey in the Jar (The Dubliners)
The Night they Drove Old Dixie Down (The Band)
That's Life (Frank Sinatra)
Mac the Knife (Bobby Darin)
Whiskey in the Jar (The Dubliners)

Chapter 3 – Police and Thieves (Junior Murvin)
Dat (Pluto)
Take it to the Limit (The Eagles)
CloudNine (The Temptations)

Chapter 4 – All Gone to Look for America (Simon & Garfunkel)
Baby Brother (War)
Get up and Boogie (Silver Convention)

Chapter 5 – Across 110th Street (Bobby Womack)
Ain't that a Kick in the Head (Dean Martin)
Fool to Cry (The Rolling Stones)
Midnight Train to Georgia (Gladys Knight and the Pips)

Chapter 6 – Mona Lisas and Mad Hatters (Elton John)
Silver Star (The Four Seasons)
I'm Mandy Fly Me (10CC)
Boston Tea Party (The Sensational Alex Harvey Band)
Skinhead Moonstomp (Simaryp)

Chapter 7 – Them Never Love Poor Marcus (Junior Murvin)
Hey Bo Diddley (Bo Diddley)
Smoke Stack Lightnin' (Howlin' Wolf)
I'm a Man (Muddy Waters)
Tubular Bells (Champs Boys - disco version)
Shake, Shake, Shake Your Booty (KC and The Sunshine Band)
Somewhere Beyond the Sea (Bobby Darin)
Dream Baby Roy Orbison

Chapter 8 – Jeremiah Johnson (Tim McIntire/John Rubenstein)
Wild and Peaceful (Kool and the Gang)
Don't Touch I Man Locks (I-Roy)
Big River (Johnny Cash)
Immigrant Song (Led Zeppelin)
Black Night (Deep Purple)

Epilogue
Silver Bells (Jim Reeves)

GLOSSARY

Arl - old
A few bob - A handful of loose coin
Burst - to 'burst' someone – to beat up someone
Cadging or to Cadge - Begging, or to beg.
Corpy - Corporation, Liverpool Corporation, landlords for council tenants rented accommodation
Dixie (keeping Dixie) - Keeping lookout
Flemings Jeans - very popular 22 and 24 inch parallel jeans worn during the original Skinhead era. The jeans were made in Liverpool by W.H Fleming. They were the jeans of choice for Teddy Boys in the 50s to Mods of the 60s, then Skinheads of the 70s
Jammy - fortunate, lucky (ie. Someone who gets the jam)
Kecks - trousers
Kit - a coordinated outfit of clothing
Flat - an apartment, a condo
Gerrin, gerrout, gerron, gorra - Get in, get out, get on, got a/got to.
Off Licence - A small shop selling bottles of beer, sprits and wine, usually next to the public house
Polis - Police (pronounced Polis in Ireland)
Scouser/Scouse - A native of Liverpool. To speak Scouse (accent). **A pan of scouse** - a pan of stew ie. Lobscouse (Norweigan), similar to Irish stew.
Sláinte - cheers (basic Irish Gaelic). Variations of this toast include **sláinte** mhaith "good health"
Terrace or Terraced house - a house in a terrace or a row of houses, usually identical and having common dividing walls
The Pool - Liverpool is sometimes referred to as 'The Pool' by local people
Thee - is used in place of they, it is part of the local [Scouse] dialect of some Liverpool people.

Printed in Great Britain
by Amazon